WITHDRAWN
UTSA LIBRARIES

THE WAX BOOM

NOVELS BY GEORGE MANDEL

Flee the Angry Strangers

The Breakwater

Into the Woods of the World

The Wax Boom

THE WAX BOOM

George Mandel

RANDOM HOUSE | *New York*

FIRST PRINTING

© Copyright, 1962, by George Mandel

All rights reserved under International and Pan-American Copyright Conventions. Published in New York by Random House, Inc., and simultaneously in Toronto, Canada, by Random House of Canada, Ltd.

Library of Congress Catalog Card Number: 62-8446

Manufactured in the United States of America by Colonial Press, Inc.

For Mayo and Laurie

THE WAX BOOM

1

Under a dirty sky threatening rain stood Colonel B. Drexel Powell on a mound of earth. He wore a steel helmet on which his insigne of rank was hidden from possible enemy eyes by a wide rubber band, and a trench coat of pure spotless white.

Old TNT, as the Colonel was affectionately alluded to when in earshot of inferior officers, was commander of a Mechanized Cavalry Group. Two Squadrons composed the Group, and each was formed of three Troops, which were roughly equivalent in strength to Infantry Companies. Invariably, single Troops were committed to assault enemy forces of superior power. A convincing reason for this never trickled down to Platoon level, where the actual fighting was done, and so the men considered themselves members of a deadly hoax, a bluff that the enemy might call at any time with disastrous counterblows. More than commonly insecure, these were men of inordinate sensitivity.

For the rest they were typical combat soldiers: very tough, very deadly—and very beautiful, too, for all were young and in the close shadow of death. The Group commander was also very tough and deadly, but hardly beautiful, being neither young nor particularly menaced. In advanced middle age and spare, he had blear, cold eyes and the pallor of a molted snakeskin. He had come up front this day to watch A Troop go rolling several miles further front.

Colonel Powell was not one to loiter in the rear: a couple of weeks back, when the outfit had been lumbering west in a change of sector and rumor was rife of a rear echelon guard mission back in Tongres, he had gone racing back to the front, as far as Corps Headquarters, and disrupted a volley-ball match bellowing at the General himself: "I got a fighting outfit! By God, I want a fighting mission!"

So the column had swung east again; A Troop was already shooting Germans out of an encircled forest and filing casualties in its morning reports when the grapevine disclosed how the fortunes of war had saved its fighting momentum from corruption. It had a fighting commander. In the approach to that forest Colonel Powell had stood amid the smokepots of Quartermaster supply units wearing the same leather face of inspiration he wore now, a man not of thunder alone but also of philosophy, as his command car behind him attested in a legend boldly lettered on its hood: *Courage is a matter of decision!* This was the principle on which he stood as resolutely as he stood now on his mound of earth.

"He's standing on an old latrine," Private Moran said, driving his sergeant past in a jeep.

"I love to see him," the sergeant said. "It's always so quiet."

An armored car followed on bouncing wheels, and in the turret a soldier swung the big .50-caliber machine gun vertical, laying hands on it in an absurd "present arms" attitude, his expression a stony one of guileless and irremediable stupidity that he had perfected saluting officers in theater lobbies and latrines back in basic-training days.

"Churney!" the Colonel barked, and his aide came barreling over from the command car as a jeep went by with Corporal Finch, who knew better than to salute officers in any theater lobby or latrine. "Churney, who's the man sticking out of that turret? I think the son of a bitch by God saluted me!"

"Gingold?" Captain Churney was panting. He always

panted. He was gifted with a remarkable memory for every last man who had come into the outfit as a replacement, and of course there were many. He encountered them all because—huge and abdominous, forever caressing pearl-handled pistols—he was always there at the Group Command Post to welcome newcomers into *the fightingest damn outfit in the* ETO. "Saluted you, sir?" He panted distractedly, one hand adjusting his glasses, the other stealing down to a pistol. "Doesn't he realize that could get you killed if an enemy saw?"

"I want names, not sympathy! Is he any damn good? Does he carry his goddamn weight?"

"His platoon leader thinks highly of him. As you know, I inquire about them all, every mother's son in this man's outfit—"

"You gonna tell me his blasted name?"

"Gingold, as good as they come, sir, and that's what amazes me about it. Perhaps seeing you up here excited him, sir."

"Didn't he ever see me up on the line before? He'll be seeing me again if he comes out of this one, the son of a bitch bastard! Now once and for all, will you tell me his goddamn name?"

"Private Gingold, sir. I said so, sir. Gingold."

"Oh, is that his name? I didn't know *what* the hell you were saying that for. Gingold? What kind of ignorant name is that?"

"Gingold, sir, is a Jew. I wanted to point that out."

"A Jew? Oh. Full-blooded?"

"I believe so, sir."

"Oh. Well. It's little enough to grant him a slight lapse here and there along the line, up on the line here." Colonel Powell cupped gloved hands around his mouth and yelled, "Get . . . Jerry . . . boy!"

"I'll get you," a corporal said in his passing jeep, "and eat hot meals off your body, you come up on the line one time."

"That's Rayhew," Captain Churney panted, both hands on

his pistol-butts. "You wanted me to point him out, sir. The one who caught a drip in Tongres."

"Oh, yas. Let's see, he looks okay. Get him a rating."

"Yes, sir. He's already a corporal. But there's bound to be a sergeancy vacancy presently."

"What's that? Hah? Right. If you can't fuck you can't fight."

The column met dusk ten miles east across terrain already laid waste by two Infantry regiments. Captain Stollman, commanding officer of A Troop, bivouacked the outfit in an apple orchard for a night of rest before mounting the assault on an enemy pocket of resistance.

Captain Stollman was a man who never raised his voice. He raised his eyebrows instead to get himself across with emphasis; this would cause his forehead to wrinkle up with all the lassitude of an excessive period spent up front and convey some hint of the burdensome responsibilities he bore. He smoked a pipe; this displayed his fortitude.

There was a farmhouse that had escaped demolition, and Captain Stollman took it over with his Troop HQ sections of Medical, Kitchen, Supply, and Communications personnel. He sat on his open bedroll waiting for his clerk, Weldon, to hook a battery to his lamp. Then, in the sudden flood of light, he lit his pipe and puffed on it, saying, "It's chilly in here."

"Shall I light up the stove, sir? They have the blackout blankets up."

"Not just yet. Get me Lieutenant Enshaw. I'm committing his platoon tomorrow."

"The Second Platoon again, sir?"

"If it's all right with you," Captain Stollman said softly. "Well? Is it all right with you, Weldon?"

"It ain't my say, sir."

"No, it isn't. It's mine." He sucked at his pipe to get it well lit. "Mine," he said again, and blew smoke into the light. "Did you ever stop to think, Weldon, how it might feel to commit other officers to take their units in? Send one platoon in and you have the other two to worry about, Weldon. For a flank move. To cover a withdrawal. You don't go in yourself, Weldon. You send others. You know how that can look to some people, but you do it anyway."

"I'll get Lieutenant Enshaw, sir."

"If I had an Executive Officer, a good one, it would be different. Someone I could trust to assume command if necessary."

"Is that new officer out there—"

"The thing is to keep from getting bitter. To do each the job he's here to do no matter what the cost. We're not children, Weldon. Do you understand?"

"I'll get Lieutenant Enshaw for you, sir."

"Do you understand what I'm saying?"

"Yessir."

For all the front-line austerity, Lieutenant Enshaw of the Second Platoon tended toward flab; still he was very active and made his presence count in each of his platoon's three sections no matter how dispersed they sometimes were. He had nothing of Captain Stollman's subtle understanding of responsibility, and allowed himself to look as scared as the next man. The men found him as trustworthy as one man could ever be expected to find another. Besides, he enjoyed an old and direct relationship with the remaining old-timers, for he had originally been the Troop First Sergeant, and had acquired his commission in the field at Saint-Lô back in France following the destruction of Lieutenant Caglower, for whom few had cared.

When Enshaw left the Captain's farmhouse, Platoon Sergeant Proctor was there to meet him in the darkness. "Did you see the new lieutenant?" Enshaw said.

"Don't start making conversation; what did the Old Man say? It's us tomorrow, ain't it?"

"You knew damn well it's us as soon as he sent for me. Did you see the new John that just arrived?"

"I didn't see his face none too good. Just a big mustache."

"He's got a goatee, too. No shit. And a sickle or something on his ass, a goddamn scimitar. Real chesty character."

Sergeant Proctor snickered. "What's his status? He coming into the outfit?"

"Yeah. I don't know where he fits. Just that he's riding with you tomorrow. He's very eager to go in first."

"Oh. Oh. In that case *you* take him in, *you* go in first and take him. And don't go wrinkling up like the Old Man and tell me you gonna be too busy running from section to section."

The lieutenant laughed, moving along with Proctor into the orchard. "I'll be right where you can see me, won't I? Go tell Riglioni his section's riding point."

"You tell him, Lew. I told him the last time."

"Okay. I'll tell him in the morning. No use giving him a bad night."

"Now why couldn't that born leader of men do the same by us? A whole beautiful night without worrying too much."

"That would be irresolution in Stollman's book."

The sergeant began to giggle softly and Enshaw shook him by the shoulder. "Take it easy, now. Get the guard set up and turn everybody in. Take it easy, Gene."

"Yeah, yeah. It's chilly, you know that?" Giggling, Proctor walked off in the darkness.

In the soul-sucking pasty mists of dawn the men were ready amid their armor to head out and attack. Each was heavy with gear, rifle or submachine gun slung on a shoulder, cartridge belt and extra bandoliers dissecting him in crisscross, grenades hung like Christmas gifts on a tree.

The mud was no more than a slimy nuisance now, not knee-deep as it had been for some time. Spotted in the fields everywhere, cows lay bloated three times their normal girth, stiff legs pointed accusingly at heaven, hides matted ugly with the dew. The scent of death was no longer a pall over the countryside; it came only spasmodically in rancid waves that then passed rapidly away. In another week or so the deepening frost would keep dead cattle from swelling, hold them to size with legs at rest beside them. All the men knew that.

Tacitly they understood other things in common. One was that every man saw a weird and demoralizing resemblance to himself around the helmet of any dead American lying face down. Another was that the enemy was a huge faceless spook, with all dead or captured Germans looking as victimized and blameless as any other player trapped in the game of slaughter.

Most of these men were long at it, yet still unaccustomed to slaughter and forever to remain so, those that lived. Unaccustomed to their fear as well. And lately come to realize how unaccustomed grown men could be to the sun and the rain of their lives, the indifferent foliage of Earth, the very air. In sun or rain the daylight picture of fleet contemporary men pursuing slaughter was too grotesque to be wholly accepted as reality. Daylight unreality was the single element that, like a narcotic, permitted sane healthy men to endure it all, day following day.

Night was different. Save for ruby gunflashes on the blackness, there was nothing to see at night; save for brief pallid landscapes cast suddenly under flares, there were no pictures to disbelieve. Night personified the enormous enemy phantom, and made a blunt reality of war. Night cornered each man, naked and tiny and alone. For some the night lingered on past dawn to blight their merciful pictures of unreality and drown good minds at last in horror.

A man wanted light whenever possible in his hidden night corners, some modest glow to make a picture or two for his un believing eyes and push him off a little distance from the presence of his jeopardy. Being full of desperation, every man needed that glow of fantasy. In his own manner each sought ways to avail himself of it as if all recognized that, in the search, life and death danced as perilously as on the whine of an incoming shell. Not only the single life that one guarded so jealously, but also the total mystifying essence of life that all shared and none began to fathom; and not merely the stinging quick death that threatened always a yard or two forward, but also the long dull dying of the race in shrouds of hypocrisy, in cobwebs of insipidness, which from birth the soul spends its precious few years eluding.

Lately the action had been too rapid for anyone to rig up a gasoline bottle stuffed with a rag, which would give a great holy light but required the construction of a tin-can chimney to carry away the black smoke and soot. In nights to come the perimeters of tranquilizing light, if they could be made at all, would have to be modest ones.

Wax was an important commodity in the outfit's infatuation with light.

2

Bivouacked in that sizable orchard, out in the open where even the spark of a cigarette had to be hidden down in an armored car turret or low in a jeep, A Troop had spent the night entirely without light. Few had missed it, however, for there was an excruciating hunger for sleep after very little of it in the weeks of shooting enough Germans out of trees to capture the encircled forest. Now, done with breakfast and the loading of gas tanks, the men were looking east for the first light of day.

Behind the wheel of his jeep, Private Joe Moran sat scraping wax from a K ration box with his bayonet. He was a little toadstool of a man with disgruntled eyes and hairy hands that worked diligently, adding wax to the tiny ball of it he hoarded in a pocket of his combat jacket. Behind him, Corporal Charles Finch sat on a ration crate waiting for the Section Two Sergeant to return, briefed for the attack.

"Moran," Corporal Finch said, blinking as a man will when preoccupied with other matters. "Why don't you just poke a hole in your can of shoe-dubbing for wax?"

"We're gonna get heavy rain."

"Huh! The dubbing'll only keep the rainwater *in* your shoes."

"Ah, shut up with that. You're always saying the same things over and over."

Finch sniggered. He slid the helmet in a low rakish tilt over his eyes. "Anyway," he said archly, "I got an extra can of dubbing out of Supply."

"Yeah, I heard about you wearing your pants backwards around the CP."

Finch sniggered again. Gangly and boy-faced, some seven years younger than Moran, he had a compulsion to rib the dour little man by way of asserting his superior rank; always getting the worst of it, he always sniggered. "Don't be bitter, boy. You can watch my light some night."

"You're a good scout, Finchie."

"You got to supply the rifle patch, though."

Moran said nothing, and this at last made a gap too wide for Finch's clumsy badinage to span. He fell quiet, abstracted with all that lay east in the encroaching light.

Soon the Section Sergeant came along, distinguishable in the lingering night by his heft and his ponderous gait, yet also by a curious economy of movement that hinted at genuine resourcefulness. One of the few left since the Normandy invasion, Sergeant Salvatore Riglioni faced Moran, also an old-timer, with eyes flattened out by fatigue and mourning.

Riglioni had a face like a bowl of walnuts. It gave his section of seven men faith in his leadership, though he deigned to bear his rank at all only because he trusted others less than he trusted himself. He trusted Platoon Sergeant Proctor as much as he possibly could another man, and that was the absolute limit of his faith: Lieutenant Enshaw only impressed him as a decent man; God only frightened him, with all the meanness of the war itself.

"We're going point," he said.

In response, Finch, who always found it necessary to appear contemptuous of danger, snorked up something to spit and expelled it smartly. Scraping wax, Moran said, "It's always us. You turn in your stripes, Sal. Old Man fingers this platoon because we got Proctor. Then Enshaw fingers. Always this section on account of you. Turn in your stripes and maybe we could live through this."

"It's not always us," Riglioni said. "Everybody thinks it's always them."

"I know. But turn in your stripes, you and Gene, and we could maybe come out alive."

This baleful kind of talk had been coming from Moran more in the past month than in all the misery from Normandy through the Lowlands. It depressed Riglioni. Moran saddened him, and in a way peculiarly familiar. Moran saddened him in the same oblique way, he realized, that his father back home did, just being older and naturally closer to his end. It was the same inevitable doom he sensed in Moran these days. "Quit being obnoxious," he said hoarsely. "This platoon's held up best. And us, since San-Germain we only got three replacements in the section. Two of them's old-timers already. We're dependable."

"Dependable your ass." Moran kept scraping wax from the little carton. "Our luck's bound to run out."

Finch hopped out of the jeep and followed Riglioni off around deployed vehicles and men, saying, "I thought they separate the men from the boys up on the line."

It stopped Riglioni. Finch was barely twenty-one and looked even younger under the big helmet. He had made corporal only because Moran declined the rating when Sandorian got his scalp rolled up like a window shade back at Saint-Lô. But Riglioni decided not to remark on it. Finch was all right. A little bit of a hotshot, but all right. Quick-witted. And almost as cool as he tried in his swaggering to appear. Looking at the boy, at his soft cheeks and dainty little mouth, Riglioni said, "Zubrowski holding up? How do you feel about him?"

Finch tipped his helmet back, deliberately manifesting resignation with a sigh. Then he set Riglioni's teeth altogether on edge with a tedious display of group loyalty in waiting for a pair of Section One men to pass before saying, "They were scraping the barrel when they sent Zubrowski up. But he's learned plenty in the last couple of months, him and Gingold both. And he can drive. He drives pretty good."

"Well, that's why I put him driving you. To learn things."

"That new guy in the turret. What's-his-name—Atman. That's the one bothers me. Stomping around and coughing, kicking things like he's in his aunt's house or something. I thought they separate the men from—"

"Shut up! Shut up!"

"What's the matter?" Finch shot glances in several directions. "What's the matter, Sal, is something worrying you?"

"Is something worrying me?" Riglioni stared at the boy, then patted his shoulder with ironical awe. "You only say that because you're a man of steel."

"Ah, the hell with that," Finch said, sniggering.

At the Section Two armored car they found the pair of drivers standing together in silence. Scarbro, a lank mountain man, was an old-timer but seldom spoke and rarely made sense when he did, so Riglioni addressed himself to the hawk-nosed little Honeycutt. "The cannon been swabbed out?"

"Gingold just got her finished. What's the score?"

"We go point."

"Shit!"

"Let Scarbro drive. I'll tell you when to take over."

"Shit," Scarbro said, "Lucky Strike green has gone to war."

The hillbilly's eye glinted, a tiny beacon of his peril, though there was scarcely any light. Riglioni thought, *The son of a bitch'll get killed on me, him or his goddamn brother*. Scarbro would return from one of his eternal visits to the Third Platoon murdered by the news that his brother was dead, or his brother would arrive to be killed by Riglioni with news of Scarbro's death. One of them had to get it in a setup like theirs, and they were detestable for it.

"Hey, Hebe!" It came from the turret, an insistent harsh whisper where Gingold, with a grip on the cannon, was climbing down, unwieldy in his full combat harness. He sprang lightly from the deck, a man about Riglioni's size but, unlike him, jocular by nature and given ungovernably to nervous gestures. "Can I see you alone, Hebe?"

This man looked doomed too, on his face a futile artlessness that, weirdly, seemed to augur the end of his luck. Chafing, Riglioni said, "You have to go back to Brooklyn for jury duty. I heard all about it."

"No, I mean it, Rig." He leaned in close, cradling his light *greasegun* sub. "It's about that new guy in there."

Replacements always aroused suspicion, even in men recently replacements themselves. Sidling off with the man, Riglioni said, "Make it snappy, we're pulling out soon."

"Maybe it's none of my business," Gingold whispered earnestly. "After all, it ain't my religion." Over his shoulder he stole a glance at the turret, meanwhile digging a hand around at his rump.

"Get to the point, for Christ's sake."

"Yeah, Christ. He's got a picture of Christ taped up inside the turret, this kid. I think he's a yo-yo."

"So what's wrong with a picture of—"

"No, listen, maybe it's okay. You'd know better. This picture, it's got an inscription: 'To Ken Atman, with admiration, Jesus.' "

Riglioni sniggered half-heartedly, like Finch. "Well, that's his own business, if he wants to be a wise guy."

"A wise guy, right? Say the word and I'll punch the bastard out and make him sit down and pray or something. I mean I don't want to get in bad with *anybody* upstairs."

A giggle escaped Riglioni just as Platoon Sergeant Proctor came by. "Sal, you goddamn foghorn," he growled in hasty undertone, then stifled a laugh when Riglioni whirled on him exaggerating a look of astonishment. In feeble light they faced one another, each wearing a disconcerted little grin at the sickly horror he saw in the other. "You know that new lieutenant?" Proctor said. "I got to take him by the hand today, gonna drive him spank into our own junk for his first kiss. Let's get on the road, boy."

He giggled and turned away with a jerky stiff erectness, a rat-faced lightweight with canteen and raincoat flapping on his seat and pants that always seemed spilled full with anxiety. Death walked on Proctor's heels like some joker in a garrison hike: this Riglioni saw, and swept a rapid hand down across his eyes. He turned to Gingold muttering, "I'm losing my goddamn mind," and reached for a cigarette.

"Listen." Gingold played the heel of his hand in a circle around his nose. "I think he's an angle guy, this Atman. You know in the woods? When we did that one hour on and one off, every time it's my hour to sleep—I just crawl into the bag and close my eyes when he's waking me up already. All night long, I'm telling you."

"What do you want from me?" Riglioni said irritably. "Go punch him out and let me alone."

"Nah, he's not a bad kid. What do you want from him?"

Gingold wore the sweet smile he could so swiftly bring over his normally obtuse expression, and Riglioni had to laugh. He had not yet been able to appraise this aquiline and adenoidal man with any sense of accuracy, but of one thing he was certain: Gingold was either a peculiarly unorthodox sort of wag or a complete idiot. If he got it today he would go out a mystery man. So would the kid Atman. He resented them both. He especially resented Gingold, who was too good a man to lose, even though his aggressiveness under fire stemmed more from a savage dread than from the hatred of Nazis that he professed.

It was still too dark to strike a match. The cigarette dangling in his mouth, Riglioni went back to Finch, who was admonishing the pair of drivers to avoid shell-craters in their maneuvers on approaching the enemy town. "You roll down into one and Gingold could slam a shell right into Rig's jeep."

At sight of Riglioni he snorked and spat and then resumed

the same advice he had offered innumerable times while, as they had so often before, Honeycutt and Scarbro gazed at him with mute and remarkable patience. "Let's go," Riglioni said.

Back at the jeep Moran still sat scraping wax. With a momentous smack of his lips Finch said, "This gonna be a real bad one, Sal?" He spoke without inflection—solemnly, manfully, bravely asking no quarter of fate.

It was a moment of colossal discomfiture for Riglioni. Five years older than Finch, he felt so much his senior that the boy's infantile flamboyance alone seemed enough to cripple him. "We're going in like a shiteating regiment, what do you think of that? Just the three platoons, with Kitchen and Supply and the rest of Troop sneaking in behind us. Nothing but the 75's for artillery."

"Where's the rest of the Squadron?" Moran asked.

"Swinging around for the forest. There's a forest behind the town and old gangle-ass wants to cut off any retreat and be a hero up at Corps. God knows where the other squadron is. So what's the difference who goes point? We're all getting our ass shot off today."

"Don't crack up on me," Moran muttered, sheathing his bayonet and stowing the K-ration box in a pocket.

"Go on," Riglioni told Finch, "bring Zubrowski up behind Scarbro." He climbed in behind the mounted machine gun, murmuring, "My guts feel like glass."

Moran got the motor running, his attention on the officers gathered around Captain Stollman's jeep. "Who's that guy with the Buffalo Bill bush on his face?"

"Some new John. He showed up last night."

"Get a load of that fancy curved knife. Who's he think he is?"

"How should I know? I don't even know who I am."

"He's got a look in his eye. A look. Like he's plotting to take over or something, like he's full of ideas how to run this outfit.

His chest, see his chest sticking out all ready for those medals? I never thought it would be my fate to see another Finch."

"Finch! What the hell's he got to do with it?"

"Full of shit like Finch. Look how he carries that little carbine of his. You know, I was just starting to realize something when I got drafted. It was gonna set me up for life. That there's hundreds of ways for people to be full of shit, and everywhere you look somebody's doing it."

"Me, I'm doing it. That's who I am. I don't want to fight. I want to hide."

Moran lit a cigarette, then lit Riglioni's. "Take some advice, Sal. Turn in your stripes. This is supposed to be a recon outfit, and suddenly we're a task force. Put a wrench in the works. Turn in your stripes before it's too late."

"Get her up on the road, Joe." With a doughy hand he acknowledged Proctor's signal. "I turn in my stripes and they'll give them to some table waiter, so don't talk like a jerk."

"No, you and Gene Proctor, the whole outfit would bog down. Be good for nothing but to guard the General somewhere back in Belgium. We'd eat good and get some pussy, boy."

Riglioni stared at him, stubby Joe Moran who looked as if he hardly stood a chance today. The darkness had dissipated; there was light and chill and a galling dampness.

Moran said, "You want to play Twenty Questions?"

Kitchen, Medic, and Supply trucks trundled aside for the armored vehicles. Motors shrilled brazenly against a flat surrounding stillness in which not even a cricket chirped. In the point jeep Riglioni and Moran played Twenty Questions and led A Troop east through country much like the country in most parts of the world yet by daylight always a thing of strangeness to the men.

3

The town stuck out like a boil on the German plain. Beyond it a vast pine forest climbed hills to a mountain range. In a copse of young trees Riglioni stood on high ground that sloped down for miles to the plain, his gaze not on town or forest but on the mountain purpled and amorphous with distance, where the big enemy guns would be situated.

On the low road behind him he had stalled his Section Two vehicles, and others were braking up one after another. There was a vague chilly drizzle now, like mist.

Cherished moments of respite were evaporating; the peace was fabulous. He listened to the chary warbling of birds, a carol of humble tenure. Impassively, leafless trees prattled. The sky was obscene with doom, and lost friends were closer now. There was no more time.

How frail he was on the planet.

Proctor and the bearded new lieutenant came up, then Finch, then Lieutenant Enshaw, and finally Captain Stollman with his clerk Weldon and a map board. Stollman squinted out from the cover of trees and said, "There's our town."

He lit his pipe meticulously, then oriented the map board on Weldon's knees. Eyes directly on Riglioni, he said, "In a couple of miles we leave this ridge and run an open stretch. Not a long one, but we might get some artillery down on us. After that—"

"From those hills, sir?" the new lieutenant asked crisply.

"What?"

"Enemy artillery. From the high ground out there?"

The Captain's forehead wrinkled up with forbearance. "Yes," he said. "After that, according to Sergeant Meskerman's patrol maps, we get considerable embankment to hug, all the way to—here, some two miles short of the town. As you all know, there has been no reconaissance of the town itself. But we do know there's a canal running through it, don't we?"

Sergeant Proctor began to giggle.

"And a railroad," Stollman said, "right in the approach."

Proctor's giggle ascended, grew noisier, his ghostly blue eyes blinking. Pale-eyed too, the ruddy-bearded officer laid an austere look on him. "What's so funny, Sergeant?"

"Let him laugh," Captain Stollman said.

"This is hardly the time for jokes, Captain."

"Nobody's joking," the Captain responded softly while Proctor went right on giggling, his eyes wild. When Stollman bent over the map again, puffing on his pipe, his forehead solemnly wrinkled, Corporal Finch left the thicket. With a seasoned flourish he unslung his rifle and caught it up at port to balance himself for the steep descent. On the road he looked around in dust settling about his long legs, slung his rifle again, and pulled his chin back in an incongruous jowly way, as if overcome by some sudden gastric plight.

Actually it was no more than an effort to contrive a wrinkle in his forehead. Maintaining that expression, he approached Moran where he sat scraping wax behind his wheel. "Watch out for that ninety-day wonder," he said, just barely opening his mouth. "Chickenshit, Moran, real chickenshit."

"Who, Buffalo Bill? Yeah, I get that feeling about him."

"Not just a feeling, Moran. I know. Keep your eyes open."

He strode off, blinking in the misty whisper of a drizzle. At the armored car he leaped up and slapped the turret. When Gingold's head popped up Finch raised only his eyes, so that prominent wrinkles etched his brow. "How's the new man feeling?"

"What's the matter with your neck, Hebe?"

"Nothing. How's he taking it? Nervous?"

Gingold stared down with a marveling sleepy smile. "Why should he be nervous? He's shining his shoes."

"Shining his—his combat boots?" Astonished, Finch nonetheless kept his chin down and his brow furrowed. "How can he shine suede, or whatever you call it?"

"No, he's got these paratroop boots he bought from a Frenchwoman. He's more your type; he thinks he's going to a birthday party."

"Yeah? Well, you tell him if we get a night patrol I'll stick them in mud right up to his ass."

Gingold vanished down in the turret; he reappeared in an instant and showered Finch's helmet with a clatter of spent cartridges, saying with a nasal gasp, "On your way, Hebe."

By the mere arching of an eyebrow Finch turned his grim expression into a sardonic one, head cocked for a scathing retort. But wryly a smile crept into his face and, walking off, he said, "All right, keep a tight hole, now."

At his jeep he unslung the rifle and climbed in beside Zubrowski, saying with a long sigh, "Handle-bar mustache. Goatee. And that dopey knife. Boy, you see everything in this man's army."

"What's the matter?" Zubrowski yapped, awkwardly working his underslung, fragile jaw. He had astonished eyes that gave him a canine aspect. "Who? What?"

"Him," Finch grunted just as Proctor came chauffeuring the new lieutenant back in his jeep. "Lieutenant Buffalo Bill."

"Buffalo Bill!" Zubrowski guffawed, and ululated with slobbering delight. "Hey, that's a hot one! Buffalo Bill! Boy, what a way you got, Finch."

Corporal Finch yawned, sinking modestly in his seat. "Big shot ninety-day wonder. The goddamn phony."

There was more open ground than Captain Stollman had been knowledgeable enough or willing to indicate. Lieutenant

Enshaw was quick to assess the situation and overtake the point jeep, a long ash hanging as if by magic to one of the cigarettes almost always in his mouth, chain-lit but seldom puffed on. Shooting past Moran, he yelled, "Go like a big-assed bird!"

Like invisible corkscrews, shells began to break the air overhead. But none hit the road; they crashed far down the slope, exploding black rancid geysers as tall as the lollipop trees bordering the ridge in a rank of doltish unconcern. Big shells, they were not zeroed in, and without trouble the entire troop sped through to the cover of towering embankments.

Proctor shot by and signaled for a regrouping pause, Buffalo Bill sitting with hands ready on the mounted gun, so ramrod stiff that Riglioni began to laugh. "That paper ass-hole—you see Gene giggling at him? Gene better find the Old Man a nice deep CP in a hurry. I don't want *any* of those fake sons of bitches near me." He snorted to break off his laughter. "They'll get us killed!"

After a long probe down into the valley, Lieutenant Enshaw drove back, signaling a clear road and good defilade ahead. Moran idled the jeep past him to take up the lead again. Nothing came at them all the way down. The country sat quiet and gray in the drizzle, dozing like a peaceful countryside anywhere else in the world.

Presently the air disintegrated in the heartening ferocious crackle of the 75-mm. guns spanking a barrage down on town and forest, and A Troop went looping the hillocks in a race for the target. No enemy fire came to demand evasive maneuvers as the vehicles crossed their run of flat ground. The 75 Platoon had the whole German town pinned down tight, but when Riglioni approached a single-gauge railroad track the big ones came hooting in from those guns on the distant heights.

Joe Moran got the point jeep across clean, but one blast on the track lifted the armored car and rocked it so violently that Gingold, exposed in position on his .50, let out a frenzied invective made falsetto by the din. With the bearded lieutenant fixed beside him as brave as a stone, Proctor accelerated straight for the flaming 75 blasts and, just as the friendly fire lifted, he led a wide sweep into the smoky black storm where buildings were ablaze. Troop machine guns hammered in both the heavy octave and the light; 37-mm. cannon pounded point-blank amid the thundering enemy shellbursts.

The Second Platoon and then all the Troop charged in, raking squat stone houses on every side without meeting entrenched resistance. There was penetration in good depth before the enemy shellfire came down on an abruptly lowered trajectory and the column had to pull up on the flagged sidewalks for a halt. Lieutenant Enshaw rumbled down the line, half standing behind his wheel and shouting but voiceless in the uproar of explosions on surrounding streets. He kept pumping his arm for an advance, so the column tracked after him. Then shells came marching up the avenue of penetration and stalled the outfit in earnest.

Harsh eruptions bit corners off a slate roof here and there and exploded the damp cobblestones like racks of pool balls. Vehicles pulled up close to the buildings. From the jeeps men fled in a clatter of metal gear into doorways while car crewmen hid down in their turrets and under hatches they quickly slammed shut. Big shells were devouring the street, but Proctor had chosen a route that put houses between the hill guns and the vehicles, so with each blast the path of fragmentation was safely away from the hiding men. In a deep doorway Riglioni broke open a K ration and found the can of processed cheese. Squatting there under him, Moran yelled, "Gimme the box!"

The noise was deafening before it fell off with an abruptness that left dank aftertones ringing in the fumes. Moran stuffed the waxed container into a pocket, saying, "I don't know if I'm cold or scared. I'm all trembly inside."

"It's sort of cold," Riglioni said. He fell to opening his can of cheese as again the shells slammed down, though in a pattern more conservatively spaced than before. He ate in slow munches. The shells hooted in and crashed all over their end of the town. Acrid fumes hung heavy in the mists.

"We got in too easy," Moran said.

"They sucked us in. Deeper inside they're gonna give it to us heavy."

A jeep shrieked to a halt and in it Proctor yelled, "Sal! Run your disciples into that next street!" His narrow face was livid, the pores visibly enlarged. Buffalo Bill sat forward with both hands on the machine-gun pistol-grip. "We got to find their OP and blind them," Proctor screamed, and winced as a shell crashed upstreet.

The lieutenant sat courageously petrified. "Turn in your stupid stripes," Moran piped, and another shell wrenched a rooftop. "It's always got to be us!"

"What?" Proctor regarded him with abstracted eyes, then giggled and drove off.

The three vehicles of Section Three rolled by with Connie Meskerman in the lead jeep. Riglioni shoved Moran out and piled into their jeep behind him; then both of them leaped out flat on their bellies as a huge one rustled in close. It sledged into a building across the way with a fantastic rubble-crushing explosion, and the smoke was still showering rock dust when Moran got rolling with Riglioni pumping his arm for Honeycutt and Zubrowski to follow.

They took the turn fast, Riglioni calling it that way and calling cannonfire over his head from Gingold against the street bend a distance away. He raked the left wall of buildings and behind him Finch machine-gunned the right; it was when they took the bend that the first enemy small arms fire came.

A shrill chatter sent slugs crackling past; metal hit the jeep with a thump and Moran wheeled sharply out of there before the armored car nosed in. Honeycutt stopped the car short.

Gingold boomed off a brace of 37 rounds and the car backed out. Finch was already out of his jeep and kneeling at the corner house, pumping his rifle empty. The German machine gun answered and Finch danced back.

The air was all smoke and fine drizzle. The bombardment sounded off to the north where Meskerman had taken Section Three. Riglioni reached Finch just behind Zubrowski and a few paces ahead of Moran. "I could send Gingold's cannon at them," he panted, "but who knows what's waiting to hit it? Sit tight. We're up ahead of their big ones. Proctor'll come looking soon enough."

Not Proctor but Enshaw came in his jeep the next instant. He hopped out and listened to Riglioni's report on the German gun, then said, "We could roll the armored car in, but they could pepper the tires and set her up for something maybe big they got." A long ash fell off his cigarette. "You know about where that Schmeisser is?"

"No, we got out too fast."

Finch said, "It's about three hundred yards. On the left side. A low window someplace." Like everybody's, his face was purple with chill and disbelief.

Shells, smaller than those from the far mountain, pounded the street behind them and tracked north, gasping, shrieking in. Enshaw said, "Finch, you get across there in a hurry and cover me. Take somebody along. I'm gonna inch in a little."

Finch tapped Zubrowski and got set with his rifle high. As he did, the gaunt little driver did, his small protruding jaw sheeny and aquiver. Finch leaped forth and Zubrowski leaped after him and they crossed the street in a tumble for the cover of piled debris just as the enemy gun cut loose.

"Separate and stay close to the wall," Enshaw told the men. "They know us and maybe got a phone to call down some mortar."

He slipped around the corner firing carbine shots from the

hip, and the pair across the street set up a rapid fire. Together they both ducked low when machine-gun slugs chewed powder out of the rubble. Enshaw plunged back in awkward haste, stammering, "There's rifle cover for that Schmeisser! Jesus, I thought I was hit! Am I hit? Jesus, I thought I was! Sal, bring your load up to right here and cut the shit out of that side! They got rifles on that side!"

Great shuttling moans sounded overhead and Moran said, "Oh, that's railroad guns they got up there, 212s or something. Oh, they're big." The detonations were monstrous behind them. Moran went for the jeep and brought it back with Riglioni on the air-cooled .30, raking the buildings across on Finch's side.

Enshaw leaped up on the jeep, waving Finch and Zubrowski down for cover as the German gun noised into Riglioni's racket. Over the high clatter he yelled, "Look, this is how, Sal. Keep those rifles pinned down and somebody can go along the wall without that Schmeisser seeing shit. Their Observation Post must be in a steeple or something back in there and we better put it out. You take that Schmeisser out, Riglioni, and we can move up on that OP too."

Then he was gone, jeep and all.

Riglioni let up on the gun to stare after Enshaw, muttering, "Take that Schmeisser out," and Moran was staring at him when something hit the jeep a malicious clang, and he cut loose again with the machine gun, bawling, "Out! Out! Back her out, Joe!"

Out they went and a corkscrew came straight down from the sky and sent them both in a flat lunge to the pavement. The shell crashed close by, rocking the whole street and spattering rock dust hard against helmets and vehicles. From the armored-car turret Gingold yelled, "What the hell are we waiting for?" and then vanished when another monster hooted down to explode in midstreet.

Riglioni ran low for the armored car, bellowing a gibberish of misery and anger. He slapped the hatches and with a leap walloped the turret. "Let's go, we're walking," he bellowed, and an incoming shell drove him under the car.

Greasegun in hand, Gingold scampered to the deck, leaped down and ran behind Riglioni to where Moran crouched between jeep and building. Honeycutt and Scarbro threw open their hatches and shimmied expertly out and down. Weapons hugged close, they ran off in the smoke.

Then out of the turret came Atman, the replacement only a week or so up on the line. As young as Finch, he had the same sort of neutral features, and wore steel-framed GI glasses over gentle eyes. He gazed about with an ignorant sort of detachment as if, in spite of the hollow pandemonium, he did not realize that someone was bound to die this day just as it was bound to turn from drizzle to rain.

4

Suddenly that abominable spook, the enemy, had produced a group of men in smug deep helmets who were determined to kill Section Two for no more than trying to advance.

Incredibly, human men were menacing them, persecuting

them in their work. Not human men at all but hateful entrenched men as impersonal as the drizzle-misted hills beyond, insufferably hostile men without emotions, motherless and childless, unloving and fatherless sudden men full of some unworldly foreknowledge and cunning and a mocking obduracy.

The shells crashing in streets behind them were just a lot of noise now that terror had focused full on their path ahead. Riglioni stared at faces, at Moran who looked doomed and at Scarbro who had a brother worrying somewhere close by, at Atman the stranger and at Gingold who was even more a stranger because of the small things that were familiar about him, at Honeycutt who wore the face of a suspicious hawk and grenades on his chest and had a wife waiting back at her father's sharecropper farm in Alabama. Honeycutt seldom carried grenades; he really trusted nothing but his rifle . . . had recently extended it one-handed out of a poker game to drill the pigeon Weldon had been trying unsuccessfully to pot at fifteen feet with a pistol . . . and drawled, "Only way to get use out of that weapon is throw it." He could shoot that way; scouting on foot up ahead of the vehicles, it was common for him to carry his rifle in a single hand and swing it like a lead pencil, muzzle so freely nosing about that he could hit sudden targets wherever they appeared. A hell of a man to lose in a stupid mission like this one.

"You, Honeycutt, go in first," Riglioni said without looking at the man, but looking at each face that he told what to do while shells smashed up the town. He put Scarbro in beside Moran, who then whispered the jeep forward with the towering hillbilly—grown so small behind the gun—sending a lethal spray to gnash glass out of windows across on Finch's side and drive riflemen down.

Honeycutt slipped around the corner with suspicious eyes and the one hand swinging his rifle. Then Riglioni went in hugging the wall that Enshaw had discovered to be out of the machine gun's line of fire. He signaled across for the two men to draw German fire, and Zubrowski rose up to pound off shots with Finch. The Germans answered with a hysterical song, and Honeycutt pointed out the vague smokeless break in the mist at ground level upstreet.

With Finch and Zubrowski hiding again, the German gun let up. Riglioni began trotting behind Honeycutt, dependent on Scarbro's unfaltering fire to keep them safe from the dangerous long wall of windows under which Finch now went crouching in a crazy dash over the rubble ahead of murderous dust spatters and vanished as the death swept past him. He was gone. Then he was up and Riglioni screamed to make himself heard above the clangor of automatic fire: "Stay down! Stay down! Who wants you up there?"

But Finch was good. He had separated himself by several yards from Zubrowski who, apparently on Finch's prior command, now rose up and cracked rapid shots at the German cellar window. When the dust butterflies tracked along the edge of debris to send Zubrowski down, Finch popped up, firing accurately enough to scare the enemy gunners silent for a while. He was good.

Riglioni waved Gingold and Atman along behind him, indicating upper-story windows for them to watch on this side of the street. Gingold rattled a burst across to Scarbro's windows and laughed maniacally, spittle bubbling over a lip. "How about that fucking Hebe!" he barked, and ran ahead.

Riglioni pursued Honeycutt, who suddenly fell to a knee pumping shots at close range into a doorway, leaped up with a grenade and let the handle fly off as he ran, pitching it like a baseball one short instant before it exploded inside the house. He plunged into the smoke, shooting, and Riglioni leaped past and turned to wave Gingold and Atman in after the little cracker.

Skinny little cracker and cold, everything personal—his fear, his mourning, his humor—buried deep. He had once lost his fire-power in a jeep crash, but he had it in there now and Riglioni was laughing at Gingold because a man's voice sounded crazy in this uncanny drizzle: *How about that fucking Hebe!* after killing a man in a window, a brave crazy man trying to sneak death to Scarbro, and Gingold's voice in the uncanny drizzle was crazier than the brave dead man, so Riglioni laughed, or giggled, and thought his face was Proctor's and poked his rifle into one doorway after another while muffled gunfire broke off in the house his men were taking behind him. He watched his own upper windows. He had to hasten things along before enemy mortar could be called down on the street.

He was tempted to call Moran's jeep in deeper, but he still dreaded point-blank cannonfire from some possible hidden emplacement in the smoking wreckage of houses at street's end. Scarbro kept punishing the windows above Finch, Moran siding him with an occasional rifle shot. With Zubrowski assisting, Finch kept the German machine gun revealing its position in broken mist. "Smokeless powder, the bastards," Riglioni sobbed, and none of it could really be happening around Salvatore Riglioni who was really the same old little kid from Bethany Road in Burbank hugging his mother's knees and saying, "Oh Ma I love you because you give me potatoes."

They were back there in the house too long. Within thirty yards of the German gun he turned and saw Atman back out of the building hunched over his rifle, mouth agape and blowing vapors up around his glasses, shellfire drumming to the north; then Gingold danced out on nimble feet, and at last Honeycutt dodged past them both in a trot right up to Riglioni. "There was two Krauts in there."

The time of his jeep accident. Rode it down a hill so steep that he lost control and when the crash sounded everybody ran around the hill expecting a wrecked Honeycutt but there he stood leaning a hand on a tree where the jeep lay over on its back, four wheels spinning, the mounted gun a ruin with perforated steel jacket split and spread out like cardboard and Honeycutt engrossed in it: "Guess I done lost my fire-power."

Now he resembled the other pair, who came running. They all looked alike. Mortar had to fall soon, Riglioni felt it, and there was no debris sufficient for cover on this side of the street. Still, if the jeep stayed close to the wall . . . He signaled Moran in deeper and held up a grenade for him to acknowledge with a nod. He waved it high until Finch poked up his head, nodded, and vanished behind the rubble again. The street stank of wet powder fumes; everyone was sodden and agleam. He pulled the cotter pin, moved up fast while Honeycutt got the others into a doorway. Rifle prodding ahead of him, Riglioni took over a more advanced doorway and there weighed the grenade, measured the distance, and tossed it high to land near the machine-gun window. He flopped back in a corner of the doorway and watched Moran call Scarbro down low in the jeep—the three in the other doorway cutting shots at the windows—until the grenade barked.

Scarbro was up stuttering on his gun again and Finch went racing out of the rubble across a flat sidewalk for what seemed a longer time than it should take for the grenade smoke to clear away from the German gunners' line of sight. But then he was down and firing from behind the crumbled stoop he had picked out for his roost, firing and giving Zubrowski his run before the Germans could dare seek a target. There was something unnatural about his talent. He had them pinned down, a big automatic weapon hiding from his rifle, and had Zubrowski perfectly trained to roost and keep fire on that cellar window while he himself loaded up and resumed firing. Then he was making charades to inform Riglioni that the house doorway was on the far side of the machine-gun window. He was unnatural, hence a fit part of the unnatural drizzle, the day of smoke, and would certainly have hit any doorway or window on this side that showed a face, so Riglioni took the three men in swiftly past several doorways and into one just short of the menacing cellar window.

All alike, as unnatural as Enshaw who stuck himself in to draw fire and wreck the Kraut plan. *Riglioni,* unnatural name. He got another grenade off his jacket and, with Scarbro's pattern of gunfire a part of it, felt he had been through this moment before. Not just some similar skirmish but this moment itself, with Gingold panting hysterically, with Honeycutt pursing his lips as if trying to recall something, with Atman gaping dumbly, the vapors bubbling out of his mouth in quick tiny convulsions—this very instant all over again . . .

He stared at Atman, who had never experienced a street fight with them before. "How's it going, kid?" he yelled above the staccato of Scarbro's firing, crazy-voiced out of a face of ashes.

"Okay."

Little boy smiling, oh familiar, oh sick. *Son of a bitch thinks I'm a murderer. I'm getting killed now.* "Gingold. This grenade goes off, you run through it and shoot up the next doorway. Inside fast. Unless a locked door, see? Then me, Honeycutt, Atman. Quick. Soon as it goes off."

He yanked the pin, carefully lobbed the grenade as for an instant Scarbro's gun was silent and a voice blossomed out of the cellar window, a mild and tremulous young voice saying, "*Es ist unmöglich.*"

Under rifles pounding shots at the windows he fell back in the doorway with a vision of piled smoky rubble where the street bent south, of rain and the hills away off. A glimpse of heaven forever—*Hey Salvie! Hey Salvie!*—and then the grenade exploded so simply.

Through smoke he chased past the window behind Gingold and saw him go hard against the door, forcing it, and Riglioni fired first with Gingold's slow *bububub* sounding then, and Honeycutt was firing up a dark stairway and dashing off where he kicked at something and said, "Right here, Sal."

Riglioni yanked him away from a slatwood cellar door, then had to deflect the man's rifle, saying, "No, you'll get a ricochet. Let Gingold, his lead slugs."

The machine gun went into action below, a consoling racket that meant Finch had started nagging to distract the gun crew. Good boy, better than ever. With one greasegun shot Gingold smashed the lock and then he kicked the door in while Riglioni got his last grenade ready. He let the handle fly off, yelled, "*Raus kommen!*" and threw the grenade just as a pistol fired in the cellar.

No one was hit. Below, the explosion swallowed up the shrieks of men and into it Gingold lunged raking shots and at the top of the stairs Riglioni triggered fast shots at three men already contorting in swarms of smoke directly under the high mount of their long, precision-built and complex gun. Gingold kept hitting them until his gun was empty, then went to stand over them, abstractedly replacing his spent magazine with a full one. He bent to take a P-38 pistol, got it into a pocket, and remained kneeling, gasping with a clogged nasal sound, his gaze on a blond boy with knowing blue eyes who had lost his helmet while dying.

Honeycutt walked over. The suspicion was gone from his eyes; now they were wide and pensive. He looked past Gingold at the dead boy and, with the most contrite smile ever, said, "What do you think of Hitler now?"

Scarbro sat pointing his mounted machine gun at Germans who stood in a litter of broken glass with hands on their bared heads. Zubrowski was lining them up along the wall and some were still straggling out of the low-flung apartment building. They were men of various ages, faces full of wives and mothers and flat naked horror, eyes fixed on Scarbro with a clear conviction that he was to be their executioner. They were feeble, futile sons and fathers, not a Nazi face evident among them.

The last came out goaded by the rifle of Finch, who was chewing on a cigar. There were eleven in all. By custom, Gingold strolled over to abuse them with an interrogation in Yiddish.

To the north, shellfire was spasmodic, and now it could be made out as frightful 88-mm. German and the Troop's own puny 37s. Motors sounded, approaching. In a violent tremor, Riglioni sent Honeycutt and Zubrowski upstreet to work the houses, and took Moran out of the jeep to send him poking with Gingold through doors on the other side. To Finch, who was patting the prisoners down for possible hidden weapons, he said, "We're getting mortar any minute. Cover these guys, I'm pulling the jeep in close."

"Nah, I cut their wire line when I flopped over there. Right on their wire I flopped, so I cut it. They never had a chance to call for mortar." Finch wore a smart-aleck grin around the cigar, though his tiny baby-lips were white. "I found a whole bunch of these cigars, Sal. You want one?"

"Huh? Listen, next time I tell you to stay down, you do it. Don't you know my signals?" Now he saw vehicles rolling in around the bend—jeeps, armored cars—with Proctor in the lead and identifiable by the Buffalo Bill lieutenant beside him on the air-cooled gun. An injured look crossed Finch's face, but he hid it in a long meditative puff as he lit the cigar. Riglioni said, "You cut their wire, huh? If it ran out that way I guess their OP is in there, not up ahead."

He shambled away to the jeep where, as he got behind the wheel, Scarbro said something the northerly shellfire obscured. Riglioni got rolling across the street and pulled up close to a house near the kid Atman, who was tilting up his canteen for a drink. A wayward notion that Atman had been absent for a while made Riglioni dizzy. Chilled, sick to his stomach, he climbed out and went to meet Honeycutt and Zubrowski, who came forth from smoldering rubble where the street bent away toward enemy terrain. With nothing to tell them, he was really taking the opportunity to get away from Proctor, convinced that the Platoon Sergeant had another mission for him. He was ravenously hungry.

Proctor called his name. He stopped, his teeth chattering. He was all alone and cold on glistening wet flagstones out in the middle of the universe.

The drizzle turned to rain. Absurdly, he thought of a pork-pie hat he had once owned, and of his blue car, and of going from it up rainy stone stairs into a warm house.

"The OP is in behind there," Proctor said, approaching.

"I know. Finch cut their wire line to it. I got no casualties."

"I know. Finch told me." Proctor blinked his pale punished eyes in preoccupation. "We lost Jimmy Caddigan. Right in the head. Listen, don't bother Meskerman too much, I'm gonna take him in that way for a look. Keep him away from everybody for a while, he lost Caddigan. I got your vehicles here with Section Three. He lost Jimmy Caddigan and you know—"

"Corporal!" A crisp loud yelp. The bearded lieutenant was standing in Proctor's jeep. "I said search those prisoners!"

"Get some table waiter to do it." Finch strolled over puffing on his cigar. To Proctor he said, "I disarmed those prisoners, Gene. I told him so."

"Sergeant Proctor!"

"Ah, for Christ's sake, Lieutenant, run their ass back to Troop and leave us alone!" Proctor's cheeks were gray and open-pored. He giggled, staring blankly at Riglioni, then abruptly went grave as Moran and Gingold came trotting along.

"Sergeant Proctor," the lieutenant intoned. Approaching, he unslung his carbine and for some obscure reason brought it up to port with a military snap. "I want two men detailed at once—"

A gunshot clanged squarely in the officer's path, weird against the distant noise of shelling, and stopped him while Scarbro swung the smoking long .30 around and began examining it in a grotesquely exaggerated way. After one panicked glance the lieutenant continued on, and stopped amid the clustered men. Raindrops danced on his enormous nose; nestled in the ruddy mustache, his nostrils flared out imperiously. "I want two men detailed to search those prisoners in my presence."

Proctor looked at him, glanced at the wet pavement, looked again at the officer. He worked his raincoat off the back of his ammunition belt and flapped it out slowly, then began putting it on. Riglioni said, "I'm putting Finch in for a decoration, Gene."

"Is this Finch?" the lieutenant said. "I'm putting him in for a bust."

Finch puffed luxuriously on the cigar, studying the officer under a wrinkled brow. Proctor giggled. "If I read it in the Bible I wouldn't believe it. All right, get spread out. You think you're in garrison someplace? Enshaw be along soon and move you all up. Lieutenant," he said, "you suit yourself. Anything. But I'm gonna tell you one thing. You leave my goddamn men alone," he went on in a rising, unrestrainable voice, "or by Jesus I'll knock out your fucking eyes, shit in the holes, and call you *ole turd-head!*"

Men laughed. All over the street men were laughing and flapping out their raincoats, unslinging their light field packs. The cannon were still dueling to the north, the spank of 75s now added to the 37s against an 88 no doubt mounted on a big maneuvering Tiger tank. The sky just hung there white and rainy and the lieutenant hung there too in the fantastic moment, holding his flimsy carbine at port.

Then came the noise of a racing jeep. But it was not Enshaw. Scarbro's brother braked to a halt, looked around at the faces of Sections Two and Three, gunned off and spun around for his race back again to the idle Third Platoon.

"Sergeant," the lieutenant began in a tone he labored to bring up out of his bowels, "I can't doubt that you know the meaning of insubor—"

"You son of a bitch," Riglioni cut in with a shaky, almost tearful, voice, "you looking for a bullet in the face? Go on and get the hell out of here, you cunt-faced son of a bitch!"

Like a rock-slide his face went at the officer and got him going for Proctor's jeep, scared white but nonetheless wearing a grim campaigner's intransigent look. He gunned the motor and swung the jeep around in a sudden silence that fell over the world as if cannon to the north were paying proper tribute to his rank. At the bend he jumped the sidewalk to avoid collision with the approaching jeep of Lieutenant Enshaw, who cut away sharp but never lost the ash from his dangling cigarette.

5

Connie Meskerman was dead.

Pinned down by a barrage for a full hour while scouting ahead with Proctor, he had come back all right. But later small arms had riddled him while his Section Three and Lindemayer's Section One were knocking out the Observation Post to cut off enemy communication with the mountain guns.

Meskerman and Jimmy Caddigan were dead; Lindemayer had a casualty; now the time was night and, after advancing several streets, Riglioni's Section Two was intact, fed, and wearing dry socks in one of the three widespread houses that formed the Second Platoon holding point.

"Evangeline," Moran whispered, and Atman snored gently. "She went rowing after her sweetheart." Moran's tiny candle had lasted no longer than a minute, and Finch had refused to make a light out of his extra can of shoe dubbing. Now Finch slept and Moran, his head under the blanket hung for blackout over a forward window, spoke in a drowsy undertone. "She rowed up the river and he came rowing down, behind some bushes or something. So they missed each other. Never saw each other again, and lived happily ever after. Sounds screwy, but I remember."

Atman mumbled something. "Jesus, even in his sleep he makes noise," Riglioni said alongside Moran. "And you—what are *you* talking about, Joe?"

"These movies they used to show us. Two colors—the world was blue at night and brown in the daytime. I remember the movies they showed us in school. But night ain't blue, it's a black son of a bitch. Whole bunch of crap they fed us."

"Pull your head inside. Better take some sleep. If the Krauts don't come up the Old Man's bound to dream us up a patrol."

Moran came groping for Riglioni in the darkness. "There's two other platoons, what's he want from us? Sal, turn in your stripes!"

Atman snorted and giggled in his sleep. "Jesus," Riglioni muttered; he lit a cigarette and glanced at his watch. He could not be sure that Atman had disappeared twice under fire, as he imagined. Both times there had been a lull in the fighting, first immediately after the street fight to knock out the machine gun, and then during their lunch in the burned-out husk of a building. But he was there for the advance, this weird kid, had even run ahead past the retreating Section One to drag Checorski out, full of shell fragments and whimpering, to the shelter of a house. "First I see him, then I don't."

A few feet away another match blazed, Gingold lighting up. Atman coughed, gagged, kicked out with a clattering foot, and in a firm voice announced, "John Brooks is not a cockroach!"

Riglioni fell forward and shook the boy. "All right, get the hell up! You want to think John Brooks ain't a cockroach, that's your business, but quit making all that goddamn noise about it!"

"What? What? Is it eight o'clock?"

"Pretty near. You might as well go relieve Zubrowski. And don't be making noise. You make too much goddamn noise. We don't know how close the Krauts are, and we don't want them to know where we are. Can you remember that?"

"Sure, Sarge. We expecting a counterattack?"

"Of course we're expecting a counterattack. What kind of stupid question is that?"

Atman cleared his throat like a claxon, coughed, sighed.

"Jesus, I just told you to keep quiet!"

"Sorry, Sarge. Where's Zubrowski at, Sarge?"

"Where's he at?" Riglioni had a notion the boy was grinning in the darkness. "You saw us mount a gun in the cellar window? Well, that's where Zubrowski is. Listen, first I see you, then I don't. Okay. Okay, Atman. Now you just haul your ass out of that bag and go relieve Zubrowski."

He crept away to find Scarbro, and woke him to relieve Honeycutt in the armored car positioned down the alley, then returned to the window and the sound of Moran's bayonet scraping wax. He sat there smoking. Finch sighed in his sleep. Nearby, Gingold's cigarette glowed. It was too quiet out front; he pictured Germans crowding closer, inevitably closer for the counterattack, vengeful and murderous with fear.

The Captain's clerk Weldon was bound to show up. To fetch him for a showdown with Stollman and Buffalo Bill. Weldon would be grim and frightened. Weldon would resent him for causing his excursion out of that safe cellar CP deep in the town. His stomach sank with revulsion and dismay. The cellar below was cluttered with piles of furniture and God knew how many booby traps. He must warn Atman against snooping around down there and possibly blowing them all to bits, but he only sat pressed back beyond hope into one of those peculiar paralyzing instants of clarity in which he saw his death. Momentarily now, a savage barrage would fall, or the Krauts would come up screaming, in a multitude too immense to roll back with the outfit's bluff of strength.

Moran whispered, "Doesn't it make you feel brave to know that Meskerman and Caddigan are dead?"

"What? What's the matter with you, Joe?"

"Very brave, and sort of grown up?"

"Listen, Joe, you leave me alone! I'll bust your head, you crazy son of a bitch!"

Scarbro passed under the rear window blanket and down into the jeep parked below. Metal clanged where Atman descended stairs, and Gingold giggled a soft curse. "Without capital initials he writes his name. A real yo-yo, what are you gonna do?"

"Gingold, go tell him about booby traps. For Christ's sake, don't let him move the furniture around."

Scraping wax, Moran said, "I can't help it, Sal. I always feel that way when one of the boys get it. Like a goddamn hero."

Riglioni could have taken some sleep by waking Finch to keep the guard reliefs going, but he lay on the floor thinking of Meskerman and Caddigan and episodes of grief and laughter he had shared with them. And Grury and Sandorian and Kaufmann and even some faces turned nameless over the long months of seasons that survived them. At midnight he sent Scarbro and Atman off to their second guard hour, woke Finch, and tried to sleep.

There was no end in sight. Winter was setting in.

He knew there were Germans prowling the shadows and open lots out front. They would run close and hurl potatomashers in the windows as they had in Orsbach, sparing him while fragments murdered Grury a yard away. The kid Atman would fail to see them coming. Scarbro would have no line on them, coming as they would in the kid's area. He fished a biscuit out of his jacket pocket and munched on it. The rear window blanket flapped, Honeycutt returning from the turret. Moran woke babbling. "Finch. You awake, Finchie?"

"Yeah, yeah. You got your rifle patch ready?"

"Sure. Give me the can and I'll set it up."

"No, take that rifle patch and go clean your foreskin." Finch sniggered. "I got no extra can of dubbing, Moran. Christ, I don't even have *any*."

"Oh for Jesus' sake, you prick! You're a prick, Finch, a prick!"

"Now shut up," Riglioni barked in a whisper.

Outside a small noise grew into grinding tank treads and swiftly advanced, intensified until it seemed a Tiger tank was charging the house. As Riglioni bolted upright, it turned into the fluttering hoot of a gigantic shell and seemed to pass directly in one window and out the other before it crashed mightily in a near street. With an insane laugh Honeycutt shouted, "Man, you ain't going back to Ala-BAM!"

"Shut up!" Riglioni wriggled along the floor to grab him. "You gone out of your head?"

"Shit!" Honeycutt yapped. "Shit! Shit!"

Riglioni knocked him over and held him down, a wiry little mass of tremors. In the darkness Gingold came awake with a wretched grunt and said feebly, painfully, "Firing squad for Rig and Proctor, they don't know how to kiss ass like human beings."

"Shit, shit," Honeycutt said, but in a whisper now.

"All he can think of is food," came from Zubrowski in a scratchy voice. "What time's it getting?"

"Shut up, you just went to sleep." Riglioni let Honeycutt up. "Now everybody pipe down in here."

Moran said, "Connie Meskerman, well, well, well, well, well. Death makes you want to die."

"Shut up, Joe! Maniacs! Section Two? This is Section Eight!"

Another shell came over and drove them all to the floor with a clatter, another enormous one that rattled like a tank. Something hit the rear blanket, someone threw himself in at the window and the shell crunched the night to disaster outside. Riglioni sat up. "Who the hell!"

"Me, Proctor." A giggle.

"Oh, leave us the hell alone, Gene! Ain't the Old Man gonna use anybody but this platoon?"

"Never mind that snow. You the only section without casualties."

"There's two more *platoons*, for Christ's sake!"

"Well, well, well, well, well."

"Joe, I'll kill you! Go to sleep, Joe!"

Proctor flopped down on the floor. "Don't get your ass in an uproar."

"No, let the bastard send somebody else out."

"Take it easy, I just brought wire. He wants wire, so I ran some wire. Here, get your hand on this field phone. Your call sign is Mayflower. Troop is Reliable. Platoon's Gingerbread but it ain't in yet and won't be for a couple hours. Enshaw's out on patrol with a couple of Lindemayer's disciples, so don't be bitching it's always you." He ground the lever and then muttered some words to check in with Troop. Lighting a cigarette, he leaned back on the wall. "Let me rest a bitty bit. I still got line to run over to Rayhew."

"Is he making sergeant now?" Finch said. "I thought Gross was in line for it."

"How should I know? Old Man and me sort of off speaking terms. That bearded mishap must've gone piss-whistling to him while me and Connie was laying under them bombs."

"Well, well, Connie Meskerman, well, well, well."

"Now go on to sleep, Joe. Please." Riglioni dug knuckles at his eyes, rubbed his face. "See, this whole section's nuts. Every one of them, from Atman to Zubrowski."

Like a tin sheet in a wind the next shell rippled through him and then became thunder at a distance. There was silence in the dark house. Presently Proctor said, "Yeah-boy. Colonel Powell committed Captain Stollman. Stollman committed Lieutenant Enshaw. Enshaw committed Sergeant Meskerman. It's like them Biblical begets." He gave an anguished giggle. "General commits the Colonel. Another general commits the General, on and on up to Eisenhower. Then Roosevelt. Then God His own Self, I guess."

"First Christ," Moran whispered. "Proper channels, boy."

"You'll kiss ass through proper channels," Gingold said nasally. "Rig and Proctor, just like everybody else."

"You ain't going back to Ala-BAM!" Zubrowski now. Idiotic.

Proctor said, "I ain't kissing no ass in this world."

"Yes you are, Hebe. Once the Old Man says insubordination?"

"I'll court-martial the son of a bitch." Proctor snuffed out his cigarette in a burst of sparks. He went over the call signs again with Riglioni and Finch, then slipped out under the blackout. Soon his jeep whispered away, and only silence remained in the dead hollow center of night that for Riglioni wore the image of his own destructible face. He squeezed his eyes shut.

"Miserable," Zubrowski gasped. "Misery, misery."

Riglioni felt dusty, ancient, weak. His brain seemed to be crowding out past his eyeballs. Moran's scraping bayonet and the breathing of men were sounds adrift and alien in this black pit of doom, the unanchored night. Where was sleep? God mocking him.

"Yeah, I know why I'm so miserable," Zubrowski slobbered toothlessly. Nobody commented. "Hey, no crap."

"What do you know about crap, Hebe?"

"He don't know shit about it," Honeycutt said, and they all giggled, a bunch of desperate Proctors glass-eyed in the dark cell of panic, all sharing the same horror that swept down now with a shell that mocked them from God above and erupted outside, voice of the night, the monstrous phantom darkness, the enemy. There was no end to it and no sleep and the scythe of Death was scraping nearby and tricked him into wanting to die and Riglioni struggled against the cold fingers of sleep. He sat up in a lurch, his bare head colliding with Moran's helmet.

"No kidding, I just figured out why I'm so miserable."

A match flared. It sent up a second, stronger, flame that continued bright and warm and made a ghostly apparition of Gingold's face above it under his helmet with its net and burlap—a wonderful flowering light that illuminated a great potbellied candle below. In a voice thin with awe Moran said, "Where did you ever get that magnificent candle?"

"I'm so glad you like it." Gingold stretched his arms with a voluptuous grunt.

"A fantastic candle. Where did you ever get it, Paul?"

"Never mind the Paul crap."

Riglioni bent toward the flame. "You made this candle?"

Studying the bright motionless light, Gingold said nothing. Zubrowski chuckled. "You know why I'm so miserable, hey?"

"Because you're a malcontent," Moran said impatiently. "You don't know how to enjoy a war. How about a hunk of wax off that candle, Paulie-boy?"

"Never mind the Paulie-boy crap. This candle's a work of art."

"How about a chunk off that work of art?"

"You got no rhythm, Hebe. People with rhythm don't molest works of art."

"It's a beautiful candle," Riglioni said. At the fluttering rush of a shell overhead he put on his helmet. Finch lay back on the floor. All wore their helmets. Honeycutt rose and leaned forward on his rifle to regard the flame. The shell exploded deep to the north.

On a fluid blubbery laugh Zubrowski said, "Hey, no fooling, you know why I'm so miserable?"

"Because your heart's in the States," Moran snarled, "your teeth are in England, and your ass is in Germany. Gingold. Professor. Give me a little wax. You made that splendid work of art. You must have wax."

Murmurously, as if to himself, Riglioni said, "He melted wax, he poured it into a vase, stuck in a hunk of string or something. Then he broke the vase. Turns out to be a genius, a genius."

"That's Venetian-blind cord in there," Gingold said on a modest note of pride, watching the flame intently.

"He made a goddamn candle." Honeycutt, in the circle now with gleaming sunken eyes, sounded a long low whistle.

For a full minute the men sat raptly studying the majestic warm glow. Then Screaming Mimis rocketed in on ghastly shrieks to crash all over town, and Finch said, "Psychological horseshit. Imagine them trying to steam us up with a few rockets. Sheeeeeeee!" He chuckled contemptuously and slid the helmet low over his eyes.

"Hey, let me tell you how I figured—"

"Zubrowski, don't be a windy bastard," Moran said. Another team of rockets shrieked by and peppered the night. "Where does a guy get so much wax? Where, Gingold, where?"

Detonations rang outside, small ones to the south. Then something exploded in the yard that faced enemy ground across a patch of buildings reduced to rubble. "A grenade!" Zubrowski yelped, snatching up his rifle.

Finch said, "This is it, men. Douse that light."

A hand moved, darkness fell, but the flame was imprinted on Riglioni's eyes; a ghost of the flame danced in his eyes while men waited for him to deploy them against the counterattack. Small detonations hammered the entire line, occasional mashers struck the house, and in the darkness each man waited alone with his jeopardy while Riglioni, though conscious of it all, sat enraptured with his vision of the dancing flame, yearning for the blaze of it again, telling himself there was no reason yet to take the noise as counterattack. "No," he said, "those are only rifle grenades from way off."

A little hysterical, Zubrowski said, "There's no Krauts out there?"

"No, or Scarbro would be cutting at them. Light the candle."

Finch said, "Somebody go see if Atman fell asleep on the gun. I ain't heard a single noise out of him."

"I'll go," Gingold offered, apparently afraid to chance a light. "Ken Atman, with small initials he writes it, crazy kid."

A grenade struck, loud amid more distant explosions. "Never mind," Riglioni said. "Sit still. Light up your damn candle, I tell you it's all right." A moment passed full of heavy breathing audible over all the racket outside. Then the flame rose, tall and composed. "Just what did that wax come off of? You don't have to say where."

Gingold passed a hand fondly through the flame. He smiled. "Zubrowski. How did you like that Frenchman and his broad?"

"What Frenchman, huh? What?"

"The one who crashed in the woods. Didn't you know he was a Frenchman?"

"What crashed in the woods? What woods?"

A thunderclap shattered glass upstairs and men fidgeted in the falling dust. "When we were in the woods last week," Gingold said, running a hand around his nose. "That plane, Hebe. What's the matter with you?"

"A plane crashed?"

"What's the matter with this Hebe? Can a guy sleep through a plane crash?"

"Because he's a windy bastard," Moran said. "Talks in his sleep the same as awake."

"Didn't you even see him come down in his 'chute, Hebe?"

"I never even heard about it. Not a word nobody said."

"Well, I'm telling you now. This nut flew over with a broad and his plane conked out. Lucky Frenchman, he bailed out okay. Plane smacked up, but he came down in one piece."

"How about that," Zubrowski murmured, picking his nose. "I never heard nothing. Jesus, I'm a heavy sleeper." Screaming Mimis broke the night open and crashed in patterns, grenades kept pounding, and for a long while the men sat transfixed around the candle. Then Zubrowski said, "What about the broad?"

"Oh, she was an old bag," Moran picked it up, "she just floated down." While Zubrowski grumbled to himself and

Finch sniggered and Honeycutt scratched his chest, Moran said, "Give me wax!"

Silently, Gingold rubbed his unshaven jaw. Riglioni said, "Just tell me what kind of wax." Gingold ignored him, studying the flame. Grenades thumped in the yard. Suddenly a machine gun barked, a short burst from Atman in the cellar, and Riglioni leaped up with his rifle, snarling, "I'll kick his ass right up his back!"

"He's the one with the wax, Hebe. He made this candle."

"He's crapping you, Sal," Moran said, and while grenades exploded near and far Riglioni ran for the cellar with Gingold's baritone laughter trailing. He reached Atman just as the boy cut loose another burst, and stopped him with a slap to the neck.

"Where the hell you think you are, at a shooting gallery? You want to give our position away? Wait'll you see somebody before you start blasting like a—see, kid, the tracers'll give our position away. You have to wait. Where'd you get all that wax?"

"Wax, Sarge?" Atman rolled around with his back to the sandbags that Germans had conveniently left behind for this gun mount. "Did you say wax?"

Riglioni ran. He leaped upstairs with the conviction that Gingold had only tricked him into believing it was Atman's candle. But when he reached the others he was no longer sure. He did not know Atman well enough to put playing it dumb past him. Accepting the candle as a gift, Gingold might have told the boy to deny everything. All of them were in place, reverently watching the flame. "Gingold. Did that joker really make this candle?"

"Up yours, Hebe."

Grenades hammered and suddenly burp guns began their falsetto clamor. "Honeycutt, get down there and send that son of a bitch up before he brings the whole thing down on us. Don't holler at him."

Gingold laughed. "You brown-nosing shit-healer."

"Shit-heel," Moran corrected. "Can't you talk decent English?"

On the way out with his rifle Honeycutt sang, "They coming after our lily-white asses now."

"Then if it ain't in the cellar," Moran mused, "it must be upstairs in that house."

"What house?" Finch said, and flattened out at a howling crash near the window.

"Never mind."

"Get down!" Riglioni snapped at the stomping entrance of Atman. Grinning, the boy squatted, red lights dancing on his glasses.

"He's the one, all right," Moran decided.

"No, it's Gingold," Riglioni said with a rasp, and cleared his throat.

The burp guns were distant; nothing from them was hitting close, but grenades still exploded outside. "Stay down," Finch said, "they're coming up now." With a snap he tightened the sling of his rifle, and Zubrowski got set with his.

"No Mimis any more," Riglioni said, "no mortar, nothing. They're ready to move in now. Gingold, can anybody get it? Is there more wax anywhere?"

"What am I, all of a sudden, a wax authority? There must be more wax *somewhere*. Shouldn't I blow out this light?"

"No, it's burning out fast anyway, you might as well leave it."

"Yeah," Gingold said, "I never saw wax burn this fast. Real *ersatz*. Cheap Kraut product."

"They're coming up," Zubrowski cried, his tiny eyes flaming. "Listen to the bastards!"

"Take it easy." Riglioni squatted there, leaning on his rifle, watching the flame. "Give them another minute. Moran, if Scarbro opens up, you get out there and traverse for him. Finch, take Zubrowski and run your jeep around into the other alley. You, Atman, take some grenades up to that little window on the landing and wait for them. Stay down now. I'll cover the front windows. Gingold, you just stick your greasegun out the back window in case any of them get past the rest of us into the street. You son of a bitch, you got the softest detail—give me some goddamn wax!"

With a laugh Gingold killed the flame in a gloved hand. Finch led Zubrowski out under the rear blanket. "It ain't him," Moran said in the darkness, "it's that cuckoo kid Atman."

"You said I was crapping you before, Hebe."

"I deducted different."

"Go on, get the hell out in the turret," Riglioni said. "Who's that coming back?"

"Sal, you want to see the CP?" It was Proctor again.

"In this shit? The Old Man can wait."

"It ain't gonna last." Proctor strode across and pulled the front blanket aside. Maddened fireflies zigzagged in the south to distant stuttering reports. "See, they ain't coming heavy. They never built up even enough to get Stollman throwing stuff back at them from Troop. There's fresh coffee at Troop, Sal."

"Yeah? They keep late hours. Go tell the bastard I turned in for the night. He's got his goddamn nerve, looking to ream us out past midnight."

Proctor dropped the blackout. "It's my own idea. I figured we be there when Lew Enshaw gets back, and hit Stollman before he gets the courage to try hitting us."

"Up his, I ain't going. I need sleep something awful."

Gingold's flame, sprouting then, illuminated Proctor where he knelt by the field telephone. He looked around with bemused pale eyes. It was still a noble light, though the candle had so swiftly melted down to a pink puddle on the floorboards. "What in the hell is that?"

"It's a candle," Gingold said.

Riglioni passed his hand slowly over the flame. "You ought to see it before, Gene. A beautiful candle. This big around. He made it. A beautiful candle."

"What do you mean, he made it?"

"Out of wax," Moran said. "A whole bunch of wax."

The burp guns shrilled distantly. Proctor stared at the flame. A few grenades coughed, and then the night sank away to quiet outside. "Where'd you get all the wax?"

"It ain't my wax. The kid made it. Atman."

"Bullshit," Riglioni said.

Moran leaned in with a crafty leer. "I know where he found that wax. I know where he made that candle."

"Where?" Gingold said.

"Never you mind."

They huddled there devoutly watching the flame tremble in the puddle of wax. All the world was quiet except for Atman up on the landing. He scraped around, he cleared his throat, he sneezed and coughed. Finch's jeep purred softly outside and grated to a stop. Riglioni blew out the flame. "Pull the kid downstairs, Joe, then go relieve Honeycutt. You relieve Scarbro, Gingold, it's one o'clock."

Finch and Zubrowski came inside. The light blazed again under the face of Gingold, who began to scrape wax from the floor with his trench knife. Riglioni said, "I need sleep, Gene; you really want that crap with the Old Man and Buffalo Bill?"

Gaping at the stately flame, Proctor said, "Nah, the hell with it."

6

The morning action was by the Third Platoon. It launched a central assault behind heavy 75 bombardment, the other two platoons raking the German flanks with machine-gun and 37 fire in high trajectory from the blind shadows of alleyways.

Mortar went over from Troop and German mortar harassed supply trucks on the streets. German 88s split the air deep into town until, just before noon, those crackling shells took shorter flight to zero in on the attack point alone, nothing but a random enemy mortar shell exploding in the rear, so Scarbro took a jeep forward in the knowledge that the Third had been stalled. He returned with the bare information that his brother's platoon had advanced an appreciable distance toward the canal before spreading out to hold a line against possible counterattack.

Then, as Riglioni's men sat eating 10-in-1 rations in the clammy house they had taken over last night, Proctor drove up to tell of Third Platoon casualties. "Nobody killed," he said, savoring some hot bacon. "Macklin got a bad one through a lung, but he's gonna live. Cafiero's got himself a million-dollar wound in the leg. Two others, I don't know them. Replacements, I don't know either of them."

Riglioni said, "Where was Buffalo Bill all morning?"

"Not with the Third. Old Man's saving him for us this afternoon."

"Us this afternoon? Oh, us?"

Proctor began to giggle. "Two o'clock. Us and the First, both. We're trying the flanks."

The men ate in silence, helmets cupping their rumps like toilet seats. Outside there was no longer any 88 fire, but intermittently both sides threw mortar. Honeycutt said, "I don't like this dump anyways. No stove. Chilly goddamn dump."

Riglioni pawed the hair down over his forehead and scratched around in it. "If we do any good at them we'll be getting out of the cars. Jesus, I don't want that bearded jerk in my way."

"He won't last long in anybody's way," Moran said ominously.

Giggling and glassy-eyed, Proctor said, "Maybe that's exactly what the Old Man's counting on. Somebody mad or scared enough to rub the beard job out and save him the need to face up and chew us out. Oh, he's a gentleman and a scholar, that one."

With a giggle he went for the exit window and climbed out. To the turret team Riglioni said, "You two go swab out your cannon."

"Can I borrow this pump stove?" Atman had his rifle slung, the little gasoline burner in both hands.

"Quick, let him go cook," Moran whispered archly. Louder, he said, "Sal, I guess you want me to go for the gas and water, the ammo, grenades and all."

"What? Yeah, okay." He ordered machine guns cleaned and sent men to cover the window with rifles while the machine gun was taken down. Just for the look of it, he told them. "There ain't bound to be anything coming around behind the Third. Take off, we have less than two hours."

They both watched Atman scoot from doorway to doorway with the pump stove, dodging shells toward the street where yesterday they had knocked out the big Schmeisser. "See?" Moran said. "Just like I figured. When you and the boys hit that cellar, Atman ran upstairs. Did he find Krauts? No, wax. Wax he found."

"What kind of wax?"

"How the hell should I know?"

Now Moran pulled up right outside that house, jerricans of water and gasoline already in the jeep along with green tin cases of ammunition, and a wooden crate of grenades. As they entered the dusty place, noise sounded upstairs. Stealthily they crept up, Riglioni in the lead, both by habit raising their rifles as though expecting to find Germans instead of Atman. The town was quiet; only an occasional mortar burst sounded anywhere. Upstairs the noise was careless: footfalls, a shuffling, a rhythmic sort of thumping.

Two flights up they caught sight of Atman pumping the little stove. Unaware of visitors, he set a number-10 bacon can on the stove and struck a match. Then he began to fill the can with varicolored chunks, apparently of wax, from the pockets of his combat jacket. When Riglioni stepped up on the landing Atman turned to regard him with a thin smile, his glasses reflecting the open gray sky where the roof had been blown completely away.

"What are you doing, Atman?"

"I swabbed out the cannon and cleaned the .50 with Gingold, and there wasn't any more you said to do."

Moran came along. "What's that you're cooking? Wax?"

Atman nodded, kneeling there. From behind him he brought forth a lovely crystal vase with a length of sturdy cord in it. "Making another candle," he said, eyeless, flat fields of light on his glasses.

"Where'd you get the wax?" Moran said.

"In there."

Riglioni went around him and up two stairs across rubble into a ruined attic under charred naked beams and the sky. Wooden crates and steamer trunks, or corners of them, were visible in the heaped wreckage. Two trunks had already been hauled free and opened; around them lay linen tablecloths and counterpanes of wonderful bright design. From one trunk Riglioni took glass pitchers, vases, and lamps all wrapped in linens. From the other trunk Moran produced silverware nestled in handsome lace curtains. Then both began to kick through the debris of plaster dust and slate and the torn limbs of furniture. They worked without pause until Riglioni said, "What are we looking for?"

"How should I know? I asked the bastard and he wouldn't say. He just offered me a little wax. I don't want his lousy wax."

"Why not?"

"Why not? I don't know, I didn't figure it out yet. But I don't want his lousy wax. I want my own wax. If he found wax, we can find wax. Anybody can find wax if he can find wax. Nothing supernatural about it."

"Of course not. Why should there be anything supernatural about it?"

"Don't waste time bullshitting. Find some wax."

"What kind of wax, for Christ's sake?"

"I don't know. We'll know it if we see it, won't we?"

Riglioni returned to the landing, where Atman was pouring molten wax into the vase. The boy glanced up with a smile. "It always comes out pink. Starts with different colors, melts down pink."

"How about some wax, Atman?"

"Whatever's left over you can have. Okay, Sarge?"

Riglioni squatted. "Where'd you find the wax in there?"

"Right in all that rubbish. I told Moran."

"What did you tell him to look for?"

"He didn't ask."

"All right, I'm asking. Tell me."

Atman was concentrating on his work now, pouring wax into the narrow neck of the vase. Finished, he extended the tin can. "Better put on a glove first, Sarge. This can's pretty hot."

"Just set it down on the floor. Come on and tell me what you got that wax off of, what we should look for."

"I don't know, Sarge, it's sort of personal."

"Personal! What—you mean you don't want to tell me?"

"Well, it's sort of a private matter of conscience, if you know what I mean."

"I don't know a goddamn word what you mean!"

"I don't want to make enemies."

"What the hell are you talking about? Where'd that god-damn wax come off of, Atman?"

A smile crept along the boy's lips, and there seemed to be a hint of mockery in it. "I don't think you'll find any anyway. I told Moran. If there's any left you ought to know it's wax right off. So there's really no point in ordering me to tell you."

"Who's ordering you? I'm just asking."

"Well, there's no point."

They squatted there staring at each other. Then Riglioni returned to Moran in the rubble. They searched under fallen beams and disemboweled upholstery, kicked aside decorative screens and old window blinds, dug with their hands in the damp mortar and the slate, but found nothing made of wax. When they walked out, Atman was gone with the gasoline stove. The number-10 can sat on the landing, about a quarter inch of pink wax congealing at the bottom. They stared down at it. Then Moran got to his knees and began digging wax out with his fingers. "Get a teeny hunk of that cord," he said.

At the edge of town a factory blazed in the night. German "baby buzz-bombs" had fired it. Forward across a cobbled avenue, in a front yard of rocky turf beside a dark squat house, Riglioni and Moran dug cautiously with their entrenching tools. "I wonder what he was thinking," Moran whispered, "when he said that stuff about why he was so miserable."

"Well, we ain't ever gonna know. Now shut up."

"He just figured out why he was so miserable. Imagine that."

"Shut up now, Joe."

Very quietly, Moran scraped with his shovel. Firelight danced on edges of his broad face. "You think maybe he knew he was gonna die?"

Riglioni quit working. He stared at Moran. "You're supposed to be so goddamn smart," he rasped. "Now this supernatural shit from you all of a sudden. Goddamn it, shut up, shut up. This house could be full of Krauts."

"Don't be silly."

"How do you know different?"

"Because we're alive, that's how I know. That factory lighting the whole street up, everybody digging in down the line, and Krauts in there just watching us? If there was Krauts, we'd be dead by now."

"So what the hell are we digging out here for?"

"Shhh. Because you take orders instead of turning in your stupid stripes. Old Man said dig in, so Enshaw hands it down." Moran began to chuckle, but it turned into a helpless sobbing. "Will you just look at us out here? Two grown men who don't know how to save their own ass. Hey, you know why I'm so miserable, hey?"

"Shhh. I'm going inside. Listen. I'm going in and clear this house. Then I'll pull the vehicles up and that's a sight better than three stupid slit-trenches with a fire lighting us up. Now quit that crying and go tell the guys. I'll pull the jeep up."

Rockets came screaming in again while Riglioni was rolling the jeep out of a back street, rockets shrieking through his head, rockets crashing with fragmentation that whined white hot and visible in flight. Bigger than Screaming Mimis, they cracked apart into huge chunks with surfaces like congealed razor blades, but there were not enough of the fragments to be more menacing than the practically harmless Screamers . . . though recently in the Ardennes six Mimis had struck around Johnson and torn half his face away.

He could locate the terror in different sickly parts of his body —first in the guts and then in the eyes, which grew icy cold and tearful, then in a dull ache at his wrists and finally in his right foot which rebelled in favor of jamming the brake and plunging away for cover.

Zubrowski was dead. The men were hugging open ground, and the only way in the uproar was to make this house safe for them and for himself. He pulled up under a window in the light of flames from the factory, which had stood intact at twilight when they passed it running hard after a squad or more of Germans. From the glove compartment he got his flashlight. Rifle extended, finger on the trigger, he climbed in the window. Impossible for Germans to be present; still, some madman, some fool of a Kraut might be lying in wait and this was the last bare rock of life where all was clarity and a man knew that his destiny was turned by madmen and fools. Rockets came, shrill and unworldly. His life depended on the likes of Captain Stollman—and Buffalo Bill, who had not appeared all afternoon to doom him with pomposity . . . another new weapon, and an additional enemy using it against him.

His fingers, shielding the flashlight lens, freed only a needle of light, and wherever this beam groped he pointed his rifle. He cleared the first bare room, then found cellar stairs and ascending stairs. With tense caution he visited four other rooms on the first floor, his heart stopping at echoes of his own small noises. They had swung the vehicles out of town to the north and returned deeper east where, amid the shrieking rockets, German mortar and 88s had met them with a fury. Dismounted, they had hopped from house to house searching, until contact came in a burst of small arms crackling in an overtone of hysteria that meant panicked Germans. Disorganized and demoralized, Germans had died on their vaunted Hitler soil under the Second Platoon onslaught of nothing heavier than grenades and small arms, until a pair of cross-firing Schmeissers racketed, opening fire too soon, to the salvation of everyone but Zubrowski whose turn had come to go scout for the length of a street. Rockets had crashed as they fell back past the ignited factory in cover of the settling night, Atman dragging Zubrowski's devastated body, having run ahead into machine-gun fire to salvage it by some mad compulsion.

Now the maddening rockets shrieked again. The cellar was full of packing cases around which Riglioni made careful search. He climbed stairs that whined to his step. The upper story was a shambles of debris, a stink of dankness, destruction, and rot. More stairs ascended toward nothing but the black sky where, just as he turned to go down again, a flare burst and flung out its widening pale blossom. Then under the shrieking night of rockets a pattern of burp guns nagged. Another flare opened the sky. Troop was anticipating the counterattack. He plunged downstairs in almost uncontrollable terror.

The big hill guns convinced them. Even Proctor was on edge. At the height of a barrage he came tumbling in through the window with a field phone and called for Riglioni in the darkness. Angrily he demanded, "What the hell are you doing in here?"

"You expect me to leave everybody out there lit up by that goddamn fire?"

"I told you this line of houses ain't safe. They could be full of Krauts—or booby traps, for Jesus' sake."

"I cleared this house. Nobody's touching anything. It's coming tonight, ain't it?"

"Well, goddamn it, it's got to come some time, and the sooner the better. What've you got set up, one gun?"

"That's all you wanted in the trench. So I got it out in the shed on a pile of potatoes."

"Potatoes!"

"As good as sandbags. What's the matter?"

"Okay. Better bring your other vehicles around. Don't position them, just keep them ready to roll out of cover if they have to. But keep a man in the car at all times. At the wheel."

"How about we wait for this to let up? The car's got nice cover in a real skinny alley, and we'd have time before they could—"

"Time, your ass. They be walking right into the edge of their barrage and hit us the minute it lifts. You bring those vehicles up close right now, Sal."

Proctor slipped out the window, through which light from the burning factory danced in at an angle to a far corner of the floor. The big shells were wrenching out a pattern of thunder, and mortar explosions filled the gaps, the 75 Troop answering from the rear, so Proctor's motor was never heard in his wire-running journey to the other pair of sections.

And Riglioni was talking in it all, with guts that bobbed as if afloat on the sea. "Scarbro, pull the car up to that house on the right, this side of it. Get your jeep, Finch, right behind mine, but leave a few yards." None of the big shells were landing this short, but mortar exploded everywhere along the wide loose line all three platoons had formed. "The rest of you spread out and cover the forward windows. Stay in the car, now, Hillbilly; I'll relieve you in an—if it—go on, stay at the wheel."

Behind Finch, Scarbro climbed out saying, "I'm just a country boy—don't be scared of this thang, girls."

Moran said, "They could walk right through us if they knew the right spots. If they put a patrol through they'd know the whole—"

"At ease! Quit talking yourself off, just tighten your hole

and stay awake." Riglioni squatted there at the window, ready to call men out to the armored car and the jeeps according to how the enemy came, with what strength, from what direction.

A front window lit up and in the roar Gingold fell back with a shriek of pain and horror. Up again, he was a harsh choppy breath in the darkness. "Rocket. Like our bazooka. They're up close enough to throw bazooka rockets!"

Another one crashed out front. Dry-mouthed, Riglioni said, "Now, Atman, don't fire at flashes because you won't know how close they—don't fire until one of us does. Gingold, where are you?"

"Right this way, Hebe."

Riglioni found him under a window. "I'll cover here. You get to the back window ready to hop out into the turret. I'll tell you where to position Scarbro."

Enemy automatic fire cut loose, heavier than burp guns. At the letup Riglioni raised his head for a look outside where, in a widespread irregular design, houses stood on unpaved ground here at the edge of town. The outfit lacked the men and guns with which to withstand any real assault. The outfit was a bluff and the enormous phantom must know it, hiding in the shadows with a faceless grin, dancing in the corner of light from that burning factory, haunting the whole dead night, and night was in Riglioni, hollowing him and filling the void with clammy tremors. But he knew that no orders would come down for them to pull back; he would have to hold the position, and try to disorganize the attack with mobile fire from the armored car.

Again machine guns clattered, a pair of big ones in unison. No flashes were visible. Tracers drifted by to the south. The enemy was firing through burlap to hide its flashes. There was no sign of men in motion.

Then burp guns and rifles sounded a tempest, innumerable weapons along the whole enemy line, and the rifle grenades came crashing everywhere. Now several gunflashes were visible in the open night. Honeycutt said, "They're coming, Sal."

"Get ready to make it to that gun in the shed, Honeycutt." His voice quivered like a panicked little girl's. "I'll tell you when." He could not stem the quavering.

"There's Scarbro pulling up," Gingold said, and fell flat as a big shell shattered a house in the vicinity. The pattern of heavy blasts was spreading thin, the mortar fire growing denser, the 75s responding with a constancy. Gingold said, "Should I go now, Rig?"

"Hold it, hold it." Like a little girl. He wanted not to speak at all but had to, so he took a deep breath and spoke in that thin voice choked by tremors. "We'll be getting flares any minute. I don't know where to run you at them yet. So we have to hold it, we have to wait it out."

Troop did send up flares the moment all enemy hill guns went silent. Nothing moved in the pale rubble of night. German small arms and mortar fire kept peppering the darkness. Occasionally a rifle grenade wrenched the front of the house, and frequent burp-gun volleys nibbled at the walls. Soon the mortar barrage lifted completely. Troop threw several flares.

"Don't let those burp guns scare you down too long." He crouched over his rifle, the silence hammering at his heart, for even the small arms had abruptly gone dead. The night lay black and then lit up ghostly under a flare and then fell black again to hide the colossal spook. "Get ready, Honeycutt. Get ready, boys. This looks like the minute."

"Who's there?" Gingold at the back window. Whispered words outside. Then Gingold again, "Rig, it's Lindemayer. He wants us to light him up one of our candles."

"What! Where's Section One?" He scurried over to the back window and saw Lindemayer, a silhouette tall and solemn flanked by two hulks bristling with gear. "You crazy, Pete? Where's your section?"

"I left Gross in charge. Let's see those candles, boy."

"Get the hell out of here! The Krauts are coming up!"

A moaning shell struck somewhere; one lonely burp gun chattered and fell silent. "Let the bastards come," Lindemayer said. A flare burst overhead and touched his face with wan light, his eyes in shadow like a pair of holes in a skull. "Us three'll plug up a gap if they do."

"Get away! Nobody's coming in here!" A bell rang. "What the hell!" He groped in the dark, found the field phone. "Hello!"

"Give your call sign."

"Huh? Reliable."

"No, you horse-faced prick, you're Mayflower." It was First Sergeant Muldoon at Troop. "*This* is Reliable."

"What do you want, Top?"

"I got a message from Leviathan for you. They want a candle."

"Jesus! We're getting hit any minute; aren't we getting hit tonight?"

"I don't know, Sal, *Der Saurkrauten* don't consult me. But if they do come, let me know right away so I can get my precious ass out of this town fast. Any messages for Leviathan?"

"I don't know any Leviathan!" He hung up. At the back window he planted a hand on Lindemayer's chest and said, "Get lost! What's your call sign?"

"Ironside. Let me dig that candle, boy."

"Then that goddamn Meskerman is Leviathan, and he wants a candle too. Get out of here, Pete, or I'll—"

"Meskerman's dead, Sal."

"What? I mean Rayhew."

"Well, well, well, well—"

"Joe, I'll mangle you! Go on, Pete, get back to your goddamn disciples."

Muttering, Lindemayer and his Section One men faded

away into the terrible silence. Only now Riglioni became aware that the factory fire had burned out. Now in the everlasting dark the phantom hung ready to strike. Now at the window he was lost in an appalling sense of eternity, an eternity of waiting, never an end to the horror, another day and another, night and night and night of it forever, unless they came and killed him now. He wished they would come and kill him now because the whole thing was not worth the effort.

7

All were waiting at their windows. Riglioni felt weak in the brain, felt doomed to collapse, to melt down into a puddle like pink wax.

Vaguely he heard the pop, and then gently like a star the flare laid open the sky and the world. Slowly it descended in a wispy halo over blanched acres of destruction that looked eternal, broken shadows of the night spook lurking, and he saw his mother's murdered eyes which meant his death, and his father might die, the noblest Roman of them all.

My little brothers are frail. Save them, save them. But God was no savior; God disarmed Gino and Eddie with fine chests and manly little legs and strong eyes. *My brothers are frail,*

frail. The night was black outside and even Atman was silent in the mass of tension. *They will get kicked, my little brothers, in their Italian balls.* He belonged back in Burbank to warn his strong brothers and to forgive Lorraine Parrine her jewelry, for he had set her free before shipping out. Another flare, and he heard stealthy movement outside.

A sinking diamond trailed by smoke, the flare moved pale shadows where he knew a thousand Germans to be standing stock-still, and stealthy movement was only in his imagination, which was full of tricks. Alone in the turret one night long ago, he had perceived a tank in the woods ahead and traversed the cannon in hopeless terror, but the grinding of treads diminished into the faint scrape of four piglets from a nearby farm, little white porkies that later made a feast for the entire platoon.

The silence persecuted him. When you heard that pop you stood stock-still on the planet, and the thousand Germans were motionless shadows stunned among the shadows that now with the death of the flare were softly blending into the vast night spook. Black ass-hole of life. These nights Lorraine glittered, dancing through the Hollywood night spots, for he had set her free of devotion and mourning and she liked to write him about new friends and parties all over L.A. and he forgave her now but could not set his mother free. *I was so lonely you were so charming tell me dear;* Louis Armstrong sang it on the thirty-dollar record player one afternoon of sun when Lorraine kissed Howler, his oldest friend, his truest friend whose true old friendship became doubtful in that innocence full of her virginity and the mystifying unfathomable sun. And later much later he was to remember the wild indiscriminate appetite her eyes betrayed that afternoon with Howler and so he set her free of sweating him out, freed her to run loose long after her white white yielding, the shocking womanly hips of experience that she swore came only from her prankish exercises alone at home, *penny penny nickel dime as if I had a nickel on my belly and a penny on each hip and a dime on my ass to practice for you Sal,* and that was how she had prepared herself for him but shipping out he set her free, practiced perfect on him for her new home-front lovers, and all those sunny afternoons ached so hopelessly now that he remembered innocent things like beaches and rumble seats full of her virginal giddy protests. Oh if he could have her now and crowd her white forked innocence . . .

Pop. Flare. Men of the enemy had to come soon, ghostly over the rubble. Men of his own were a sound of breathing around him and gripped weapons jealously to guard their breath for another hour, a day or a week to death. The vulnerable world lay spectral in the night which, split open in silence by the sinking flare, yet hid the terrible spook, the patient spook. *Hey Salvie . . . You were so lovely I was so lonely . . .* Howler was in Africa now on a Coast Artillery gun, humping Arab girls ten years old. Connie Meskerman well well well. In Africa Connie fired his rifle at the MPs—*pang!* right through the chill of night at MPs in their chickenshit white helmet liners and webbing. Jesus, Africa? Moran at the wheel and who else was there? One more, four in all. Lipschitz the crazy bastard, his fancy tanker's suit: *The sonsabitches made me dive in the mud and now look at my suit the Kraut bastards!* A Hebe like Gingold but softer. Gingold was tough, a tough Coney Island Hebe but soft Lippy never panicked like Gingold and now he was over there mourning Connie and taking orders from Rayhew.

"Hey, Sal."

"Huh? Who? Finch?"

"Yeah."

"What the hell do you want?"

"You put me in for that decoration?"

Pang! for the chickenshit MPs. Well well Meskerman and

Caddigan and Zubrowski. "Decoration! You'll get plenty of decorations when they come at us tonight! We'll get decorations, all right!"

"Yeah, that's the kind of feeling I have tonight. That's why I want to know about that decoration. Did you put me in for it?"

"I told Gene, Proctor, he'll put you in. Now get the hell back to your window."

"I hope he puts in for it. I got a bad kind of feeling tonight. I feel they're coming soon, the whole goddamn *Weermack.*"

Finch crawled away, a quiet cat in the darkness. Men breathed. Atman maintained a remarkable silence. Scarbro waited alone in the car outside. Meskerman was stiff, his wife and kids were stiff, all the sounds he had ever made in the world were stiff, but he had fired on MPs in the Tunisian night that brought in wintry sea winds. *And I was Sal Riglioni with cognac,* all of them getting drunk village by village away from Bizerte half on pass and half screwed up with some notion that the outfit had pulled back for a rest, and now at the window choked with night Riglioni laughed because the outfit had only pulled back overnight to change sector and the four were AWOL in this town seeking Maggie's place, for they knew the town, had liberated it a month back and already the rear echelon heroes occupied it and had Maggie's place and the whole windy square, statue and all.

"We liberated this shiteating burg," Moran had announced in the din of dissolute voices while Maggie and her old mother bellowed fervent greetings in a recital of obscenities the outfit had taught them.

"Bullshit," some drunken clerk-typist responded and Riglioni lifted the safety on the greasegun that he later traded for a passing doughfoot's rifle, and for laughs he pointed it around the place in his desert rags and his beard, and heroes crawled over each other in flight while Moran roared and Connie got under Maggie's dress to negotiate for cognac and Lippy taught her mother new obscenities. The wild exodus carried him out bodily to the jeep Moran had parked hard by Maggie's door and there he roosted on a ration crate locking down the safety to keep from getting hurt in the unruly mob, when climbing over his knees a distraught man warned him to get away fast—"Some crazy GI's in there gonna shoot up the place with a tommy gun!"

The whole tavern emptied, but Maggie and her mother took it with grace and they all drank cognac amid endearing obscenities until the MP wagon came sirening across the wintry square. They were back in the jeep to see the wagon brake up with a fancy shriek and spill out four fancy MPs who, in white helmet liners, yanked fancy pistols out of white web belts and pumped white leggings through moonlight that resembled snow. A very brave voice barked, "All right, who's the guy was gonna start shooting around here?"

Seated on the crate Riglioni lifted the safety and, placing the muzzle against the MP's forehead, said, "Me."

So the MPs backed off unable to get their pistols put away fast enough. One even ventured a smile before they vanished into the wagon that then roared off, the bravest of them sticking his head out to yell, "You got ten minutes to clear out of this town!"

Pang! Connie Meskerman standing in the jeep. *Pang-EEEEeeeeeee* went his second shot whining across the square and away in the night. *Pang-pang*OWOO*eee-pang*EEEOW-*eeee.*

"I don't think that's allowed," Moran said, "even MPs."

"No, I'm elevating," Connie said, a dumpy desert hobo with freckles and a wife and kids, and if he was dead now anyone could die and Riglioni saw his mother's eyes murdered. Noise sounded outside, a whisper, an illusion.

No, it was real, growing louder. Sweat burned his face; his

ankles and wrists were chilled. Tense, he peered hard into the night. He was raising his rifle, ready to bark orders out of a crippled mouth, when the loud whisper turned into a snarl, a jeep coming in and throttling to silence. In a moment there were whispers and Proctor climbed inside saying, "Set up a guard mount. Can't wait on them Krauts forever. Pull everybody in and set up for the night."

Riglioni sent Honeycutt out to the shed gun. It was not over, yet his sense of relief was voluptuous. He sent Finch to call Scarbro back from the car. "Bring blankets, it's cold in here."

Proctor collapsed in a corner. Nobody spoke until, returning with Scarbro and equipment, Finch said, "What's the score, Proc? The Krauts just making a lot of noise?"

"Now how should I know? They could start the whole thing up again in a minute."

Well well well die. You. The spook ran out of his guts, leaving him limp and cold, but lingered in his brain tight as a cold steel coil. Matches flared, men smoked, but Riglioni knew it was not over and sensed that others in the darkness realized it too. You waited for that gargantuan phantom, the monstrous stranger that was at the same time so familiar because some edge of you was haunted by a notion that you had known this spook all your life and had only just grown up enough to take your place in the world of waiting, all grown-up and brave among the dead and waiting, waiting.

"Why don't we go after them?" Gingold said with a clogged nose that gave his voice a whining unstable sound. "What's this, a law in this town against night attacks? Why the hell don't we burn their asses and be—"

"Aaah, shut up!" Proctor exploded. "You fixing to give the orders around here? All you goddamn—you New York wise guys all think you know better than everybody, always looking to go into business for yourself and all. And then you belly-ache when people say . . . aah, shit, you give me a pain in the ass."

The night was silent again but for the breathing of men, the clogged nasal gasps of Gingold loudest. Then there was a click, the snap of a greasegun safety latch in the darkness. "You can be more specific than that," Gingold said. "You don't mean New York guys, not just any New York guys."

In the silence a match flared and blossomed into a bright flame, Atman's face above it with glasses agleam under his naked helmet. Alongside him sat Gingold, and Riglioni saw the greasegun on his lap with its safety latch down. Gingold had only now remembered to lock his safety so that nobody would get hurt by accident. Proctor's eyes were on Gingold and he looked hurt. "Jesus," he said, "what a candle! Where'd you get all that wax, kid?"

"In an attic," Atman said.

"What do you mean, attic? What did you find, that much wax?"

"I melted it down and poured it into a vase."

The men all gathered around. With a quick furtive glance at Gingold, Proctor said, "What's this joker dodging my question for, Sal?"

"I don't know, he just won't tell what the wax came off of. You can't order a man to tell."

"Why should I get anyone mad?" Atman murmured sheepishly.

"What the heck you talking about, kid?"

"I told Gingold."

"Yeah, and then I didn't want any part of his candles. But maybe now I'll go into business for myself. I fuck you all where you breathe."

The men watched the flame, less in fascination with it than to keep their embarrassed eyes down between Gingold and Proctor. Cryptically, Scarbro said, "Ladies, thrill your home-front hero with this here smoking jacket." He drew his blanket tight around him, and stared at the flame.

"So where was Buffalo Bill today?" Riglioni said.

Proctor giggled. "Can't you wait to see him killed?"

"I didn't mean anything like that. I was just wondering."

"Beats me where he was. Maybe the Old Man reamed him for complaining about us. I know he called Lew Enshaw in about it to tell if orders are obeyed around here."

A burp gun opened up in the distance, and then another, then several more. There were remote explosions, probably rifle grenades. "Did you put Finch in for that decoration, Gene?"

"No. You do that. It's early—come on over to Troop and do it yourself." He puffed on his cigarette, then killed it, sneaking a quick glance at Gingold. "Bound to get Buffalo Bill flapping his jaw and I'll let you watch me give it to him—but good. Get the Old Man giving it to him too, by God. Now Lieutenant," he drew out in a soft monotone to caricature the Captain's voice. "Now Lieutenant, you see the realities of combat. Something the books won't teach you at OCS. Us combat officers learn fast that we need those noncoms or by God I'd have to lead the men my own self. A man could get hurt that way. Even disfigured. Sheer hell. So kindly lay off those noncoms. Backbone of the army. Somebody's got to have a backbone around here."

"No, more like this," Moran said, and went on in the same poor imitation of Stollman's voice. "Won't do to get rid of our proven noncoms, Lieutenant. Us proven officers would have nobody to command but a bunch of table waiters. Men won't take orders from a table waiter, you know." The flame danced and all the grinning men watched it, entranced. Moran pretended to be sucking on a pipe, to gag on something foul. "Can this be horseshit I'm smoking? Well, war is hell, sheer hell. I realize full well that it's frustrating, Lieutenant, but patience, patience, and those upstarts will get theirs through proper channels. Cold steel, by God, and I'll make major, you'll get promoted to corporal, and if you persevere—"

"Now, Lieutenant," Finch interrupted with a snigger, "go shine my shoes and—"

"Oh shut up," Moran whined with an expression of painful disgust. "Shut up, Finch, go play with someone your own age."

Squatting over the candle, leaning on his upright rifle, Finch kept sniggering. "Don't be bitter, boy. We don't want too much bitterness in this man's outfit. Gingold's enough bitterness for one night, going into business for himself and all."

"A waste of talent," Gingold said, his eyes fast on Atman's flame. "Finch, he should be in Special Service, he's so clever."

"Oh, you noticed that?" Finch tipped his helmet forward. "Well, I been noticing something too. How come you're always calling everybody Hebe? Now that's something I been noticing around here."

"See how clever? Nobody bothered to ask me that till now. It's a matter of rhythm. You're just too busy being clever to get the rhythm of this universe into you. Go on, Moran. Pardon the interruption."

"Thank you, professor." Moran fell silent until a sudden spatter of burp-gun fire trailed off. "Now that mustache, Lieutenant, that goatee. I seem to have seen them before. It may be merely the rhythm of the universe that gives me the illusion, but then again it may be Arkansas. Yes, Lieutenant. This group is an Arkansas outfit, you know. I recall this back-road barmaid near our old Arkansas post. Wonderful fat thighs, Lieutenant, and a goatee just like yours. Same red mustache, by God. May I touch your mouth? Ah, yes, how familiar—wrap your beard around this, Lieutenant. By God, I'm putting you in for the Silver Star!"

"How many of you stretched that back-road stuff?" Proctor said into the laughter. "I heard nobody could touch her."

Moran said, "Not Belinda, no, but her sisters. Man, we had one whole night when—"

"And her ma," Scarbro said. "Old Shorty Sandorian fainted putting it to the old lady in a front porch rocker. *Eep, eep, eep,* I'll *never* forget that night."

"Fainted right in the middle of it," Proctor laughed. "I wasn't there but I heard it so often. Old Sandorian gone now, but he had his time with the ma while the rest of these jokers went down that line of Belinda's sisters right to the youngest, who wasn't but fifteen." He was addressing Gingold, staring right at him across Atman's flame. "There was four of them sisters, I remember."

"You don't have to be hand-shaking me, Proctor."

"What?"

"You give orders, I take them. That's it. I ain't your goddamn friend, Proctor."

In Gingold's voice Riglioni detected the same stifling tension he himself had suffered a short while ago waiting for the night to explode. He said, "Come on, Gingold. What did this kid get the wax off of?"

Glancing once at Atman, Gingold ruminated awhile with his gaze on the flame. Then he said, "Dolls."

Abruptly, Atman leaned forward and blew out the flame. He made scraping sounds in the darkness to gather wax back onto his candle, and then went stomping away to another part of the house. "Gingold," Proctor's voice rose. "I ain't hand-shaking you. You want to, I'll fight you big as you are. Just say the word."

"You give the orders, I take them, Hebe. That's all."

"I ain't hand-shaking nobody. I was just sorry you took me the way you did. I didn't mean nothing like that at all."

A light blazed. Moran looked up from his thick stump of a candle and in a sober voice, hardly more than a whisper, said, "You're oversensitive for a thinking man, Paul."

"You can all line up and kiss my ass."

"Dolls?" Finch said, lighting one of his German cigars. "Wax dolls, Gingold?"

"Yes, Finch, not wood, not rubber, but wax."

"Come on, Sal." Proctor let out a long sigh, then giggled. "Tell Finch your guard order and we'll go see about his decoration."

Stars glittered but there was no moon and in the night of dark shapes Proctor rolled his jeep ahead, softly rumbling, bouncing on rubble. "You let me do the talking, Sal. I'm gonna ream them officers out."

"No, let's just put Finch in for his medal. Don't start in with Stollman and that bearded prick."

"Don't worry about it. It's got to come out and there's no use letting the Old Man choose his own time for it. He keeps looking at me fishy and I know he's just waiting for his right minute."

"Listen, Gene, I don't know if I can make it with Stollman tonight. I feel funny, Gene."

"What's eating on you?"

"My head, it feels very funny inside. I don't know, Gene, I swear. The Old Man. I don't know if I can take any of his crap."

"Just let me talk. You say nothing."

Houses covered them except where several had been bombed out of existence, and after some slow minutes of crawling they turned away toward the rear quarter. Proctor had just spun the wheel when a flare popped and bathed them in its unearthly pallor. Instantaneously he stalled the jeep and they were hanging there in light.

"Who sent that up?" Riglioni whispered.

"They did, take it easy."

"No, we did. That fucking Troop, I know it."

"No, they did. Shut up now."

Darkness settled again. The jeep whispered off. In a shuddering soft voice Riglioni said, "Oh Gene I swear I don't know if I can take it any more. I don't know. Connie Meskerman now. Look at this—what the hell are we doing here? Those Krauts hit us once and we're finished. I can't, I can't any more!"

"Hoo boy, shut up, Sal!"

"Jesus, you realize it's four months now without a rest? Those jerky garrison officers—"

"Will you for Christ's sake shut your hole?"

"My men are cracking up. Moran's out of his head. Honeycutt. Scarbro was always a nut. Now you see this Gingold? How you like Gingold, boy? You can't say a word without him thinking—"

"To hell with him. If he can't take it, fuck him, let him go psycho and we'll send him home to his momma. I don't trust none of them anyhow."

"None of who?"

"Those goddamn Sheenies with their big mouths."

"Yeah? So why'd you apologize to him?"

"You think I want a bullet in the back?"

"What? He's gonna sneak up on you because he's a Sheenie?"

"No, for Christ's sake, because he thinks I called him one. What are you trying to make me out, a Jew-hater or something? Boy, maybe you *are* a combat fatigue case at that."

"Me? Listen, I think you're losing your—sh. Sh. Listen, what's that? Shh."

"That's a Signal Corps Radio 131 with some hero cranking the generator, you never heard it before? Look, there's the ack-ack detail gonna shoot up any Messerschmidt comes after Stollman's ass." Proctor sniggered. "A Kraut patrol could take this whole CP with two grenades."

He pulled up a few yards short of another jeep parked close to a building, then led Riglioni over a hump of debris toward doorway shadows where a challenging guard said, "Who's there?"

"Gingerbread. Who the Jesus you think—Colonel Powell?"

Pitch black and silent, the street floor of Troop HQ smelled of mildew and plaster dust. Cellar stairs brought them down into the light of a battery lantern hung from the ceiling. Under it Muldoon, once the red-headed Third Platoon Sergeant and now the gray Troop Topkick, raised a china cup of steaming coffee from its saucer at his desk, which was an ornate mahogany table. "Sorry about Connie, Sal. I was just trying to cheer you up on the phone before."

"Tea cups now," Proctor said. "You got it made."

"Sheer heaven. Sheer hell right through there to your left." Muldoon sipped coffee. To Riglioni he said, "Look at that ceiling, boy, solid brick, ten Stukas couldn't shake dust through her. And tea cups? Christ, we found silverware, tablecloths, potatoes. Coal bricks we found, right down here—everything. Eat your hearts out, I'm writing my mother not to worry any more."

Proctor said, "You could always cut yourself shaving. That bearded wonder still hollering Articles of War at the Old Man?"

"Simmons? Not any more today that I heard of." Muldoon rose from the table. "I'm going in there after my morning report. You want to see the Old Man about anything?"

"Sal wants to put Finch in for a ribbon. Finch been doing good. Buffalo Bill put him in for a bust, by any chance?"

"Nothing reached me about anything like that. I don't even understand that beard-job's status in this outfit. He's a First Looie, though. By God, maybe he's making Exec, maybe at last Stollman's got someone to mind the store while he gets out there fighting like he's just pining to."

"Quit biting the hand that feeds you, boy."

Muldoon turned a sheepish grin on Proctor. "Yeah, there's worse Old Men. I just flap my jaw too much since I quit soldiering." He led them through a large empty area where five Supply and Kitchen hands sat on the concrete floor playing cards around another battery lantern. They all raised guilty eyes that lent them a family resemblance. Through another doorway Weldon the clerk had guilty eyes and Captain Stollman raised a pair in lamplight that etched his wrinkled brow with deep weary shadows. He was drinking from a cup and saucer.

8

"Care for some coffee?" Captain Stollman said.

"No, thanks. Wouldn't care to dirty our mess cups. Nice diggings, right, Sal? Looks like this outfit aims to stay in this town awhile."

"Fill them some cups," the Captain directed Weldon.

Several men moved about in the large room—Sergeant Reeves of Supply, Mess Sergeant Goodspane, a couple of Medics—arranging cannisters and crates in the deep shadows. Departing, Lieutenant Spiro of the First Platoon greeted the two line sergeants; others muttered salutations and drifted out as Muldoon spoke with the Captain. Buffalo Bill got up from a blanket roll to come marching forth with tight expectant eyes.

The big room was freshly swept clean; around the sides lay overseas bags and blanket rolls where Troop HQ men could rest secure under the arched brick ceiling that made a fortress of the place. Men kept filing out until only the two officers and two noncoms remained, Buffalo Bill standing there in his stocking feet, Riglioni squatting, supported by his rifle. "Captain," he said, "I'm putting Finch in for a Silver Star."

Stollman watched from behind his desk as Proctor unslung his Thompson and squatted beside Riglioni. The Captain glanced at Buffalo Bill with a sad look of fortitude, and began tapping out his pipe. "Make your application through Lieutenant Enshaw, Sergeant. He'll take your full report and submit it to me."

"We never did anything like that on the line before. I can talk my report a lot quicker than writing it. Any clerk can—"

"We're in attack. Channels work best, save time in the long run. We're busy, Sergeant," he added dryly, filling his pipe.

Alongside the Captain's desk, erect and stony, Buffalo Bill stood looking down at the sergeants. All four men remained silent until Weldon brought the coffee and departed. Temperately, the Captain said, "Was there anything else, men?"

Proctor spoke up at last. "Has Finch been put in for a bust by anyone around here?"

"If any noncommissioned officer is broken, his Platoon Leader will be informed and in turn will inform the Platoon Sergeant."

"Well, I can see we're shaping up into a nice chickenshit outfit, all right. If that's how you want it, Captain, you can have it all the way."

"Sergeant Proctor, by now you ought to know that I have a reason for everything I do in my command. When this town is secured, and when those concerned have all cooled down a bit, I intend to look into a serious matter relating to the chain of command."

As Proctor took his coffee Riglioni sipped his, a hot sensual luxury. Proctor downed a great deal of it, gasped, and said, "Captain Stollman, you gonna have to give me a few hours to sink my feet in this new chickenshit. Right now I'm gonna remind you we been up on the line longer this trip than the ninety days it took some garrison joker to get his bars."

"That's hardly the point," Stollman said evenly as the lieutenant turned a gaping affronted look on him. "The real point —I was hoping that you two sergeants would cool yourselves down enough to face certain facts."

"Now that sticks the pig right in the ass. There was a good many facts I understood before this here man come along and started hollering a whole crock of shit I ain't heard since I last stood Saturday inspection. You got some facts in that morning report, ain't you? Just names to this man, expendable, and we might just as well quit all this—"

"Hold on, Proctor." Stollman took a tranquil moment to light his pipe. The sergeants sipped coffee and the lieutenant stood his ground with shoulders squared, eyes cold, nostrils flexed like two great muscles. Riglioni drank deep for heat with which to tamp back his nausea, eyelids suddenly heavy with an unnatural sleepiness. "Your rank," the Captain said, "carries a considerable responsibility. Now yes, you don't have to say it, I'm aware that cuts many ways. But it all boils down to a simple principle of command. This is not the time to go into it, however, so—"

"Right. Let's get out of here, Gene."

"Hey, I told you to keep quiet, Sal."

"Did you put Finch in for a bust, Lieutenant?"

"Sal! You gonna shut up?"

The lieutenant's voice barreled forth at last, resonant and

trained to a pitch of confidence. "It appears there's insubordination among the noncoms themselves, combat conditions notwithstanding."

"Aah, you ain't fit yet to talk about combat, you piss-bellied—"

"Now that will do, Proctor," Stollman said with exemplary calm. "Don't make me talk Army Regulations. Not to you. I'm used to depending on you. I'm not used to seeing you blow your top."

"I got a wife and three little kiddies. I may not come out of this, but it just ain't gonna be because of no fucking clown with a finger up his ass like some goddamn movie show hero!"

"Sergeant Proctor, it begins to seem as if—"

"Now just hold your horses, Captain, I ain't no—"

"Sergeant—"

"I'm turning my stripes in," Riglioni said.

Proctor whirled on him, pale with exasperation. "Didn't I tell you to keep out of it?" To Stollman he said, "I ain't a goddamn school kid and I ain't a fool, so let's please don't waste time throwing the shit around. If you want a principle of—"

"Sergeant Proctor," the Captain intoned with sublime equanimity, "I have three platoons to direct on a plan basis of . . ." and Connie Meskerman went drifting across the words that rolled slow and slimy through Riglioni like ping-pong balls in grease and there was a crash and then many voices and Proctor's giggling face and hands hauling him up, hands returning his rifle. "Sorry. I fell asleep, Gene, I just dozed off."

His cup lay shattered in a small puddle of coffee. Beginning to rise, the Captain decided instead to remain seated, and maintained an expression that reflected enduring pride in his self-control. The lieutenant stood there with his granite face flushed red amid its shadows. Stollman expelled a subtle sigh of weariness and said, "Proctor, will you for the sake of God calm down? I make no bones about it. I can't afford to lose either of you men. But I insist on having a command of the utmost—"

"All right, Captain, we'll be on our—"

Out of the night came the rustling of a huge shell. It hissed sharply overhead and hit hard. Another crashed in the forward area, another and another while the Captain drew calmly on his pipe. Then some vast infernal hostility crashed on the roof and laced a shudder down into the very ground that supported them.

"Yeah-boy," Proctor said, squatting next to Riglioni. He gazed up at Buffalo Bill, who faced him bravely from above. "Connie and me laying under them bombs yesterday, I seen something. We was patrolling some street and mortar caught us, we never heard the first pop out of them taking off. So we run into this house, but it wasn't worth a damn. No roof at all. Nothing like what you all have up there. And that's exactly where the big ones started to wallop, right in that goddamn house, which they must've ruint themselves. Zeroing in, you know? Oh they had that house, smack down on us they come. Railroad stuff. Like this here right now—*look out!*"

Buffalo Bill ducked in a whirl as a mighty shell crashed in the street, but quickly he came up standing again to stare down at Proctor, who giggled. "You wasn't in that house with Connie Meskerman and me, Lieutenant, but I guess you heard the barrage all right. You remember Meskerman. No you don't either, you don't know none of them on that morning report. Well, we was caught, we couldn't *move*, Connie and me. We laid out there under them bombs just shaking like a couple of dogs shitting peach pits."

"Sergeant Proctor," the Captain said, and hunched his shoulders as a shell wrecked something in a roar close by.

"No, let me tell you, I seen something. Them shells busting all around us, it looked like time to go, you know? Scared to Jesus, and right over me on this window sill sits a Kraut beer stein. A face carved on it, real fancy thing, just sitting there with a fishy eye on me. Man, what a face on that beer stein, like the principal back in grade school. Like the mayor, you know?"

Shells thundered in pattern outside, but Buffalo Bill was a rock, not even the shadows moving in his face high above. Riglioni leaned hard on his rifle, blinking his eyes against sleep. Another shell rippled in and made a hollow boom in the night while Proctor sipped coffee. "Nice CP you got here. So anyway this face on the beer stein was looking down at me. Real knowing kind of face, see, this knowing little smile, heavy eyes sort of dropped down to look me over. Like the Congressman come to town at us, the State Senator looking down at me, you know? Real big important man looking down my duster and them shells just *plaguing* us, closer and closer. And poor Connie—he's dead now, of course—Connie laying out there keeping a tight hole, and that U.S. Senator looking down as calm and brave as you please, staring down his cheek, telling me *all* my sins." Tilting his head back, Proctor drained the cup. No shells sounded outside. He got to his feet saying, "Well, you know that barrage lifted at last and I got up to study that face. That important face, Lieutenant, that high and mighty face. Know what was behind that face? Why, just nothing. Just an empty old beer stein, of course. And down inside it, way on the shiny bottom—just some bitty specks of dust."

"That's all very interesting," the Lieutenant said sepulchrally, and began to say more but the Captain waved a restraining hand and a shell hooted overhead and, drowsing, Riglioni told himself that the counterattack was coming now, but he wanted only to watch the light and believe nothing. The flame with Gingold's astonished turkey face behind it. He dreamed of a Gingold with steel-framed GI glasses and a ruddy goatee like Farmer Brown.

"Where's your mustache?" he said amenably, no demand in his voice.

Gingold laughed. "Chickenshit. Watch the wax. I'll get you some light, kid."

Then he was awake again and Proctor was standing up there saying, "Anyone's a fool to come up on the line and try pushing men around."

"And it's a damn fool who gets himself shot for insubordination!"

"Lieutenant Simmons!" Stollman was standing now, forehead wrinkled, eyes grim and moist. "Let me remind you of Lieutenant Enshaw's statement on the faultless obedience of his men. And you listen to me, Gene. Hereafter—"

"Your ass ain't worth two bits around my men, Mr. Lieutenant. I can't be responsible for him, Captain, keep him away from us until he grows outen his goddamn knickers!"

The lieutenant quaked with pained restraint; Stollman said, "Damn it, Gene, you're forcing the issue! Don't hang yourself on your own rope!" Shellbursts silenced him, and when he spoke again his perfect calm had returned. "I'm afraid this doesn't end it. By God I'm a line officer, not a judge advocate. It's sheer hell to sit here like a school marm and arbitrate petty disputes, but I have a mission to accomplish and I mean to get it done. No, this doesn't end it by any means. Get back to your platoon now."

"You're telling all that to the wrong one of us, Captain. You want my stripes? You can shove them!"

"The hell with that malarky. You wouldn't trust another man in your boots and neither would you, Riglioni. We're going to work this thing out and until we do you'll respect the chain of command to the letter."

Locking eyes with the Captain, Proctor began to giggle. Then he faced the bearded officer with a soft smile. "A man got nothing but his one old life to take serious up here. When you down to brass tacks a high and mighty face don't fool you none, and an ass-hole voice is just plain shit."

"You're excused, Gene, that'll be all."

"Come on, Sal, you need some sleep." Proctor slung his Thompson and shambled toward the door where he turned, still smiling, his eyes lost in round shadows. "I taken that old beer stein and busted it under my foot. I don't wish you no harm, Lieutenant."

Proctor's jeep rolled away in the night. Entering under the blackout blanket, Riglioni kicked into somebody in the darkness and tripped over an extended rifle. "Jesus, watch out."

"If you was a Kraut," Honeycutt whispered, "you'd be a dead one now. How'd you all do with the Old Man?"

"Proctor court-martialed him." And then he refused to talk about it, just giggling all the way back.

"It's breed, not breathe," Moran rasped in the shadows. "I fuck you where you breed, not breathe. Common sense'll tell you—"

"You can't say that to boys, Hebe, use your head. Let's go with that light, Atman."

In light blossoming now from Atman's candle, the room was full of men squatting with the support of their weapons. Lindemayer was there with Field and Munzer from Section One, Lindquist and Smith were there from Section Three. To Finch, Riglioni said, "Who's on the gun?"

"The hillbilly." Finch came out of a blanket removing his helmet, wiping at the leather headband with such apparent concentration that Riglioni knew he was preoccupied with something else and could guess what it was. "Sal, did you—"

"All right, you guys, get the hell out of here, I want some sleep. What is this, a goddamn floor show?"

"Blow it out your ass," Pete Lindemayer murmured with an abstracted gaze on the flame. "Go sleep in another room."

"I ain't gonna argue with you," Riglioni said, squatting in front of the sallow blond man. "I'll just grab you by the neck, one by goddamn one, and throw your ass out the window."

"Don't be a drag," Lindemayer sniggered, and went into a comfortable yawn.

"Now listen—" The field phone jingled.

"Mayflower," Finch said into it. "Yeah, wait a minute, boss. It's Enshaw, Sal."

He took the phone and Enshaw told him to get ready for a patrol with one man; it had to be him and any other man. "Is that Stollman's orders?" he asked. Yes, Stollman had been adamant about it, too. Enshaw told him to bring the man and get their faces dirtied up with burnt cork at Troop.

"We'll blacken up ourselves. You better come pick us up here, Lew. Bunch of idiots from the other sections are here and I can't get them out. I had enough bullshit for one night so you better do it. What?" Enshaw spoke and when he was done Riglioni said, "Okay," and hung up. "You bastards better take off now."

Rising with the others, Lindemayer said, "Chickenshit Riglioni."

Atman blew out the light and the visitors clambered out the window. "Patrol?" Moran said in the dark.

"Yeah. Don't light that candle, Atman. You're coming with me to Troop. Enshaw doesn't know his goddamn way here."

Their cheeks and noses corked black, wearing knit caps in place of helmets, they moved north on foot up a dark street, Riglioni, Enshaw, and Atman.

"Winter's a cinch," the lieutenant said.

It was not that cold. But fear was like a hint of winter in Riglioni's fingers and toes and every dark slimy organ within the secret of himself, making him conscious of all his separate parts. "Is Stollman gonna keep my neck stuck out now till I get it?"

"Gene too, he's going out later, the other way around for a look. It's gonna be you and Gene until you decide to behave, that's my guess. Don't put Finch in for that medal, Sal, listen to me."

"And let that creep Simmons get the kid busted?"

"Right, let Finch take the bust. You and Gene shat all over the Army Commissioned Officer. You can shit on a man, but not on an institution. Wise up, that's the law of life."

"We're supposed to throw Finch to them, is that it?"

"He started the whole thing anyway. Listen, what the hell do you care about Finch's vanity? Big deal, his corporal stripes!"

"His vanity? What do I care what makes a man earn what he wants? Everything's stripped down so raw up here that vanity's like eating, or praying, or whatever a guy has to do for himself. Don't be a windy college professor with me or I'll start vomiting right now."

"Come here." Enshaw drew them into a doorway, where they all squatted. "It's not men you're bucking, it's an institution. Stollman, Simmons, they can't fight it any more than you can. Because to fight it you have to disown it, and none of us are about to join the Nazis."

"Even if we did," Atman whispered, "we'd still be part of the institution. You almost got it right, Lieutenant."

"Huh? What the hell are *you* talking about?"

"The institution. It hardly matters what shape it takes, so long as it's got people to rule."

"What . . . hey, what are you, a Red or something?"

The boy tittered. "It hardly matters what shape or color."

"What the hell is this?" Riglioni said. "Let's move out."

"Faith, loyalty, status, honor—all institutional bait."

"You quit that noise, Atman."

"That's why you keep your stripes."

"Now shut up, Atman!"

At the edge of town Enshaw found the guard point and said the password for two Troop men who then guided them around a halftrack and camouflaging trees to the meadow beyond. They advanced in the moonless night at intervals of a few yards, sweating out the possibility of land mines, studying the terrain, and watching out for each other. Ten minutes east a flare burst overhead and the three men froze, each in the posture of his gait.

The exposure in pasty white light seemed endless, but at last dark fell again and on they pressed through the windless cold breath of the spook until Enshaw held them up on a small rise. "Canal," he whispered, "stay down. They got to have an outpost on it."

Riglioni lay there looking until he saw a chip of light so pale as to border on apparition, light reflecting some reflection of a distant star. "Listen hard," he whispered to Atman. "You hear a pop, hit the ground before the flare opens or we're finished."

They veered south toward the town, in cautious advance on the lowest ground Enshaw could find. Soon starlight dimly outlined the walls of an enclosed farm community, and the patrol crawled around scrub hedges down to the adjacent watercourse. Atman was remarkably quiet. Into his ear Riglioni whispered, "Squat here. Fire only at gunflashes, not at noise. Keep an eye on the top of that wall, there has to be a gun there."

A few yards closer to the wall Enshaw stationed Riglioni and entered the canal without a ripple. High on the wall a man coughed, but up the canal Atman remained silent. A few interminable minutes passed before Enshaw returned, and they withdrew, satisfied that the canal was shallow and not very wide.

Section One went point with Enshaw. While Riglioni held his Section Two poised for the attack, aircraft silenced the enemy hill guns.

No sound of planes reached them, but a white blaze outlined the mountain against a black predawn sky and the bombs transmitted an unfaltering shudder along the ground. Then out of the mute blaze a blossom soared, unfurling on the sky huge wonders of red only a shade too bright for purple. It seemed hallucinatory, an eerie sudden miracle billowing out of itself on the silent sky. Larger and larger it grew, slowly rising, slowly blooming, a brilliant crimson rose. And even when the rumble of the bombs reached them, the gigantic rose hovered in a silence of its own.

But finally the roar came, the sound of holocaust, and the great tranquil blossom turned into fire that licked out in countless tongues across the far flat of night.

"We hit an oil dump," Moran whispered behind his wheel.

Riglioni said, "Move out."

9

The pain was behind Riglioni's eyes and at his temples, a mild nuisance of an ache. Lately it came more and more at the end of action, with the last crackle of small arms, when the heavy guns were silent and the Medic wagon was focal point for the miracle of life remaining, the miracle of live hands and eyes and vaporous breath around the dead.

Now in the whispering noon rain the moment was full of miracles—light, chill, the crunch of moving feet—and full of echoes thumping in his brain of shellfire that had breached the surrounding community wall, echoes of women's frenzied screams and Enshaw's last bellowed demand for surrender from the encircled German rear guard. Riglioni stopped at the gateway to the thatch-roofed silage pit where he had just delivered a pair of German farmers to Enshaw; he stopped to listen, to treat his ears to the quiet miracle of his people rounding up the other people from outbuildings overlooking the barnyard of corpses in green. There had never been such a gentleness of sound, it seemed. But the ache in his head persisted, and with it a hint of nausea.

He had lips of his own for a cigarette, clean unviolated lips in the echo of screams already scattered off into history. Down in cellars the women had wailed amid dying blond boys. Pole and German alike, liberated slave and captured civilian, all had wailed over the corpses in field greens. Then, being herded apart from the men into a stable of plows and wagons, the women had shrieked at an isolation that could mean only rape, a fate worse than the sight of death. Forced like animals to remain on this side of the canal as a hindrance to the attackers, the civilians could have little faith left in their own troops, let alone faith in the enemy or the international law against rape. So they screamed, and beyond the canal there would be more such screams from other trapped civilians, and more feeble rear guards of the lunatic *Vaterland* ready to die for an arrogant clown with a Charlie Chaplin mustache.

Striking a match, his hands were strong and vital with large veins, beautiful hands without pain. He was enraptured with his hands. The smoke he inhaled was delicious.

Stacked munitions crates had never been opened by the enemy party of twenty or so. With a single machine gun as their heaviest piece, they had failed to surrender even after cannon had razed the walls. With grenades useless against the armor, they had tried to resist until it was too late to save themselves because Enshaw with dry spittle on his lips and outraged horror in his eyes had cried, "No prisoners! Only civilians! No prisoners in uniform!"

"No prisoners," Riglioni murmured now, the words hanging precariously at the brink of significance, threatening to fall apart. "No pri-son . . . ners." Enshaw. He had shouted the command this very morning, and this very morning they had slaughtered, and this very morning the German language had been spoken by men who now in the barnyard were knees and chins and yellowing hands all out of relation, bodies as incoherent as the words Enshaw had used by way of saying *Kill them all!*

One paltry machine gun: the Master Race. The Krauts had nothing in this town, that was becoming evident, although Moran—and Proctor too—still anticipated a heavy counterattack around the canal. "They're saving it up," Gene had said not half an hour ago, his Thompson still smoking over a dead man in the little chapel. "Wait'll we try the canal, you'll see what they got waiting for us."

Pessimist.

Pessimist Proctor, he came now with that Thompson prodding a scared little Pole ahead of him, a woman trailing them with screams. Riglioni's head ached. With one glassy look at him Proctor shoved the man past toward the silage pit. The woman, hopping along with wild yodels of terror, stopped short at sight of Riglioni, horny little hands plucking at her sweater. "*Mein mann! Mein mann!*"

A frail little blonde in her thirties, she wept in German, but he knew her as a Pole slave by her threadbare skirt and rag slippers. She kept staring at him with beseeching eyes and he suddenly realized that she took him for a guard posted to shoot all who interfered. Obviously she was convinced that Proctor's purpose was to shoot her husband as dead as the green corpses everywhere. She saw only murderers; Proctor and Riglioni were murderers. He shrugged his shoulders, invited her past with a flick of his head, and she ran screaming, "*Mein mann! Mein mann!*"

From the farmhouse, from the smaller outbuildings, men of the platoon came. The search was over; there were no more civilians hiding out. And now Enshaw came back through the gate, blinking his eyes, a fresh cigarette dangling unlit. He wore a two-piece rain suit that was issued to keep officers from getting wet. "Sal, go tell Pete to bring the women to the farmhouse."

"We gonna line up on them before Squadron gets them?"

"What? Don't be ridiculous."

All the civilians converged on the farmhouse under guard, the men and women greeting each other with outcries of unconcealed relief. Most of the men were Poles, but there were four German farmers with proud ramrod backs and guilty faces, fearful eyes. Three German women wore modest but sturdy dresses; two of them were wrinkled crones and the third was barely young enough for a hump. The four Polish women easily made the age limits, but Enshaw was responsible for the laws against imposing love in the wake of murder.

Riglioni mused on the possibility of lining the one usable German woman up for the whole outfit. Husband, father, uncle, brother; whatever those Krauts were to her, they would look on with groveling smiles: the Master Race. No equals; they recognized only inferiors and superiors—that was the tyrannical Kraut mentality all right, and there lay their beautiful sons all sacrificed to a mustached loudmouth, a Kraut Buffalo Bill Simmons.

At the end of Enshaw's column, just ahead of Proctor and his Thompson, the ungainly little Pole in wet slippers, following at her husband's heels, turned a smile of swollen gratitude on Riglioni, and he loved her with all his heart. His insides sank voluptuously; he was suffocating in the pall of rain, wounded by the sheen of rain on her face. Her face was prematurely lined and her body had no shape, but he yearned to undress her tenderly in a warm room and invade her with himself, with all the love he would turn into hate for the same purpose if he could get that German mother's fat ass in his hands before Troop came to deliver the civilians to Squadron.

"Holy Mary mother of Christ!"

In the racket of automatic gunfire Moran spun away from the window and fell back against the wall, rifle clattering, helmet slipping askew as he sank down the wall crossing himself. Shellfire broke out now where the First Platoon was driving south from this captured suburb to cut German units off from the canal, and here in the shelter of their private respite Riglioni's section sat around a table cleaning weapons. From their midst Gingold rose.

"What's the matter, Hebe?"

"Look out there! Look out there!"

Gingold gaped past him out the broad window. "Jesus, the kid's making a bunch of chickens dance."

The men got up to look out the window while Moran babbled and sputtered. Out in the barnyard Atman stood between two corpses in green, waving his arms like a bandmaster. Around him danced half a dozen hens, in a frenzy of flapping wings. The dull ache glowed at Riglioni's temples. "Now how's that possible?" he muttered.

"Oh, my God!" Moran piped. "Don't you see? Those chickens got no heads! They got no heads!"

Riglioni rubbed his face with both hands; in the babble of

voices he dug knuckles at his eyes. The hens had no heads. Hopping, springing high off the ground, fanning their wings, six headless chickens danced around the corpses to Atman's rhythmic directions. Suddenly he lurched, rifle slung on his back, and scooped up a seventh hen which came strutting out of a doorway with loud protesting squawks. Atman ringed the hen's neck with two fingers and deftly plucked its head away like a button.

"Burn the bastard at the stake," Gingold murmured.

Misty rain quivered around Atman; seven severed heads gleamed in the dirt; seven headless birds danced across the corpses in cadence with Atman's flying hands as he grinned behind his glasses.

"That's how he gets wax!" Moran yelped, and with an overbearing meditative expression Finch nodded slowly as if he were above it all, forcing wrinkles in his forehead and puffing on his German cigar. Moran cried, "He makes the wax! He gets it from bodies!"

"Get faggots! Burn the bastard!"

"Out of the thin air he makes it," Moran wailed in earnest horror.

Scarbro watched dumbly. Honeycutt was a hawk-face, smoking one of Finch's cigars and laughing, insanely laughing. And to the south guns rumbled and men were falling and bleeding. Riglioni knew the ache in his head was real, the rain and the day were real, and Atman was making headless chickens dance. Corpses moved in the rain. He said, "A trick. I'll go out there and see what he's—"

"Let Atman be," Scarbro drawled, "he's just a country boy."

"Lots of folks kill their chickens that way," Honeycutt laughed. "The nerves is what's dancing them. They're all dead, and the nerves have to play out is all. Whatever can you city idiots be thinking?"

"Sheeee," Finch exploded with bored contempt.

And Atman kept waving his arms, kept grinning behind his clouded glasses while one by one the hens expired and fell as still as the corpses in green. He was gathering them up when a jeep swung into the glistening barnyard with Scarbro's brother in time to see dead chickens amid the corpses in the rain. There stood Scarbro regarding his brother out of the same old expressionless face. Those same blond eyelashes, the same Scarbro and his time was running out, his or his brother's, one of them was doomed and the plain fact of it doomed Riglioni too in a revulsion of inevitability, a hopeless nausea.

Out of a hole gouged by shellfire in the side of a brick building came Lindemayer; the scene had the character of nightmare, for around Riglioni all the men had fallen silent. Guns crackled to the south and in the silent barnyard Lindemayer crossed to the jeep in a lank weightless stride, pointing to the window where Scarbro watched without expression. His brother leaped from the jeep, snatched up a headless hen, in another instant gunning the jeep away.

Lindemayer and Atman were alone in the barnyard, some ten yards of rain between them, each standing tall in a pensive stance. Dead hens and dead Germans lay between them against a background of parked vehicles prickly with harmless-looking guns.

Lindemayer watched Atman gather his chickens. Then the two came together and spoke in the dreamlike mists of rain. Accepting a chicken, Lindemayer carried it back to his men, through the hole in the brick wall. Atman headed off toward the remains of Section Three, which today had lost Lipschitz with a hip wound.

Men spoke. There would be four chickens for Section Two. Finch would take a jeep back to Troop for a can of bacon fat. Riglioni slung his oiled rifle and walked outside, his temples throbbing, all the chill and rain crowded into his head, weighing heavy on his eyeballs. Nothing was credible. The whole day was a lie, people filing out of the farmhouse now to take shelter elsewhere, Enshaw's interrogation over, women with their sheltered nests all warm and wet and hidden out of reach in the protection of law or sentiment or some other lie of time, and now the truck was rolling in, the weapons carrier to haul all the women jealously to Troop before anyone could possibly run down warmly into honey once before he died.

But no, that was Blaymer from Squadron to take them away before anyone from Troop could dip his wick. No, it was not Blaymer at all, he realized, walking over. Everybody was smiling, Enshaw, Proctor, even Brown of Group, who had come smiling with his burial men to gather up the corpses. Riglioni listened to speculations on whether the presence of civilians kept the enemy from shelling this walled suburb. More important targets occupied the German guns but, grasping at straws, everybody sought more than a transitory reason for this respite and chose to ascribe it to the civilians, smiling in the discussion of it—some of Lindemayer's men, Brown who had come for the corpses, Enshaw who had ordered the corpses made and now cocked his head to keep the smoke of his dangling cigarette from getting in his eyes. Just behind him Gross and Lindemayer were dispersing the civilians, sending them off to houses and huts, over a dozen men and half as many women who by now must be accustomed to more than one man each to service. As he drifted forth the little Polish wife cast him another warm smile and left her grinning husband's side to whisper something incomprehensible into Riglioni's eyes, touching his arm before she went off. Fried chicken and pussy tonight. But it would not work out that way under the laws.

"What's eating you?" Proctor said, smiling.

"Me? Nothing." Brown's men were dragging corpses toward the truck. "Nothing. I have a headache. I just feel lousy."

"Cheer up, boy, we got it made today."

"No," he said, walking off, "no, it's bad today, bad."

"What?" Proctor was following him. "What's wrong, Sal?"

The rain had stopped. "I don't know. Something. Those women, I don't know."

"Yeah, well, forget about them, don't start in on that or the whole outfit'll go to pieces."

"No, it's not the women. I don't know. Where was Buffalo Bill all morning?"

"I hear he's with the First Platoon." At the Section Two doorway they stopped and looked at each other, Proctor smiling. "Listen at that noise. Any one of them shots could kill that bearded jerk."

"A bad day. Somebody's getting killed today, that's how it feels." He went inside and saw Gingold look up from the 10-in-1 carton the section had emptied at lunchtime. He had his hand in the carton like a ragpicker, and brought it out with a sheaf of toilet paper. Riglioni said, "Where's Atman?"

"Out back plucking chickens with Scarbro," Honeycutt said at the big woodstove. To Moran, sitting by, the cracker said, "Yeah, I know all about that picture he's got hung up in the turret. When he first came in you sized him up as an aunt visitor. Now all of a sudden . . ."

"What's wrong?" Proctor asked Riglioni, meanwhile stealing glances at Gingold, who dropped his gaze and strode between them and out of the house. "What made you say that just then, Sal?"

"What? I just want to know where Atman is. He's always disappearing, like a goddam ghost or something. This morning he—"

"No, I mean about somebody dying today. I never heard you say something like that; you know, sounding off a scared hunch."

"Well, I don't know, I have this sick headache. I'm cold."

He went over to the stove, into the radiating heat of it where Honeycutt and Moran were discussing Atman.

"Funny thing," Proctor said, removing his helmet. "You said that and suddenly there's Gingold giving me that look, like he'd be proud to put a hole in my back. How'd he look this morning?"

"Killed his Krauts, took care of his ass. How'd you expect him to look?"

"Whose piece is this?" Proctor said, shambling over to the big round table. "Gingold's greasegun? The damn fool went and left it here."

"The son of a bitch," Riglioni said, "like a goddamn recruit."

Staring at the greasegun, Proctor sat down. "I guess I upset him."

Riglioni passed through a door into the little room that, with the kitchen, was the full extent of this house. It was completely empty, and it desolated him. The ache in his head kept fading and returning, and he wanted desperately to lie down. A random thought that this had once been a carriage house sparked the headache to a razor acuteness for no accountable reason; his legs grew weak. Sinking to sit on the bare floor, he found the room mysteriously and intolerably familiar and hurried out looking for the cellar door. He had to hide himself.

"Watch out for booby traps," Proctor said, and the remark infuriated him, the abrupt silence of guns to the south magnified his sick eerie sense of familiarity, and suddenly a shriek of burp-gun fire rattled outside. He ran. "His greasegun!" Proctor yelped, and ran too. Everybody ran.

The burp gun shrilled in new light rain and heavier automatic fire cut into the noise, pounding the drizzle off by a demolished community wall and Riglioni knew that Gingold was in the death of it without his weapon. He saw Lindemayer and Gross and Proctor among other familiar faces, all spreading out, all slowing down to approach the death of it clattering there in deep octave among the tall bordering hedges, and the burial wagon went bumping out of it all and a jeep came racing into it with a man diving out for cover and over by another jeep a bare ass gleamed. It was Gingold's ass and his pants were down around his ankles and he worked a mounted .30 of thunder to maul the hedges close by.

A dead man in German greens bounced up and down on his side to the pattern of Gingold's machine-gun fire: he was a madman firing at a corpse. Atman and his dancing headless birds were in Riglioni's brain as he lunged and grabbed Gingold's shoulder to stop his gun, and the voices, the voices, the dead man in green bouncing, bouncing, bouncing, and he shoved Gingold in the face to tear him away from killing the Kraut a thousand times over.

"Right in my face!" Gingold's face was stone gray, his voice was a feeble shriek. "Burp gun right in my face!" His lips were blue. "He jumped out of that hedge and snap-snap-snap they're cracking past my ears and my hand goes I got no greasegun like in a dream, a dream. So this. I grabbed this air-cooled and oh the Hitler bastard tried to kill me oh that filthy scum tried to kill me oh that—"

"Man, you shit twice, didn't you?" Lindemayer cut in while laughing men hauled up Gingold's two pair of pants, his ODs and his grease-stained combat pants, and there stood Proctor raising abstracted eyes to Gingold from the German corpse that would rot where it lay now that the Group truck had already raced away with the dead.

And Riglioni had seen it all before: Gingold's murderous terror and Proctor's baffled eyes full of youth and fatherhood and the coldest deadliness. And Muldoon. That jeep. Had he seen a jeep go past? Yes, he had even seen it stop and throw the Topkick while Gingold's gunfire agonized the drizzle, Muldoon diving to the mud. Now Muldoon. White hair under his helmet, he was mud all over and full of panic, like Lippy cursing Krauts for muddying his tank suit.

"You sons of bitches!" Muldoon howled. "I told myself no, don't go there, the bastards'll start in with the stupid war again. Bunch of wet-nosed kids. It's for kids and I'm through with it, I promised my mother I'm safe. I'm safe, Ma, no more war, I promised her."

"Must be some wild hair in your ass to get you out of that cellar," Proctor said to Muldoon, though his crystal gaze was on Gingold babbling a few feet off in the midst of laughing men.

Muldoon threw an arm around the shoulders of each, hanging on them like a casualty as they followed the crowd walking Gingold back. "Old Man's cooking a pot of oil to fry your asses and I had to warn you. I'm in his confidence, he knows he can trust me not to go flapping my jaw about it to you. Soon as we sew up this town he's gonna shove an umbrella up your pants and open it to ream you out."

"He's already doing that," Riglioni said. "Both of us got patrols last night and then *this* goddamn mission."

"Yeah, you want to be smart, start getting your noses a little brown or don't say I didn't warn you. At the risk of my own indispensable ass, too."

A drop of rainwater settled on Riglioni's nose. His headache was gone. "How'd the First make out, Top?"

"Beautiful," Muldoon panted, "beautiful. No real resistance, so says Lieutenant Simmons. Brought in a whole squad of Sauerkrauten holding onto the tops of their heads. He's a real combat man now, good enough maybe to sign morning reports and turn Stollman loose out of the CP to be a combat man too, you betcha."

"Yeah, when Eisenhower shows up on the line," Riglioni

said, squirming under the weight of Muldoon's arm, "that's when Stollman will."

Proctor said, "You see the tool on that Gingold? Like a goddamn silo. If I read it in the Bible I wouldn't believe it."

"Why didn't he use the goddamn farmhouse toilet, for Christ's sake? Gene, there could be a couple more Hitler champs in those hedges."

"Stollman's got his troubles, boys, you know that."

Proctor giggled. "Yeah, I'll flush out that patch. I think that was a real psycho, not just a champ, but I'll take a man from each section. Send me one."

"Sheer hell and all that, but he can be a real straight guy, boys. You put him in a box, fighting that joker Simmons."

Irritably, Riglioni said, "Look, Johnny, thanks for the warning, but don't be giving us a snow-job about that phony. And kindly get off my back; you're a worse wreck than Gingold."

"No, I shit you not," Muldoon said with an adolescent laugh, a gray-haired boy. "Stollman's hard but fair, once you let him relax. Right, Gene? Jesus, here comes Enshaw, don't tell him I warned you." He ran for the jeep and pulled out past the incoming jeep of Charlie Finch.

Beyond the approaching lieutenant some of the civilians attracted by the delirious machine-gun fire stood agape in the wet like people gathered to a blaze by fire engines. Riglioni saw the little Pole in her bulky green sweater. He hurried inside where in the pleasant warm glow Gingold was still babbling at the round table full of men. By the stove Atman, bareheaded and with his combat jacket off, was taking chicken parts from a can of water and laying them out on a bench. Riglioni went straight to him and said, "Get out to Proctor and help him flush the woods for Krauts. And make sure you take your rifle along."

"Here's Finch, Sarge, with the bacon fat."

"Good. Get going, Atman."

"Why me, Sarge? I have to cook these birds."

"Don't be asking me questions. Do what I tell you."

Finch began to talk and Riglioni hurried to escape the sound of it. Passing the men he heard laughter and Gingold's hysteria, saw the eyes of Lindemayer who had called him chickenshit as only a friend would, saw Rayhew whose section was being wiped out man by man, and then he was outside looking for the Polish woman whose hair was matted and whose knuckles were knobby and whose ruined angular face hardly mattered because there was no time and no hope.

Noticing his approach she smiled at him and shuffled away from one of the German crones. He looked at no face among the men ordering civilians inside. As he overtook the woman she cast him a backward glance so plainly beckoning that his ardor soared and overswarmed him and struck his brain like a lance, the headache returning, the silence returning, even the drizzle abruptly muted in this dream of rain and corpses.

In an outbuilding doorway she stood waiting with an extravagant smile that he remembered from dreams of witches. A raggedy bulk of wool shrouded the tiny miracle of her; he felt his pulsebeat everywhere. Dirt was everywhere; dank shadows dirtied her sickly long teeth; her haggard face seemed dirty. She murmured something to him in a language like broken bells, and in this rainy day of death his family receded to pallors and sorrows of distance, too safe, too clean to exist between them.

As he followed her up creaking stairs she kept turning that obsequious smile on him. Her rag slippers were drenched with war; her gray cotton stockings were a filth of terror-stricken wrinkles. The drab skirt swung freely before his eyes and he knew there was not very much of her inside it—but she existed, she existed with temperatures and varying degrees of moisture and he worshiped the little of her for that. The stair ended in a small room clammy with a chill that cut deep. On the bed her husband sat up and smiled.

That was all right. The blond little man meant nothing. His smile was a surrender.

In a babble that rose from husband and wife, an ingratiating gibberish both German and Slavic, the man leaped up hitching his pants around, and bent to haul something out from under the bed. The woman invited Riglioni to sit on the bed, and she too sat down on it, her husband rising between them with a cardboard carton. From the rubble of its contents he dug out a sheaf of newspaper clippings, meanwhile joining his wife in meaningless talk and deft charades to indicate aircraft. Planes had come over, they communicated, many planes, or frequent ones. *Bomben, nein,* he heard, no bombs.

Riglioni sat there nodding, the woman sneaking frightened glances at the rifle across his lap with pale eyes seasoned to brutality. Hadn't the Germans abused her, wasn't she used to the need he had brought behind her up the stairs? "*Deutches,*" he said in one language and in another asked, "*Sauvage?*" punching a fist brutally to his knee.

No, they assured him, their civilian masters had not been cruel—*schpatzier,* or some such word; they had been allowed occasional evening walks together in the fields. Yet they had endured the risk of arrest, the man conveyed, showing him what turned out to be not newspaper clippings at all but propaganda leaflets rained down by *Amerikanische* planes over the past several weeks. They had risked arrest to gather and hoard a pack of lies; maps dated a month and more back showed the Allied lines to be a hundred miles east of here, whereas American units, whose guns even now rumbled with enough distance to sound like silence, could not possibly have advanced more than ten miles beyond this pocket of resistance. The couple talked on in the voice of eternal victims, their eyes befouled with all that war was yet to visit on them, and his temples ached with sympathy, his chest heaved and fell with suffocating ardor.

Speaking, the woman nodded vigorously, waved her frail arms, and rubbed knuckles that were red and raw. The man backed into a wooden chair and sank down on it, talking, gesturing, smiling, constantly smiling. In the cloudy window behind him Riglioni saw men crossing the barnyard toward parked vehicles and hedges. Somewhere a woman yelped or screamed or laughed and her voice rose while here before him the gesticulating couple raced on in fervent chatter as if sound and activity were myth beyond this bleached cell of a room. And indeed all was silence outside; he sat at the center of a dream, as in a dream compulsive, breathless, intent on wild carnal overflows with a homely stranger in the very presence of her husband. They seemed to see it all take form in his face, because suddenly their mouths closed as if on command, and with folded hands they leaned back, waiting where they sat.

Gunfire crackled. Beyond the window men ran. Waiting, obedient, the couple sat facing him with old embattled eyes full of a resignation that mimicked hope. Proctor and his men quit firing in the woods. The woman's smile was vacant enough for him to see a wanton spark flash through it; the man's was the persistent smile of guilt, as if the single emotion any longer possible to him was shame at his accustomed helplessness between two plundering, insensate armies. He hated the man for his impotence. Fumbling, he took out his cigarettes and offered them. The woman shook her head, the man accepted, both of them smiling and smiling.

Riglioni's hands shook as he struck a light for the man. He stood up and pulled him to his feet by an arm, turned him to face the window beyond which men were gathered in front of the small chapel building. He turned the chair around and had the man sit on it facing the window and the men and the stucco chapel, the wet barnyard, the breached community wall. A confused gaze followed Riglioni until he sat down on the bed; then the man jerked around to face the window, aware and subdued, back again in the war.

Sitting there, the woman began chattering through her slavish smile, panting in fits of anxiety at every small pause between phrases. Riglioni licked dry lips, his head tender with keen throbbing pain. Out of his pocket he dug a package of malt tablets and handed it to the woman, who examined it with vigorous nods and an endless gibber of gratitude. He turned away from her and stared awhile at smoke curling around the man's head, which looked so fragile, and at the rims of white light around his ears. Then he rose and left the room, descended a couple of stairs, but with deep sick sighs turned back to take her and be done with it. The woman smiled; the man turned quickly on his chair to look out the window, smoking.

Riglioni sat down and laid his hand flat on the woman's thigh, felt it stiffen, and leaned forward with both hands on his rifle. He took out his cigarettes and got one lit, then put the pack on the bed and departed with the woman saying, "*Danke, danke, danke.*"

Later, tonight, I'll throw the little bastard out and get to her.

10

The gunfire had come not from Proctor and his party scouring the hedges but from Lindquist of Section Three. He had attacked the matronly German woman in the chapel and then had fired at friends of his who responded to her screams. He had fired a greasegun like Gingold's but too hysterically to hurt any careful friend. "That's it," Enshaw had lamented, "we can't keep these women here. I'm calling Troop."

Now Lindquist sat surrounded by friends between the ornate coal-heater and the farmhouse mantle, under a large crucified Christ flanked by statues of the saints. Unlike the others, he was clean-shaven; he had spruced up like a hopeful lover before dragging the portly woman behind the altar. As flabby as Enshaw though no older than Atman or Finch, he had woebegone eyes that raced across faces of the gathered men as he huddled there calling them all crazy.

"Where's it get us?" he said to Enshaw. "You take the high road and I take the low road. Benny Goodman. He goes to Meskerman anyhow. Ask Rayhew, that's his name."

"Just take it easy, kid," Enshaw said.

Lindquist took a furious deep breath. "In . . . sane," he drew out incredulously. "Don't you know? Don't you realize? No matter which way, it's death. I mean death."

"You *said* death," Lindemayer muttered.

"Oh, I thought I said hell."

Riglioni poked Enshaw. "Why don't you let him sleep or something?"

"Sure, sleep," Lindquist said slyly. "You're Charlie."

"No, I'm Sal."

With a shrug Lindquist murmured, "Charlie Sal," and picked

his nose. "Lunatics horn in, what's the rush? All my years. You go right to hell anyway."

"You mean hell," somebody said, and men laughed.

Riglioni walked away from it to the doorway where Finch met him, gleaming wet. The afternoon was dark with heavier rain. Smacking his lips, his forehead wrinkled with profound solicitousness, Finch said, "Gingold is sinking a great distance into himself."

"Huh, who taught you to say that—Moran? You pain in the ass!"

"No, Gingold's strange since that Kraut jumped him. Go over and look, Sal, just look at him."

"That idiot had to go and forget his gun. What do you mean, strange? Like Lindquist? This whole outfit's losing its marbles."

"I don't know. Maybe. One minute he won't answer anybody, the next minute you can't shut him up. Come on and look, Sal."

"Go on, I'll be over soon." Lindquist's voice rose in an incoherent babble; he was finished all right. There came Jevere and Smith through the rain with his gear from the Section Three armored car. And the Troop two-ton truck, bumping along now, was here to take Lindquist back with all the captured and liberated civilians, including the woman he had tried to rape.

So Section Three had still another casualty. Of the full eight including Meskerman when the attack began, only Jevere, Smith, and Kallenson remained under Rayhew. They were leading the civilians out now and Riglioni stood aside at the top of the stairs. There in the shadows stood Atman and Scarbro among others of the platoon, all looking as insane as Lindquist had pronounced them, heading nowhere but to hell and, like Riglioni himself, just barely managing to obey the law against stopping en route for a hungry plunge into honey. Proctor looked crazy too, heading over to the Troop drivers for some gossip. Weapon slung downward, Riglioni trotted across the barnyard while others scattered in different directions.

The chapel was no larger than the Polish couple's room; it was just as clammy, just as drab in spite of the altar which, two months past Saint Ursula's Day, was still decorated with her effigy and countless tiny candles. He had never seen so many candles standing in one place. A high table of boards had been erected across half the room to support them, a couple of thousand candles to represent the eleven thousand maiden pilgrims massacred with Ursula by the Huns near Cologne. What a rape that must have been: thousands of Lindquists and Riglionis hacking off heads and ravishing in lakes of blood until the heaving and quivering headless maidens played out their nerves and lay still.

He knelt before the altar and crossed himself with a limp hand, meaning to pray at Saint Ursula's shrine for the sister he once had. But he rose again with a sense of hopelessness; one by one, Cesare and Anna Riglioni were fated to lose the lights of their eyes. What agonies would they suffer if they realized that the likes of Stollman and Simmons were wheels in their destiny? He took out matches on a perverse impulse to light all those miniature candles made for the fun of parties but destined to commemorate a massacre and never be lit; they looked less like the assaulted saints than like phallic symbols of the rape. About to strike a match, he heard a noise and turned.

Atman's glasses glinted. He grinned, his gaze sweeping slowly across the altar, and Riglioni lunged to beat him to the candles, only now aware of them as wax. But instead of grabbing all that wax for himself he turned and stood there protectively against the desecration of a shrine. Grinning, Atman opened his mouth to speak, but all that issued was the hiss of an incoming shell.

No illusion, it was an 88 hustling in and Riglioni leaped to drag Atman down just as it crashed with racketing echoes outside. He plunged into the wet stink of smoke and the screams of civilians around the truck. Men were rising from the mud in apoplectic bewilderment and the big truck was rocking, and a fresh shallow crater smoked nearby. Someone was hit; men were jabbering about it. Enshaw, shoving civilians toward the truck, shouted commands with Lindemayer translating them into loud arrogant German before he reverted to English in a yell: "It's one of the women, she's hit all right!"

Riglioni hurried over and saw his little Polish woman's bloody hands in wild gesticulation as she leaned screaming out of the van. He reached up to bundle her down, to have her now in some bloody warm pool of mud before it was too late, but she vanished back into shadows and in her place came the bovine *frau* Lindquist had attacked, raising her black skirts high to reveal her country bloomers. With panicked bleats amid all the gibbering cries she threw herself at Riglioni and they spanked down into the mud where her quivering naked thigh wet his mouth. He wiped it in a convulsive tangle of her limbs and saw his hand as bloody as the Pole's. Wrenching over on her belly to escape him she showed a muddy backside oozing blood and there went somebody's hand at a bark from Enshaw, Copley's grin of tiny blackened teeth and his hand in her crotch and Proctor's hands and in all the shrieks and wails Riglioni helped them to heave her back in the truck among her relatives and slaves.

"Tell her she ain't hurt bad," Enshaw yapped, and Lindemayer shouted in German and through it the lieutenant in his two-piece rain suit bellowed, "Pull that truck out of here before they throw more!"

But no more shells came in after the two-ton lumbered away with Lindquist laughing in the cab.

Men wore neither helmets nor overclothes in the warm kitchen, and some were barefoot, drying all their pairs of socks at the stove where Atman stood melting wax in a can, wax in chunks and not in the form of tiny candles. Riglioni said, "It stopped raining. Go on out and swab down the cannon, Atman."

The boy looked around from one man to another, Honeycutt frying chicken, Scarbro and Moran drying their washed socks, looked around as if to state without speaking that everyone knew it was somebody else's turn for a detail since he was the section man who had scoured the woods with Proctor. "Guess I better give you some of this wax," he murmured, "or I won't get a minute's rest."

Gingold, who had been silent for half an hour, said, "Shit, Captain, I'll go swab the cannon."

Facing him at the big table Proctor laughed in an ingratiating way, but Gingold remained expressionless, even when Riglioni, flushing, said, "Never mind, it can wait." To Atman he said, "You didn't cut back to that first street for this wax, did you? It's over a mile."

"No, Sarge, I found it closer by."

"Dolls you found?" Moran asked in an awed voice.

"Made of wax. And vases, cord."

In his full combat gear Finch looked like a dangerous invader among the bareheaded men as he came in with a large carton full of china that clanked with a kind of domestic elegance. He dropped the load between Gingold and Proctor, then unslung his rifle and tipped his helmet back, gasping ecstatically. "Somebody wipe these dishes down. I got nice tablecloths in this box. Kraut bastards buried everything that's worth taking, but at least we'll eat in style."

"More shit," Gingold said. When he had spoken at all in the last hour it was to apply that word or imply it in some connection or other, and Proctor sat by uneasily to observe him, to see if he was shattered like Lindquist and a threat to the outfit. "Everybody talks it instead of truth and eats it instead of food. The whole world's a great big ball of it, whirling around and around."

"Hey boy," Proctor said, "hey boy. I don't want you folding up on us. I don't feature losing you, boy. We need you, Gingold."

"Shit," Gingold said, looking right through him. "My brother-in-law swam out of it and died. He wasn't my brother-in-law yet because . . . I mean . . . I tried to talk him out of it but he saw the color too plain and had to wash it all off in the ocean. So he swam and he swam until he was out of it and died."

"No, now look, boy, you don't want to swim away on us. You're too important to this outfit—why, that Kraut caught you bare-assed and I almost crapped myself right then and there." The look on Proctor's face, as Gingold sat staring through him, was of wariness, even fright, and yet of something more, to which Riglioni, sinking to a seat at the table, felt profoundly akin.

"I tell you true," Proctor went on. "I got no grudge on you like you think, boy. I'm gonna tell you. You shot up that poor Kraut with your ass hanging out and that ass of yours looked as hurtable and holy as my very own."

He looked around at the others with the same abstracted gaze he had earlier turned on Gingold from a fresh German corpse condemned to rot, an aching gaze that Riglioni vividly remembered. "Like that was my own ass sticking out in the rain. Like for a minute in there, you know what I mean?" Scratching his stubbled jaw he turned back to Gingold. Then he found Riglioni's eyes and said, "That little minute I even pitied Captain Stollman, but I can't explain that. No, I don't guess I can explain that at all."

At last Gingold focused on Proctor. "I'll explain that for

you, Hebe. That's the shit you're paying attention to instead of the holy hurtable ass, Hebe, and it was no surprise to me when that Kraut jumped up because my attention was on the same damn thing and so I forgot my gun. No surprise, I even *knew* it was gonna happen because my brother-in-law wrote me a letter about it."

"Your brother-in-law?" Proctor said, aghast. "He's dead."

"What! Who told you that? He's in the Pacific fighting Japs. Just a kid eighteen years old, what do you mean dead?"

Choking with confusion, Riglioni said, "Let's eat those chickens before dark."

From the stove, from the small sink, the men all turned to him as if he and not Gingold had spoken in derangement. Men regarded him with eyes haunted by their common doom out here at the lowest bottom of the universe, where Gingold had killed one man a thousand times to save his vulnerable ass and where Proctor had found pity for Stollman who would kill a thousand men a thousand times to save his holy ass—and get canonized for leading them all to the butchering Huns. Pity for Stollman seemed fantastic, a sly trick Proctor's mind was playing on him, yet no one stared at Proctor, no one stared at Gingold; their attention was on Riglioni who, ashamed that he had seemed to be singling Atman out for details, could only say, "Jesus!"

"Sight better off if they left them women for us," Scarbro said out of his private ruminations.

"Well, they didn't," Honeycutt turned on him irritably, "so don't be thinking about it. Least we can shave, and bathe off this filth."

The afternoon was going to dusk in pale rays of sun at the window. This whole side of the canal was taken now, and in wide deployment the Third Platoon held the entire front. No gunfire troubled the day and the enemy, licking its wounds on the other side of the watercourse, was probably glad to have it this way. Clean, the men of Section Two sat eating chicken and luscious French fries on true Dresden china and a tablecloth of the finest linen. In the luxury of it all Riglioni felt so restored that not even Finch's prattling could dishearten him.

"Pass the salt, Walt," the boy said, or, "Shove me some hen, Ben," bothering nobody but Moran. "Thanks, Hank. Have some bread, Ned. More spud, Bud?" Finally even Moran ignored him, concentrating on Atman with questions about wax.

For all his deranged talk and reticent withdrawals since killing the enemy who had shocked him, Gingold ate fried chicken like Henry the Eighth, ravenously, with blazing eyes and the grunting snorts of a hog. Nobody protested; this was the day for humoring Gingold and even Finch played the game, complying in quick puffs of cigar smoke when Gingold asked him to open the window. As if he were asking for air that way in subtle ridicule of a remark Proctor had just made about Stollman, a self-conscious smile crossed Gene's face, and dark twisted roots seemed to sprout through the moment.

As a joke Riglioni had been picturing Stollman consulting Buffalo Bill on logistics for the next Troop action when with a full mouth Proctor made his remark: "What the hell, Sal, the Old Man's got his problems and his pride just like us."

Busy with the last of his chicken, Riglioni was willing to grant that point without questioning its relevancy—but then came Gingold's request to Finch, and Proctor's masking smile which all at once suggested that his need to defend the Captain stemmed from more than his queer flash of pity in the rainy slaughter of this day. He sensed that Proctor was on some secret hook in the snagged chain of command and, suffering for him, he lowered his eyes. A signal of sorts must have passed then, because the next instant Proctor and Gingold each took the tablecloth by an end and heaved it, bones and costly dishes and all, right out to the barnyard with a crash.

Proctor howled, less with mirth than with reassurance now that Gingold's true reason for wanting the window opened was apparent. *You think I want a bullet in the back?* Proctor had said that night after stinging Gingold's pride, and now that same fear was exploiting him: he was not merely humoring Gingold, he was toadying to him. Stollman could keep Buffalo Bill away from the Second Platoon until its sergeants agreed to honor his rank and not shoot him, but Proctor was in no position to avoid Gingold; he had no alternative to staying close to a man who in his horror and derangement could easily take the notion to shoot him in the back.

This dilemma of Proctor's seemed to encompass the whole day of rain and corpses and words in strange defense of Stollman. But Riglioni could not link it all up well enough for satisfaction, so he decided to forget about it and enjoy the luxury of peace in which now, as dusk swarmed down fast, men gathered to watch Atman break glass and free his pair of candles. They were marveling at his virtuosity when Lieutenant Enshaw arrived to eat a drumstick and confer in private with Proctor and bring back the pall of war in announcing a mission for the night.

It was to be not an attack but a simple guard mission in relief of the Third Platoon, a long, long night of waiting in the lap of the spook. They were to be spread out wide along the canal, only two men to each outpost, alternating one hour of sleep with one of guard which the night of visions would stretch into an eternity. In the abstracted gaze of Proctor, Riglioni saw Captain Stollman's threat of special missions, but no longer for the two recalcitrant sergeants alone; now the entire platoon was threatened.

Until dawn each man must wait alone with the spook. All three sections of the Second Platoon must wait and imagine and brood on the parade of eradicated friends while the other two platoons hung back in respite, section by whole idle section holding in reserve. He and Proctor were the reason; Riglioni caught the Platoon Sergeant's eye to ask what he thought of Stollman now, but instead he said, "How about lighting a candle, Atman?"

The presence of so many bathed and shaven men seemed to consecrate Atman's gallant flame. Its altar was the big table around which Riglioni's men sat in reverent silence. On surrounding benches and inverted helmets men of the other sections sat as if in some cultist church, leaning with a ritualistic sort of uniformity on their upright weapons.

Lindemayer was there with Gross, his chunky corporal, with Munzer, Field, Copley, and Spoldren, the entirety of Section One which had entered this town a man short and was now still another short. The remains of Section Three—Rayhew, Smith, Jevere, and Kallenson—hid with the others in the light of Atman's candle from the unacceptable reality that Meskerman was dead, Caddigan was dead, a stranger to them by the name of Zubrowski was dead and the names of three living men had like so many before them turned ghostly: Lipschitz and Checorski and Lindquist.

Six casualties in three days, just in this platoon alone, and Captain Stollman with his wrinkles of fortitude sat distant from it, deep in a ready-built fortress—to which Proctor had gone racing his jeep when he could have rested in Atman's flame instead. Riglioni remembered Proctor leaving for Troop, his robbed eyes, his threatened eyes, and it occurred to him that the man's reason for defending Stollman, whatever it might be, put him in a danger of mental breakdown far worse than Gingold's.

Dismayed, chilled, he hid in the flame, let the hypnotic flame take him home to visions of his parents and brothers sheltered in a bright warm room of music, where often Lorraine used to come with her Friday permanent and home-loving smile. Her hair was always groomed to a convincing counterfeit of permanence, those radiant threads of time now passed like glitters on a morning sea . . . vanished time . . . vanished white majesty of limbs that used to welcome him, and all these men hid in the flame remembering such limbs of grace and dignity and sudden willing awkwardness . . .

Blinking, he looked around at men soon to be cut off from the light of their fantasies because of two insubordinate sergeants. Some chewed on K-ration biscuits or cheese, some smoked; all stared at the flame with composure, though aware that Stollman meant to persecute the entire platoon as a pressure against two sergeants until they truckled to the rank of Buffalo Bill. The stately flame bathed them all in luxurious respite, and into the flame went Riglioni to unburden himself, pursuing Lorraine again to escape the complex and cunning images of Stollman. But he saw her dancing, giggling in a Hollywood carouse among the old men and invalids left at home, so he hurried past the spectacle of it to a bulky green sweater and plundered Polish breasts, his own kind of woman, to comfort.

"She gives me a hard-on," Scarbro said, and a pang of jealousy cut Riglioni right down the middle.

"What?" he said, turning away from the flame, blind with it. "What? Who does?"

"Axis Sally. Tuned in on the radio, other night when I pulled the car up. Axis Sally was talking one of her dry humps at us."

"Shit," Gingold said. "Exactly what I mean. She wants us to grab our spouts and forget the Krauts."

Many laughed who would soon go numb in the lap of the spook, and Stollman sat plotting against the platoon in his distant safe cellar. "There's no law of nature that guarantees fairness," Moran said like a mind reader, and Riglioni gaped at him.

"What did I say? Did I say anything, Joe?"

"No, but you sit there shaking your head and it's easy to guess why. Don't bother your head so much."

No law of nature guarantees fairness. All through his life a man kept running up against that plain fact and endured it with just such little homilies in all his despairs. Riglioni had endured it from Arkansas through Africa, the old Army game, but it was different now; there was the extra ingredient now of Buffalo Bill Simmons. The ingredient of arrogant sham had intruded where the lives of men were the stake. In his nauseating affectations of strength and resolution, Stollman was at least dedicated to saving his own skin at all costs, but Simmons . . . Buffalo Bill aspired to nothing more than an egotistical posture, was nothing but a pointless phony.

"Shit," Gingold said, and that was the word for it all right, the image, the perfect reeking symbol of Simmons' sham, an insult to the whole human race. Yet the men laughed; Gingold said it and the men, focusing on Atman's flame, all laughed. Gingold said it all in one stupid word that would be his whole reason for shooting Proctor in the back. Riglioni contemplated strangling him, even began to raise his hands but drew back as a jolt of pity for Simmons struck him so hard that he was sure his mind was slipping. Watching the flame, going blind with it, he remembered the two black dogs in Africa . . .

They had taken the French town. The civilian celebration was over; in Maggie's place men were drinking and teaching her mother to be obscene in English when the two big dogs locked together in black death-worshiping snarls. Civilians surfeited with disaster ran screaming across the square to separate beast from beast, but no man or woman could unlock them until one mustached giant struck down with a door and wedged it between them. "Don't fight each other!" Jevere translated the civilian's frenzied cries. "Kill enemies, not each other!"

What was an enemy? His mind was slipping. If he pitied Simmons he could pity any German with eyes and arms and parents; if he had killed blue-eyed boys no older than his brothers he could kill Simmons—and for the same reason: to save himself. He could kill Finch, who plagued him and endangered him too, even if his manner was different from Buffalo Bill's. All men were his enemies by that count and, blind in Atman's flame, he was mad at last with war.

"What are you supposed to be doing?" Moran said. It was Moran's voice but there were no features on his face. "Why don't you just turn in your stripes instead of shaking your head so much?"

"It's him," he muttered, and closed his mouth to keep from speaking the name of Simmons, because it was Stollman himself, yes, Stollman was the other black dog, the enemy, lining up special missions for the entire platoon. No. No . . . it was all wrong; he was thinking in circles, creating attitudes to fit his confusion into simple patterns like a crossword puzzle.

While Atman struggled with the quick-melting *ersatz* wax his flame died, and now in the sudden silent night a shell crackled away over the canal and wrenched something asunder in enemy terrain. Another sputtered across and another, a parade of 75s in a wide pattern of destruction. The candle came alive. Nobody spoke; all gazed at the tall motionless flame. In counterpoint to the shelling came the spatter of machine-gun fire, and Lindemayer approached the table saying, "Atman, give us some chunks of wax for tonight. We're all gonna be in separate emplacements."

"In holes, probably," Rayhew said. "We can't make lights."

"Maybe there's houses, cellars. Give us some chunks, Atman."

"Much as I'd like to, who's gonna give me wax if I run out?"

"You can get more," Moran said, adding in a smaller voice, "can't you?"

"No guarantee of that. See, that's why millionaires don't just up and give money away." Sculpting wax back up on his candle, Atman seemed to be hiding a grin. "Much as they'd like to."

The outer door slammed, and shells crackled away, and Proctor strode into the candle-light, back from his visit to Troop. "What are you all doing in here? You expect the Krauts to just sit and take all that junk without throwing back at us? One direct hit and the whole platoon's wiped out, you goddamn jackasses. Wait a minute. Get your gear and haul right out to the vehicles. Soon as we relieve the Third they're pulling south to hit over the canal tonight, so don't be bitching that we're the ones getting the wrong end of the stick."

Eyes turned on Scarbro, who had begun tapping the table with his knuckles. "So then Bob Hope cut in on Axis Sally. Big speech to say what a wonderful country to fight for is the USA. Had a checkered vest on him."

"What you talking about, boy?" Honeycutt sang in a high Southern lilt. "How would you know he had on a vest?"

"Heard it on him. His voice was fat, fat, with a checkered vest."

Moran said, "You'd think they'd get some GI to say that, somebody up to his neck in this disgust."

"That's it, Hebe, just more of it to take our attention. No surprise, no surprise when that Kraut jumped up at me because I got that message from the kid and knew . . ."

Cutting through this deranged babble and the friendly fire came a hoot, a fluttering rush of air. Riglioni tensed, disbelieving but too clear-headed all at once to miss the meaning of the monstrous enemy shell overhead. The German hill guns had not been knocked out at all, at least not completely. The explosion boomed not far to the south, and another shell struck at greater distance, and another tore up the night a short way to the rear.

"Hoo-boy," Proctor giggled. "We cooking ourself up some turkey tonight. Get going, boys, we got to lay wire and all."

Riglioni took him aside. "What happened up at Troop?"

Proctor blinked at him and giggled, then wetted his lips. "Old Man talked at Enshaw and then he talked at me. Now he wants to talk at you, but not tonight. Hey, Gingold, you're riding with me."

"Sal, come here," Moran whispered slyly, with cautious glances to the side. "I know where there's a whole bunch of wax for us."

In those far hills the Germans were hysterical, firing in a wide pattern instead of seeking out the 75s to concentrate on; they were hysterical and so was Joe Moran at the wheel beside him, saying, "Since when are you such a Holy Joe? We could've written letters or something tonight. Candles are candles! I never heard of—"

A shell lit up the hedges before them. Riglioni waited for the bark to sound and fade, then said, "How many times do I have to tell you? It's a shrine. If it didn't bother your conscience why'd you wait till now to think of taking those candles? Now shut up and watch where you're driving."

"I didn't before because I didn't know we would be separated from Atman tonight, that's all."

"You're full of crap! You knew in good time, but you needed me along to share the guilt or something."

"You're crazy, crazy! Saint Ursula and her—you believe that insulting nonsense! You remember the eight thousand Krauts surrendered in France? Did you ever see so many people at once in your life? How can you believe eleven thousand broads went walking across Europe? Stupid! Who fed them? Could there be enough Huns in one gang to—"

Moran ducked and spun the wheel as mortar erupted in a terrifying loud pattern throughout the approaching hedges.

Shrinking with fear, Riglioni knew that Moran felt the same horror and would maintain silence now in order to hear the remote sound of mortar popping at its source. A flare burst overhead but they were covered from the canal by embankment hedges and Moran kept driving, an ear cocked to pick out distant thuds through the racketing small arms and shellfire. In the spooky light his face looked at once as old as Riglioni's father and as young as his brothers, his poor little pasty-faced brothers.

Spare them spare them God you bastard!

11

In the fury of the German hill guns, where the canal was a continuous blaze, the Second Platoon broke column formation to spread out in advancing through the hedge growths. Billy Field drove Lindemayer in the lead jeep until it met an inferno head on and soared in the fiery spurt that turned it the color of pink cherry candy, with Lindemayer thrown into the trees.

Field was lost but Enshaw found Lindemayer in the uproar. Ordering withdrawal at last, he raced him back by jeep all shaken and black and searching his hide for punctures, meanwhile screaming for his driver who suddenly bolted out of the hedges like a flying rainbow. Billy Field ran some thirty yards, not on fire, yet reflecting every color possible to this roaring night of havoc.

Men leaped from the retreating vehicles to chase Field up the first street that cut away from the canal, and in exploding flashes of light they overtook him where he collapsed. His face was blue and his blood was purple except in the flashes that turned it bright orange in rivers on his green face, in jets and puddles all over his corpse. He was already a corpse with startled eyes, saying, "Udn, udn, udn," like some child imitating the sound of a car, saying, "udn, udn," until he died.

And before Riglioni's eyes the skin of Billy Field, in patches between the channels of blood, turned a deep muddy yellow, like suet.

Several streets back from the canal, where Enshaw deployed the vehicles, Gross volunteered to guard the street from a turret. He preferred the open night. He minded the shells very little, or so he insisted, and Proctor took the others inside with blankets for warmth and for blackout, to wait until Enshaw returned with new orders after disposing of the corpse at Troop.

But in the house nobody bothered to cover windows. While Finch descended to investigate the cellar with his flashlight, the others squatted around, stealing glances at Lindemayer whenever a shellburst or flare threw light in at a window to touch his face. Like a catatonic he sat there, head hanging low, hands limp and white, his rifle on the floor. In the long light of a flare he turned up his palms and they were as black as his sooty face.

The shells of both armies thundered, but within that world of noise the house was a silent cocoon until Moran said, "Well, well, well, well, well."

The house shuddered to a near crash. Finch returned saying, "That cellar's been cleared by somebody. Swept clean like your aunt's front porch."

"Well, hit it!" Proctor shrieked on the run and in a bloody ooze of light men fled from the sudden howl that shattered the world in dust and plaster and the clammy odor of death; down a staircase they stomped behind Proctor, coughing, cursing the hill guns and the planes that had failed to silence them.

A light blossomed bright. Panting, Atman crouched above a new ornate candle perched on a sizable porcelain jar. Proctor giggled, and his frightful giggle ascended to laughter: "I was first man through that door and when I get down here this guy's already here setting up that crazy candle!"

Many laughed; none were hurt. Forming a circle around Atman's flame, some sat in their upturned helmets; others rested back against potatoes piled in a bin. Only Scarbro remained erect, pacing one way and another in the fringe shadows until he too came to squat and stare at the flame. Moran whispered, "Sal, how'd he get down here first with that candle? How could he do that? Tell me that."

"Get away from me, Joe." Enshaw should have pulled them back from the canal earlier. Back when the missions were solely to locate the enemy and run, Enshaw could roll a column into sudden point-blank fire and swing it out again, whole, in a minute. That took a concentration that amounted to the closest thing Riglioni could find to true courage. Tonight the man seemed to have changed; his courage seemed changed to bravado. He should have pulled back sooner.

Riglioni saw Lindemayer staring at the flame from the potato bin, and then he looked at Gingold through the flame. Lindemayer seemed the calmer; possibly the soul-shattering episode of Field's destruction had been less of a shock than Gingold's this afternoon. Lindemayer's explosion came in the loud filth of battle, when he was dry in the mouth with death, whereas Gingold had been luxuriating in a sensual moment of relief when the berserk German leaped up to kill him. Helplessly, Riglioni snickered.

Small arms nagged in constant chatter; the shelling moaned and thundered. Scarbro sat focused on the flame with feeble-looking eyes full of Third Platoon action at the canal. From face to face Moran glanced, absently moving his lips to say *well well well* without voice, and Gingold cleared his throat for speech and said, "Shit."

What an experience, Riglioni thought, to be shot at while relieving oneself. The enormity of it was only just reaching him with full impact. He snickered again in spasms that bubbled out of him. A weaker man than Gingold would have died on the spot of heart attack. It was no wonder he kept trying to make such unwieldy significance of the event. The snicker turned into an open bark at a sudden recollection of old Howler pressing a toy pistol to his head while he was in the sack with Sally Devencort. He laughed, and beyond the flame crazy little Spoldren, whose jaw was reminiscent of Zubrowski's, began to titter as men turned blank bemused gazes on Riglioni.

Howler had sneaked into Sally's beach house ahead of them to hide under the bed. Once they arrived, Sal and Sally, employe and wife of the Drive-in King, the idiot Howler timed himself to rhythms of the bed and then at a certain pitch leaped up in the dark like a spook. When the cold metal touched his forehead Riglioni thought it was Devencort himself and screamed from the bottom of his heart.

He laughed, and shaggy Munzer chortled, and Proctor giggled in the tones of his new self-consciousness. He should have pulled the platoon back at Enshaw's failure to do so. *To hell with it, to hell with it.* Gingold uttered his word again, and shells crashed, and Lindemayer laughed; everybody laughed looking at Riglioni in his laughter.

"Bob Hope's right proud of the USA," Scarbro said, "and

Lucky Strike green has gone to war. They ain't ashamed to print that. Get this smoking jacket for your home-front hero, I seen that in *Yank*. They don't care what all we see up here."

"That's it again, Hebe, take warning from the smell of it. That means watch out, something's gonna happen. My wife—"

"Shut up!" Riglioni barked through his helpless laughter. "That's enough of your goddamn crap, Gingold!"

"Let him talk," Proctor leaned over to whisper. "He's off his knob, Sal. Let him talk it out, maybe he'll calm down and be some good to us."

Punch Proctor in the mouth he's bucking for something to hell with it let me alone Sal. Riglioni lit a cigarette, and staring at him through the flame Gingold went on: "I mean the real thing too, like a hint from Heaven. My wife's kid brother, eighteen years old and he knows all about it. He understands it, he saw his brother swim out of it."

Through the belling of cannon came stomping footfalls and there stood Enshaw looking around, already accustomed to the death of Field, with somebody else a rigid shadow behind him in the darkness. "What is this?" Enshaw said on a note of mild indignation. "Gene, you just set there and let them all gather like a flock of cows?"

"We already got our direct hit upstairs," Proctor said. "We're okay in this cellar."

"You want us outside in this shit?" Lindemayer said.

"I want you separated into three sections. There's hardly anything left to this house upstairs, and it's a wonder none of you got—"

"Well, we didn't," Riglioni said. "Sit down, we're about to open a keg of nails."

"Too goddamn clean, that's the trouble. Bathe and shave and your ass gets so precious you hang together for protection or some—"

"We'll be dirty again soon enough," Smith ventured softly.

"That's no shit," Honeycutt said.

"How you feeling, Pete? You cleared up any by now?"

Lindemayer looked at his palms. "You want us out in this shit?"

Now the rigid shadow, stepping forth, turned out to be none other than Buffalo Bill Simmons all ready to face the platoon now that Stollman had consulted Enshaw and Proctor. With his goatee and fancy mustache, with his hands clasped on the little carbine behind him, he looked sternly from face to face in the candlelight. "You men might extend yourselves beyond that single word when addressing officers . . . and each other as well. There's nothing manly about foulness."

Gunfire grew louder in the silence that fell, and then Scarbro murmured, "Lucky Strike green got a gun."

"Drown us in it," Gingold said, rubbing his nose beyond the flame, "and there's no denying we're foul. Call it perfume and you're a phony."

"That'll do, soldier."

"When the shit stops, Hebe, I'll stop calling it—"

"At ease, by God!"

It was an arrogant snarl, and Finch got to his feet raising his rifle, his grim gaze on Simmons such a transparent affectation that it galled Riglioni and he hastened to speak before the boy could. "All right, what's up, Lew?"

In the groaning aftertones of an explosion Enshaw said, "This is Lieutenant Simmons, our new Executive Officer. First Lieutenant Simmons. He wants your attention."

Simmons butted his carbine to the concrete floor and struck a Parade Rest stance, feet apart, his free hand behind him. Somebody farted. Men laughed. "At ease," he said and, with nostrils flexed, recited, "Beans, beans, the music fruit, the more you eat the more you toot." His chuckle was met by silent stares.

Gunfire cackled; shells assailed both sides of the canal.

"Very well, men. Minutes ago our assault over the canal was mounted. Probably at this very moment the Third Platoon is making vehicular progress over engineer bridges. Centrally. Within the hour, at Twenty-one hundred hours, I will lead the First Platoon across in the southern sector."

Several men applauded.

"At ease! Men—now let's get together on this, by God. Now some of us got off to a bad start. I'm sorry about that. But I strongly advise you against pushing me too—"

"This light," Atman announced with a kick and a scrape, "is beginning to sputter!"

Hurriedly Proctor said, "When do we go over? I thought it was supposed to be in the morning."

"At Twenty-two hundred hours the Second Platoon vehicles and men will be deployed by Lieutenant Enshaw in reserve position. Here, pay attention! What the devil are you doing?"

"I have to gather up this *ersatz* wax," Atman said, aiming his rump at the officer, "or this candle will go out, sir."

"What's that? Reserve position, then. Striking point north. No guard mount will be necessary as the enemy is well engaged on the line and Troop is in holding position on the flank approaches. Are there any questions?"

Smith said, "What's all that mean, Corporal?"

Rayhew tapped Lindemayer. "What's all that mean, Sergeant?"

"Could you calibrate and interpolate that, Staff?"

"All right, let's stop this crap," Proctor said, cutting the game off. Riglioni was sure Gene would have passed the question on to Enshaw if it had not been for his talk, earlier, with Stollman.

Killing his cigarette he watched Proctor turn a subdued glassy look on Enshaw, who said, "It means we're probably out of it tonight. At ten o'clock I'm taking you back into town and unless the other platoons run into trouble we can hit the sack in peace tonight. You have about an hour and a half before we move back. Now split these sections up, Proctor."

"Oh, shhhh-ucks!" Atman cried, and the sputtering flame died. "Has somebody got some cord?"

A match flared, the face of Simmons dimly illuminated above it, his jaw descending to produce those visceral tones of authority. "Maintain five yards between you outside. And, I would suggest, inside too, for all the good your kind of conversation'll do each other."

The man was insane with arrogance, unable by his very nature to quit asking for a bullet in the back. As he made for the stairs a blaze flared on the candle Atman had lumpishly molded together and something flickered with the light in Enshaw's eye, a look Riglioni had not seen since garrison days; not even Finch ever betrayed quite that degree of craving for promotion. And Proctor, guiding Sections One and Three past Enshaw, seemed to be wearing that same guarded, covetous look. No, it was an absurd idea. Neither of them could possibly give a damn about anything as meaningless as promotion, not Gene, not Lew, who turned just then to face him saying, "When you're in position, Sal, report to the Old Man. I think you might find him at the CP."

Billy Field was dead but there was respite now and Enshaw could joke that way, the men could laugh; everybody was happy. Respite, respite: little mice feeding on crumbs and on each other. Up yours, First and Third, we're in Reserve Position Striking Point North, as Buffalo Bill put it to get himself killed. Whether his bullet proved to be American or German, his killer would be Hollywood, all the asinine movies he had swallowed whole in his harebrained life. And Enshaw knew the man was doomed, Enshaw wanted those silver bars . . . But that was ridiculous; what good would they do him, and what good would Enshaw's brass bars do Proctor? "Jesus," he grunted.

"Shit," Gingold said. "We can say it now, you foul bastards. We're alone now and nice people like Buffalo Bill can't hear us say it."

Section Two was alone; Proctor and Enshaw had departed with the rest, bona fide members of the *institution* trained to feed on crumbs, trained to feed on each other. That was his persisting sense of the two who could have pulled the platoon back ahead of Billy Field's disaster. He struggled with a frustrating sense that he could almost but not quite name what it was whetting the appetites of two friends who in one day had turned into strangers. And he sensed also that Stollman's demand to see him was a part of it all.

"Foul is right," Moran said. "Foul is how I feel because I ain't Bob Hope or Lucky Strike green or anybody's home-front hero."

"That's funny but it hurts," Scarbro murmured by the potato bin. "It's as funny as it hurts, or it hurts funny or something."

Honeycutt said, "Cheer up. Listen at them bombs, and man, we ain't going over tonight, and the Krauts got nothing big. Cheer up."

"Don't you know that's just more of it, Hebe? Didn't my brother-in-law . . ." Riglioni closed his eyes and began drifting away from the gasp and twang of Gingold's nasal voice. To escape the taste of foulness he tried to focus on a dream of Lorraine—her hair, her teeth and lipstick—but instead saw the haggard Polish woman's face and found himself lost in the sputtering flame. Blind, he closed his eyes in shell patterns that were spaced out wider now through Gingold's garbled talk of relatives and foulness. "Just eighteen and he knows, he wrote me all about it. Got himself engaged—he's old for his years, it's a long story. Before he was drafted—"

"Well, don't tell it then," Moran said before Riglioni could.

"No, not the long part . . ." And on Gingold went through gunfire, on and on about an engagement ring and a toilet bowl in which some girl had lost the diamond for some boy to retrieve, on and on while Riglioni vanished into the flame losing weariness and filth and all aching sense of himself until Atman complained that the candle would not last and everybody fell silent in the gunfire and Moran said, "What's the point of that foul story, Paul?"

"That he looked at the diamond instead of the foulness. All his life the kid knew what to look at, Hebe, not like his brother. Can't you handle abstract ideas?"

They argued and the flame died and distant automatic fire took Riglioni off to the First and Third Platoons, which seemed to be doing well south along the canal. But he could feel no relief in the heartening advance of the noise, no repose with Billy Field a technicolor death in his mind. Scarbro insisted in the darkness that he comprehended Gingold, and told a story of his own to show the other side of it all, the diamond that somebody missed by concentrating on foulness. Riglioni tried to escape the foulness, but with no flame to hide in he was trapped in the hillbilly's images of a squeaky-voiced little soldier who, disgusted by his wife's toilet nonchalance, divorced her. Chilled, miserable, he found himself laughing in trills and rumbles to Scarbro's lazy drone: "He swore he was that disgusted, telling me it with that beady little voice. Just turned my stomach, so I clouted him one on the mouth and to this day I reckon he never figured out why."

Laughter had broken out all around the darkness and in spasms of it Moran argued with Gingold and Honeycutt simpered a demand that Gingold make some sense and Moran said, "It's just that I don't pretend to understand what I don't That's for phonies like you, Paul."

"Yes you do," Riglioni put in, "you pretend to understand shrines, and history, things it takes people a lifetime to figure out."

In a sudden halo of light Atman put his glasses on. Moran

wore a hurt and charitable smile, saying, "Don't get into that with me, Sal. I might start explaining what fouls guys like you up till they start looking for special meanings in everything."

"Well, don't be calling him a phony and starting a lot of trouble on me around here. Can't you just disagree without calling people names?"

"All right," Moran laughed, moving closer to Atman's flame. "I'll tell you a story featuring that great holy symbol of Gingold's. Sal can back me up that it's true, he was there. Connie Meskerman. Jesus, it was Connie," he murmured, the laughter stopping on his face and lurking there like a meditative grimace. "How's that candle, kid? It ain't lasting, is it?"

"No, but I'll make a new one tomorrow. I can find the wax."

"Oh. You can find the wax. Just like that, you can find it. Little wax baby dolls, right? You know, I'd like to . . . I feel like rapping you one in the mouth like Scarbro did that squeaky little freak, you know that?"

"Tell your story, Hebe."

"All right. Connie, rest his soul. In the squadroom he had this lush in the next bed. Remember, Sal? A real alcoholic, drunk as soon as he could get a sniff at anything. One night he comes in after lights out and pulls all his clothes off in the dark. Falling all over himself. I was across the squadroom and didn't wake up till later, but Connie told me . . ."

Riglioni remembered that night back in Arkansas, Connie Meskerman shoving the drunk away to his own bed which was the toilet of Moran's foul story now, remembered the man's disgusting accident and Connie's shriek when the man sat down on his bed to tell him about it—*My sheet, my sheet, he fouled up my sheet!* He laughed the tears out of his eyes in recollection of Connie's mortified voice and mourned him in barks of laughter. There was more silence than gunfire outside and Moran wheezed describing the riot in the squadroom, the officers arriving, the MPs, the men all doubled up with laughter while Connie Meskerman tried to get hold of an MP's pistol with which to shoot the drunk down. "So the officers, they made this lush take his sheets and Connie's sheets. Naked in the woods they made him dig a hole, six feet deep, six feet long, six feet wide. Made him bury all those sheets in the hole, he was falling into it and they were dragging him out. Now. What's it mean? Does that story—hey, hey, what's the matter with him?"

Amid the laughter Scarbro sat up straight in a strange and silent paroxysm, his eyes agleam in the flickering light, his open mouth a cavern of brown teeth. He raised his rifle and stared at it, his face falling grim, then dropped it to his lap and commenced his weird silent laughter again. "What's laughing?" he said. "Hey, what's laughing? You do your face this way. Inside here, your guts, you laugh. What is it? Laugh? Laugh? That the word? Hey, what's this sling, a sling? Is this a sling? Is that what you call this, a rifle? Hey now. Laughing. My, look at this. My hand, look here. Another hand. I got two of them. Hands? Can that be the—"

"Sheeeeee," Finch exploded, "this hillbilly's bucking for—"

"Hey boy!" Honeycutt barked. "What's eating on you?"

Softly, Scarbro said, "Rifle. Rifle. You know, that's a funny word. Sling on it, too, with these doohickies. Is that a word?" Atman's flame perished again, and in the dark Scarbro said, "Now it's all gone. See? Just words."

Riglioni said, "You feeling all right, Hillbilly?"

"Sure. I guess."

Outside the night was silent, no shellfire, no small arms. In the flat blackness Riglioni had a vision of Scarbro's brother dead on his back, a bloody rainbow of colors. Beside him he heard the tense panting of Moran, who then whispered, "That scared the shit out of me, Scarbro. Don't ever do a thing like that again."

"Scared it out of you is right, Hebe. That was a good story you told."

"Buffalo Bill," Riglioni muttered in the black, "he's fouling up our sheets."

"That's true," Moran laughed uneasily. "But it ain't Gingold's point, the goddamn phony. He's trying to—Atman, for Christ's sake, can't you make a light?"

The boy cleared his throat, but it was Gingold who spoke. "Why do you call me that, Joe?"

"Because . . . because you're a human being and that means there's a hundred ways for you to be full of crap. Atman, for Christ's sake!"

"I need some cord," Atman said. "Wait, I'll use a rifle patch, I'll make some light for you."

As he rattled around in the dark Finch's voice rose. "Sounds like the goddamn First and Third's pulling back. Man, if we don't do it ourselves, nobody does it for us."

"Is Finch a human being, Joe?"

"Human, all too human, Paul."

There was no sound but that of Atman scraping around, his rifle clanking against the porcelain jar, his inverted helmet rattling on the floor. Then the flame blossomed, and in its light Gingold wore an expression of incipient horror. "Now that you mention it, I guess I am a phony. I look to act like a tough Coney Island character, a hard guy. But that's phony. I was never tough in my life."

Moran laughed, ambushed by a swift embarrassment that aged his eyes. "Who the hell ever took you for a hard guy, Paul?"

"He's an intellectual," Atman said with a proud grin. "His mind's too good for this world."

Gingold flashed a glance at Finch, as if in fear of some mordant comment, then actually winced when Honeycutt began to talk. But it was Atman the cracker addressed. "What do you know about what's good except wax?"

"I was in Liberal Arts when I got drafted. I know."

"That's it," Riglioni sounded off, "you college jerks with your—"

"My wife's brother," Gingold interrupted, looking demented again, babbling aimlessly again. "A real killer, the guy, and I been trying to look like him all along. You talk about foulness —boy, he hated it, he hated it. And you know something? He got himself killed hating it. He died only a little ahead of us." Gingold gave a crazy laugh. "I tell you but you don't care."

"That's right," Riglioni said with mounting irritation. "You can cut that crap right now. I'm sick and tired of it. Go on patrol and I get it from Enshaw, I get it from this jerky punk here with his jerky Liberal Arts and his jerky wax. Atman, for the last time, are you gonna tell me how you get that wax or not?"

The candle was small in Atman's hand, and he stared at the flame pursing his lips. Then he looked up with benign eyes, smiled, and said, "Sarge, do you . . . do you believe in the hereafter, Sarge?"

"Jesus Christ!" He shot to his feet. Dragging a blanket he went for the stairs. "I'm getting some sleep. Wake me up in fifteen minutes and pull out the cars."

"Twenty-one forty-five," Finch laughed. "If I'm full of crap, Moran, what do you call Buffalo Bill? Man, it's coming out of his ears."

"Yes, Finchie. It's very sharp of you to notice that."

Riglioni mounted the stairs, Gingold saying behind him, "You're a human being, no, Moran?"

"Absolutely not."

Now it was dark. It was silent. It was dank and smelled of rot. He huddled with the blanket around him, cold and miserable. There was a pressure on his brain, as if it were wrapped in a blanket. His mouth was dry; echoes of his own laughter, dancing around the brazen colors of Billy Field's death, seemed a proof of madness. One more action and he would crack. They were all on the verge, Moran with his *well well well* and Gingold with his preposterous foul symbol and Scarbro burdened with a brother shooting up the canal and probably dead by now. Finch was insane with vanity, and Honeycutt with secret brooding. Atman, dancing headless hens and digging out wax and mocking everything with his eternal grin . . . a lunatic.

They were all off their rockers and driving him mad with the same collegiate blather that had driven him home after two years at UCLA. Lorraine had always wanted him to go back and resume the tedious ordeal to become a doctor; once long ago he had passionately wanted to be a doctor. But the general lust for sophistication had bored him to his guts ("Everybody wants to be an Englishman," he had complained to Lorraine). That was it: people fouled up your sheets and Enshaw named the process an *institution* and Gingold called the world a whirling fecal globe because of it and Sal Riglioni made a mental crossword puzzle of himself trying to blame the war on Stollman to a point of utter and distracting confusion. And he was doing the same sort of thing right now. "I'm losing my mind," he whispered.

Lorraine. There was nothing to prevent him from creating visions of her in the darkness. Her sleepy smile and long silk neck, the perfect breasts for his hands to cup. But she could laugh and dance while he rotted here. In mind he fled from Lorraine to Sally Devencort with the same vindictiveness that had driven him to her so often in life, when time was so cheap that one squandered it. But he could not seem to make Sally exist. Amid loud laughing home-front faces she faded away with Lorraine and he pursued the sight of them, but they remained without dimension in his mind, powder things. The little Polack was enough to make ghosts of Sally and Lorraine. He saw the Polish woman with wrinkles of life across her pathetic face, blond hair limply jeweled with raindrops. He remembered her mortal teeth. Hope sparkled vividly, disguised as resignation, in her eyes; they touched his heart with pain. Wet rags enslaved her feet; wet rags were a shroud over the frail body that took his breath away, and he longed to hold her naked against him, to warm her, to teach her a tenderness she had never dreamed of and let her see through his brutal face to joy. If he could find a moment with her in some warm room he would love her spindly shoulder blades and cherish her gangly shanks. *Because she exists.* He would carry her back and forth just to let her rest like a child in his arms, because she existed.

Full of tremors, afraid for his mind, he got a cigarette and lit it, trying again to create a vision of Lorraine. She formed, all white and smiling, but turned vaporous before the slave woman, who existed, whose meager heat and haggard breasts could replenish him in this cold clammy hole of night.

"Rig. Rig, it's time." Clothes rustling as he squatted, Gingold was there. "Listen, I don't want them to know, but I think I'm in danger."

"Danger?" Faint with sudden panic, he sipped on the cigarette. "In danger? You said danger?"

"No, I mean my mind . . . maybe it's going, I'm scared. This afternoon. Before it happened I knew that Kraut was gonna jump up."

"Gingold, don't try to pull that crap with me."

"I knew what was gonna happen a couple of seconds before he jumped up at me. Like I was asking for it, like I went without my gun because I wanted to die. Moran says death makes you want to die. So what does shit make you want to do? Do you realize we're up to our necks in it and there's no way out?"

"See, Gingold?" he quavered, weak with panic. "We're all starting to crack up. But we can't afford to. Stop thinking. Gingold, don't let yourself think too much. It's a trap—don't think."

"Are you religious, Rig?"

"Huh? What does everybody want from me? Go get them rolling out those cars. Go on, get away, get away!"

Was he religious? Did he believe in the hereafter? He sat there quaking with chill and horror to the creak of Gingold's descent. He had better believe, because it was only a matter of time before his mind fled or the wallop came and cut him away from the earth.

He felt death lurking in him on echoes of a faint sound: *udn . . . udn . . . udn . . .*

12

Captain Stollman had a small private bedroom off the big subterranean room that served as his Command Post, and in it he had Riglioni wait while he spoke with Sergeant Reeves and a Squadron Supply driver. Lighting a cigerette Riglioni sat back on a cot full of blankets, under a battery lantern spiked to the stone wall and blazing extravagantly beyond all laws of conservation.

Outside the CP was a hive of commotion. Stollman, considerate of the men close around him, maintained contact with Squadron on an SCR 131 that operated right there in a corner of the cellar, a man with headset working the Morse key, another cranking the hand generator, and a long wire run outside to the antenna. Mess Sergeant Goodspane's boys kept the coffee cups steaming where code clerks scribbled and men prattled over maps, all wearing their helmets like soldiers and grimly speculating aloud on the distance of shellbursts in the area.

On arriving, Riglioni had seen a squad go out to take a guard shift on sandbagged cellar guns at the flanks, crouching away as pale as men in a dawn attack. The ack-ack detail huddled near the Kitchen with ears cocked for the sound of enemy aircraft that would never come. The only one who seemed to recognize the precious safety of this position was Muldoon, who had led the Third Platoon through Africa and most of France. The rest wore embattled faces of dread: it was all relative and the mere thought of it nudged his brain toward the brink, like a blob of jelly on a knife.

"Sal, let's not horse around," Stollman said, entering. "What do you suggest we do?"

The Captain sat down on the cot puffing on his pipe. He removed his helmet and without it in this brazen light he looked almost as boyish as Finch, as vain and narcissistic. Waiting for an answer, he wrinkled his brow, so Riglioni wrinkled his and said, "Captain, I didn't come here to horse around or anything else. You sent for me, Captain."

"Look, we just got wire into the First and learned they lost an armored car. Two casualties—nobody killed, thank Heaven. I'm expecting wire to the Third any minute, so I don't have much time. Look, Sal, I'm sorry about that scene the other night, the chickenshit stuff, but I had to act like a captain for that garrison joker, Simmons. Now, what would you do about the situation if you were I?"

"I'd bust Simmons out of here and give Finch his decoration."

The shadows flinched around Stollman's eyes; for an instant they reflected pain and fatigue, making him look real, deeply involved in all the devastation and waste. Then he arched his eyebrows in a mustering of fortitude, saying, "Sal, you're a mature man. One like you is worth ten like Finch. That's the plain—"

"Yeah? How many Simmonses am I worth?"

The Captain heaved a weary sigh. "It's noncoms like you and Gene who make combat leaders out of officers like Lieutenant Simmons."

"Well, don't underestimate Finch. He's good. That kid got the outfit into this town, you know. I wouldn't be much help to you if I let some phony idiot foul him up just to make himself look like a hero."

"Your help to me is exactly what this interview is—"

"*I have returned.* That kind of crap, like MacArthur over there in the Pacific."

"Screw Simmons," the Captain snapped, and struck a new light for his pipe. "You think I give a damn about him?"

Riglioni almost laughed at this sudden display of good fellowship. Just this afternoon Muldoon had remarked on what a decent fellow Stollman could be. And he remembered Proctor commenting on it weeks and weeks ago in France, what a *regular guy* Stollman used to be among the noncoms back in the States and in Africa, too. Riglioni had not made corporal till Africa; never having witnessed this aspect of the man, he found it hard to face with tact the democratic smile he was being treated to now.

"Screw him," the Captain repeated, and engrossed himself in puffing up a good light in his pipe.

"Well, Captain, I just don't know what to do with him when he sticks his two cents in. He came around tonight and—"

"Just call him Sir and make him happy—that's all it takes. You know the old malarkey about saluting the uniform, not the man. He's an officer and he was sent to me, I can't treat him as less. So what do you say we just bury the hatchet and forget what happened, carry on as usual."

Stollman had already hinted at the extra missions he could heap on difficult noncoms and their whole platoon; he had shown how he could favor them too, as he was presently doing by keeping the Second in reserve. Now his gentle manner was a tacit threat as well, yet Riglioni could not help saying, "To carry on as usual would mean a Star for Finch the first thing, at least a Bronze Star."

"Forget about Finch. That's sentimentality. Be realistic. What leadership qualities does a boy like that possess? You, on the other hand, can go as far as your ability to lead is required. Hard realities, Sal, no malarkey. Platoon Sergeant, First Sergeant, even a commission. I don't mean to sound cold-blooded, but the sheer ugly truth of it is that vacancies open. Vacancies open. You could wind up Captain of this Troop. I'm as mortal as any man."

Sporadic eruptions were remote; it was so safe in the Captain's cellar. With revulsion, picturing Enshaw and Proctor taking this same kind of lecture, he said, "None of that interests me. I have to put Finch in for that decoration. I promised him."

"And I'll have to reject it—or allow Simmons to put through a bust for Finch." Gravely he said, "Believe me, Sal, Simmons would be on safe ground if he went over my head about it to Squadron. I'm trying to reach a compromise. If you both give in a little we have the whole thing settled. Meanwhile, expect to see Lieutenant Simmons in action with the Second tomorrow. Teach him a few things."

Safe ground safe ground. He pictured Lew Enshaw coveting silver bars on *safe ground.* A lunatic vision. "Can I depend on him to lay off my men?"

Heaving to his feet, putting on the helmet, the Captain said, "He has a refreshed and perfect understanding of the chain of command as it pertains to combat conditions."

Riglioni stood up too; he puffed on the cigarette, staring at Stollman, thinking, *This guy believes I'm here just because he sees me here. He thinks I'm sane just because I act like it.* "The morale is low in my section, in the whole platoon."

All at once in smoldering conflict, a spark of exasperation passed across Stollman's face, a swift application of restraint, a swallowing back of sarcasms that were not to be uttered where irony had no place in his role as regular guy. That facial turmoil could only mean Stollman's deliberate caution against any display of pomposity. It was a pose, as vacuous a trumpery as the Colonel's command car inscription: *Courage is a matter of decision!* And it was funny, a paradox: determined to be no clownish Buffalo Bill but the *opposite,* the sweet likable American *regular guy,* Stollman was being more pretentious than that red-bearded fool could ever be. Rumbling, the laughter began to ascend through Riglioni even before Stollman said, "I'd give my right arm to pull this outfit back for a rest."

His right arm o boy so easy to talk in this cellar about losing an arm no blood to it no grief. When the laugh broke free his cigarette shot out of his mouth and he caught it and fumbled and dropped it, laughing as he stepped on it, laughing in hopeless gasps and loud barks of mourning. *This guy thinks I'm here. This guy thinks he's a soldier this pointless mission Billy Fields was so nice you never hated him for being handsome.* "Did you hear about Gingold today?" he babbled inanely. "Killing a Kraut with his ass hanging out?"

The Captain had heard about it; the Captain laughed with dead suspicious eyes, a hell of a regular guy. Then, as his clerk brought in a coil heater and battery, he led Riglioni out where Medics could be seen carrying litters past the CP doorway, and said, "I knew all along that I could depend on you, Sal."

In muffled warfare Lieutenant Simmons woke them. "The other squadron is attacking the enemy hills," he announced, flashing a beam of light around the cellar to rouse men from their corners. "A firm beachhead has been secured across the canal."

"A beachhead!" Finch laughed. "Man, you can jump that canal with a good run."

The beam pinned Finch to a wall. "Corporal, I have submitted a request to break you down to private. At the Captain's request I have agreed to leave it pending. A word to the wise is sufficient. All right, men, everybody up! We move out in ten minutes!"

Riglioni was waking slowly to it all, trying to make sense of the moment and at the same time careful not to crack the fragile shell of sleep. He remembered telling Finch about his talk with the Captain, and now as a candlelight brightened under Atman's face he remembered to look for Scarbro. He was there, all right, rising; he had returned from his jeep ride to the Third in time to turn in. The boy's candle was a brand new one. Riglioni looked at his watch. Midnight. "What's going on? Where we going, Lieutenant?"

"You'll be informed by your Platoon Leader. Formation in ten minutes, so get a move on and let's have no bitching. I've been in action all night and I don't expect a break before morning. I ask no man to do what I won't do myself. Here, you, get your boots on, don't be gaping at me."

He was addressing Gingold, who sat propped against the cement wall in his blanket, scratching at his stockinged toes. In a voice like a bass drum, as if out of his sleep, Gingold said, "Show me a tin Jesus with ethics and I'll show you a saint named Hitler."

"What was that remark? Was that a reference to me, soldier? Aren't you the same man who—"

"Lieutenant, you want us out of here in a few minutes?" Riglioni said, still clinging to the tail of sleep. "How about leaving my men to me?"

The pause was a short one in which nobody laughed: every sleep-drugged man seemed to have wakened to a clearer sense of the situation now, even Finch. Then Simmons said, "Very well, Sergeant. I'll leave your men to you. See that you keep them in line."

Simmons waited there; it was time for Riglioni to call him Sir. From years back came the voice of a First Sergeant reporting *Troop all present and accounted for* to some CO, in his sing-song bark actually shouting, "Up your ass for the count of four!"

As Buffalo Bill took steps toward him in the light of Atman's flame, Riglioni drawled, "Yeah son."

"The enemy's flank has been turned, Sergeant. His hill guns are being destroyed by the other squadron. In desperation he may strike at our flank for a break-through. This trip *is* necessary. Carry on."

"Yeah son."

During the ride down to the canal, and in the work of setting up machine guns and field phones, Riglioni had struggled to keep the edge of sleep fresh, but he could not swarm back into it in this little plaster hut of an outbuilding. If he had light he could have hidden with it under his raincoat to write his parents in the eighty minutes left to him before he must relieve

Moran on the entrenched gun in the doorway. Or he could write Lorraine just to re-create her for himself. His flashlight belonged in the jeep; he was responsible for preserving its batteries. Down the line Atman had that whole new candle made of the wax he seemed to get out of thin air. Spooky kid.

The telephone jangled like Christmas bells. In the trench ten feet away Moran said, "Mayflower One. No. Nothing. Don't call us, Gingerbread, we'll call you. Over."

"That Proctor?"

"Gingold. Proctor made him call the line. Giving him responsibilities. They must be having a ball together. Like arbitration instead of fighting. Can't you sleep, Sal?"

"No. You might as well crawl into this sack. Come on."

"The cold doesn't close your eyes for you? I can hardly keep mine open. Supply better be coming around with heavier clothes soon, or we'll have to use those drag-ass overcoats."

"Quilted jackets, Reeves told me. The requisition's in a long time. Now keep your voice down, Joe." From the sleeping bag he crawled into the moonlight haze while Moran moved out of it. "Supply's pulling details on the ack-ack .50s, but the Kitchen's just cooking for Troop. Goodspane keeps coffee going around the clock. I told him one of these days he better send up hot food or we'll invade him. I had flapjacks." *Shut up shut up stop talking so much.*

"Ack-ack. I didn't know there's any more Luft-waff. Oh, yummy-yummy, wake me up soon as you feel sleepy, Sal."

Another moment, and Moran was gone under rhythmic soft gasps. The canal was not visible though he knew it ran about fifteen yards in front of the hedge-fringed hut beyond barren shell-pocked earth. No more than three hundred yards across open ground stood the squat suburban houses still enemy-held on this north end of town.

Fanatical Krauts, insane to try holding out with the pitiful little they must have if a bluff of an outfit like this one could advance so steadily. Unless they were saving it up to strike one mighty blow for a guaranteed break-through. The real maniac was this outfit. Men were dead, men were maimed. And the rest were doomed for no better prize than a lousy little pocket encircled by Infantry short miles away. This mission was to keep Colonel Powell busy playing cops and robbers, to keep him out of the General's hair; that was the mission. History books would hail A Troop as the heroes who kept the volley balls bouncing at Corps.

Sitting there, he dragged the grenades in their crate away from the gun to leave more room for traversing. It was absolutely still; he knew the Krauts were gathering to attack. They had to counterattack; the rules demanded it. "I wish," Moran said, startling him, "I wish you went and let me take those little candles."

"Can't you sleep? Keep your voice down."

"Since when did you get so religious? I gave you credit for brains, I never once saw you go to church back home, and now all of a sudden. All of a sudden. Like those bastards who never saw a shell go off closer than a hundred yards, they go around saying, 'Oh dear, there's no atheist in a foxhole.' "

The chain of command, I'll command him to be more religious. Now he along with Enshaw and Proctor had knuckled under finally to Stollman's chain-of-command principle, even though in the Captain's mouth and reflecting on Buffalo Bill it was plainly a lie and an insult to the whole human race . . .

"Well, there's *one* atheist in a foxhole, and don't be getting in my way the next time, you bastard. Just remember I ain't any member of your church. You can make me eat it, but you can't make me call it candy."

You gonna manage this joint for me, Devencort used to say, *you do it my way or get the hell out.* Stollman would have seemed a better man than Devencort back then, a regular, considerate, fair-and-square boss instead of the big butter and egg man whose wife you had to tumble just to get even. Back then Stollman would have fooled the world, the whole drifting muddle-headed world, but he fooled nobody up here where the game was for life and the simplest men saw right through him . . .

"Murderers," Moran said.

Enshaw, of course, was an officer, and moreover felt trapped by the *institution* rather than by men and so had to accept the *chain of command* religiously, as a way of life you might say, regarding even Stollman and Simmons as bona fide members of the insulted human race . . .

"I'll tell you the true story of Ursula and her maidens, you simple bastard. Eleven thousand symbols of the church's guilt. For all the little maidens the church kills in cold blood every year with its disgusting laws. A little slip and they have to die, because the church won't let hospitals help them. A little slip —don't call it fun to make love, call it a mistake, anything— and they have to sneak out and get killed by drunken witches with pipes and wire hangers. Big deal, a stupid little fetus to get rid of before it ruins them and their whole family, so they got to die instead of going to a hospital. And the church talks about human dignity! Huh! They're *against* human dignity, the dirty rotten murderers."

Stollman was the Colonel's pratt-boy in this disgusting game, and Enshaw had to support the Captain. But what was Proctor's stake in it? And what was Riglioni's? Yet he and Proctor and Lindemayer would go right on serving the philosophy of clowns until the big noise swallowed them away with Meskerman and Caddigan and Field, and poor witless Zubrowski, each of whom wore the face of a sucker now in his mind . . .

"I was once a little fetus myself. And my momma was sick, and my old man and all my brothers and sisters prayed and prayed, so some jerk with a long black dress ordered the doctors to kill my momma because I was such a holy fetus. It was my momma or the fetus, and the law said save the fetus and kill the momma of all my brothers and sisters. And they almost made a fag out of me loving me so much to keep from hating me. My old man and my brothers and sisters. They always knew that God had His reasons and they loved the fetus and prayed for the fetus and would've made a fag out of me if I didn't have a brain to think with, and God in His infinite wisdom grew the fetus into a man, and sent him here to die in the worst filth the world ever saw. And guys like you, Riglioni, are the scum of the earth, forever bending your knee to a lie."

"Keep your voice down. You know you're losing your mind? It's easy to talk like that. Sure, just turn them in and Finch'll take over, or some other eager beaver, and make heroes out of everybody to kill them off ten times faster. And Buffalo Bill, he'll wind up Troop Commander—that's an amusing idea but not worth dying for. Now go on to sleep and quit—"

"Sal! Sal!" Suddenly Moran was upon him, clutching his arm. "What are you talking about? Do you feel . . . do you know what—"

"Turn in your stripes, turn in your stripes. You're just like Finch, always saying the same thing over and over."

"Shhh, don't talk so loud. I didn't say that. You didn't hear me right. I was talking about—"

"I heard you, don't hand me that, you goddamn pest. 'Turn in your stripes,' you said. 'Give them up and the whole stupid outfit collapses,' you said, 'the whole disgusting war dies out.' "

"You feel all right? I mean you're not cracking up on me, are you, Sal? Look, why don't you go in and—"

"Me cracking up? You're the psycho around here. You get back in that sack, that's an order. And keep your hole shut, that's an order. And if you disobey that order I'll shoot you for insubordination under combat conditions. I mean that, Moran."

"Jesus, you had me scared for a minute, Sal." He scrambled away and from the darkness his voice came on a weak flutter. "Don't be fooling around like that, Sal. Everybody's cracking up, it's no joking matter."

It was no joking matter, because his brothers would be the very same kind of swaggerers as Finch, who kept looking at him with eyes yearning for nothing in the world but that stupid decoration. He had coupled Finch with Atman for the night, to give him some moments of light—if they could manage it in their outbuilding—just because he could not produce that decoration the fool coveted so, and it was no joking matter. "Don't be looking at me like that," he muttered. "Don't get suckered in like Finch, they got to him when he was just a kid, that's the trouble with him."

"Ohhhhhh, Sal, Sal. Sal, you're scaring the bejesus out of me."

"Then get the hell to sleep." The pest, *turn in your stripes,* that was all he could think of to say, day and night, *turn in your stripes.* And Finch swaggering all over the pale pock-marked earth all his life right up to this moment of hell when the enemy realized at last what a fake the whole outfit was and massed all their tanks and cannon and automatic weapons to strike like a sudden storm. He could hear them faintly grinding in the distant reaches, and then like echoes, like notions of memory, distant shellfire sounded.

The Nazi captains were prancing now; he could see them through the wall of dark. Low in the trench he got ready on the machine gun. He felt them in his sinking guts, faintly heard them yapping guttural oaths to the Fatherland, swearing blind faith in Holy Hitler, slapping swagger sticks to their thighs and pledging by their souls to butcher all the grown and hairy fetuses. He bent his face into both hands and rubbed and rubbed, then looked up again carefully scrutinizing all the broad shadows of the night. He saw nothing, heard nothing but the remote and hollow shellfire. Somewhere in the hills and beyond, squadrons and battalions of other men fought in other worlds. Other knees bent to generals with maps and morale-building ball games at HQ.

The night was aimed at him.

In desperation the Germans must hit a flank; Simmons had said so out of his holy OCS books right down the chain of command from God the mocker. This was the flank they must hit, he knew it as an inescapable truth. In moonlight the far houses confessed it, hanging there as eternal as the immemorial moon that lit them bright and cold and numberless, the night spook's ageless eyes.

He seized the machine-gun pistol-grip and searched for sneaking enemies to kill. He could feel every tooth so tiny in the night, every hair and bone and muscle so tiny in the night. Desperately he tried to contradict his knowledge of disaster, for the knowledge itself menaced him now as the enemy massed to strike. He knew they must come within moments to ridicule his existence with steel, knew it with a degree of perception so keen that the knowing, the fact of knowing, was too stark and final and awesome to endure and carried him the last frozen inch over the brink of his being to madness.

I am not Sal Riglioni. I never was. I am a button on the tit of the world. Help me. God. There was no God in this pale black pit of madness. He was a quaking shambles of glass. *God. Holy holy.* Soft summer rains and fresh aromatic pies and the knowledge of father and mother were all delusions in this doom where nothing of spirit or substance existed. *Spell dog backwards. Big dog, black dog. Enemy dog, friend dog. Spell tit backwards, penny nickel dime, spell hips backwards and belly and ass and add them all together to spell* Mother of God *backwards to catch my brain before it goes ass backwards after the tits of a slave* . . . Oh those sapless breasts . . . if he survived this night he would take what belonged to him and grope with war-black hands for the hot moisture of her life and kiss her brutalized face. He would lead a patrol around pine woods to Squadron and claim her. Men who saw his face would stand out of his way. He would teach her something about clear skies if he survived the burp guns shrilling now somewhere under the setting moon.

At last they were coming with gunfire, at last in his long life of waiting. Flashes pierced a broad sweep of the night and he trembled. If he survived . . . and became Sal Riglioni. He would teach the world about clear skies . . .

He pictured clear home skies. Trees whirred in winds from the sea. He saw himself in white tights racing over domes of grass. He saw a sun that gilded and inflamed him; he remembered life lucidly. He remembered mountains and splendors of laughing faces and if he survived this cold breath of the spook he would go home again to be Sal Riglioni in glories of his youth. In air and radiance. On lit city roads to the long hills of Elysian Park, its gurgling lake. City of Angels. All he had to do was live again. In a rapture of hope he sank down in the trench. Swarms of passion flooded him; he swelled and grew hard with love.

Come on Krauts I got something for you.

He wriggled in firmly behind the long gun, and the feel of it in two powerful hands calmed his stomach. Moran, snoring gently while insects bit at the plaster wall, would stay down low if he woke. Watching the distant flashes, he was safe in this trench, a throbbing rock of life to live.

The field phone tinkled through the clatter. He lifted it and listened to Proctor calm in the gunfire saying, "Line, this is Gingerbread. Don't nobody open fire until they show up on the canal. Line, this is Gingerbread. Don't open fire before they rush this canal. Check in, Line. Over."

"Ironside One, Roger." Lindemayer and Munzer.

"Ironside Two, Roger." Gross and Copley.

He waited, then remembered that Section One had only the two Ironside positions to report. Spoldren was the odd man like Gingold and off with him at Platoon. Only five men left in Section One, only four in Section Three . . . He quit comparing casualties and said, "Mayflower One, Roger."

Finch said, "Mayflower Two, Roger."

Honeycutt said, "Mayflower Three, Roger."

He hung up. Moran said, "They coming, Sal?"

"Yeah. Stay down in there. If I open up, you take some grenades and crawl out to the other hole."

Along the perforated steel jacket of the gun he sighted on gunflashes; he listened to death snap by unobtrusively overhead, and resolved to kill, and resolved to live, and waited, throbbing with power.

The Captain was quick to rely on Enshaw's hunch that the Germans had shot up the canal only to disguise the maneuver of pulling back to tighten their line of defense. In fact, he was so enthusiastic about the speculation that he ordered an immediate Second Platoon advance without vehicles or 75s. With only the 37s of the other platoons shelling the houses ahead of them they shattered ice across the shallow stream and went over the bank in a wide stalking line like trench fighters of the First World War.

The Germans threw half-hearted mortar, blindly and without pattern enough to locate the narrow line of advance, and no man suffered so much as a scratch. Amid the plaster dust of bombardment settling in the chill, each section took over a house of its own to form a line.

All through the advance Scarbro wore a big coat of shaggy black fur; now it remained over his light pack as he sat impassively in a corner among men sobbing and cursing frozen wet feet. Honeycutt wore a silk high hat, his helmet strapped to his pack. When Atman lit his candle, men opened their packs for blankets and dry socks, and Finch rode across the room on a bicycle he had found in the cellar. They were all insane, Moran cursing the Church and Gingold calling all creation a turd. Riglioni huddled with his blanket in a corner, without changing to dry socks and without bothering to set up a guard, but before he could sleep Proctor came and ordered a detail to be sent back for the vehicles.

Riglioni made Atman his first choice, in order to be rid of the candle so that men would take their sleep in this longest day of his life. He sent Finch along just to be rid of his puerile comedy. Dispatching Scarbro upstairs to cover a window with his rifle and some grenades, he got back into his corner with the blanket wrapped around his soaked and aching feet. If he changed his socks the dry ones would only be soaked by his boots; the Germans, throwing token mortar in occasional bursts, would be back, and though he was miserable enough now to let them kill him without resisting, he wanted his boots on in case he should change his mind. The distant hill battle still rumbled as he tried to sink into a dream of lying in a warm bed with his Polish wraith.

He dreamed of his father instead. He saw his father at a window with a greasegun on his lap. There was nothing soldierly about the old man save for the gun; he was dressed in the vest and baggy yellow pants he liked to wear pruning his gnarled fig tree—his peasant clothes as Sal called them to amuse Gino and Eddie. Yet old Cesare seemed in dead earnest waiting there as it seemed he had waited for years. Poppa, you don't belong here, what are you doing here, Poppa? *Hey Sal, hey you boy.* All lumpy bone, what a beautiful face on the man! What a smile, fading now in griefs of memory. *Me, I wait for your sister to come home.* Hey Cesare, hey Cesare, you're not supposed to have daughters. *Okay, I just wait.* So long you wait, what are you waiting for? *To see her face again.* When the face began to crumble Riglioni turned his back on the dream.

He woke with chilled feet, knowing loss. Craggy old Cesare waiting all these years; his sister had died when he was eight and he remembered only her swift chubby shadow and yellow hair. Theresa whom they called the angel—she would have been twenty-one this year. They said Eddie resembled her.

He lit a cigarette. Men were snoring. Upstairs there was noise and Atman came to mind, but he recalled that it was Scarbro up there stealing last moments from his inevitable death. The noise was a sneaky shuffling in the soft cacophony of snores. His feet were numb with cold, but he could walk on them as if on stumps; cupping his hand on the cigarette, he took his rifle carefully around men to the stairs.

No silhouette sat at the window rich with starlight, yet Scarbro's noise was close upon him as he mounted a few stairs; the rhythm of it stopped him with some wayward sense of being meddlesome. Something brushed his cheek, so softly that he was not startled but reached up and with the back of his hand felt fur. From the upper staircase, the sleeve of Scarbro's crazy coat dangled through the banister, swaying by his face. Abruptly the separate noises came together—the soft creak of wood, the dark shuffling, a hoarse windy panting—all in the rhythm of the fur sleeve that swayed like an arm outstretched in submission. Riglioni yanked his hand back, swiftly turned, and with quiet care escaped, dragging on the cigarette, killing it underfoot before he went into the night and around with his rifle to cover the cold yawning street lit weirdly like a graveyard by bright stars.

Half an hour later he climbed the stairs. Seated at the window, Scarbro had the fur coat hanging from his shoulders like a dead black beast. "You want some sleep, Hillbilly?"

"Sal . . . I think we all best stay awake. Them Krauts are coming. I feel it in my bones."

"They'll get up quick enough if anything happens."

"I feel queer, everybody sleeping and us holding nary a single machine gun on this whole line."

"That's all right. Vehicles be back soon enough and we'll mount a gun. Why don't you get some sleep?"

Rising, Scarbro left his coat on the chair, then turned and picked it up. "Krauts be coming tonight. I just know it, Sal."

"That's all right. They don't have much in this town." As Scarbro creaked down the stairs dragging his fur, Riglioni sat down and began to wait again, facing eternity.

Come on, Kraut bastards, come on and get it over with.

13

Under the bright morning sun, in the hoarse incoming thrust of a shell, Finch came toward them peddling the bicycle for his life. He had a cigar in his mouth. Scarbro's black fur coat blew out around him like wings. He pumped his flashing legs to outrace the shell, but it crashed and he vanished in the spewing gray geyser.

As the sound of impact reached them, the bicycle shot forth

from the smoke with Finch still peddling desperately and chewing his cigar and crouching to make himself small. Moran shoved Riglioni back in their doorway until Finch raced by, then said, "Don't call him! If he's hit he'll drop. We got no time for him—come on!"

They dashed across the street into an alley that Atman had entered, and there Riglioni paused for a look back. Finch lay sprawled on the cobbles, facing the clear blue sky. The wheels of his bike still spun where it rested on the corpse of a mud-spattered horse. Both Finch's hands danced about his body searching for wounds. Then he came up sitting, his slung rifle jutting high out of the fantastic fur coat, and puffed attentively to see if his cigar was still lit. Riglioni watched him pick up his bicycle and ride it around the dead horse, then trotted after Moran.

It was a fine day. Even the frost was mild. Incoming mortar and 88s were too infrequent to hamper truck movement across the canal. To the south, where the First and Third held a line, the gunfire was only spasmodic. There was no heavy artillery at all because the other squadron had overrun the enemy hills and all the big guns and rocket launchers were silenced forever. Best of all, the Second Platoon was at rest until Simmons completed his patrol with Troop personnel. It appeared that the Second had crossed a mere branch of the canal last night and Simmons had to discover the main stream, determine the size of this island, and see if it was held by enemy troops. It had remained for Buffalo Bill, of all people, to drag Troop men into at least a semblance of action. The First and Third had suffered only five casualties and not a death among them; it was a fine, fine day, with men washing socks and underwear and roaming about at leisure. The pale sun glittered; the sky was clear.

"Shhh," Moran cautioned, peeking around a corner. "There go Rayhew and Kallenson. They never spotted Atman."

"Did you see where he went?"

"Yeah, he went in that—shhh, hold it, there's Gingold."

"Baa-aaa. Baa-aaa." Crouched and pointing his greasegun, Gingold moved warily toward a narrow alley like a man on patrol. With a tense gaze down its opening he let out another bleat and suddenly dropped to a knee firing his greasegun in short bursts. Away down the alley he ran, crying, "Baaaaa, baaaaaaaa . . ."

"That's it, he's gone," Riglioni said in despair. "Gone, gone. We better get him before he hurts himself. Last night I knew he was on his way. Come on."

Somewhere a shell boomed. "Later, later, we got no time for that. He'll be all right."

At a slow trot they entered a rustic stone house and stopped in the clammy shadows. Moran whispered, "Shhh, listen. He's kicking around upstairs." Step by step they ascended, treading lightly. "Listen, he's knocking things over. Wait. He stopped somewhere, the bastard found wax—come on!"

Up on the landing they began to enter rooms. This house had not been hit but, searching through at dawn, the men had overturned furniture and emptied drawers on the floors. Riglioni and Moran loitered in no room but looked and tip-toed on to search for Atman, pausing for silence at each creak of a floorboard. In one doorway, finally, Riglioni planted a hand on Moran's shoulder to stop him. There knelt Atman, praying at a shrine of the arrow-pierced Saint Sebastian.

They backed out of the room. A pair of shells struck outside. Moran whispered, "What's this, a church or something? Like Lutheran?"

"No, this whole Rhineland's Catholic. That's a sanctum or something. Patron saint. I didn't know he's Catholic."

Atman poked his face out, grinning under his big helmet. "Gentlemen," he whispered, "if you'd like to worship, come right in."

In the same reverent undertone Moran said, "Whose shrine is that, Saint Sebastian?"

"Quit whispering!" Riglioni barked. "What are you guys whispering for? If—"

Atman shot forth, catapulted by an enormous blast right behind him in the room, and headlong they threw themselves down the stairs to a pattern of mortar thumping across the area. Atman darted to the doorway and by the ammo belt Moran yanked him back from a flashing orange flame and all three were flat on the floor in the hot bark of it. "Lousy Krauts just showing off," Moran panted, beckoning them into a corner behind the stairs. "All right, did you dig out any wax?"

Squatting there, Atman grinned. "Can't say as I did."

Outside it was quiet. Riglioni sprawled back. "No, you just came in here to pray. Sure. You were just looking around for a retreat to pray in."

"Oh, I just did that to impress you, Sarge. I heard you on the stairs. I wanted to impress Moran, because he's so religious."

"Religious? I'm an atheist, kid."

"So I heard last night. When you said all human beings are full of crap."

"Crossing yourself over those dancing chickens," Riglioni laughed. "Saying Holy Marys, getting more and more superstitious every day. What a phony."

They all fell flat to the crashes nearby of mortar. "That tickled me," Atman said, sitting up, "Gingold letting you get away with it. Funny for a smart guy like Gingold to miss the point that atheists are the most religious people in the world. The biggest fanatics."

Still flat on his belly, Moran looked up at the boy, agape with amazement and affront. "Me a fanatic? You crazy or something? That Holy Mary stuff is just a habit from when I was a—"

"Not that," Atman giggled with relish. "I mean your enthusiasm and passion when you talk against God. As if there's nothing more important to think about. Are you religious, Sarge?"

"What's it your business? How come you're always asking me that? You and Gingold, how come you—"

"Tell the truth, it's got to do with wax, that's the only reason I ask. You believe in the hereafter? The existence of God? All the other so-called essentials?"

Red with congestion, Moran said, "Boy, you been talking an awful lot of wise-guy stuff around here, Atman."

"Yeah," Riglioni said, sitting back against the wall. The mortar shells were striking elsewhere now. "You talk like you're on a campus somewhere. That's sort of disgusting to grown men, kid, so cut it out. Especially on a nice day like this."

"I just asked if you're religious," Atman said, mocking him with a superior grin. "Are you?"

He stared at the boy awhile, caught Moran's appraising cold glance, and decided not to equivocate. "I guess I believe. I wouldn't make a spectacle of myself about it, but I guess I do."

"You bet your ass you do," Moran snarled. "You miserable disappointment. It's meddlesome imbeciles like you that get guys like me mad—or passionate, as this jerk calls it—guys like you with their ignorant superstitions that they ought to be ashamed of, making laws out of their stupid ignorance and demanding that guys like me obey them. Like those little teeny candles!" Angrily he started to rise, but fell flat again with the others when an 88 crackled overhead and gonged nearby. As they sat up, he said to Atman, "Now cut out this nonsense. What do you mean, it's about the wax? You gonna insult my intelligence saying you get wax by praying for it?"

"Oh, no, Moran, I'm an agnostic by nature."

"So what the hell were you doing in that sanctum?"

"That's no sanctum, that's a sacristy."

"You don't believe in God?" Riglioni said.

Grinning, Atman toyed with his glasses. "It tickles me. If God was what the books say, what a bore He would be. No better than a human being, so petty He insists on people praying to Him, reassuring Him. So petty He's full of recrimination and self-doubt. In other words He's been concocted in man's image, just like some folks say."

"Exactly," Moran snapped. "So what in sweet hell are you bothering me for? God is a ridiculous concept to anyone with an ounce of brains and self-respect!"

"I don't know."

"What do you mean, you don't know?" Riglioni said irritably.

"I don't know if there's a God or not."

Beside himself, Moran was red, quivering, showing his teeth. "Make up your mind, you goddamn nitwit!"

"I did. I made up my mind that I don't know and don't care. Neither one of you *knows*, and you get mad at me for admitting I don't know."

Something began tapping in Riglioni's head, or on his helmet, but he ignored it saying, "What if there *is* a God in Heaven? How will you face Him?"

"I could vomit," Moran said.

"Easy. If He exists He'll like me very much, I'm sure. I'm a pretty decent sort. He couldn't ask for better."

Simultaneously and in the same exasperated voice, Riglioni and Moran said, "What's that wax come off of?"

Atman looked at one and then the other, back and forth, grinning. "No. I can't tell *you*, and I can't tell *you*."

Only vaguely conscious of the tapping on his helmet before, Riglioni now heard it in a precise and perfect rhythm; he moved aside with a jerk that brought glances from the others. Something hit the floor, a drop and then another and another, some sort of liquid dropping from above in a widening pink puddle. He touched a finger to it, looked up at the ceiling of planks, then touched the puddle again and said, "Wax. There's wax dripping down. Wax!"

"Baa-aaa. Baa-aaa."

"Hey!" Confused and unnerved, Riglioni leaped to the door and signaled across the street to Gingold. "What's the matter with you, Paul?"

"Did you see a sheep go by here, Rig? I been chasing the bastard all over this—hey! Hey! Get out of there! That goddamn house is on fire!"

They raced across to Gingold. The house was burning, all right, ignited by the mortar shell that had struck upstairs and almost murdered Atman, who now with half a grin said, "Right in the sacristy."

Winter fell before noon, suddenly, like a bomb. In spite of the bright sun there was no question about it: winter had arrived in earnest. Cold cut through the house the platoon was holding, and men moved their card table close to the big coal stove where others were heating bath water in their helmets. There had been no shelling at all since the crackle of small arms and Buffalo Bill's return with the Troop men who reported enemy contact as they passed to the rear behind the reticent Exec.

At noon Enshaw drove up to announce Rayhew's promotion to sergeant and after a moment of private talk with Proctor sped off for the CP again. He left the men in an embarrassed silence, turned away from Gross, who by seniority had been in line for Meskerman's stripes. He stood naked by the stove, bathing out of his helmet and smoking one of Finch's German cigars, a squat furry man like Moran, balding and with prominent features. At length Rayhew turned to him from the card game saying, "Eddie, I'm sorry. I didn't buck for it."

"Oh, that's all right. I expected it to go this way when Gene didn't stick me in Three as Acting Sarge."

"I wanted to make you the Actor," Proctor said. "Enshaw told me no soap, the Old Man said no."

"That's all right," Gross said, rinsing himself. "I'm used to the game. I'm only in this for kicks, not profit."

Proctor looked around blinking those pale eyes, then gazed for an instant at Riglioni where he was pulling pants over fresh underwear and concentrating on the ecstasy of heat from the big stove. Dropping his gaze, Proctor said, "Well, anyway, Buffalo Bill's coming by for one noncom and three men. Bringing the same from the other platoons. Combat patrol. See just what the Krauts got set up before the canal on this end."

"Never mind, Finch, I'll go," Gross said, toweling himself down. "Where's Finch?"

"He already volunteered for something," Honeycutt said in his high hat. "Gone back with Copley to the CP after some trimmings to go with Gingold's sheep." Eyeing Gross, he looked like a little Indian medicine man in that hat. "How come you're bucking to go on combat patrol?"

Gross ignored the question. The silence became cumbersome. Then Proctor said, "Honeycutt, Lew says for you to get rid of that hat when we move up. Shines too much. Attract gunfire."

"I ain't volunteering for no patrol."

"I once had a colored girl friend," Gross said. "Sweetest thing in the world, but she never trusted my reasons for liking her. Just didn't trust white people, so I lost her. But when I had her we went through a bad neighborhood late one night. Bunch of hoods surrounded us, young punks but real mean. Closed in ready to kill me for going with a colored girl, and I guess to kill her for being colored. So I saved us. I said, 'Don't mind me, boys, I'm only a Jew.' " He looked around from one perturbed face to another. "They let us alone. Didn't know what to do and let us alone. See, Rayhew, being a Jew comes in handy *once* in a while."

Rayhew dealt cards to Scarbro, Jevere, Smith, and Kallenson. Nobody spoke until Proctor, staring at his shoes, said, "One man from each section goes with Gross."

"By the numbers," Gross said, and puffed on the cigar, flapping out a fresh OD shirt. "Section One—pick him, Pete."

"Spoldren," Lindemayer said.

Riglioni was about to name Atman when Gross said, "Don't finger Honeycutt, Sal. If he bitches I won't know if it's because my father was a Jew or my girl was colored."

"Did I ever pick on you, Gross?" Honeycutt said, removing his high hat. "I mind my business, you ought to do the same."

Proctor got in front of Honeycutt as he reached under a bench for his helmet. "Don't be starting a fuss, Cracker. Gingold, you talk to Gross, tell him some things I told you last night."

In a corner, wrapped in his blanket, Gingold said, "Proctor told me to stop calling everybody Hebe. It shows how self-conscious I am." He faced the wall, as if to sleep.

With his eyes on Honeycutt, who was yanking the camouflage net off his helmet, Proctor said, "Gross, you got it all wrong. Nobody thought to bypass you on that rating. Rayhew was pegged for sergeant away up in Group. That's what the Old Man told Lew, and don't ask me why because I just don't know."

Rayhew stared at him, then at Gross, then at some of the others, and finally said, "I don't know why either, and don't nobody make a crack that I do. You're it, Smitty, you're on that patrol."

"See, that's what it is about you Jewish guys," Honeycutt said. "You think everybody's picking on you all the time. You make everybody uncomfortable." He looked deranged, bent over the helmet and high hat and camouflage net before him on the bench, pulling at things, wriggling around. Gross kept puffing blandly on his cigar, getting dressed. At last Honeycutt turned, putting the high hat on his head. His camouflage net was on it now, full of burlap rags. "I'm volunteering like my name is Charlie Finch. Ain't nothing a nigger-loving Kike'll do that I won't do."

"See what I mean?" Gingold shouted, sitting upright to face Proctor, who was already chuckling along with Gross. "You see what I mean?" He scrambled out of the blanket and reached Honeycutt in two long strides. Bending to get his face close to the cracker's, he spoke in booming spasms, short of breath. "I'll tell you something about your whole fucking kind, Honeycutt. You're shit! You don't believe in yourself! You use words like that . . . for other people . . . to exalt your*self* but . . . all you do is betray . . . betray your *lack* of self! Like one of these fairy-baiters! Imitate a fag . . . that's supposed to show . . . what a man you are! It just shows you don't *believe* you're a man and that's what all you fucking bigots are, you little son of a bitch! Plain unadulterated shit!"

As he stood there panting, Honeycutt grinned in his face and pointed past him, saying, "You done gone and forgot your greasegun again, Paulie-boy."

In Scarbro's fur coat and smoking a cigar, Finch brought in two prisoners at the point of his rifle. They were cooks from Troop; one of them was Fergusen, who always bragged that he was a master butcher put to improper use as an ordinary cook. Convinced that Finch was dangerously insane, they obeyed his every command and strung up Gingold's sheep, butchered it, dressed it, and set it up to roast in the big oven before they were released to ride back in the Mail Clerk's jeep. Men who had gone searching in vain for wax brought in several eggs which, along with the three bottles of wine uncovered by Copley, made a decent meal of the tough and tasteless mutton.

The patrol returned in good time for the meal, which was there for the taking in a huge pan on the stove. Honeycutt and Kallenson got out of their gear and fried eggs for themselves. Smith got out of his and took his place in the card game alongside Munzer. But Gross, frozen and miserable, sat on a stool between stove and table in all his gear. "They got a lot of strength left on this side of the canal, about a company."

"Yeah, we heard you sound them off," Jevere muttered.

By a window Riglioni kept looking over a letter from Lorraine. Like the one from his mother, it seemed to be a carbon copy of others she had sent over the months, a recital of all the fun she was having. As always, he kept reading it until it added up to an obvious attempt to cause him pain, and then he read it again, recognizing the message of injured love but finding no joy in it, no reaction at all. He thought of the Polish slave with indignation—as if he had been robbed of her, the very least he deserved.

Gross said, "We'll be hitting them before nightfall. Buffalo Bill said so."

"This platoon?" Lindemayer said.

"I'm not sure." Gross reached to the stove and picked a greasy shank to chew on. "Wait'll Enshaw shows up, he'll tell us."

Atman kicked around in a corner, making noise, then brought a number-10 can to the stove and said, "Wax."

"You ought to make small candles," Riglioni said, putting the letter away.

Prone in a sleeping bag, eating mutton, Gingold said, "If you make enough candles we could spread them out. A guy could read, somebody could write letters."

"Be split up tonight," Lindemayer said. "Be nice to have a candle of our own."

Atman wagged his head, grinning. "No, they wouldn't last a minute, the way this wax melts down so fast."

They all regarded Atman in obsequious silence, all but the card players and Gross, who suddenly reached down for a wine bottle and, muttering distraughtly to himself, brought it around in a slow arc to swiftly crack it down on Munzer's head, knocking him to the floor in a loud collapse. "The son of a bitch wasn't anteing. Caught him doing that all morning but I wasn't sure. You schmucks don't even watch him. Keeps saying, 'I see you,' and puts nothing in the pot, the bastard. Get up, Munzer, I didn't hit you that hard."

"Yes you did," Munzer said, flat on his back. "I'm unconscious."

"Didn't even break the goddamn bottle," Gross muttered. Heavy with all his gear, he sat there eating sheep.

Lindemayer rose and stood over him. "Can't you control yourself? You going crazy? Ain't we getting enough casualties in this platoon without your help?"

"Stop rifling questions at me. He ain't hurt."

"Yes I am. I can't move. I'm numb."

"Numb. D-U-M-B, numb."

"Combat fatigue," Finch laughed, cleaning his rifle at a bench. "First Lindquist, now Gross . . . be shooting up the outfit in a minute. Sheeee, can't you take an hour with Buffalo Bill and come back sane, boy?"

"Maybe he did get me crazy, I don't know. That jerky champ, he can get you crazy. Kept calling me Corporal."

Some had been laughing but now they fell quiet, glancing at Rayhew, who studied his cards. Finch noticed nothing amiss, and laughed. "What should he call you—Mister Gross?"

"No, the way he says it up out of his hole, like those gangle-assed guys on yachts who call each other Commodore. Turned my poor stomach." He looked around at the mute faces. "No, that's all I meant. Rayhew, that's all I meant, I don't give a damn about that rating. Hey . . . hey, get the hell up, Munzer."

"I can't move."

The sun had slanted off the window and Scarbro's face hung in brown light over the card table; Riglioni saw his eyes tawny and round and nested in shadows like an owl's, staring through the moment to his death or the death of his brother. Time . . . it was not infinite; it had an end, and if Riglioni could feel it closing in then Scarbro must doubly agonize in that sensation, must doubly pray—at random instants, maybe right now—for the end to strike down and be done with it.

Men gathered around Atman, who was grinning, not complacently but as at a joke. They asked him questions aimed at the night that was a whole battle away, desperate questions about wax.

Rolling in from Troop the weapons carrier killed the day, for it was the first palpable signal of battle. In spite of bright sunshine a pall fell over the men hauling shells, tin cases of ammo, and jerricans of gas and of water.

"I thought we're walking in," Riglioni said to Proctor. "Is this Buffalo Bill's order, to load up?"

"No, we got to stay ready to roll vehicles, don't we?"

"You gonna take Simmons by the hand? What kind of deal did you make with Stollman, you and Lew? Did he throw you a whole lot of shit about promotions like he did me? You two bastards are bucking for something and you make me sick."

Proctor stared at him without giggling, without the shifty look that never failed to glint in his eyes before battle; through layers of frozen sun he stared as if at some lunatic, and looked guilty as he never had before. Turning off to join Enshaw at his call, but keeping that flat gaze on Riglioni, he said, "Don't be simple."

14

In the sunny frost the Second Platoon danced nimbly through streets torn by mortar. Doorway to doorway they leapfrogged the smoky loud flashes in pursuit of the spook.

Buffalo Bill Simmons paced the way with his chest stuck out and no man ahead as scout. He had chosen Finch to stay abreast of him on the opposite side of the street.

They could both be killed as far as Riglioni was concerned, Simmons who against grumbles of complaint had demanded the fixing of bayonets, and Finch who, recognizing his designation as point-man for the obnoxious challenge it was, had sniggered in the lieutenant's face. They could both die, he told himself, though as he ran his mouth said, "He's just a dopey kid, give him a break."

They ran out from under the mortar patterns and when the street was too still, too full of sun, Riglioni aimed at the officer's back, knowing a time to kill as all his life he had known when to trust and when to suspect, when to race a motor or brake it. In the pale sun and the stillness, with the bursting sound of mortar hollow in the other world behind him, he began to kill Simmons when Finch in his doorway held up a hand to call the platoon to a halt. Riglioni sprinted ahead to be there for the lieutenant's reaction. Apparently on the same impulse, Proctor raced over from the other side of the street. Finch trotted across wearing a smart-aleck grin. "We're under their mortar, we got to find the bastards now."

It amazed Riglioni to find Simmons still alive, a travesty of indignation pointing his little red goatee, flaring his nostrils out, squinting in his tension this thin first instant past his moment to die. "By God I'll be the judge of that! How dare you signal back—"

"Lieutenant, we better split into sections now," Proctor put in, the four of them panting in the mixed cloud of their vapors. "They're bound to be waiting on us right up to the edge of their mortar, and we best spread out a front to find them."

"Don't you think I know all that?" Simmons sputtered, blotchy and alive as if Riglioni had not just killed him. "We're advancing one more street! The yardage is only—"

"Fuck the yardage," Proctor giggled. "This ain't no shiteating football game and we're losing good time flapping our goddamn jaws like a—"

"Sergeant! By God, you signal this platoon to—"

"You're gonna be cut down before ever you see the face of a Kraut! I'm trying to save your hide, you goddamn—"

"Walk back, Proctor!" Enshaw was among them now with his dangling cigarette. "Pull these men back!"

They ran, leaving the two officers with Finch, and Riglioni could not understand Proctor. "You take him by the hand! Why? Why? You ignorant bastard, I ought to kick the Jesus out of you!"

"Shut up, Sal." Proctor giggled, then shoved him into a doorway and giggled again. "Get a hold on yourself. Grow up and don't be looking to kill another man's son."

"Why don't you let me shoot him out of the goddamn way? You son of a bitch, don't tell me you and Lew don't want him put out!"

"Lew gonna arrest him if he keeps acting up, he told me so. Christ, those mortars gone quiet, the bastards must be pulling back. They got away on us because of that bushy-faced—"

"Holy Christ! Stollman and Buffalo Bill both in the same outfit! And Colonel Powell up on top! Degenerates! What idiots we are! It's our *life* and we let degenerates run us. Jesus, maybe at Corps the same thing, at Army, maybe even Eisenhower is surrounded by degenerates, maybe Roosevelt even. Clowns, monsters! Can that be? Can that be? The President of the United States fouled up by clowns and degenerates?"

Giggling, his eyes running water, Proctor shook him by a shoulder. About to say something, he instead turned to Finch, who came in saying, "Sheeeeee, what are you gonna do with a yo-yo like—"

"You, you little jerk, why didn't you signal *him* instead of us?"

"Let up on him, Sal, for Jesus' sake. Maybe we be peppered good by now if Finch didn't hold us up. You think that bearded confusion would ever take a hint from—"

"Hey, don't be telling me to grow up! I see the trick now! Grow up! Salute! Kiss every degenerate's ass just to get yourself a Good Conduct ribbon! That's what you're bucking for, a Good Conduct ribbon, and you son of a bitch I thought you were Gene Proctor!"

"Gene," Enshaw said in the doorway, his face flabby and green, "leave a holding detail and take the rest back for the vehicles. We're gonna bust on through."

"You know what you did to that beer stein with a U.S. Senator's degenerate face? You son of a bitch, Buffalo Bill's face is—"

"That's right," Proctor said. "I want to go home and be Gene Proctor."

One jeep was gone in the rainbow of Billy Field's death; there were not men enough to operate the other vehicles left behind.

Section One brought no armored car, Munzer driving Lindemayer and Copley driving Gross in jeeps. Section Three brought no jeeps, Rayhew commanding his three remaining men in their car. Section Two was at full armor, Moran driving Riglioni, Scarbro driving Finch, and Honeycutt alone in the hatch of the car, with Gingold and Atman in their turret.

Proctor was at his own wheel, driving Enshaw. In Enshaw's

jeep Spoldren drove Buffalo Bill who, as cannon and machine guns struck at a community of apartment buildings, quit firing his mounted .30 to leap up and actually bark commands for the platoon to stand and make battle instead of racing past the contacted enemy rear guard. At Enshaw's signal Rayhew kept his armored car back to demolish a couple of German machine guns and their rifle cover with his cannon and .50 and pair of .30s, while the rest of the platoon rolled forward. The presence of Spoldren saved Buffalo Bill's life when Riglioni, hot in the momentum of his .30, rode by too fast for confident aim.

Forward and crosswise they searched streets in a thunder of enemy shelling. A sudden madness of civilians—a mustached man here and a wild-eyed old woman there—darted across cobbles as if pursued by Hitler himself, shrieking at the invaders and vanishing in doorways or explosions. Gingold's cannon destroyed an escaping Volkswagen painted in camouflage like a battleship, and at last it seemed they might overtake an enemy column to wipe out. But the day thickened with scurrying civilians and Enshaw swung the platoon around to secure the area they had penetrated, shouting to each passing jeep in the shellfire, "Spare civilians! They may be slaves!"

In Riglioni's tumbling brain the roar of platoon cannon and machine gun was in such full storm that he failed to recognize the tightened concentration of 88s until Moran pulled the jeep over and shoved him out for a dive to the sidewalk. Separating the 37-mm. wallops from the accelerating swish and crack of enemy shells, he saw the platoon vehicles all hiding in shattered crannies down the street amid leaping belches of smoke and stone. Then the 37s fell silent all at once and, with Buffalo Bill in determined pursuit, Gene Proctor raced past yelling, "Cut around that corner, we got the bastards locked up in there!"

Through green oceans of confusion Riglioni leaped around the corner to kill Simmons. An explosion knocked him bouncing off a wall and he pumped shots at two men already dropping like sacks from Proctor's raking chatter that caught them on the run. Another German fled from a doorway and Riglioni's shot knocked the helmeted head to one side but the man turned to look at him before falling. Men swept by in the uproar—Moran, Gingold, Copley—none of them recognizing him though he knew them all. Where shadows moved he fired into windows; he ran reloading around the corpse of a woman with legs so white in a dirty black shroud. He looked for the red goatee and somewhere in the din he killed Lieutenant Simmons, firing at him to save his own life for all that might still count some day.

He saw Honeycutt's high hat in its net of burlap rags. Two men with big mustaches and pathetic eyes and baggy yellow pants hopped awkwardly ahead of Honeycutt with arms folded atop their heads, and now the platoon foraged toward the rear to clear the houses while 88s struck everywhere in unfaltering parade. In the din the running stopped, the small arms fire ceased to chatter and only popped here and cracked there, and all the sundered world slowed down. Now the enemy shells began to seek him out, and rang like gongs.

ShhhhhhhhhhhhpONG!

Shhhh-shhhhhhhSHHHHHHHHPAWEEEeeeeeee . . .

Seeking the small of his back every shell dogged him, each thumping knell of doom, and men spoke in hoarse unfamiliar voices. Greasy Moran in a rubbled kitchen: "They got tanks, plenty of 88s on that canal." *Shhhh-shhhhhhSHHHHPONGEEEowowwww.* Grimy Gingold in a tranquil bedroom adorned with silk drapes and a ponderous crucifix: "Scarbro killed the officer and they crapped out."

Gunfire crackled and he ran outside, saw Honeycutt on one knee pumping shots upstreet in his netted high hat, saw Finch and Moran race ahead, saw a boy in green trotting forward: "*Kamerad! Kamerad!*"

Leaping the corpse of a civilian came Buffalo Bill Simmons with a noble face, shouting, "Prisoners forward! All prisoners forward to the vehicle positions!"

There was nothing incredible or shocking about this resurrection; he would simply have to kill Simmons again. He saw green movement and bolted after a man who staggered and reeled and fell backwards through a doorway, vomiting blood. He was dead when Riglioni overtook him on a dark staircase; beyond sat an open crate of potato-masher grenades in the cellar. The corpse sprawled head downward with Christ hanging from his neck on a cross, and the 88s kept thumping, echoing down in the cellar toward which this German had run full of death to hide. Two Mauser rifles lay on the stairs, so Riglioni went searching and found a second corpse on a table in the middle of the clean concrete floor.

The gong of a shellburst rang. On the table lay the remains of a youngster with open sad eyes and a blood-soaked chest. The green uniform pants had been taken down to expose a tiny penis in a region innocent of hair. For some inexplicable reason someone had undone the pants of someone else's bloody-chested boy—but weirder than that, Buffalo Bill kept springing back to life each time he killed him. The whole house convulsed to the wallop and the gong of a shell.

He searched, poking the rifle ahead of him. Dusty burlap haphazardly covered old furniture in the shadows. Coal bricks were piled neatly on one side. He looked into the root bin under a window; there were potatoes and potatoes, thousands upon thousands of potatoes that never trembled when a shell roared outside. He knew that someone was in the cellar. Pointing the rifle where he looked, he saw someone behind a baby carriage, and advanced. It was a woman crouched on her haunches in a cold pool of darkness. She wore a gray tweed tent of a coat that reached the floor; her eyes were wide and white on his pointed bayonet, and they flinched to the gong of a shellburst.

By an arm he hauled her to her feet, up and up until she stood as tall as he, an angular big woman close to thirty with shadowed facets to her thin long nose and scared eyes on his bayonet and black hair combed neatly into a bun and lips that were tiny and soft as a child's.

Joists sighed to the crack of a shell. She flinched with the roar and when he let go she sank back down on her haunches in terror of his fixed bayonet. He squatted to face her, his eyes frozen, his breath short. The flesh of his face felt heavy. Her coat had fallen open to reveal a black homespun dress over knees upon which her tiny folded hands were bulky with prominent veins and knuckles. As he laid the rifle aside and dropped forward on his knees, her eyes rose slowly from the rifle to his face with a hollow gaze. A shell swished in and struck with a howling aftertone in which, as she shrank and for an instant showed her teeth, he heard a second sound, a strange distant whistle that he recognized as the choked sound of her whimpering only when another shell struck and she winced fearfully and her mouth opened wide to free the whimper in quavering bleats.

He knelt there facing her and she wept openly into his face, the tiny soft mouth turned cavernous and hard with terror. The shells hammered down, struck the earth, the buildings, each blast echoed by her wails. The enemy was hammering at its own, the trapped rear guard and the civilians left behind to hamper the invader; enemy eyes flinched to each gonging knell of doom, and intimately she showed her wet tongue and tiny teeth as German shells rocked the ground; before him the Master Race wore the face of Meskerman's exile and Gingold's dread and Moran's inevitable doom. Staring at her open mouth he reached under her coat with both hands and she gasped through her wails and he gasped at the incredible softness of the enemy as a shell crashed down to send the baby carriage rolling away.

ShhhhSHHHHHHPONGGGGG in her eyes, her open wet mouth.

The dead in witness, he revealed himself like the dead boy, but alive, alive. She gaped, then limply in the thunder obeyed his search with tremors, falling back, meeting his eyes at last without malice. Each shell made her shudder, each made her shrink as though to a wallop on the head, but at the instant of her final capitulation the horror spilled out of her eyes, leaving a vacuum of all sense.

SssssshhhHHHPONG! Moist miracle; God was in the hair that grew. He drew back from tumid heat and returned in shudders and thunder, and with sallies of ardor the enemy consumed him too soon. He sank to her; in her delirium she held him, her hands on his grotesque field pack.

His helmet fell with a clang and rolled around in a half circle, rags and a mesh caked pink with wax that had dripped from above in a burning house. The breath of the enemy was on his cheek. Her eyes, inches from his, were inexpressive in the joined vapors of their panting. He disengaged himself, threw the graceless bloomers to her, and rose with the rifle and a trembling cold hand at his belt.

The shellbursts and gunfire seemed distant now. Let them go, he thought, let them all go to hell with Simmons, the tiny penis on a corpse. Yet, sheathing the bayonet, he turned to hurry her along and go forward to find the outfit.

Just as he had left her she lay there, as if stunned, or afraid to move without permission, or intent on having him gaze at the shape of his pillage. Exposed that way she looked raw, like something hung upside down in a butcher shop, exactly like the dead boy. His stomach turned. "*Raus*," he said.

She began to babble in German and tears drenched her face,

but she moved not a limb and her white legs were like those of the corpse on the street. "*Raus,*" he barked, "*mach schnell!*"

She babbled on in mounting hysteria; his head echoed with noises. It was only when he pointed the rifle into her face that she moved at all, rising in awkward haste, mincing over to the table where she draped her bloomers across the exposed hips of the corpse.

On the stairs, where pale light fell on the dangling Christ and the yellow face of the corpse, she cut her babbling off with a stifled animal grunt and fell. He dragged her to the top where she fell again and began to vomit in shuddering spasms and outcries of pain. Weeping, jabbering, she reached out to him with those tiny gnarled hands and he showed her the muzzle of his rifle to move her out on the empty street of echoing shellfire.

The sunlight seemed full of disease in the gunpowder fumes poised over the ruins. He heard motors, and shoved her forward, shook her by a shoulder to shut her up. Rounding a corner he saw an armored car bumping along past platoon vehicles stalled in the cover of buildings. To one side he saw his men all walking off behind Atman. Spoldren came out of a street with two prisoners and said, "The whole Third Platoon drove through to the canal. There goes the last car of them."

He did not quite know what that meant. Nor did he understand Rayhew at all when, at the vehicles where all the prisoners were gathered, he said, "Section Two's working that part." He understood nothing—not the fading winter sun, not the faces of grief and mourning, not even his sickly shame which, wearing the face of the Polish slave, brought back visions of acquaintances he used to dodge as they came walking down the avenue with homely dates on their arms. German soldiers were wounded and so were some civilians, most of them old and most of them women for reasons he could not understand. "*Alles kaput,*" an old grandmother wept, wringing her hands, and Riglioni's prisoner wrung her queer hands and in a deep hollow voice he had not heard from her in the cellar bawled, "*Alles kaput, alles kaput,*" and Rayhew, his face parched and wrinkled in the sickly sun, said, "You all right, Rig?"

"How can anybody be all right?"

"Your section's in there, working those houses. Proctor said to keep working them till Enshaw gets back from Troop."

"Yeah? Where's Buffalo Bill?"

"He moved right up with the Third. That joker's a real volunteer."

"Yeah, well, I'll . . . well, maybe he'll get it today."

"This is some day, Rig. Not a casualty, nobody scratched. Like angels watching over us or something, you know?"

He smiled for Rayhew and walked north toward his section's area. Behind him the women let out a louder wail in unison; trucks were coming, weapons carriers to drop off crates of ammo and take prisoners back to Troop. It was always the same and there was no point to hanging around for it because they would not be bringing hot food. Up ahead stood Scarbro looking east, as always preoccupied with the Third Platoon, which had carried the war forward and left the Second in an isolated dimension of silence.

Coming out of a doorway, Moran said, "Where you been, Sal?"

"Don't be pumping me."

Moran laughed. "Come on, we're looking for wax."

"Yeah, dolls. You believe that phony kid? Dolls?"

"He never told anybody dolls. That's Gingold's story, and you know him."

"No, I don't know him. You know him? I don't."

"Hey, what's the matter with you, Sal?"

"Oh, I feel fine, just fine. You feel fine, don't you?" Beyond a battered wall that exposed the whole bottom story of an apartment building, he saw Honeycutt kicking through a pile of rubble. "Hey. You looking for a booby trap? Move your ass out and clear some houses."

Under the preposterous high hat Honeycutt's tight pensive hawk-face stared at him. "You got a wild hair or something? A booby trap in rubbish?"

Moran pulled him along in frost that had cleared the air of gunsmoke. "You act like you're cracking up, Sal. I think it's really time, boy."

"Time, yeah, time for what?"

"To turn in your stripes. I mean it. You sound psycho, Sal."

He trotted to get away from Moran and again saw Scarbro against a darkening easterly sky of shellfire. He chose a house and followed his rifle into it, scaled rubble from room to room and climbed stairs to the shattered roof, from which he saw clean new smoke puffing out of a window nearby. Downstairs he found Moran gaping at the large crucifix hung on a wall and said, "Come on, there's somebody in a house over there."

In a shattered room Finch stood over Atman with his rifle slung, the bayonet still fixed. Atman was crouched over a small fire built on the floor, and grinned as he glanced up from a black kitchen pot. "He's cooking wax," Finch said.

There was a mahogany chiffonier on which plaster dust had settled—over undisturbed gilt brushes and framed pictures of children. Beyond, half covered with rubble, stood a dresser, a large crucifix above it on the wall. Another Christ looked down on the torn and shattered bed, and quivered faintly to each thump of a distant shell. Riglioni said, "Where'd you get that wax, Atman? Don't be a jerk all your life."

Atman stood up wiping a hand on his chest, spewing short smoky puffs of breath. "Most of it's this morning's wax—there wasn't much. There's a nice vase for it under that window, it never broke. And I have a pocketful of cord. We'll have a nice candle tonight."

"Yeah? Well, stick it up your ass." He took Finch aside. "What did he get that wax off of?"

"Beats me, he won't tell me. I lost sight of him a lousy minute and he's got one busted down to a million pieces."

"One? One what? A doll?"

"Yeah, I guess. You see any dolls around?"

"You get him and move out of here. I mean right now."

"Sal, Sal, wait. Listen. Something's queer about this guy. I think they sent us a real lunatic, you know? I'm only following him around to see that he doesn't do some crazy goddamn thing."

He looked at Finch and saw an expression he could read only as dishonesty; the contempt Finch displayed was nothing but a transparent disguise for the awe he felt for Atman. Moran felt it, they all felt it; Atman was becoming a big shot in the outfit with his wax. Without another word to Finch he stomped out and, Moran following, hurried into the next house to look around for wax dolls.

They found none and moved on. The shellfire was dissipating into echoes of itself, and there was very little fire-fighting to be heard in the east. Every house they entered had religious articles for Moran to mock. "Christ on the Cross, saints, beads, shrines, a bunch of disgusting hoo-doo. Shows what phonies people are, those Krauts praying to Jesus one minute and kissing Hitler's ass the next. How do you match that up with your holy goddamn devotion?"

"In all the time I know you I never heard you blaspheme like that. Then last night, all of a sudden you—"

"Me all of a sudden? You! I never saw you sober for church one single Sunday back in the States. Me, I hardly ever thought about it until the chickenshit started closing in from all sides. Colonel Powell. Stollman was okay, you didn't see him too much anyway, but now Buffalo Bill. Impossible, a guy like that, and Stollman protecting him. Why? That's a question. And Enshaw and Proctor protecting him. That's a different question. And these crosses the Nazis kept, the saints to protect them. The answer is everything is a filthy lie."

It unsettled Riglioni to hear Moran speak as if out of his own mind. Poking his rifle around a doorway, entering a room behind it, he said, "You don't have to throw everything together and call it shit like that psycho, Gingold. You—"

"Yeah, Gingold," Moran laughed as thunder broke again to the east, rumbling off into faint gunfire. "He wouldn't let anybody go down in that cellar before. He's a fatigue case, all right. Tells me, 'Rig's down there relieving himself.' That's the first thing comes to his head. Did you post him there to keep guys out?"

He felt his face drown in heat and turned away, but looked at Moran again, saying, "Why don't you let me alone?"

"One look at his face and I knew you weren't using any cellar for that. It's just the first thing came into his head. I knew you were down there praying. I just knew it in my guts."

"So what's it to you, you little bastard?"

"It's shit to me, that's what it is."

"Yeah, yeah, you know everything. In your guts you just know everything. You think you can understand religion all the way, like a crossword puzzle or something? You either have it or you don't. Now stop bothering me about it."

"Jesus, you can look me in the eye and say you have it? That *you believe* you'll go right on thinking and feeling if you . . . like if you get . . . you know . . ."

"If I get one right in the head. What's the matter, can't you say it? How can you be so goddamn superstitious and still—"

"I don't know; it's my Catholic boyhood. Stick to the point. Can you look me in the eye and say—"

"Here, I'm looking you in the eye. I believe that if I die my soul will continue. I'll go right on thinking. I'll exist." They stepped over a pair of bare legs sticking out of rubble, peered into a totally wrecked house and turned, stepping over the legs again. "Now, you want to know why I believe it? Because I want to believe it. Because I have to believe it."

The sun was down, the chilly blue sky was pale with twilight. Moran walked ahead, then turned with a perplexed smile. "It must feel pretty good to believe that. To be able to believe that must be nice." He scaled a pile of charred bricks and beams, then turned again in whorls of smoky breath. "But you ought to be ashamed of yourself, you damn fool."

"I'm ashamed of myself. Now will you let me alone? Will you please stop bothering me?"

Up ahead Proctor and Gingold were entering a house. Moran said, "There go the sleeping-bag buddies. Come on, that lunatic Gingold knows."

Gingold did know. Riglioni hung back, sick with shame. From the direction of the sporadic shelling came a jeep at high speed. When it braked, Scarbro went running toward it, the first time he had ever openly acknowledged the arrival of his brother. Trotting over, Riglioni was swept with a forlorn sense of finality, of something failing, of life stopping. Corporal Tobias of the Third sat grinning behind the wheel beside Scarbro's brother, who stood up with a bloody grin, waving black and bloody hands, saying, "I'm hit! I'm hit! Old 88 whacked some old house and I got me a million by God dollars' worth! Gunpowder, boy! Slate! Brick chips! Both these hands and my big long chin! Looky! Looky," he cried as the jeep geared off and spun away. "I'll be crawling through all that English poontang and they'll never get me back . . ." Muffled shellfire drowned out his song.

Honeycutt strolled over to stare with Scarbro. Riglioni turned to meet Moran's eyes and they blinked at each other, turned to watch Scarbro stare, then moved off to find Gingold, who knew about wax. Standing in the doorway while Gingold went through the house, Proctor met them with exhausted eyes and said, "You feeling better now, Sal?"

"What do you mean by that? What did that son of a bitch tell you?"

Both of them gaped at him, Moran with half a smile, Proctor blinking and perplexed, saying, "Gingold? I wouldn't worry too much about him. About knowing it was gonna happen, that Kraut jumping up at him? That's okay, that's one of those things, like walking into a room and thinking you been there before."

"It's what he calls it that worries us," Moran said, his grin broader now on Riglioni. "That's what bothers us, when he says taking his pants down told him it was gonna happen. Calling everything shit, even when a guy gets down on his knees, right, Sal?"

Burning, Riglioni went through demolished rooms searching for Gingold. And the room he found him in seemed a room he had been in before; the moment itself seemed a repetition of one recently gone by. But that was not hard to fathom, for Gingold was kneeling wearily before a shrine just as Atman had knelt by one this morning so many noises and corpses ago.

Going closer, he recognized Saint Anne being visited by the angel in her domed bower. Gingold was handling the angel, fixing what was left of it in place. The angel was headless and Saint Anne's extended hand was missing. Looking up, Gingold said, "They were on the floor."

Riglioni squatted beside him, expecting a smirk of insinuation. But there was no mockery, nothing even conspiratorial in the man's puzzled and obtuse expression. "What are you gonna do now, Gingold? Pray here? Is that allowed in your church?"

"I ain't praying. I just fixed it to see how it looks."

"How does it look?"

"Tired. Everything looks tired." Gingold rubbed at his eyes, and panted a little before he spoke again. "Ridiculous too. Everything looks crazy, like in a dream. What are we gonna do about Buffalo Bill? He'll get us all killed."

"I don't know. I guess somebody'll get frantic and take care of him. I'm tired too, I don't know."

"Rig, you know what's allowed in my church? Whatever you need to do is allowed," he said, tapping his belly, "right here in my church. Right here I knew he was gonna jump up at me. I dropped my pants and knew. I reached for my greasegun before he jumped up. Now I know something right here in my church, Rig. Some shit's gonna kill us. Not this war we been fighting all our life. All our life, this war? That's not what'll kill us, it's a big lie'll kill us, a big mistake; I know, I know."

"Now you mark his words now," Moran said in the doorway. "When it's all over and you're waiting for the burial detail, remember what he just said. You'll be able to exist and think and everything, won't you, Sal?"

Over his shoulder he studied Moran's grim face and saw nothing familiar in it. He did not look like Joe Moran, and the man behind him did not look like Gene Proctor. Squatting there, he turned to the grimy man who did not look like Gingold. "Tell me about that wax, Paul. I don't think I can take another night in the dark. I need that wax."

"Everybody needs it, Rig."

The remark stirred something in Riglioni that felt like a scream, trapped and struggling to escape. Everybody. Everybody was doing the same, seeing the same, feeling the same, even thinking the same. Everybody was the same; they even looked alike in their cumbersome gear. Through the threat of a scream his voice emerged weak, in a wan flutter. "Every night we wait in the dark. Every goddamn night of our lives we wait and wait and wait. Sometimes I forget what we're waiting for, Paul."

Gingold danced back in alarm and fell sidelong over his greasegun. Proctor hurried over to assist him but he fell back again on a shambles of draperies and dust. "I knew you were gonna say that about all our lives and waiting. Before you said it! Jesus!"

"What's that wax come off of? Please, Paul."

Gingold used his greasegun as a crutch to rise from the debris. He stared down at Riglioni with an expression as sublime with agony as Christ's on the Cross, then turned away rubbing his nose and approached the shrine. He handed down the ten-inch statue of Saint Anne and said, "It's wax."

From his squat Riglioni went to his knees, examining the little effigy. It was handsomely carved in great detail, and in its harmonious colors it looked like Dresden china. The face was neither as tragic as the Polish slave's nor as arrogant as the U.S. Senator's on the beer stein that Proctor had crushed. It was not as pathetic as the German woman's face in a cellar of raw butcher's parts. It was just a doll's face, a wax face.

Moran squatted beside him, his face purple with dusk, turning the headless angel over in his hand. He held it up with its wings spread under his chin so that his head became the angel's, dwarfing the tiny wax body as in some quaint cartoon, and in a thin falsetto he said, "Lady Anne, I came to tell you your daughter Mary's gonna have a baby named Jesus. And he's gonna come from God to save the whole human race. Wait and see. Wait . . . wait . . . wait."

So that was why Atman kept asking officious questions about his faith. He giggled; Saint Sebastian himself had dripped down on him from the holy room that mortar had set ablaze. All those saints were wax; on the ornate mantles and in all the rubble every saint was wax. What had kept him from recognizing them as wax while Atman saw through the paint on sight? His gaze drifted across the grimy combat boots of

Gingold and Proctor, their automatic weapons dangling in the silence. He looked at Moran, who was watching him intently.

"The hand's broken off this one anyway," Riglioni said, and shattered Saint Anne against the floor.

15

From the far mountain came a haze that shoved the last twilight colors to the top of the sky, and the day fell dark as men ate K-ration suppers in the echoing forward shellfire. Then Enshaw returned to roll the platoon ahead a couple of hundred yards. In the glooming frost they linked up with the Third Platoon, which had withdrawn from the barrage that had cost them Scarbro's brother.

Each section took a house for itself in an arc formed by both platoons, and in the evening, when all the enemy guns were still, Riglioni left Moran to melt their wax and took a jeep back to the combined Second and Third HQ. He returned to candlelight in the cellar with good news.

"There's replacements up at Group. Enshaw got it from the Old Man, so it's not just a latrine rumor. How many men nobody knows yet, but we ought to be getting them tonight. Because Stollman figured it out at last that the Krauts got nothing but a tank or two. So the whole outfit's slamming into them tomorrow and that'll be it in this town. That'll be it."

Silence hovered over the circle of men around the candle, until Honeycutt said, "Replacements," and heaved a long sigh. "That sort of kills Connie off for good. And Field . . . Caddigan . . . Zubrowski."

Snow fell. Except for the guard mount in each section house, the entire platoon gathered to watch the candle Moran had made. Except for Scarbro, who drifted around in the shadows, all the men sat still, peering under their helmets at the hypnotic flame.

Men arrived from the Third Platoon, first Gundersen, Muzakis, and Reilly, then Austen and Fry who were drunk on vanilla extract. Their sleepy grins, as they told of stealing the juice from the Kitchen, induced Finch to say, "Fry is fried." Men reacted to that with annoyed complaints, which broke the spell of bemusement.

"They had tanks lined up on that canal," Muzakis said. "Four, five of them I figure."

"Bullshit," Austen laughed, "you take everything too serious. You exaggerate, you ignorant Turk."

"I'm no Turk. You're always calling me a Turk."

"You're Spanish, aren't you? That's what we always called Spanish guys where I come from. Turks we called Gypsies. They got maybe two tanks."

"They blew up their bridge," Reilly said. "They had a nice bridge and blew it up on us. I took a patrol in and saw it go up."

"Who told you I'm Spanish? I'm a Canadian ten generations."

"You're a Turk," Fry said. "Austen's a Canadian, an Eskimo."

"Everybody shut up or get out," Riglioni said. The talk had brought back faces and noises: Buffalo Bill and Stollman and the primeval skinned crotch of his plunder in a gonging cellar, everything he could escape so well in the motionless yellow of the flame, the tall static shadow at its center.

Fry said, "Rig's a Turk too. Spanish."

He wanted to demand silence again, but instead said, "Listen. Did Buffalo Bill foul you up today? That lieutenant with the red goatee."

"Oh, is he a lieutenant?" Reilly said. "I wondered why he was shooting his mouth off so much."

The flame sputtered. Lindemayer sent Spoldren off to relieve Copley, and Rayhew sent Smith for Kallenson. When the candle had run down into a useless puddle and the flame was dying, Riglioni relieved Atman upstairs with Honeycutt, and the boy who could be quiet enough on patrol came stomping and clanking down to put a light to the finest candle the visitors had ever seen.

Cannonfire went over from the 75s, but the Germans returned nothing. Like a big shaggy vulture in his fur coat, Scarbro circled the crowd noiselessly. No man of the Third ventured to discuss his brother's luck or their envious resentment of it. Escaping into the flame, men cared about nothing else; they shifted on their haunches, silent in the light until finally they began muttering the inevitable questions about wax. Lindemayer put a cigarette to the flame and lit it. "Didn't he foul you guys up at all, that beard job?"

"The other day he almost did," Muzakis said. "But Morgdahl took him by the hand. Stuck with him today, too, kept him busy."

Reilly said, "What do you mean, dolls?" and Riglioni lost his temper.

"If you came here to flap your goddamn jaws I'm gonna throw you all out ass by ass."

Atman turned grinning to Moran. "How come you don't tell them, Joe? There's plenty of wax in this town."

"How come you don't tell them, Sal?"

"Don't be a wise guy. You want to start a riot in this outfit?"

As the 75s grew more thunderous Proctor kicked through to the light. Dusty with snow, he unslung his Thompson and looked around. "What the hell is this, a revival meeting? You men get the hell back to your positions."

"Come on, it's Friday night," Munzer whined.

"You want to see Saturday you get your asses out and make it fast." Proctor's voice shook. "Don't you know they coming over tonight? You be caught with your britches down like whores in a raid."

Snuffing out a cigarette, Rayhew said, "We got our guards mounted. It's Friday night, for Christ's sake. There's no school tomorrow."

"Go find your own wax!" Riglioni barked above the jabber. "Get the hell out of here and take this chickenshit Proctor with you!"

Amid the stirring men Proctor said, "What in the hell is the matter with you, Sal? Stollman ever find out the Third Platoon's over here on top of us and—Jesus!"

"Yeah, and what, you brown-nosing bastard? Suddenly all you got on your mind is to be a gentleman and a scholar like Stollman."

Proctor squatted to face him. "I don't know what's got into you, boy. All's I want is to finish this war and go home to my kids."

Men swarmed babbling through the doorway, where Gundersen boomed, "This miserable snow now. Why couldn't they send us to the Pacific? Palm trees! Naked broads! Sunshine! Sunshine, by God!"

"Bugs too," Scarbro said, hulking above the flame. His silence had lasted for hours, and now in dancing shadows his face looked like a madman's. "Mosquitoes on them islands could fuck a cow standing flatfooted." The laughter made him blink. With a curious squint he stared at each face that passed him. "What's a joke about that?" he murmured, drifting off to walk the shadows again. "Joke . . . joke . . ."

The 75s kept punching into German ground. Behind the last silent man, Proctor stole one perplexed glance at Riglioni and joined the shuffling ascent. Section Two closed in around the flame, each man huddled into himself for warmth, each solemn in his helmet. Scarbro came out of the silent shadows. He planted his rifle, took a stance, tucked his fur coat tight around him, and began to recite.

"Was these two fellers walking in the snow. Butcher and baker. Said the butcher to the baker, said he, 'Well, looky here, my son John has went and pissed his name in the snow.' Said the baker to the butcher . . . no, he looked down at it, at the name, and he clout the butcher one in the mouth. Said the butcher to the baker, 'Now how come you clout me one? No concern of yours if my son John chose to piss his name in the snow.' Said the baker to the butcher, 'It's in my daughter's handwriting.' "

His lifeless eyes blinked to the laughter. Sniggering, Finch said, "That was a Cohn and Lapidus joke when I heard it. No offense, Gingold."

Scarbro withdrew to the shadows; Gingold took out a handkerchief and blew his nose. Moran said, "Finch, did I ever tell you that you're a low-grade prick?"

"Sheeeee, it's the truth—I just told the truth. Gingold don't mind, do you, Paul?"

"From head to toe, Hebe, you're made of shit. I do mind, because you loused up Scarbro's joke."

"Scarbro's joke! All of a sudden Scarbro's a comedian. Soon

as his brother takes a furlough on us he turns into a comedian. With a dopey old joke I heard a hundred years ago. Pick on him for a change instead of me."

"Quit asking for it," Riglioni said, "and nobody'll pick on you. You just keep asking for it."

"I just told the truth about it," Finch whined.

Molding melted wax back onto the candle, Atman giggled. "You got to be very careful with the truth, Corporal."

The 75s sent over another volley, and then the silent night closed in again. Scarbro came forth to say, "Mr. Harlow Yates told the truth." He set his helmet down and sat in it, hunched forward on his rifle in his mangy black fur. "Told the truth behind a lie every time, told it when he thought hisself alone. Sheriff Carl Hoffman learned to tip-toe behind him for it. Sheriff looking for Lester Malloy's still. Mr. Yates good and drunk mostly, so the Sheriff asked him. Says Mr. Yates, 'What, has Lester got hisself an illegal still? By golly, a God-fearing man like Lester stooping that low! Of course I wouldn't be knowing the whereabouts of no such, not I.' Sheriff thanked him kindly and took off. Mr. Yates went on down the road home just tickled with hisself, said, 'No, not I. Only been cutting back of the sawmill and around the long pines to Lost Hollow for near twelve years after that panther piss, but how would I know?' Snap goes a twig and there's the Sheriff turning away. Mr. Harlow Yates go shouting after him, 'I never said no such! That's a lie, Sheriff Hoffman, I never told you so!' And Lester Malloy went to jail."

Man by man Scarbro watched them laugh, blinking his faded eyes in the corona of the flame. "Old Jackson James reported a guinea hen missing, so Sheriff Hoffman went alooking. Seen feathers in a trash can out front of Mr. Yates' yard and called him on out. 'Now, Harlow,' said he, 'them speckled feathers come off a guinea hen, you can't deny that. Old Jackson James lost him a guinea hen and it sure looks like you ate it.' Well, sir, Mr. Yates wasn't fit to deny it. So he said, 'Sheriff, I tell you true. Heard a noise out here sounded like a hoot owl. Just hooting up a storm. So I taken down my gun and shot it. When I seen it was a guinea hen I felt right sorry. But there she was all dead and wasn't no use but to eat it, so I did.' Yup, yup, Sheriff thanked him kindly and took off. But then he whip about after Mr. Harlow Yates on his tippy toes. Old Yates go shuffling up that yard toward his door, go talking, 'Humph, imagine me not knowing a guinea hen from a hoot owl. Haw. Knowed it was old Jackson's hen when I seen it and knowed it when I ate it.' So Sheriff collared him and Mr. Yates went to jail."

Intently again he studied the laughing faces, without any laughter of his own. Finch rattled with deferential mirth, crouching there. "Jeez, all the months I know this hillbilly I never heard a joke out of him before."

"Shut up, Charlie," Moran said dismally.

"Joke," Scarbro whispered. "That is a joke, isn't it?"

Gingold said, "Yates is nice. I love Yates. You got any more about Yates?"

Riglioni loved Yates too and wanted more with a deep, famished yearning. "Emcee Yates," Scarbro said. "That's old Harlow's boy. Grown man, full grown. Plank ripper, worked with me down to the sawmill. Lived down Biggers Road close by the river. One Saturday found him on line with us all to get his pay. Taken it off in a corner to count it up, and then he come back to the pay cage. Says, 'Miss Lily, I believe I been fucked out of some pay.' Oh my, we hustled him away just slapping hell out of him for that, and Lily Gaines, she ran into the back office flapping her hands like a moth burned his ass on a storm light, her with a preacher daddy and all. Boys assured Emcee Yates he insulted her, we went begging Lily back into her cage.

Emcee stood there rubbing his hat like a squirrel, boys kicking him to apologize. 'Miss Lily,' he says, 'Miss Lily, it wasn't you I meant, it was the goddamn company fucked me.' "

Now, tentatively, Scarbro laughed along with the others. As if astonished, he looked from face to face, and laughed in choked little gasps. Then, his tone childishly ingenuous, he said, "Funny about jokes. Jokes, they make men laugh. Grown men laugh. Jokes. Funny kind of things, jokes. Joke, joke, craziest goddamn word I ever did hear. Joke? Joke? What's that? That wasn't no joke at all. That was the truth. True. Joke. True—"

"Turn in now, Hillbilly," Riglioni said. "Let's all turn in. Save that wax, kid."

"Not worth saving this melted stuff, Sarge."

"Stuff. Wax, wax, hey, that's one. Hey, that word, wax. Hey, stuff, wax, you call that—"

"All right." Riglioni put a gloved hand down on the flame and the night fell in on them all. He reached over to see that the safety was locked on Scarbro's rifle. "Get your blanket, Hillbilly. Where's a sleeping bag for him?"

"Where's the *replacements?*" Finch said.

Sitting at the machine-gun window, Riglioni heard the creak and rustle of someone approaching, heard the clogged snorts that meant Gingold, yet it was Moran's voice that spoke his name. The darkness turned one man into another; the misery and foulness made them all alike.

"How is he?" Riglioni whispered. "Talking a lot?"

"You can hear him from here?"

"No, I can picture him raving about words in the dark."

"Who, Scarbro? No, he's fast asleep in a bag, fur coat and all. Gingold. He's talking—he's off his head again. He says they're coming tonight."

"They are."

"Jesus, how do you know? How does he know? Everything, he says he can tell everything before it happens. Sal, he scares me, the bastard."

"It figures they got to come over tonight. When the 75s hit them they didn't answer; they're saving it up to hit us all at once. They know we're hitting them tomorrow, so they got to hit us first."

"How do they know we're hitting them?"

"It figures. I know they're coming tonight."

"You know nothing! It's just a hunch!"

"Shhh. Ask Finch. He's the one who knows things before they happen. He stopped us all from getting killed without even going through channels this afternoon. Shhh."

"Shhh. That's what I came up here about. What do you say we knock him off tomorrow?"

There it was again: they were all the same. Wrapped in his blanket, Riglioni watched the snow coast down outside against the black. "Yeah. Yeah, I guess we better. Just the sight of that fancy goatee any more and I—"

"Who, Buffalo Bill? I meant Finch, but okay, him too."

"Finch! What's the matter with you?"

"Shhh. Life is short. Especially for us, and that bastard bores you to death just opening his mouth. That insipid son of a bitch, he makes you wish you were dead—you could just quit and get killed in a minute on account of a guy like him. Grow up, this ain't a joke. Finch, Simmons, Stollman, we got to knock them all off. It's us or them."

Combat fatigue, the little bastard's gone, gone. "How about Enshaw? He's a good man, but after all he has to pass orders down."

"Okay, Sal, Enshaw too. Shhh."

"Gene too. He's bucking for a field commission and doesn't give a damn about us."

"No, not Gene. You're just upset. Not Gene, Sal."

"No? Okay—Atman? How about Atman? All I can think of any more is candles. He got us crazy with those candles. Knock him off."

"Hey, are you pulling my leg?"

"Shhh. And Gingold. The Jews got Hitler mad and that's why we're here. Gross too, then we go over to the First and take care of Goldring."

"Okay, okay. Just Finch, Simmons, and Stollman. And Colonel Powell."

"If you kill Finch, I kill Proctor."

"You know you're nuts? Out of your goddamn head! I'm trying to be sensible and you make a stupid joke out of it."

"Joke. Joke. Stuff, wax. Joke? What's—"

"Cut it out! Cut it out! You stupid nut!"

"Shhh. Tell you what. If one of us lives through the counterattack, he kills all the Turks. No, all the Eskimos."

"Listen, you keep saying it and those bastards *will* come over, you goddamn psycho!"

"You superstitious jerk. Get down on your knees and pray."

"Jesus, will you—who's that coming?"

"Me, Gingold. Come on down—the kid sprung another candle."

"Send Finch up to relieve me, Joe. Don't shoot him."

"Shhhhhh. Be serious."

"Well, we can't chance the noise. Don't shoot him."

Moran scurried away. They were all the same, all insane. "From Atman to Zubrowski," he laughed. "That was a pretty good one."

"Rig. They're coming over tonight." Facing him, a bulky silhouette, Gingold had a blanket around him too. "Take my warning. I'm an educated man. Don't let this get around, but I wrote three articles and a short story and sold them all. One was about the James family. That Kraut, when he jumped up at me I knew—"

"I know they're coming, Paul. I'm expecting them."

"What! They're coming? How do you know?"

"Shhh. I used to manage a drive-in joint in Englewood."

"Hah? What? Rig, are you feeling all right?"

"Sooner or later every nut in this outfit asks me that."

"Listen to me. I got to tell you something. Listen. This intuition—I'm not trying to impress you with something unnatural. Intuition is all your experience and intelligence that comes together at times of crisis to show you what's bound to happen." He cleared his throat quietly, then sniffed to clear his nose. "Rig, how old do you have to get before you start trusting your intuition?"

"Okay, the quick and the dead, that's what you're talking about. Be quick, Paul, and beat it away from me with that schoolboy crap before I rap you one."

In the dark of dawn the 75s set up an earnest barrage, and Proctor roused the platoon. Riglioni passed the word on to his men: "No vehicles. We walk through the last sector to the canal. If we get through, we slip down the canal to the north end and over. If we contact Krauts in that last sector we go back for the vehicles. Meanwhile, we're taking bazookas. Anybody volunteer for the BAR?"

Gingold looked to the left and pointed to the right at Finch, who said, "I'll take the goddamn thing."

Wincing with exasperation, Moran said, "You stupid idiot! The whole Kraut army'll pepper you!"

"If they can find me," Finch drew out complacently.

Riglioni caught Moran's eye and said, "If the Krauts don't pepper him, some psycho table waiter will."

Moran shrank from that gaze and turned away saying, "You let this kid take that BAR and you're a criminal."

They cooked and they ate, they argued and they joked, and Finch strutted around with the long automatic rifle, courting doom—but the doom Riglioni saw in Finch was no plainer than the doom he saw on every face in the cellar, or the doom he felt in his own glassy middle. Atman sat polishing his glasses; Moran was packing clips into a bandolier; Gingold and Honeycutt were comparing snapshots of relatives over their C-ration cans in a ritual of murmurs—a ritual, it seemed, of reconciliation, as if because of their quarrel yesterday each was using the other to make his peace with the world before the attack he was trying so hard not to think about.

Scarbro sat hunched over in his fur coat; he had taken no breakfast, not even any coffee. Riglioni said, "Hillbilly, you drop that coat off in a jeep before we move out." Open-mouthed, Scarbro nodded. "Honeycutt, you wear your goddamn helmet today."

In his camouflaged high hat, ignoring Riglioni, Honeycutt said, "How you mean it's your wife? I don't get you."

"Here," Gingold said, "look at this picture. It's my wife. What are you doing with my wife's picture?"

"It's my wife, you Brooklyn Sheenie. Let's see that picture. Yeah, she resembles my wife a little. Pretty much. Same hair, same skinny legs. Hell, my wife's down on her daddy's farm."

"That's what you think. What's your wife's name?"

"Huh?" Honeycutt looked around sheepishly. "Petunia."

"Petunia! That's my wife! Petunia Gingold! Allotment checks she's getting—from both of us!"

He slapped a hand to his helmet, gaping at Honeycutt who, squinting suspiciously, pursed his lips and said, "Uh-uh. I got you that time. Nobody calls her Petunia. Tooney. Tooney, that's all she's ever been called."

"Tooney! No wonder she made me call her Tooney! I couldn't—"

Honeycutt sprang and caught Gingold by the throat, shouting as they fell over, "What about your two brothers-in-law? I never heard of guys like that!"

"My sisters' husbands!" Gingold shoved Honeycutt away and they came up facing Scarbro, who sat there staring at his extended hands, at one and then the other, his mouth hanging open. Men quit laughing and turned with Honeycutt and Gingold to watch Scarbro study the rifle in his lap, swinging his gaze slowly from one end of it to another. Gingold got his helmet back on and rose to stand over Scarbro. Slowly Honeycutt began removing the camouflage net from his high hat, watching Scarbro run his slow scrutiny from the rifle to his hands and back again.

Even when the first 88 walloped into the area and everyone else tensed by reflex, Scarbro never flinched but merely sat there gaping back and forth between the hands he held up before his face. His eyes were full of disbelief. Bending forward, he stared hard at one boot and then at the other, ran fingers over the sidestraps and laces, then looked up as if in reflection before he reached slowly for his helmet and removed it. With his head cocked, he plucked delicately at the camouflage net; he looked at the webbing inside. Then he pulled out the helmet liner and looked back and forth to compare it with the helmet itself in his other hand.

The 75s crackled away; the 88s hustled in and crashed. Watching Scarbro, aghast, Riglioni felt filthy in his uniform and was struck by a sudden vision of the German woman's queer hands, her tweed sleeves frayed at the edges. Nausea swept through him; his helmet felt so heavy he had to remove it.

The fur slipped off Scarbro's shoulders and pack, falling in a heap beside him. With one hand he put on the empty steel shell of a helmet, down over his eyes; with the other, ceremoniously, he handed the helmet liner to Honeycutt, who stood up wearing the same tight look of vigilance that he wore during every skirmish: Slowly Scarbro ran an obtuse gaze up Honeycutt's little body, then dropped it again and groped with a trembling hand at his boot, as if unable to convince himself it existed. A crashing shell shook the ground without causing him to wince, and when he drew his bayonet from the sheath on his pack Riglioni shifted over ready to grab him if necessary. But Scarbro fell into an absorption with the bayonet, trying to lock it on his rifle but apparently unable to remember how. Then he noticed Riglioni, and extended the bayonet, handle first, like some conciliatory offering.

Riglioni's glances met the darting glances of others; every face was agleam with the filthy sweat he felt all over himself. The rifle seemed to baffle Scarbro. One end of it or the other stayed with the hand that tried to reach the cumbersome empty helmet on his head, his left hand with the muzzle, then his right hand with the stock. Seated on the concrete floor, he shifted around in circles, struggling with the rifle until Moran relieved him of his helmet. With both hands, panting but weirdly composed in the face, he surrendered his rifle to Gingold. Then he looked around; panting harder and quicker, he tore at straps to get his field pack off. Atman helped him remove his ammunition belt along with the pack, and that was when, to the angry patterns of shellfire, Scarbro's eyes rolled up into his brow and he fell straight back with his head striking the concrete a hollow crack.

Finch and Honeycutt took Scarbro back to Troop in a jeep, his fur coat wrapped around him. Distributing grenades, positioning the section in doorways to wait separately for the advance to begin, Riglioni could not erase his last sight of Scarbro unconscious, chest heaving as if in a struggle for air. Shells flashed and crashed and the snow was an aimless flurry in the black dawn sky, a tranquil snow in which he saw his death. The day was idiotic, and idiotically—an image in his mind of Scarbro bubbling at the mouth—he kept muttering, "I could've caught him before his head hit."

Every negative fact had an eerie positive quality: the morning was suddenly bereft of falling snow; a strange absence of cold haunted the sector; the gaping windows conveyed an incontrovertible sense of desertion; even the light, turbid with warnings of death, seemed less a matter of encroaching day than of the darkness receding before them. There was no shelling, no noise at all: it was the very void of reality they entered to spot-check houses where the spook lurked only in soundless echoes, the ghost of a ghost.

No German gun could possibly exist here, yet every face was livid with reflections of the pitiless sky, every stubbled cheek and lightless eye seemed marked with a cross for destruction. To Gingold, whom he found kicking through heaped beams and plaster in a house, Riglioni said, "You expect to find Krauts under there?"

Gingold rubbed his nose with a limp hand. Under scraggly majestic brows his shapely eyes seemed the quintessence of worth, of reality. A sort of chiseled soft lobe in nis upper lip—what was that? His condemnation, and Riglioni wanted to warn him but had no words with which to do it sanely. Gingold said, "We might be waiting again tonight and want a little light."

"That another one of your hunches, your fancy intuitions? Move out, Gingold." One fanatic on a machine gun could wipe them all out, yet all they could think of was wax. In the next house he found Honeycutt searching through debris and ordered him out. On cobbles agleam with melted snow he saw Moran trotting toward a doorway and overtook him at a dead run. "You see something in there?"

"Yeah. Atman. Shhh."

"What! Hey! You still following him? You know what to look for and still you follow him? He's magic? Idiot!"

"Shhh, let me alone. You're turning into a real pest."

Moran darted inside but Riglioni's next remark stopped him. "You gonna kill him, is that it?"

As he turned, the injury in Moran's eyes was doom itself. *Oh save this little bastard.* "I was just scared last night. I didn't mean any of that. You know that, Sal."

"Look," Riglioni said. Beyond Moran in the house, emerging on his knees from a cave formed by crossed beams supporting a mountain of rubble, Atman looked up at them and blew out a puff of vapor. He slid his rifle ahead of him, using it as a lever to help him rise and at almost the same instant swinging the other hand in an arc to smash a statue on the floor. He looked up again and grinned. It seemed the last grin possible to him.

All of them were skeletal, with a deathly iridescence in the shadows of their faces—Finch whom he found giving the whole platoon cover with his big Browning Automatic, Lindemayer and his men who were searching through debris in the neighboring houses, Proctor who goaded what was left of Section Three with giggled admonitions against wasting time to hunt for wax.

"They know what kind of dolls to look for?" Riglioni asked him.

"Yeah. I told Pete last night. He told Rayhew. Whole platoon knows all them saints are wax now and the chickenshit's over. Let's go."

Gingold approached with his eyes full of dread and the breath coming out of him in choppy puffs. "Rig, Finch says Buffalo Bill is coming with us today. Proctor told him. Wait a minute, don't be snapping at me. What I want is your attitude on it. You give the orders, I take them. What do we do about that man? If he starts to screw us up."

Riglioni smiled inanely and saw the breath of his life dance into Gingold's. "I don't know, Paul. You know how it is. We figure and figure, and then we play it by ear."

Gingold smiled too, but his eyes retained their shape of dread. "In other words," he said, this poor man who must die today for Colonel Powell, "Simmons better take care of his ass." He turned at the sound of a motor. Two Troop men were in the cab of a weapons carrier creeping past. Several yards in its wake came a jeep with Buffalo Bill driving and alone. "Sometimes," Gingold muttered, "sometimes I think I'm dreaming."

Where the vehicles pulled up behind him, Lieutenant Enshaw signaled for the noncoms to deploy the men at five-yard intervals and then to assemble for final briefing. From his mouth dangled the cigarette with its long ash; his cheeks sagged as if with age. The noncoms followed him into a house, and there stood Buffalo Bill Simmons, waiting, eyeing Finch and the BAR, finally drawing a deep breath to barrel out his chest and say, "Do you know how to handle that weapon, Corporal?"

The boy grinned, showing dimples and teeth. It was a grin unlike anything normal men could manage at a time like this, a true unpreoccupied grin that involved his eyes as well as his tiny baby mouth. "There ain't a weapon in this outfit I can't handle, Lieutenant."

"I want you to fire in short bursts. Twos and threes."

There it was; the bearded buffoon was asking for an argument, throwing a training-book rule right in the face of an experienced combat noncom. Riglioni began to sputter after words with which to intercede, but Finch spoke out. "Now don't make me disobey the lieutenant, you Kraut bastards."

He said it with a snigger, and others laughed. The face of Buffalo Bill was a red mossy rock. "Remember one thing, Corporal. You obey orders first and ask questions later."

"Yazzuh, boss."

The huge nostrils flared. "Watch your impertinence, Finch."

"Yazzuh, boss!"

"Very well." Simmons turned to Enshaw, who was busy

chain-lighting a fresh cigarette and would not raise his eyes. Blandly regarding Finch again, Simmons said, "From practically my first action with this platoon I've had nothing but impertinence and insubordination from you. The chain of command is—"

"Lieutenant," Enshaw interrupted, "this isn't the time for that."

"Let me be the judge of that," Simmons intoned, keeping his arrogant gaze on Finch. "My request to break you down from Corporal will definitely be executed today."

"That's a funny word to use," Lindemayer said.

"You're the only thing'll be executed around here," Finch laughed.

Full of tremors and in a frail voice Riglioni said, "What the hell do you expect to accomplish with this chickenshit, Lieutenant?"

Lindemayer, ghostly pale, spoke again, stammering. "You be a goddamn school marm and *somebody's* gonna shoot you in the back. Don't you realize that?"

Not a word came from Proctor; Enshaw only puffed and blew out smoke and puffed again. Simmons' face was a haughty mask of patience, an intolerable thing to behold. "Are you all through?" he said. "Now listen to me. It happens to be the duty of an officer to isolate any man who is a threat to the chain of command, which is the lifeblood of efficacy in the combat unit. I have patiently tolerated insubordination in all its various forms, but there will be an end to that right now. Do I make myself clear?"

An unwieldy silence followed. Apparently, like Riglioni himself, the others were strangled by frustrating disbelief. Stiff, disdainful, Simmons eyed each man in turn—Rayhew, Lindemayer, Gross, Riglioni, Proctor, Enshaw, and finally Finch again—as if confident that his sham of pluck and candor had stunned the group with reverential awe.

And for that alone he deserved to die.

On the face of it Simmons seemed ten times as false as Stollman, ten times the hypocrite, but here at the brink of death, where the pure misery was a vision that cut through the subtlest of disguises, every man readily perceived Stollman to be made of the same filth as Buffalo Bill: the *regular guy* and the pompous ass were two sides of the same counterfeit coin. Yet at the last instant, when the trigger must be squeezed, the Captain could be spared in his safe cellar while Simmons must be killed. The difference had nothing to do with convenience; it was a matter of taste . . . just that.

A small matter, a gap in taste so small and yet so acute that it insulted the entire human race . . . as photographic pages in newspapers had all through Riglioni's life. He remembered a photo of West Virginia coal miners' children, potbellied with starvation, flanked on one side by a shot of half-clad actresses flirtatiously showing their knees and on the other by Mrs. Herbert Hoover in her Girl Scout uniform. And the smuggled photo of Balkans hanged by Hitler—one with a face so like his father's that he had suffered personal grief—which had been juxtaposed with one of Madame Chiang Kai-shek, surrounded by senators, laughing in her white satin gown at a Washington ball. The whole game of living used to stand naked for him in pages of that sort; now, where men starved of life stood on the path to Hitler's noose, Buffalo Bill Simmons had to die for seeing no more than his own fatuous posture at stake in the game. Anus of insipidness, unwashable stink on the world, he had the cracked narcissistic brain of a politician, and because of it he had to die. And it seemed to Riglioni that if souls existed, this man's must descend to eternal fire for his insult to the human race.

In the silence where no man moved, Riglioni fixed the bayonet on his rifle to open the flesh of that rot, to uppercut the butt into that foul red beard, to slash and butt, slash and butt, to kill him in the sight of Enshaw who clearly had no intention of arresting him . . . who wanted him dead and out of the way—this stood out suddenly as plain fact in an instant almost mystical with intuition, and Riglioni hung there immobilized in tremors of a soul-crushing restraint.

And part of this sudden knowing was Proctor; part of the tenuous insight that saved Simmons from him once again was Gene Proctor who looked weary and old, a vulnerable rodent with a wife and three kids all wrapped up in his dread. Enshaw stood there squinting through the smoke of his dangling cigarette, beyond a doubt determined to let Simmons talk himself to suicide.

In their rusty bed of hair the nostrils expanded and Simmons commenced his unedifying harangue about forward observers from the 75 Troop, about the deployment of the bazooka and rifle-grenade teams, and Riglioni saw the barnyard of Enshaw's rainy slaughter, of Gingold's thousandfold murder in defense of his tender ass, of Muldoon defending a Captain eternally in search of the Executive Officer competent enough to free him for combat missions—the big joke in the outfit, and there stood Lew Enshaw believing in it as he himself believed in God . . . because in this small corner of his existence each had nothing else to believe in.

Poor Enshaw and Proctor! What a job the Captain had done on them! They had come away from the CP bucking, all right, but for life, not rank. Those silver bars meant survival to Enshaw and he would not hesitate to slaughter Simmons for them. That was true, Riglioni told himself, and not some quirk of his brain: the proof was in the calculated silence now of Enshaw, who with a word could place Simmons under arrest and remove him. But to arrest him meant countercharges or at least delays, a barrier to the one safe spot in Lew's *institution,* the Command Post fortress of long safe days and nights with Stollman out fighting the war.

And poor Muldoon too. No wonder Proctor had begun to defend the Captain right after their last meeting: not he but Muldoon was in line for Enshaw's rank, which would leave the First Sergeant spot for Proctor to hide in and write letters home that he was safe forever. But *forever* was short in this circle of disaster that blinded Proctor so, this merry-go-round that, having sent Enshaw from Topkick to Platoon Leader, was soon to do the same with Muldoon and would before long bring Proctor as well full circle to his doom.

Riglioni sank down to a squat in misery and confusion. Stollman had captured his two friends by appealing to the instinct that reduced even the best to fools—the blind, murderous lust to survive that made them susceptible to gross irrationality. Lew Enshaw knew as well as anybody that only a miracle could pry the Captain loose from his deep holy vault of security. Desperation . . . it was desperation, finally, that bred a belief in miracles.

What did Stollman expect me to buck for? he thought as Simmons thumped pointless words up from the hollow drum of his soul, and he suddenly recognized himself in Buffalo Bill, an ignorant cog in somebody else's wheel, a fool and a fraud, a lie on the earth for submitting to more treacherous liars.

He is a caricature of us all.

16

A whisper, a crackle overhead where death hung still and gray, and the 75s began the action, signaling the Third Platoon 37s to help raise thunder in German terrain.

In the brittle ice and shallow slime of the canal, the men of the Second lay back against the five-foot forward embankment. Trembling, Proctor said, "Sort of hoped those replacements would show up just in time."

From up the canal Enshaw returned in a crouch after some words with Lieutenant Angell of the 75 Troop, who as forward observer was operating a walkie-talkie; from down the canal, where he had gone to instruct Rayhew's section on the launching of their rifle grenades, Buffalo Bill Simmons came marching upright, chest out and goatee pointing forward, showing off for unimpressed men who were rising up to peek over the bank in the barrage guaranteed to pin the enemy down too tight to look for heads to shoot at.

Tall hedges camouflaged the Medic wagon; over the bank on their bellies came Posner and Farnsworth with red crosses on their helmets and no weapons in their hands. The last crumb of respite was gone. Riglioni tightened the rifle sling he had already tightened before; he could not manage to bring moisture into his mouth.

Ahead he saw the main house and some outbuildings of an open farm upon which the town in its ambitious growth had encroached over the years; beyond lay some flat ground and then houses clustered uphill to form this second part of a useless prize. The black smoke of shellbursts cavorted in the first tier of those buildings and beyond. Down the line rifle grenades popped off Rayhew's launchers to crash against walls and light up windows of the nearer structures.

"Move out!" Simmons boomed.

Enshaw held up a forestalling finger, cigarette smoke shivering past his cocked head, his face gray with horror. Before Buffalo Bill could mount his voice of indignation there came what all but he knew enough to wait for, a hollow boom and a rip in the air that described an 88 in crackling flight toward Third Platoon cars on a far bend of the canal. Enshaw spat out his cigarette and led the way crawling forth over the bank, with Finch moving men up, his long black BAR pointed at the sky, which hung in idiotic witness.

All mud, they rose in a run behind Buffalo Bill until he veered left and turned, barking over the uproar a command that came out sounding like, "Eef ife eat a beat a fife!" He was a clown placed between men and their masters and Riglioni was a clown leading men to the farmhouse where Lindemayer ran two men inside to clear it.

Alone Simmons continued left and Proctor aimed his Thompson, but Riglioni caught the barrel and deflected it, bellowing, "Let him draw fire for us!"

Germans were killing Simmons for them now, knocking him flat with small arms from the wall of shelled houses, and an enemy tank was pounding away at the Third Platoon, so men raced forward for the outbuildings in separate lunges, Finch diving to his belly in a rut to fire a wide sweep of single shots from his BAR. Like snapping fingers an enemy rifle fusilade passed overhead and through it in plunges Riglioni saw Enshaw making for a sparse hedgerow, saw Honeycutt and Scarbro fall, flanking Finch with smoky toy rifles, and knew there was no Scarbro any more, yet saw him, and that was when the spook looked full at them in the whiplash crackle of an 88 ahead of the bark that sent it off, which meant it was coming straight this way, and he dived flat but heard it corkscrew down and wallop a hole in the day.

He floated free in a soundless void, touching the mistaken

earth in sight of Copley's voiceless screams, Enshaw's voiceless roars of command, the voiceless day of flaming black columns and Buffalo Bill marching somewhere in summer khaki and Finch in flames. Then a ferocious velocity cut his ears open for the day to pour back chattering and swift, with lunatic grass fleeing beneath him and Enshaw screaming for the bazooka. Not Scarbro but Gingold was the man firing on his run forward toward a hut that went up with a splintering howl. Finch was not on fire at all with his little face yelling, "I got it! Spotted them in holes not the houses gimme tracers somebody!"

Somebody yelled out of Riglioni's mouth, "You'll bring it all down on usssss-o-o boy," it was all down on them already and Enshaw threw M-1 clips past upright Simmons marching in a red circus suit now and Riglioni pointed out roosts for men to take behind a hump of grass and dry brush. With his magazine filled Finch quickly pumped fireflies out of his long piece to make a target and run right instead of left, good boy drawing fire to let Riglioni have men lay fire with him and kick up dirt around the target for Angell to see and destroy it with a walkie-talkie: down came the 75s to silence enemy small arms and there went the Medics hauling Copley.

Enshaw was screaming; he wanted them in the forward hedgerow thicket and there went Moran with Gingold, their pumping legs, and Finch would not stay frugal with his shots and knelt to make a long line of tracers while Rayhew and three more darted forward beyond, and that was it for Finch in the boxcar rattle of an 88 that he ran to outrace but only met head-on in a black storm that vomited him forth without his bicycle, and he coughed and reeled and fell and clawed and leaped up to run again but straight forward now raking long bursts and his talent was that of an actor: so convinced he was a hero, he acted like one every time. The spook caught up to him at last with a chattering scrape of death across his hips to twist him down in the muck while Simmons ran ramrod stiff through the doorway of a flimsy shed.

Charlie Finch dead without his stupid decoration was the final outrage, and Riglioni had to kill Simmons despite all pity for fools. At the end of his run he dived behind the concrete base of the shed with Atman diving too behind concrete on the opposite side of the doorway. Inside Buffalo Bill stood tall amid farm junk, peering between vertical wood planks of the forward wall. High in the uproar he stood looking for the tank-mounted 88s and Riglioni pointed his rifle but into his line of fire went Atman like a snake yelling, "Get down! Down, Lieutenant, down!"

Simmons brushed him away looking for the cannon which now cracked the sky apart, a stammering loud whisper down into the bowels of the day. Atman the Wax King came plunging out ahead of the almighty blast and up went the world in black fumes.

In pungent black odors he tumbled over while Atman coughed and gaped and clawed to grip the unreliable earth. Down it all came in the shape of wagon wheels and wall planks and the end of Simmons, who had outlived Finch by a minute. Out of the flaming rubble the big Tiger listed toward the cars of the distant Third until shells hammered a black chain of its treads skyward and it keeled big-assed to a halt like a lost gamble. He fell and commanded Atman to fire with him at the silhouettes, but Moran was there instead of Atman, Gross and two others firing with him to knock silhouettes down as they leaped from the blazing turret.

The Medics carried Finch in a dash for the canal. Men raced after Enshaw to his thicket away forward, though another tank still lived somewhere and kept tearing at the earth, the heaving sea of earth black in Riglioni's path to Enshaw where Honeycutt fell back to slip down against a tree pumping off shots.

Enshaw screamed for the bazooka and Riglioni plowed through the black morning to reach him and suddenly some unseen scythe clipped the tall grass before him and he fell, rolling over to signal two men past him and behind the hedgerow, to urge unfamiliar friends away from the error into which he had followed Enshaw. Then he burrowed into the sheltering earth.

"Bring up that bazooka!" Enshaw on all fours in the ditch beyond two corpses, Riglioni flat behind a ten-inch treasure of earth to hide from a whirring machine gun. Enshaw on all fours in the shrill chatter and the *tak-puh tak-puh* of deadly toy rifles, two corpses in high-pitched chant like occult music and Enshaw wanting to hug the ground but up on all fours in his obligation to lead and win his silver bars. "Let's go with that bazooka! Gimme that . . ."

Abruptly silent, he began to go over slowly on his side, slowly, without reluctance, slowly, pitching over without any expression but a look almost of relief. An 88 gonged and showered the ditch with stones.

Riglioni was pinned down by small arms that sounded like toys, by 88s hissing to stretch instants into hours and years and centuries before striking close by. Low in the ditch he lay on tangled bramble while the hedge withered to the shrill scythe and black earth leaped to the sky. Then Proctor sprang up from the ground and advanced a bazooka team instead of pulling men back from the massacre until the 75s could finish their job. He saw them fly around to the other side of the hedge where he had already sent others and where now on an endless hiss the idiot phantom struck, where now again it hissed and struck, two blind 88s crashing behind the hedge. Then in the whining echoes he saw the grass stand still before him. He ventured some inches down the ditch and still the grass stood free of the phantom scythe. The machine gun was dead but somewhere the Tiger still thundered to kill him.

SsshhhhPONGGGG! They want Sal Riglioni. Inch by

inch he crawled down the ditch, for hours and years and centuries of shells hammering down, an age of crawling to the corpses of Honeycutt and Gross. Clay was all that remained of them, putty, strange gaping effigies of Honeycutt and Gross that seemed never to have breathed or sung or cared about a thing. *Why don't I care about Honeycutt and Gross?*

Sssss-haw-ssss-haw-ssshhhSSSHHHPAHHH! In a new burst of small arms he found Enshaw dead too, and somewhere a remote female voice, or a recollection of one, said, "Pretty please."

Lew you son of a bitch you look like wax. Enshaw had brought them all in too far and had them die for his silver bars. *SsshhhOWP!* Yelling, screams, the crackle of rifles. "Please . . . pretty please," rose the voice, and it could only be that his brain had cracked at last, for he imagined not merely a woman or child but one who knew English in the death.

Sal has no sense no temperature, everybody is dead. The whole front was a storm of tumbling black smoke in thunder grown suddenly distant. He reloaded, then plunged through the sparse gray hedge and came out on the other side amid small outbuildings where the tender girlish voice was real: "Pretty please a tree on me . . . get me out, pretty please . . ."

In panic he realized that it was not a woman's voice, not a boy's voice, but the voice of a man pinned under a tree, wailing in a high thin squeak like Moran imitating the angel of Saint Anne: "Help me . . . take it off me . . . pretty pretty please . . ."

He saw the helmeted man lying flat by a little stucco house of white and, crawling toward him, saw the Thompson sub in the grass. There was no tree on the man. Flat on his belly with his face turned sidewise, the man was Gene Proctor with an infant's voice saying, "Get it off me pretty please . . ."

Proctor stared at him through beads that were eyes no

longer. "Come on out of here, Gene, there's no tree on you."

"Pretty please . . ."

There was no small arms fire, but cannon still walloped at enemy terrain; the sky still hung moronically above. He saw Proctor's back, and it was some kind of trick on the world because Proctor was dead and yet said, "Please," like a little girl and stared out of glass chips of blue, "pretty please." Proctor was turned inside out and cut in half and in the middle of his back sat a shimmying big bowl of cherry Jello. "Pretty please."

Sound stopped and time stopped and Riglioni lay in the grass with his rifle, looking at the shattered glass of Proctor. He lay there in the soundless void looking at the whole vast error of the universe. He wanted never to move again. They were all dead. There was one sound left in the world and it went: "Pretty please . . ."

He lay close to the blind beads of glass and looked for Proctor whose voice survived him in a persistent high echo of all the world's pleading: "Take it off me . . ." For a long time he lay listening to the final sound of the race: "Pretty please . . ."

His rifle came up to confront the penetrating sound of men. There came the enemies he must not kill: Munzer, Spoldren, Gingold, all the fakes and victims living just to die. "Suckers," he muttered and, lowering the rifle, looked at Proctor and listened to the high polite voice that would not die in its corpse. The feet of men kicked through grass and stopped, then came on again to gather round. A face descended; he saw glasses, saw Atman, said, "Beat it, kid."

"You hit, Sarge?"

"No, Proctor. That's Proctor there." Another man bent to him; at sight of Gingold's ghastly face of grime and mourning he said, "I know, I know. Moran. Moran, right?"

"No, he's on the other side with Muldoon," Gingold said,

and started to cry like a kid all blubbery and clogged up in the nose. "Why don't you get up, Rig?"

"Oh, I'll get up after a while. Who's dead?"

"Finch," Atman said. "Honeycutt and Lieutenant Enshaw."

"Gross," Gingold said.

"Pretty please . . . off me . . ."

Riglioni said, "What about Proctor? And Copley?"

"Proctor's right here," Atman said in a puzzled whisper.

"Cope's doing good," Gingold sobbed. "Lindemayer took him back in Muldoon's jeep."

"Muldoon? Jeep? Where's all the Krauts?"

Sniffling, gagging, Gingold said, "Rayhew's boys knocked out their machine guns, two of them with rifle grenades; 75s put out a tank and pretty near a whole company maybe. Spoldren hit another Tiger right in the ass with two bazooka rockets—it's burning back there. The Third went through . . . Get up, Rig."

"Pretty pretty please . . ."

"What about Simmons? I guess he counts too."

"Well, you saw him go, Sarge. There's nothing left of him."

"I was sort of expecting him to show up again," he murmured, rising with his rifle, and for the first time he realized that Munzer and Spoldren were also there with the bazooka and one remaining rocket, their rifles slung pointing at the stupid murk of sky. Moran and Muldoon came to stare down at Proctor, who said, "Pretty please . . ."

"Walk the platoon in," Muldoon said, pale as his hair and grim with grief, and Riglioni said, "What platoon? I don't understand, Top." They were all dead. "Where's the replacements?" he demanded without really caring, while Farnsworth and Posner gathered into a litter all the parts of Proctor still saying, "Pretty please."

Three replacements were all that came down to Troop, Johnny Muldoon explained, and with a ponderous sigh thanked God that Stollman had kept them back and saved their lives. "I want you to keep moving up just to get them walking. The Third rolled in deep to cut those Kraut bastards off. I'll drive ahead of you with Lindemayer on my gun as soon as he brings back the jeep. All we can run into is maybe a few foot Krauts."

All that talk in the incredible stillness, words and eyes of grief slipping away into history with the dead and the noise, the scorched field and the dismembered Germans. Now time was setting in again, but slowly. He led the skeleton of the Second behind Muldoon's jeep and felt akin to Scarbro. Scarbro could not rejoice in his brother's good luck, for it left a vacuum with the sudden loss of a responsibility that had come to be his reason for existing in the madness. Now, robbed of all the actors in the game of survival that his own mind had staged, bereft of all the interchanging villains and victims, Riglioni was too depleted even to feel the sensation of grief. He could think only of God, that immense and twisted prankster—what other force could, with such sublime deftness, handpick Finch and Simmons, Enshaw and Proctor for destruction? Robbed of those actors and his hate, robbed of the ungainly Polish woman and his hope, he had only God to abide with in the madness—a fear and a revulsion that added up to worship.

Then he was alone, advancing alone with his rifle in both hands while all the men followed Atman down a side street. He followed along behind them and saw the mission turn to plunder. They were not looking for cameras or German silver trinkets, and so made no tent-rope lines with which to yank out dresser drawers from a distance against the possibility of booby traps. These madmen obsessed with candlelight took only vases of glass and china from the rubble, and shattered saints where they found them upright on mantels or buried in debris like ordinary destructible objects.

Obsessed himself, he joined them for wax with which to burn out the night spook in holy flames of diversion. The tanks were destroyed, the enemy units were shattered, but the enormous phantom endured to make men await it in the darkness of their lives. Flame, wax; he followed Atman. Where houses burned they followed Atman in and out of streets, finding Muldoon's jeep where it foraged at a slow crawl and losing it again to search in the smoldering devastation.

Suddenly there was gunfire and Atman led them all toward it at a trot—Moran, Gingold, Munzer, Spoldren, Smith, Jevere, Kallenson, Rayhew, all miraculously alive in the wreckage of the Second Platoon. And Lindemayer too was alive, lanky blond Pete who sat behind the mounted .30 hammering captured civilians to death in spite of Muldoon who pulled and punched at him in front of an armored car with Gundersen of the Third standing appalled in the turret.

Hammering the gun Lindemayer screamed and ineffectively Muldoon fought him screaming and women screamed with their men in the grotesque labor of dying. Youngsters were dying grotesquely among their parents, a dozen human beings were leaping in all directions but screaming Lindemayer raked wide to capture them again in his din of bloody murder. Then silence rang and Lindemayer sobbed in fumes and frost: "That's that! Court-martial me, you rear-echelon son of a bitch, that's that, that's that!" A chant rose up from the bodies, an eerie music of wails, so Lindemayer swung at Muldoon and opened fire again, screamed again, and again rang down a silence, through which he leaped at Muldoon's throat shrieking, "You come up on the line all of a sudden and tell me—go on and court-martial me, prick!"

The Topkick heaved him away shouting, "Pete! Did I say anything about—Pete! Pity the poor bastards I said, just it ain't their fault that a goddamn—"

"Don't be telling me! It's their fault, their fault! You rear-echelon pig, Hitler captured them? Re-educate them? Every fancy bastard on the home front feels like a hero talking that shit! This is how you educate Krauts, every last mother and son down the line till they're wiped out, that's how you—"

Riglioni grabbed him; leaping out of his trance he hauled Lindemayer bodily from the jeep and stood him up at the end of his arm. He pulled back his fist to punch him out of his delirium, but saw his mortal wet eyes and just held him there until, blinking, sniffling, Lindemayer broke free and ran screaming, "I'm sorry! I'm sorry! You lousy bastards, I'm sorry!"

He hopped and leaped among the twisted corpses, apologizing and cursing them all to hell, and when he began to kick at bloody faces of the dead, several men grabbed him and Muldoon cried, "Pull these bodies into a house. For God's sake get them in that house. Tobias," he bellowed at the man standing up in a hatch. "For God's sake back her up! Gundersen, you're gonna shell that house till it burns, burns!"

"I'm sorry! I'm sorry!"

In the knot of men Atman said, "We got wax, Sergeant Lindemayer, wax, plenty of wax. All kinds of light tonight, in every room. We'll play cards, and read, and write letters home."

While the shelling of the house of the dead still echoed, Lindemayer went dry of tears. To send him back as a *fatigue* case meant to confess his massacre to Troop. There was no question of that and with Riglioni's help Muldoon rationalized other reasons to keep him: Lindemayer was mad but so was everyone else in the wake of this morning's disastrous battle; the vengeance that provoked his outburst was in them all; he had not become incoherent as Lindquist had and unlike

Scarbro he was reasonably in control of himself now. That was the end of it; they would simply have to watch him. Now they had to get their vehicles across the engineer bridges while the guns of the First and Third Platoons—which had suffered no casualties today—blasted away at the town.

It was an impressive column that the Second rolled forward past Squadron wagons transporting the dead and Troop carriers hauling ammo to the line. The jeeps of Enshaw and Proctor stayed back at Troop, but every other vehicle crossed the canal in convoy, two men to each armored car and one in each jeep. Eleven men were inadequate to so many vehicles in attack, but once deployed in a line with the First and Third they made an awful noise and caused a mighty destruction.

At noon Muldoon returned from Troop to pull the Second into a house for lunch. In the continuing din of the First and Third guns, while men kindled the big coal stove, the Topkick squatted in Riglioni's corner and said, "Nothing's coming back at us—it sure looks like the Krauts are finished. How do you think the boys'll take to walking it forward?"

"Go on and ask them. What do you want from me?"

"Listen, you're Acting Platoon Sergeant—move your ass."

"I'm Actor?" Seated on the floor with his coffee, Riglioni stared at the ashen face under Muldoon's naked helmet. "Top, you better not get on me like the chain of command, now. I'm telling you, Top, you better not or I might go off at you like Pete did before. I might, Johnny, so don't be making me the Actor and all that kind of crap."

In a nervous spasm Muldoon rubbed his hands together. He glanced around at the men muttering near the stove, and presently said, "Look, Sal, you think I like being up here instead of in that CP? The minute word came about . . . about the damage, Stollman sent my ass up to take over."

"Well, that's just tough shit, Mr. Topkick. You're breaking my goddamn heart. Why don't you tell the Old Man to send up a new lieutenant to chain-of-command us, the son of a bitch?"

"He's doing just that. And I'm the boy."

They stared at each other a moment. "You accepting a field commission like Lew Enshaw did?"

"What should I do, Sal? Tell me straight."

"Tell you straight? I'll tell you. Take those bars, tell Stollman to take those lieutenant bars and shove them up his yellow ass. Wasn't the desert enough for you? Wasn't San Lô? Stay in that cellar, you damn fool, and let him jam them up his ass."

Confusion pinched Muldoon's clean face. He blinked his eyes and looked at his feet; he looked at Riglioni in the shadows and said, "I don't have the guts. I don't mean guts to tell Stollman to shove them, I mean guts to hide in cellars for the duration. It's those morning reports; I don't have the guts to write up everybody else's suicide any more."

Riglioni could think of no way to tell him what a fool he was, how soft in the brain his weeks of safety had turned him. Somewhere glass shattered, and Atman held up the first new candle.

"He's already put in for the commission," Muldoon lamented. "Rush job up to Group. Rush job for new ratings in this platoon, your staff stripes and stuff. I don't have the guts any more to save my precious ass."

"You let that dirty little coward push you that way? That—"

"Sal, I don't have the guts," Muldoon whispered with a demented stare. "And Sal . . . Sal, Stollman's guts, to keep himself in that cellar no matter what . . . he's the bravest man in this whole shiteating troop."

After lunch the Second Platoon did not resume its cannonade because Riglioni failed to give the order and Muldoon was back at Troop. Through hours that echoed with shellbursts, men created their marvelous candles. Sturdy pink specimens flamed in every corner where weapons were taken down for cleaning. Candles blazed against the afternoon gloom and men wrote letters home. By candlelight they divided the booty of friends who were gone, and by candlelight they searched for still more booty in cellars. Nobody stinted on wax, for the outfit basked in abundance.

The barrage ended at 3 PM, and soon after Muldoon came to lead them forward on foot. Nobody protested, and the column of a dozen men pierced a street for half a mile in the flutter of a soft new snow. They encountered civilians, old women wringing their hands, old men who only stared dumbly, and there was no need to watch over Lindemayer because he remained in control of himself and even complied when Muldoon asked him to requisition all firearms in the district. Obsequious with fright, old grandfathers brought forth ancient hunting weapons along with some Mausers and a few grenades. Muldoon elected these men special police to go back and command other civilians to dump all weapons in midstreet.

The column moved up a few more streets before gunfire stalled them, and Muldoon went ahead to scout alone. "He's yellow," Lindemayer said as they waited in cover. "No guts to order a detail on patrol."

"Johnny always was all right," Riglioni said. "He just went and forgot some things." It was too quiet. He stepped outside, signaling men in other doorways to follow.

"Do you believe in the hereafter, Sergeant?" Moran said behind him.

"Don't flap your jaw at me, Joe, I might bust it."

Moran laughed. Caked with grime he looked like the desert rat Connie Meskerman had been in Africa. Instead of his rifle he had a Thompson. His whiskers caught snowflakes, which sat on his eyelashes too, giving him a lunatic aspect. "They're all in heaven, ain't they? Why be so touchy?"

"Where'd you get that tommy gun? It's Gene's?"

"Yeah. He turned it in with his stripes."

"Well well well, huh? This is your well-well crap, huh? All grown-up and brave just because everybody died all at once, huh?"

"That's it. Laying out there this morning, I told myself if I live I'll never give a damn again. And that makes me invincible. Nothing can touch me any more because I don't give a damn in hell if it does or not."

Snow on his eyelids—he was insane. *So am I, walking into this disgust for Stollman.*

Muldoon came back with a squad of the First Platoon and what remained of a German platoon, some fifteen men trotting forth with hands on their bared heads. Where Muldoon halted them Gingold went from prisoner to prisoner saying, "*Nu, vus zugen zee tzu ein yeed?*" They smiled and they scraped, as if none of their number had ever died for Hitler.

At Muldoon's command Riglioni sent men back for three jeeps. It looked as if this town was taken, with only mopping up to go. He glanced at his men in the drifting snowflakes. The prize was Stollman's, not theirs.

One truck in the relay hauling prisoners back brought mail. All the vehicles had been rolled forward, and in the broad avenue Riglioni sent a detail to drive gaping civilians inside; concentrating on the mail clerk, men tended to lower their guard and be exposed to attack from any wild fanatic. And he was sure that very thing had happened when an outcry cut through the gentle drift of snow and women began shrieking. On the run with others he found Kallenson butting a German boy with his rifle. Riglioni lunged to yank him back. Blood was a mask on the boy's face and ran orange into the snow amid females wailing in a swirl of flakes.

"Lip he gave me," Kallenson panted. "The dirty little bastard gave me a wise-guy look and said something."

Lindemayer helped women raise the boy, who began to weep and jabber. A girl responded to Lindemayer's German with choked fearful words, and then the boy shrieked something that ended with "Heil Hitler!"

"Stand him up by that wall and shoot him," Lindemayer said, and turned shouting in German at the women, who reacted in panic with hoarse bleating cries of entreaty. One crone fell to her knees in the snow, tugging at Lindemayer's pants until he kicked her over. Men dragged the boy off, another woman fell screaming to her knees. The mail clerk's face stood out among the rest, pale and disbelieving.

Riglioni shouted, "Throw this punk in the truck! He's under arrest as a Nazi. Tell Stollman I said so. For Christ's sake, Pete, he's no more than fourteen!"

Instead of protesting, Lindemayer turned to the women with a broken roar that brought immediate silence. As he shoved them toward a door Moran said, "Start the goddamn mail call."

Twice the clerk called dead names before Riglioni stopped him and said, "Don't call Proctor, Finch, or Honeycutt, okay? Don't call Gross or Copley."

A few cries later the man called Finch's name, and somebody yelled, "Here!" It was Moran, insane with snowflakes on his eyelids and Proctor's Thompson slung on his shoulder, grinning at Riglioni, saying, "Sheeeee, I thought they separate the men from the boys in this man's outfit." When Riglioni turned away he said, "I don't think Charlie Finch made heaven, what do you think of that?"

Again there was a scream from the houses. Riglioni fought back an impulse to punch Moran's smirking mouth and instead said, "Go see what's happening there, will you, Joe? I'll get your mail."

He had gathered one letter for Moran and two for himself when Jevere called him over to the house of the earlier trouble. Jevere was trying to be secretive, but mail call ended and men followel aimlessly along. In the house, the sizable and intact home of people once well to do, women hung back mutely from a staircase where Moran stood pointing his Thompson up at Lindemayer, who had a girl by the wrist and was saying, "You wouldn't, you bastard."

"I'll shoot you right down," Moran said. "Let her go. Keep that sling on your shoulder and let her go."

"Get this little bastard out of here, Sal. I'm taking this nookie."

"*Raus!*" he barked at the women, and began shoving them out of the big kitchen, shouting, "*Raus!*" over their eruption of pleas and prayers. Jevere was staring at him, and Moran, Munzer, and Gingold who had protected his privacy in a gonging cellar. But this was different. The other had been a woman, not a child; she had submitted willingly and even with a manic hunger to match his own in that hour loud with doom. Yet he heard himself say, "Let him alone, Joe, get out of here."

"You're all under arrest," Moran snarled. "You goddamn Sal, you ignorant fanatic, you're under arrest. I give you three, Pete. One . . . two . . ."

He turned to the laughter, blinking. Jevere was laughing; Gingold and Munzer joined in. Then Lindemayer laughed, releasing the girl, who dashed away through the door to her people, trailing a long low cry.

"What is she," Moran said, "sixteen years old? You and your disgusting Saint Ursula—candles you wouldn't let me take. Now you're busting saints like you believe Jesus Christ got killed in a crap game."

"Here's a letter for you, Joe. Come on, let's find ourselves a nice house for tonight."

All of them were laughing except him and Moran, who lowered his Thompson at last and said, "Confession—that allows you to do anything at all, doesn't it, you low-grade bastard?"

"Listen, goddamn it, I thought you didn't give a damn!"

"Don't change the subject, you low-grade bastard. I have principles, and that's more than you'll ever have on your goddamn knees."

Gene Proctor was still alive at the Group hospital tents. Facing Riglioni across a small table in his candle-lit cellar room, Muldoon said, "They been operating on him all day. He could pull through, Sal."

"Yeah? He'll be in some shape for Missouri. His kids'll be proud of him." He was penning congratulations to Lorraine, whose letter today, written just one day later than yesterday's euphoric barb, told in simple convincing language of her concern for him and then said *Surprise, surprise, I'm getting married on Christmas Day!* "What do you want, Top? I'm busy."

"Tony Stearnes is Topkick now, I'm Lieutenant Muldoon. You're Platoon Sergeant Riglioni. Munzer, Jevere, and Spoldren are corporals. And get this—Moran goes from private to section sergeant. All down from Group in one day. Yeah, yeah, don't tell me, seven noncoms and four privates in the platoon, I can count. Except I brought you two replacements, and Moran said shove the stripes up my indispensable ass. So it's six noncoms and six privates, with Joe Moran in the—"

"Will you quit flapping your jaw? Who gives a damn?"

"That guy Gingold scared the Jesus out of those two kids. Out of me too. He halted us from a turret and pointed the .50 right down our rainbarrel till I said Reliable. Jesus, I ain't Reliable any more, I'm Gingerbread, and I'll—"

"Listen, Johnny. Listen, buddy. Why do you think I'm down in this freezing cellar? Because I don't want any conversation. What the hell do you want?"

"Okay. What did you set up besides that car with Gingold?"

"One gun in a forward window. Gingold opens up on anybody that gets around the street and the boys'll make it to the other vehicles fast. I oriented them before dark."

"Okay. Come on upstairs and meet your two replacements."

"Up yours. Bring them down here."

Muldoon removed his helmet which, without a camouflage net, looked bald. He glanced around the small whitewashed cellar room, then gave Riglioni a nitwit smile. "I'm scared of Pete Lindemayer. I think he wants to shoot me."

"Don't be ridiculous. Listen, am I gonna have to take you by the hand? I'm trying very hard not to lose my mind. I admit it. It's hard work. You went and let him stick bars on you, now be Platoon Leader and let me write a letter home."

Muldoon rose. "Okay, Sal, I'll send down your replacements."

"Who wants them down here?" Getting up, he snuffed out the flame with a thick hand that no longer felt heat and led Muldoon up the stairs, meanwhile slinging his rifle and putting his helmet on, saying over his shoulder, "You tell the boys you're a Second John now?"

"Yeah, and they all look like they want to shoot me, as if Johnny Muldoon is a ninety-day wonder fresh from the States."

In the big kitchen of light from flames that flickered and flames that stood up tall, two young boys wearing full field packs sat together on a bench with rifles in hand and bulky overseas bags at their feet. One had long black sideburns and the other had a scraggly blond beard. Under bald helmets that looked enormous their uneasy eyes darted around at men who totally ignored them, playing cards, cooking wax, or sitting on blankets with their mail. Riglioni had seldom seen them looking so grimy; this morning's mud was still caked all over their boots and stubbled faces. "You boys take those packs off, make yourselves at home. How come you let these guys sit here wearing full field packs?"

Rayhew said, "Nobody told them to."

"All right, set them up. Light packs, and show them how to tie the rest of their gear on a car deck. Tell them the situation, where to go in case Krauts come up. You come with me, Atman."

He took a cigarette from Muldoon who, lighting them both up, whispered, "Why doesn't some one of these guys hook the phone into the wire I brought in?"

"For Christ's sake, Johnny, tell them to. Rayhew, give these guys early shifts on the window gun and tell them what to shoot it at." He sped downstairs before any voice could assail him, lit his candle, picked up his pen, and began thinking of kindly things to write Lorraine. Stomping footfalls sounded, and there stood Atman. "What the hell do *you* want now?"

"Me? I don't know. I don't want anything, Sarge."

Look at this he came down to stare at me. Insane, they were all off their heads, especially this one who was already caked with mud though not two weeks up on the line. At least Atman knew enough to keep his weapon with him. Riglioni looked around for his own rifle; it was gone. Then it slid off his shoulder on its sling. He stood it against the wall, puffed on his cigarette, and said, "Don't you see I'm trying to write a letter? Why do you have to bother me, Atman?"

"You told me to. I mean Jesus, Sarge, you said to come with you. That's what you said, Sarge."

"Oh. Yeah. Let's see. Listen, you son of a bitch, did you ever kill a Kraut?"

"What? What do you mean, Sarge?"

"What do I *mean?* Oh boy. Kill. Aim your rifle at a Kraut and squeeze the trigger. Did you ever shoot to kill in this town?"

"Sure, I guess so."

"You guess so! Don't you know?" He was being mocked, and with something more potent than a grin, with gravity and simple statements of fact . . . Or maybe not. Could anyone be as simple as this man looked? "Listen, I never saw you knock a Kraut down. I never even saw you fire that rifle."

"Oh, I fired it all right, Sarge. Lots of times."

"Yeah? At what?"

"At Germans, where they were, sort of."

"Sort of. Sort of. Sort of?" He took the pen and wrote *Dance and laugh yourself off, everybody's dead.* He was sitting at a table and Atman the Wax King was shifting from foot to foot above him; that was it. His brain dangled like a slab of veal on a hook, but he knew exactly where he was. "Listen, did you ever see a Kraut, aim your rifle at him, and squeeze off the shot to kill him?"

"Maybe, I don't know. I get pretty excited, and sometimes when it's over I don't know if things happened or I just imagined them."

He wrote, *I'll die anyway by and by,* and crossed it out, then wrote, *You know I wish you a long happy life,* and crossed out *life.* His candle began to flicker and shadows danced on Atman's simple face. *No, not simple. Inside he's laughing. A lunatic . . . help him.* "Atman, listen. There's still Krauts in this town. Fanatics. You're up here to kill Krauts. You see them, you shoot to kill them. You get me, Atman?"

"Well, gee, Sarge, it doesn't come natural to me. I want to do what's right, but I never seem to be shooting exactly at any particular German."

Riglioni found himself chewing on the pen. *Clamp down hard and I could bite it in half but who wants to bite pens in half and blue Jello bowl in the middle.* Down on his helmet in a burning house this kid had melted Saint Sebastian, commander of soldiers at Milan until Emperor Diocletian found him out to be a Christian and melted him down with arrows.

Dio-cletian, what a name for the pagan, Dio, Dio. "You think killing is supposed to come natural? You got to *make* yourself do it. You can't be sentimental, you have to be realistic. How do you expect to make corporal and all that?"

That struck the boy funny: laughing, he squatted, leaning on his rifle. "Gee, I can't just promise I'll aim at a guy and kill him. I might never get around to that, so how can I promise?"

"You might never get around to that so how can you promise. Stop laughing now. From now on you kill Germans or your name is Stollman."

"I'll try my best, Sarge. I realize I ought to be ashamed of myself."

"Why ashamed of yourself? No, just—"

"For not killing people. I ought to be more realistic."

The flame started a crazy dance in its widening pink puddle. Feeling faint, Riglioni said, "There goes Saint Barbara. How do I know? It must be. She was the patron saint of dangerous crafts until she melted down. Look at her go. Vacancies open. She's as mortal as the next saint, and that's the sheer ugly truth of it. Hard realities. You could wind up First Sergeant, even Captain."

"If you say so, sir," the boy laughed.

Riglioni laughed. *He thinks I think he's me.* "What do you say we just bury the hatchet and cough up some wax?"

Dark and light, dark and light, Atman's face flickered like the dying flame. "I already melted down all my wax, Sarge, it's all upstairs in candles."

He twisted the letter to Lorraine into the shape of a wick, ignited it, and watched the flame grow wide in the puddle of wax. "You got no wax to give me, huh? So why do you come down here and bother me?"

"You told me to, Sarge."

"That's no excuse. Get the hell back upstairs."

Atman kicked and scraped and coughed and stomped away

upstairs. The paper flame grew brighter in its wax bed on the table. Above, he heard voices rise in argument while before him the flame dimmed and flared up strong and died. In the darkness Sal Riglioni laid his head down on folded arms to escape the voices of anger and affront, the assertive men, the emphatic men all ready to swear they were alive.

After a while he slept, and dreamt of waiting by a window with his father in the deadly silent night.

17

"Sal. Sal."

The sound of shelling was massive but distant—far, far, like a memory, and he knew the dream into which he was being urged by a familiar voice, so he ignored it and stayed on the white sand where Mimi out of his boyhood was taking him away from the crowd *for just five minutes,* she said, and he was laughing at the joke because she had matured in her swimsuit and so it would certainly take more than five minutes in the warm subsurface cave to which they would swim.

"Sal, Sal, come on upstairs, they're all coming to watch the lights."

"What's that shelling?" he said to Muldoon's voice somewhere in the sunny water sparkling lucidly off Playa del Rey; he blushed then, sheepishly smiling as Mimi turned a puzzled gaze on him.

"Never mind that, it's miles away. Come on, they're piling in from the other platoons on account of that goddamn wax."

"No, you got it all wrong, she means business, she's a doll, a doll."

"Hey wake up, Sal!"

In the dark he rose and clawed to gather his cooled puddle of wax. "Freezing. Be wearing goddamn fur coats if Reeves doesn't come up soon with winter—what's that shelling out there?"

"Sal, will you wake up! It's way south of here, far away. Listen, Sal. Guys are here from the First and Third Platoons, all over the joint up there."

"So what do you want from me? Kick them out if you don't like it. I remember you when you were a man, Johnny."

"This platoon's psycho. I mean it. I wouldn't take crap from a normal man, you know that. But these guys have had it, boy."

"You don't say." Furiously he kneaded wax in both hands. "Why don't you tell that to Stollman instead of me?"

"I did. I told him to pull this platoon back before it explodes and guys start killing each other. He looked at me like I wasn't there. He was busy shaping up the CP . . ."

Back into his arms he dropped his head in the rumble of distant shellfire, and tried to swim off with Mimi through the warm glittering sea. How nice to dream of her full grown; he had loved her at fourteen, her long coppery hair. *I never had the idea about girls . . . they're really like guys except so sweet . . . and I was a wise guy because I knew I didn't know and acted like I did and . . .*

". . . to sweep up and make it all neat and when the Major came the radio generator was grinding and Intelligence maps all over the joint—"

"What, what? What major? What?"

"Jimmerson of Squadron, what other major we got? Pinned the Silver Star on Stollman and told him what a fine—"

"A Silver Star on Stollman! What are you trying to—"

"No, I mean it. Jimmerson made some speech. About remembering the Old Man to everybody up at Group. I think Jimmerson's moving up to Group—that's why he came right into this town like a reckless hero. If Stollman gets wind that Oakes and Dixon and all their disciples are here—"

"Yeah, yeah, that won't do. Go clear them out for Stollman, don't louse up his chance for Squadron. He's in line for Squadron, ain't he? With a Silver Star and all, up to Squadron and no son-of-a-bitch line man is gonna stand in his way, right?"

"Maybe, I don't know. What's it to us? Our problem is the Krauts might get it in their heads to try us tonight and all those guys up there won't be on the guns if—"

"You just said if Stollman finds out. Now you turn it into a snow job on me, that the Krauts might come. I never thought just a couple of brass bars could turn a good man into shit."

In the dark he got his rifle and went upstairs, into a blessing of warmth where men crowded the rich light of candles. Most of them were without helmets or combat jackets, even those of the other platoons, dozens of men in OD sweaters and dirty beards. Kneading wax, Riglioni said, "Who's standing guard, Rayhew?"

"The two replacements. You said to mount them on early shifts."

"I said on the window gun. You stuck one of them out in the car *alone?*"

"Why not? He's a trained man. He can traverse and step on a floor trigger. What's eating you, Sal?"

"Sheeeeee, I thought they separate the men from—"

"Who said that?" Riglioni's flesh crawled. "All right, Joe—"

"Sheeeeee." A snort like Finch's, and somewhere, hiding behind knots of men, Moran spat with an exaggerated quaggy sound. "Scraping the bottom of the barrel for platoon sergeants these days."

"Where are you, Moran? You lousy little rat, I'll—"

"You low-grade prick."

Laughing, jabbering, men stared at him. He fumbled a cigarette into his mouth, saw Muldoon watching him from the cellar doorway. "Everybody out of here. Get going. Back where you belong."

"You pulling rank on me, boy?" It was Oakes, platoon sergeant of the Third. Beside him sat Hawley, a section sergeant, grinning.

"Lieutenant Muldoon," Dixon of the First said with a note of sarcasm. "How come I didn't make the extra stripe like Riglioni, now that Stearnes got your stripes?"

"Go on and ask the Old Man," Muldoon barked angrily. "Now get the hell out of here, and that's an order!"

"Chateau Thierry," Gingold said, warming his hands over the stove. Men had begun to stir at Muldoon's command, to mutter irritably, and now they used Gingold as a reason to fall quiet and swallow words that might cause them trouble. "This side-show in Coney Island gave you Chateau Thierry and it sounded just like this shelling, miles away. But lights flashed, and it was scary."

"Here," Riglioni said, taking the candle from a shelf nearby, snuffing out the flame and holding it out to Oakes. It was still thick and good for half an hour's light. "You take one for your platoon too, Dixon. Now get out of here. You know those goddamn Krauts might still come at us. You ever hear of them not counterattacking even once? Go on, what's the matter with this outfit?"

"Scary as hell, Hebe. I wonder what people would've done if that side-show simulated a real close one—BAM!"

"You ain't going back to Ala-BAM!"

"You're asking for it, Joe, I'm warning you!" Where men were rising he found Moran in a sleeping bag, back against the wall, his sub and helmet beside him. He was grinning; his eyelashes still seemed dusty with snow, his teeth seemed pointed in the dancing shadows, his face seemed a hundred years old and near death.

"You know where Lindemayer is? He took Munzer on a pussy patrol. Because you said it's okay. Like John Tetzel selling indulgences."

"Huh? What troop's he in?"

"*He-he-he,* you ignoramus. That's the history you never learned, the Reformation. Tetzel the holy monk, for money he pardoned sins past and future. He—"

"Shut up! Shut up! Get your ass out of that bag and go relieve the kid on that window gun. You, Atman—where are you?" He shoved through the bodies milling past Muldoon. "Atman, soon as these guys are out of here you take over the car and send that boy inside."

There was no way out of doing Stollman's work. To survive you had to help Stollman get even further away from the war than he was. The low morale of these men was a sign of suicide more than mutiny. He sat down at the table in the rumble of voices and distant shellfire, and Moran sat down across from him with outraged eyes that brought to mind Stollman's eyes, which were comfortable despite their guise of agonized responsibility. Enshaw's *institution* towered between the two men, protecting Stollman and dooming Moran, dooming all in this room just as it protected all the powers above Stollman.

"Joe," he said. "Joe, don't make an enemy out of me. Stollman's bucking to make Squadron and really be out of the war for good. And to get there he'll see us all shot by rear-echelon commandos in white helmet liners if he has to."

Men on their way out were stopping to listen. Muldoon hurried over saying, "Sal, you ain't sure of that, you're just guessing."

"What else am I gonna do but guess? What do you want me to do, be fair and reasonable and a good sport and all? You're telling me to play the old shit game, huh? A Good Conduct ribbon for me and Finch's Silver Star for Stollman. Squadron for Stollman and—"

"What's this Silver Star?" Moran said.

"That's it, the Major pinned it on him tonight. And you go to that window gun, and Atman goes to the turret. That's who you are and that's who Stollman is—there's nothing in nature that guarantees fairness. Tell them, Joe, tell them all about it."

Voices rose angrily and drowned out the distant echoes of gunfire. Dizzy, full of hate, Riglioni felt compelled to settle with Stollman once and for all, to seek him out now and kill him. But then his glance caught the open face of Atman who would not give him wax as a favor, the glass-blinded eyes that of course saw him as a mere extension of Stollman and it occurred to him that he might just as well shoot himself to exterminate the object of his hate.

Brubak, the wispy-bearded replacement, saw Germans in the snow and opened fire from the armored car. He had already served earlier as guard in the turret so, with manpower cut down still further by the failure of Lindemayer and Munzer to return from their patrol, Riglioni honored the boy's experience and let Rayhew send him out when his turn came again just before dawn.

Awakened by the gunfire, Riglioni lost no time in getting to the forward window to keep Heggenrich, the other replacement, from cutting loose on the machine gun by something like sympathetic detonation. By the time he got outside Moran and Smith were already walking the prisoners in at rifle point, Smith making a joke of it but Moran grim and frightened even though the captured pair, disarmed and with hands on their helmet tops, turned out to be none other than the pussy patrol itself.

Once a candle was lit it appeared that Lindemayer, unlike Munzer, was not sharing the joke at all. As grim as Moran, he sat at the table wiping snow from the rifle he had dropped ahead of him in his dive to escape Brubak's fire. "Sal," he said, "take this little bastard away from me before I kick his ass up his back."

Moran said, "How many dead civilians you leave behind, you goddamn SS man?"

Munzer laughed. "What the hell you bitching about? We got an address for you, for Christ's sake. Two fat sisters, I swear. They loved it, man."

Riglioni wrapped himself up in his blanket near the stove and turned to the wall as Moran droned on with malice. "That's fine, gold-bricking us like a couple of recruits. Everybody has to pull guard for you and tomorrow you'll be out on your feet and we . . ."

Sleep was all that counted and he tried to fade away. Long ago in Arkansas . . . when everybody was still alive . . . at a KP sink he was all alone in the suds because a little jerk named Doby or Roby or something had decided to hide out behind the mess hall, his fatigue pants stuck down into his socks; he remembered the disgusting look of those socks when through the window he spotted the man signaling him for secrecy with a quick finger to his lips, disgusting socks over his pants and that nauseating demand for secrecy while Riglioni stood there doing both their jobs. *Hey Cook,* with a finger pointed out the window at Roby or Doby who, as the cook spotted him, shook a fist at Riglioni, promising an assault that of course never materialized. And Enshaw and Proctor somehow formed a parallel to all that but it mattered less than the sleep . . . Brubak with his blond wispy beard . . . like Sal Riglioni as a youth crossing the ocean to war and praying for an attack by planes, for he had it all planned—the deck guns he would reach before a Navy man and track the Stuka with a line of tracers arcing out ahead of it to get a medal to Cesare's great pride. He must remember to watch those eager beavers before they got what remained of the Second killed just for the romance of being heroes . . . how incredible that Sal Riglioni had once lived in that dimension . . . how long, long ago. But sleep, sleep was more important than Enshaw and Proctor fouling up everybody's sheets to reach the heart of self or something, and that was their trick, those crafty captains—they made you so drunk with self you fouled up people's sheets and surrendered all your little brothers to survive and that was the dirty trick on you because you wound up in a deep hole with all the sheets you ever fouled . . . the trick was that the self you learned to cherish turned suddenly as inhuman as the captain who taught you contempt for all the brothers who might have saved you along with the race . . . and now it was too late, now he lay dying among dead friends. He dreamed of a candle to light with a crisp new book of matches, but it was far too late and he wept in the distant rumble, yearning for the smell of grass.

The snow kept the Kitchen from rolling hot breakfast forward to the line; Muldoon told them so as if the Kitchen had ever brought hot food, but nobody laughed. The deep snow, slowing the armored cars and jeeps, would render them more vulnerable to whatever heavy power the enemy might still possess, so the entire advance had to be on foot.

Raw cold drove men to their overseas bags for galoshes that cut down their speed; some even hauled out overcoats, which made it doubly hard to be nimble. The cold was bitter on faces and on the trigger finger everybody poked through one glove. No snow fell, but the air was white with mist and the dancing breath of men who went forth searching for enemies and saints to destroy.

Carrying by turns a tripod, an air-cooled .30, and two cases of ammo, the men followed Atman into houses, looking where he looked, bypassing ghostly ruins for houses that stood untouched by the week of shellfire. There they shattered saints in the sight of old women who wailed and invoked Jesus Christ.

"You hear them?" Moran said, burly in his coat. "It's just the name, Sal, not the word of Christ they ever bother with."

"Stay five yards away from me, Joe."

Moran made no sense, but neither did the day of weird stillness which, haunted like a cathedral by the infinite and eternal, promised reward yet harbored threat. The frost rumbled with echoes of that other war whose distance gave one the illusion of respite; it was far away like Gingold's side-show Chateau Thierry and left one as brave as a sightseer in this abysmal Coney Island of snow and peace. "Christmas is coming," somebody said nearby, "Six more shopping days left." Riglioni's nose ran, and it seemed a crueller plight than the threat of death a yard or two ahead. He thanked God for his galoshes, heavy though they were, and wished that he had worn his overcoat, and said aloud, "Watch out, watch out, don't fall asleep."

At the end of a street Muldoon signaled a halt. Riglioni kicked ahead to him and said, "What's up?"

"Look."

Where Muldoon pulled back, Riglioni peeked around the corner of a big stone building. Before him lay a large open square of trackless snow, a slumber of half-wrecked stores and buildings gaping concentrically at a fountain statue of some goddess or muse with an extended arm. Her hand was shorn away like Saint Anne's. Beyond smooth mounds of snow that indicated rubble towered the spires of a Gothic church. "The town square," Riglioni murmured, with some semblance of exultation in a small glow at the breast. "Today might be the last day in this town, this is the main part of it at last. Look, Johnny, over there to the right. That's the pine woods."

"Well, the snow cuts your idea of distance down. There must be another mile of town before the woods. Boy, B Troop must be freezing its nuts off in those woods."

"Yeah, it's just a pity on them, ain't it? Johnny, there's either a rear guard in this square or this is where they got to surrender the town. You better contact Spiro and Morgdahl and make a decision."

Crouching beneath him, Muldoon stuck his head out far for a look, then came up standing in cover of the building. "There's an escape route to the hills on the left, Sal. They might have pulled out of here to the hills last night. There might be a rear guard left behind or there might not be."

"That's the story, Johnny. You and the other Platoon Leaders better get together and decide. I'll set up the machine gun, meanwhile."

The breath came out of Muldoon in long curling banners as he stood there, his back flat against the building. "Imagine locking up this town today. On a Sunday too. Anyone wants to could go pray in that church."

The open square lay silent and white, the sky shut down tight around it and dense as clam chowder. German rifles would sound like cap pistols.

Riglioni signaled the men forward from their doorways up the street. Moran's nostrils were wet. Gingold breathed in choppy puffs of calamity. Atman came up looking around like a chicken, his glasses clouded, and men of the other sections followed him. Two weeks on the line and already he was a big shot in the outfit, like a religious leader, like some half-ass crooner or comedian back home.

Leaving Rayhew's section to cover the square with the machine gun, Riglioni sent Lindemayer and his section—comprised now of Munzer and the two new men—to the left side of the street and Moran to the right with Spoldren, Gingold, and Atman. But Moran said, "Where do you get that crap? I ain't any section sergeant."

"Joe, will you please for the sake of—"

"Not on your life, buddy. Get some table waiter to shovel your shit."

"All right, Spoldren, you're Actor. You take orders from Spoldren, Joe."

"Yazzuh, boss."

Riglioni stared at him. Both of them were trembling with cold and horror. "Who told you Finch said that?"

"Gross."

"We could infiltrate," Brubak said, coming over to intercept Muldoon on his way to the machine gun, and Riglioni turned toward them just to escape Moran.

"Infiltrate what?" Muldoon said. "What's there to infiltrate?"

"Like on the Infiltration Course in basic training."

Gingold had to explain to Muldoon and Riglioni. "I guess it was developed after your time, but they fix these machine guns on wooden boxes. Then everybody goes crawling out on his belly while the guns fire live rounds above them. It's very scary."

"Yeah?" Muldoon said. "Okay, soldier, you're elected. Go ahead."

Brubak glanced around in several directions, the wind in his wispy beard. All morning he had been looking for war and now that it was here for him he seemed in no hurry to meet it.

"It's your idea," Muldoon said, "go on and do it. Go infiltrate, we'll fire all three machine guns above you."

"Come on, Milt," Brubak called to Heggenrich.

"Never mind him," Muldoon said. "Get going."

Where Kallenson knelt holding a belt of ammo into the machine gun for Jevere, the boy stretched out prone, took a deep breath, and crawled forth sinking deeper and deeper in the snow until he almost vanished in it. "Get up," Riglioni called, "and head for that statue." He signaled to Lindemayer as the bearded kid rose shaking off snow like a wet dog. "Don't look around, just—"

At the crack of a shot he lunged forth and with Jevere cutting loose on the machine gun behind him he knocked the boy flat and dived for a hump of snow some ten feet ahead. Behind him from three streets came the machine gun fire of all the platoons; following the tracers, he found a target to hit with rapid shots in the cap pistol and automatic din. Brubak was firing too, and in came Lindemayer pumping shots with men following at intervals to crouch and fall, rise and lunge past Riglioni. Reloaded, he opened fire again on the forward run for a new roost behind snow-decked rubble while men popped out of the First and Third Platoon streets with grenades exploding now before two targets on opposite sides of the square.

He leaped for the fountain and pumped his arm signaling the machine gun forward and there came Jevere and Kallenson toting it in a running crouch with Moran picking up the chatter on his Thompson, walking upright as if invincible in a straight line for the store that was a target, Gingold to one side of him firing in a crouch and then lurching upright to heave a grenade and call everyone down for cover.

Men pumped shots at windows with Riglioni while the First Platoon machine gun entered the square and opened fire point-blank into the smoke of Gingold's blast, so Riglioni turned Jevere's gun around for a fusilade into the opposite target allowing the Third to run its air-cooled in on four pumping legs and set up a noise in the unsullied middle of the snow.

The whole troop was in and deployed, falling and hopping up in powdered snow flurries, in the relentless crackle that shattered upper windows and brought cries of persecution in German, and Riglioni knew they had the square and maybe the town and sat up in the white fountain to crack shots at windows and fell flat again to reload, sick and laughing in the crackle with crazy images of another campaign weeks ago, a barnyard in which he found a caged black rabbit quaking like a wound-up toy with one ear sheared off at the skull and the other a stump of gore, the cutest, most sickening beast ever seen. Up firing again he laughed recalling the chicken he found sitting on hay in barn shadows of that same yard, the fresh egg he found and fried in his mess kit, each succeeding day an egg under the hen, "Hello chicken," each morning until the one when all he found was the severed head and in outrage ran sticking his rifle in every face of two platoons, roaring, "Where's my chicken?" until he smelled it frying and scared First Platoon men into throwing up their hands and ran off with the deep smoking saucepan as if from a bank job. He laughed in the crackle and laughed even louder because they were out falling in the snow, yelling, "*Kamerad! Kamerad!*"

Up stood the three lieutenants bawling commands that silenced the three machine guns. Riglioni hurdled the fountain rim with his noncoms bawling the platoon forth from doorways while other men deployed other platoons around the enemy positions. Turning toward Moran, who jammed a new magazine in his piece among other advancing men, he yelled, "Watch where you walk," and giggled at the nonsense of warning men against mines and booby traps in this white mystery, giggled and trembled at the sight of nothing but upright men where the snow was torn into ruts and vapors, shuddered voluptuously at the exquisite absence of inert twisted bodies and motionless helmets in the frost. To Brubak who came trotting up, he yelled, "Like nothing, hah, kid?"

"Is that all the fight these Krauts got in them?" the boy panted, and laughed, with the look of a man about to fold over sick.

"Yeah, yeah, that's about it, that's about it." *Words, words, look at me flap my jaw.* "Go on, start working those buildings."

Bareheaded scared boys stumbled out of the stores now with their wounded, out of doorways with hands on heads blond and black and bald. There was no longer a sound in the white square. It all looked familiar: there the black dogs had locked in snarling battle, there the MPs had come for Connie Meskerman to frighten off with shots echoing in the night, and the arrival of replacements had killed Connie off for good just as Honeycutt, outliving Connie by four days, had said.

In this white hallucination of familiarity he saw Lindemayer light a cigarette like any civilized man who killed only soldiers. And there came Gingold whom he remembered as if from all his life though he had come up recently enough to know all about the nonsense they called *Infiltration Course* back home. By how long would Gingold outlive Honeycutt—another minute, a day? There came Moran through the incredible air, outliving himself minute by minute. Across the square Lieutenant Spiro and men of the First had all the prisoners heading into a street for the Troop truck to gather up when it came plodding forward warlike on its chain wheels. Some platoon, the First—only four casualties in the entire week under a lieutenant not two months up on the line; Spiro looked magic with his heavy jaw and dead pan. Spiro was something, all right; they said he spoke only to give commands and then only when absolutely necessary, a magic bulldog who kept his men alive somehow and never laughed. Lieutenant Morgdahl, who had lost nine, came trudging along with Muldoon and others now, as if anxious to roll on and lose more in order to match the Second's fourteen. *Fourteen men, God, that's who You are.* Frail with cold, he wanted to get inside, but instead responded to Muldoon's signal and hopped along like a robot, sensing the start of a brand new mission.

Just behind the square, the town ran down in a steep descent to its edge less than a mile distant. On one side were the woods held by B Troop, on the other open snow that rolled higher and higher into foothills of the far German mountain still rumbling with battle. While Muldoon and Sergeant Oakes scrutinized the snow where light vehicles and foot troops had broken it in withdrawal, Lieutenant Morgdahl muttered into a walkie-talkie and then began again to look out through his binoculars.

As the others returned Morgdahl lowered the glasses and said, "Cheese and crackers, it's too misty to see anything."

"Well, we got the goddamn town," Oakes barked. "Call it a day, Lieutenant, mission accomplished, let's go."

"If my guess is right," the officer said, "Captain Stollman won't quite agree with you." The man belonged in a government office somewhere, stamping papers and being polite with forbearance, a stocky, blue-bearded efficiency expert full of ethics and determination, Mrs. Morgdahl's best son. Riglioni turned away as he said, "When the Captain gets here I'm taking a patrol out. Who's game?"

"Christ," Oakes shouted, "you see any tank tracks? Only way they can come back at us is in Volkswagens or on their frozen goddamn toes! Uphill too! Man, what kind of wild hair you got?"

"Easy Bob, easy Bob," Morgdahl laughed, his little nose red. "They could swing around wide to a flank, if they're under those hills. And that battle noise in the mountain means something, that's my hunch. Ask the men for volunteers like a good scout, Bob. Just for a couple of hundred yards out of town."

"Let's bring the vehicles up," Muldoon said, hopping up and down to keep warm. "Set them out on the other side—there's a good line of fire across the square. Nothing around any more to catch us rolling in slow in the snow."

"Fine, Johnny, you take a position here. I'm sure Captain Stollman will want the First and my boys on the flanks, deeper in."

Riglioni walked off before Muldoon could order a march back for the vehicles. Morgdahl was keeping a finished mission alive to impress Stollman, whom he probably admired. He was every son of a bitch that raised his hand in the question period after a tedious lecture back in training; he was every garrison officer who came on with a broken heart whenever his platoon failed to win the weekly pennant for the best-scrubbed barracks floor; he was Mrs. Morgdahl's son Chickenshit without whom no war could ever be fought.

Out of an office building came Tobias of the Third with a small statue to show Atman. Riglioni veered left toward the gloomy old church, which seemed to have escaped the tons of shelling that had struck the town. He heard a chugging sound and dropped his gaze to see Gingold heading toward him with Moran, who waddled in the big coat, his Thompson dangling.

"What do you want, Joe? I'm going in to clear this church. You don't have to."

"Yeah, well, I better. Just to keep you from praying yourself off on a booby-trapped altar. Those jokers figuring out a new mission for us?"

"Go ask your section leader, Moran. Get lost."

Riglioni led the way up broad stone stairs soft with snow. Beyond the unviolated façade the inside was a shambles; shellfire had punched straight down through the roof, churning up benches and cabinets like an egg-beater. Upended and split benches protruded from snow that rose in undulant hills almost to the top of the altarpiece, where the carved heads of angels peeked through, small hands extended, holding snow.

"Well," Gingold said, "no booby traps in here. No tracks, they'd've left tracks."

"No, they could've trapped it before the snow," Moran said, peering over the smooth white hills and into shadows at the rear where snow blocked the light in a gaping shelled wall. "It just looks too goddamn pretty to be true. All sweetness and light, it must be loaded."

"You get dumber and dumber," Riglioni said, but before he could continue Moran was raking shots in a sweep across the place, kicking up clouds of snow in short bursts from his Thompson. A white avalanche descended from the altarpiece, revealing a masterpiece of woodcutting, an angel-trimmed bas relief of the Nativity with the haloes of Mother and Child in golden glass that had somehow escaped harm. The shots kept ringing but stopped short amid echoes when another mountain of snow fell in at the shelltorn wall. In one corner, revealed in a sudden shower of light, stood a statue as imposing as God. At least eight feet tall and alive with brilliant colors stood Jesus Christ of the Bleeding Heart.

Silence fell over the three gaping men; even the distant war, the muffled clatter beyond the mist and the mountain, went mute where Christ stood tall and inviolate, as if newly risen.

Men edged in at the broad entrance with weapons raised, but without a word Riglioni signaled them to clear out. In a shaky whisper Moran said, "You know what that's made of, don't you?"

Gingold snorted to clear his nose. "Moran, for Christ's sake!"

Moran hung there fixed in a stiff crouch, as if urged forward and held back by conflicting forces, rooted there in all the mystery of himself. For a moment Riglioni watched him struggle in that paralysis of fear and mourning and deranged anguish; then, his scalp crawling, he said, "Joe, let me alone. Let yourself alone, Joe."

With the wounded sleepy glance of a man caught masturbating, Moran blinked up at him and cleared his throat to say, "Huh! I just think it must be booby trapped, that's all. All that wax, all that light for us, it just looks too good to be true. The sneaky bastards must've set it up for us, good and loaded."

There was a noise behind them and they whirled with weapons aimed at Atman, who had tripped over something and now went tumbling over wreckage in blown clouds of snow. A careening bench bounced and thudded into snow; Atman fell, tumbled, rose, and fell again with legs that kicked and hands that searched for the ground and at the same time held his rifle high and dry. The boy fell and fell, rolled, tumbled for what seemed several minutes, and then sat up with his glasses hanging from one ear. Grinning, he adjusted them in place while Gingold murmured, "Something like that I never saw in my life."

Up on his feet, Atman slung the rifle on a shoulder, looked around, and then kicked up new snow clouds as he plowed with a happy grin past the three men. On his way to the enormous Christ he swung the rifle off his shoulder without breaking stride. One hand on the pistol-grip and one on the balance, he brought the rifle around from behind him in a butt-smash that wrenched a hole in the effigy of God.

They watched Atman draw the rifle back and slam the butt home again with wax chunks flying. His next smash cracked the statue in half and it swayed, it toppled, the upper portion sailing off in a headlong arc of descent, a thick hollow shell of wax that struck like Scarbro's head and cracked into several huge chunks.

Atman glanced around at the transfixed men and then concentrated on butting with his rifle and stomping to pulverize the Christ. Cannon moaned in the distant east. Wrapped in smoky mists of his breath Gingold said, "Should I punch him out, should I punch him out?"

Nobody spoke again. They watched Atman undo his field pack and haul out his blanket and shelter-half. He took the raincoat off his ammo belt and flapped it out. On his knees, taking swift suspicious glances behind him like a miser, he spread out the blanket, then the shelter-half, and began gathering up his wax. Gingold ventured toward him, but Riglioni turned and Moran followed him out, waddling along over white snow where men were showing each other the little saints they had found.

"Where are we?" Moran said, and Riglioni stopped to face him, running a sleeve under his wet nose. It pleased him strangely to see the unconcealed confusion in Moran, who panted, saying, "This is a business section. Offices. Stores. And there's these statues all over. This place is crazy with saints."

At the sound of approaching motors Moran reeled away, turning as others nearby turned to watch an armored car chug and grind into the square leading a jeep; it was a Troop car protecting the jeep of Captain Stollman, who came triumphant now like a general with his clerk Weldon driving him. Across the square both vehicles stopped between Lieutenant Morgdahl and Sergeant Oakes, but the sound of motors continued; the morning was venomous with an oncoming drone of aircraft. Moran kept reeling in drunken circles, then leaned back against Riglioni as if he were a tree and looked uneasily in several directions.

"Business?" he said. "Saints? Where are we? This ain't real. This is the middle of hell."

18

If Captain Stollman had remained at the CP, the Stuka attack might never have occurred. By threes in V formation they passed high overhead in greater numbers than seemed possible any longer to the shattered *Luftwaffe*. Only two of the formations keeled off to go screaming in a dive at the town, but not even these would have made more than one reconnoitering pass if the Troop ack-ack detail had not erupted in fervid heroics like a trigger-happy pack of replacements.

The Captain, Riglioni knew at once, would have ordered those .50s to remain silent, less in application of proper strategy than by his keen instinct to save his own skin, and on that insight he ran to hide where Stollman hid as the keening dive bombers chattered from wing guns on their way to target, ran to survive with the man whose instincts even told him when to leave that haven of a CP. "Hit some cellar," Moran shrieked. "Where you *going?*"

"To get orders," he shouted with a giggle crazier than Proctor's had ever sounded. "Hit some cellar," he bellowed at men who stood rooted in the snow with saints in their hands even as the first team of bombs gonged at the CP. "Get cover!"

He saw Stollman pumping an arm to bully his armored car into the church through that gap in its wall where, instead of Christ, Atman was prey now to the blind wheels. In the shrieking a pattern of fragmentation bombs pummeled the day and Stollman bolted, lead man of half a dozen including Riglioni who plunged into the bowels of an edifice with the attack caterwauling louder and the town cracking wide open to an enormous blast and bombs thumping like a mighty sledge in rapid unrelenting advance.

Then marble stairs heaved to a silent tide of concussion that sent them all flying, but no man lay where he landed and all were down another flight when in the very next instant came the colossal hollow clap shuddering through the gray dungeon, amid the pipes and dials of a furnace room where the six lay stunned and panting.

Down with the settling dust came a tomblike silence. "Look here," Lieutenant Morgdahl said, "central heating."

"Nah, the furnace is blasted out," Oakes panted. "Goddamn Krauts put a grenade in it before they pulled back. Don't you see?"

Muldoon said, "They sure as hell just blasted out this town. That's what we get for letting Squadron give us ack-ack to mount."

Weldon sat watching the Captain light his pipe. Morgdahl said, "Strange that they can still gather that strong an air power. Must have been close to forty planes up there, and in attack, to boot."

"The enemy has made a major break-through," Captain Stollman said, and drew on his pipe—slowly, as if to give them all time for a thorough comprehension of his remark. "Because of morale considerations, I hesitated to break the news until it became necessary. This seems a most appropriate time."

"Morale!" Riglioni giggled; he could not help giggling. "Come on, Captain, come on. Where. What. How strong, come on."

"Three prongs of an assault were launched yesterday on a front perhaps a hundred miles wide, the northernmost aimed at Liége through this very sector. Intelligence was brought this morning personally by Major Jimmerson who—"

"Christ!" Oakes barked. "Krauts in this town strung us out right to their own time-table! What's that battle in the mountain—the north prong, Captain?"

"Some phase of it, yes. Apparently we're holding with some

success up here, because south of here the enemy has broken through the Ardennes and reached Bastogne."

Muldoon said, "Then we pull back?"

"We do not. The other squadron is withdrawing into the bordering pines, and B Troop will roll out of them this afternoon to deploy forward, below this square. But not before *we* capture and occupy that last sector. This town will be taken in its entirety by A Troop. Before lunch, before C Troop arrives with Squadron and—"

"Christ, Captain, what makes you so sure we got a town left out there?" Oakes was panting all over again, this time with anger. "I think those Troop jokers of yours went and got their asses bombed off this time. I don't think you even got a CP left to work out of."

"That's to be investigated right now," the Captain said calmly. "Whatever's left is what we have, Oakes. We can't afford the luxury of grief, that's our orientation. Nothing counts but the fight, remember that, nothing counts but victory. This position will be at Group strength, ready for orders."

"What's our individual missions?" Muldoon said. "I mean now."

With a glance at Riglioni, Stollman puffed on his pipe and said, "Transfer one armored car to Lieutenant Spiro, John. The First and Third Platoons will advance to complete the occupation, the Second Platoon holding, then taking police and traffic action while the First and Third establish our holding positions in the rear."

A smile attended those last words: the rear holding position, with B and C Troops on the flanks and the other squadron forward in the pines, was A Troop's paltry reward from Group for the mission accomplished, and Stollman was acting as if he had bestowed it. Men were moving for the stairs behind Stollman, but Riglioni sat back in a sort of collapse against the wall, searching for some response to this latest condescending hypocrisy of Stollman's. Snow seemed to be sitting on his eyelids; his brain felt like the inside of a mattress.

"Oh yes, Riglioni," Stollman said in the doorway. "Sergeant Proctor has been brought through. He's been evacuated with a better than even chance of recovery."

"Pretty please," he squeaked.

The Captain blinked, and vanished with Weldon and Morgdahl. Uncomfortably, Muldoon said, "Let's go, Sal."

"This whole damn town never meant a thing. I don't want this town, Stollman wants it. It's his prize, not mine."

"Sal," Oakes said across the hollow place, "there ain't a thing you can do about it, so don't eat your heart out."

"No, he had to take every last inch of this town to kiss the Colonel's ass. They put us into a pointless fight. Pointless. Just to get us killed, that's all, just to kill a bunch of suckers."

Oakes came forward a couple of steps saying, "Yeah. We belonged up on that mountain if anywhere. Not in this shit hole. The Krauts just tied us up here, that's all. And Stollman . . . he wasn't even in it the way we . . . I mean he was in it for that decoration, and to buck for Squadron, not to kill Krauts. He's so full of shit when he talks fight that I—"

"Wait a goddamn minute," Muldoon barked. "You going off your knob? What's that got to do with us? Listen, Sal—"

"You listen. You signed something, didn't you, Johnny? To get him that Silver Star. You and Morgdahl and Spiro, didn't you?" Officers had to sign for a line commander's decoration and Muldoon could not deny it. Embarrassed, Oakes backed off through the doorway. Muldoon turned, but stopped when Riglioni said, "I quit, Johnny. Tell Stollman to take that decoration he stole from Finch and shove it up his ass with my stripes."

"Sal, I didn't sign anything. Sal, that paper was ready, without a date, when I was still First Soldier of this troop. Sal, Lew Enshaw signed that paper with Morgdahl and Spiro."

"Oh, Jesus." He laughed in all hopelessness. "And he sent it in with Lew dead? Oh Jesus, turn in my stripes and let me alone. Just let me alone, will you please?"

"He dated it Saturday morning, the minute the whole outfit was over the canal, while Lew was in there dying with you guys. And Sal . . . if he gave me that paper to sign I would've had to sign it. I'd sign it because I'd have to."

"No. No. You could always just die instead, you could always just lie down and die instead. Better men are doing it all over Europe, half of them in phony missions like this one for phonies like Stollman and Powell. Get lost, you bastard, and let me alone."

Muldoon shuffled out, dragging his puny carbine, and Riglioni sat there, deep in the safe earth that Stollman had found by instinct while better men lay hiding from the bombs in shallower cellars. And now Stollman was off playing his repulsive game, probably out there right now watching men recover the bodies of Gingold and Atman and Moran, watching men, stunned by the gigantic bomb that had struck just outside, drag bodies out of rubble without recognizing them as the remains of Gingold, Atman, and Moran.

Stollman functioned with equanimity in the middle of other men's wars, all brave and grown-up in the death of others; resolution like his was a simple matter of staying aloof. He had no more to do with the fighting than a general at Army HQ, no more to do with the bleeding and grief than a priest had with the deepest anguishes of his flock, no more to do with the horror of single moments than a senator back home had with the bread a man had to earn—and like them all he prospered by the careful process of maintaining his exalted distance.

Captain Stollman prospered at self-preservation, holding all others expendable toward that single end. He was a super-realist, of all possible enemies the deadliest.

With the weight of snow on his eyes, his brain quivering like Jello, Sal Riglioni rose a private and went out to see who was dead.

The hunt was on for Atman.

Men of the First Platoon, who had miraculously escaped a beehive of fragmentation bombs, came with reports of disaster and took the officers back, for Stollman's jeep was nowhere to be found. A blockbuster had struck just alongside the church, pulling half of it down into the enormous crater by suction. In the debris men searched for Atman while jeeps of the First came and went in relay, each driver describing a little more of the havoc before he took Third Platoon men back for their vehicles.

The ack-ack crew of four men were gone in the blast that demolished the whole Troop HQ house above surface. Fortunate enough to have been cowering in the cellar fortress, the rest of Troop were badly shaken up and agitating now for removal as casualties. Another blockbuster had turned part of the canal into a lake, and across the town eight-foot craters left by smaller bombs were surrounded by houses shorn of walls where bloody civilians screamed over their dead.

Now in the monstrous crater Gingold was hysterical once again. He kicked at rubble and threw beams aside and babbled about having foretold Atman's doom while the boy was wrecking that giant Christ and turning the whole day spooky.

Gingold had just hauled away the shelter-half of wax for Atman when suddenly an armored car was in the church on top of the boy and bombs were crashing everywhere. The next moment Gingold was burrowing his way out of snow and debris under which he had thrown himself, rising into what he called a wet dream of surviving the mighty final blast, when the armored car came at him in tumbles and leaps where nothing remained of the church but a wall and a half and the tall carved altarpiece with two glass haloes still intact. Wherever he ran the armored car pursued him, down the stairs and across the square, aiming the cannon to kill him until he leaped flat into the fountain of snow, and the car, knocking the goddess statue down on him in stony chunks, bumbled crazily into a street and away.

Looking for Atman now, Gingold was hysterical and so was Kallenson, whose teeth chattered in the smoke and dust; he kept falling down the slope of the yawning huge crater, and complained in loud stammers as other stumbling and hysterical men hauled him up again. "Bastards! This whole town they had to hit! Why didn't they just knock off the CP and blow the hell out of here?"

"Because they're GI's," Moran bellowed. "All they wanted was to get rid of their bombs and go home instead of looking for a fight!" He saw Riglioni watching from the rim of the crater and went rolling down to the bottom with men chasing after him in great belches of dust. Up he came again, yelling, "Hey, Deacon, when do we eat lunch?"

"Ask Muldoon. I just turned in my stripes." Everybody began to climb up the slope toward him and while Lindemayer sounded off a chatter from his maniacal face of soot and smears he shouted, "Don't be climbing up on my goddamn back any more or I'll kick the Jesus out of this whole platoon!"

At first he took it for an illusion when he saw a curl of smoke in the demolished church, but going toward it now he knew the smoke was real; it crept up the far wall that still towered, and he turned his back on it with revulsion. Irrationally, smoke sickened him; his brain had turned glutinous and foghorns lowed in his ears. The square was entirely deserted now; men were gathering around him, all as insane as he. In a dismal tone Moran said, "You turned in your stripes?"

"You told me to, you told me to. They sewed Proctor up, he's alive, they sewed up all the parts."

Implausibly, it seemed that cattle lowed somewhere. Men murmured; some tried to smile. Lindemayer said, "Don't believe any of that snow they hand you, Sal. You know he ain't alive. Let's get on with looking for Atman."

Chickens too; chickens clucked and cattle moaned. Behind Lindemayer men crossed the rubble and mounted the high lip of the crater and descended, all but Moran, who stood there fidgeting, licking his lips, while behind him cattle came over the crest from the last unpenetrated enemy quarter of the town. Civilians came, carrying bundles, pushing wheelbarrows piled with crates and cartons, toting slat cages of fowl that clucked. Moran did not turn toward the noise, but said, "What did you go and do that for? I know I told you to, I know I sound crazy, but what did you do that for? Don't you realize I'm crazy?"

Through snow on his eyelashes he saw the parade of beasts and people crossing the square. Moran did not seem to hear them, but Riglioni believed what he saw: men, women, and children herding cattle across the square, not many beasts but a drove of people, the bulk of the town's population suddenly returning home on some fantastic impulse. Moran kept staring at him. "Don't you hear anything, Joe?"

"What? Cows, I hear." He turned and looked, then faced Riglioni again through smoky puffs of his breath. "We got this town locked up. This is no time to turn in your stripes. I don't understand you, Sal."

"What do you understand? Do you understand that?"

Moran looked behind him again, then turned back and said, "Sure, it's civilians. And cows. Stick to the point, Sal. Why—"

"Where did they come from? Krauts must have sent them. What's to keep a counterattack from coming right up that way?

Do you understand why there's no roadblock set up? Not an armored car, not a .30 anywhere up front."

"Oh, sure there is. Muldoon put ours right up there, where those people are. Brubak is on it." Fidgeting, squinting at him, Moran said, "Sal," and licked his lips, then changed Thompson magazines from one pocket to another of his bulky long coat. "Sal . . ."

"No he isn't. Isn't that Brubak with Atman?"

Moran turned to watch Atman and Brubak come along behind the civilian horde pointing enormous muzzles, each with his rifle slung vertically on his back and carrying some eerie weapon with a ten-inch bore. They veered away from the parade that, circling around the crater, crossed into a street clucking and lowing and kicking up snow. Now on the far side of the square Riglioni could see the platoon .30 set up with Heggenrich seated behind it in the snow. "See?" Moran murmured. "I told you we got a gun."

Atman and Brubak came on toward the ruin, their strange weapons growing longer and longer, some nine feet of gray tubing under an arm of each. In contrast to the bearded blond Brubak, Atman seemed old and seasoned, but when he came nearer and grinned he seemed nothing but insane. "What's that you got there?" Moran said.

"Cardboard. Linoleum came in these, I guess. We found them in a cellar down that way."

To Brubak Moran said, "How come you left the machine gun? You know you can be shot for that?"

"Oh, Heggenrich relieved me on it. Atman got Heggenrich out of that crater to relieve me, so I could get the stove going down in the cellar here. Heggenrich doesn't know how to start a fire so I—"

"You got Heggenrich out of that crater?" Moran asked.

"With Lindemayer's permission. I asked him first."

"You did? Okay, Atman, go tell him it's time for lunch. Tell him we can look for you again after lunch."

"You tell him, Joe. I have a lot of work to do. I have to cut the sides down on these things before the wax hardens in them."

"What? Oh, I see. You're gonna fill them and make nice candles. What made you go down there where it could be full of Krauts?"

Atman turned to look, one hand toying with his glasses. "No wonder there were so many civilians. I got mixed up, I guess."

"You went all the way down that hill?"

"Yeah, I was dizzy. That bomb knocked me right out from under the armored car and I was so dizzy I didn't even remember taking the rest of my wax downstairs. So I asked Gingold but he said he only took one load of it down, so I must've taken the rest. In fact—"

"You asked Gingold? Where, in that crater?"

"Yeah. I'm still pretty dizzy, to tell the truth, so you go see Lindemayer. Okay?"

"What about?" Moran said, and Riglioni began to walk. Over hills of snow and disaster he walked toward the smoke that was no illusion and followed it around the standing wall to where it spewed out of a stovepipe protruding from a cellar window. The war in the mountain seemed to have ended; he wondered if he had actually heard any gunfire from that sector at all. Yet the air raid had taken place, of that he was sure, though it seemed that not enough time had passed this day for a fire-fight in the square and a bonanza discovery of wax and a Stuka attack and the surrender of his burdensome rank. Not even enough time had passed for Atman and Brubak to vanish, yet back in the shell of the church again he saw one of the long cardboard tubes disappearing into the snow and debris. Now only Moran was to be seen in all the white square, descending into the crater—no doubt to help the others search for Atman.

All the beasts and people were gone, if they had ever existed at all. He circled around to get a view of Heggenrich on the machine gun, and waved when the boy waved to him. Numb with cold he searched, and found a hole in rubble on the church floor, the hole through which Gingold had probably hauled Atman's shelter-half of wax just before the bombs deranged everybody.

There was a stair in the hole. Descending, he found that Atman and Brubak had already relieved themselves of their helmets and overclothes. In radiating circles of heat they lifted a black kettle to the top of a white-hot potbellied stove, and began to fill it with chunks from the blanket and shelter-half, Brubak doing what Atman did as assiduously as Zubrowski used to emulate Finch. From the raincoat they dumped more chunks on the central heap, and then emptied Atman's field pack of still more wax.

Beyond them the cellar was a cold stagnation of shadows full of church paraphernalia. Riglioni took off his heavy helmet and sat down in it, leaning forward on his rifle. Upstairs, voices approached; there was the noise of vehicles. He removed his pack to get at the K rations and, meeting Atman's smile with a small one of his own, he felt puny and feeble but content to remain that way as long as the world would let him alone.

Courage is a matter of decision!

The Colonel's command car bumped along amid Troop trucks and Squadron trucks relocating civilians and helping them gather their dead. From the western heights with Group HQ came the entire 75 Troop in its column of self-propelled guns too stunted to look real, advancing to the canal for a central low position from which to pump shells in any necessary direction. Civilians wept at its passing as if at a fresh invasion, little boys and old men and females of every age crowding the doorways of habitable buildings, family packed in with family of the weeping Master Race.

B Troop had rolled in from the forest with grimy men festive at the prospect of occupying houses instead of holes. Squadron HQ had arrived, guarded by C Troop and snapping orders down the line of rank in voices proficient at rear-echelon war. Group police appeared at the crossings, their status lettered in yellow on their helmets, to direct traffic that tamped snow down and opened the roads wide to a corruption of the conquest, an influx that resembled a plague of spoilers flocking to a boom town. Through it all Weldon drove Stollman in his new jeep, leading two half-tracks full of salvaged equipment and personnel on the way to a new CP, cooks and Supply hands barking loud sarcasms at Squadron men in derision of their fear at having to come up front. In the same spirit Squadron clerks ridiculed Group drivers who transported civilians and prisoners in uniform through the town.

Lindemayer found it all amusing, not only the sickly antics of non-combatants but the panic and confusion of civilians dragging mattresses and utensils from one ruin to another, the mothers stumbling with children in their arms, the crestfallen old Prussians assisting their wounded to ambulances, the wrinkled crones who wrung their hands and wailed, "*Alles kaput, alles kaput.*"

"Oh, these poor bastards," he laughed, "so God-awful sorry for themselves. Bragging themselves off one day about bossing the world and begging for pity the next. Suck this, you creeps!"

The First and Third Platoons, returning from a quick uneventful foray into the quarter already penetrated by Atman, had ferried the Second back to its armor, Riglioni riding a car deck with the boy and his two long tubes that looked like giant fire crackers with cords protruding from the wax. One section stayed with Muldoon to position vehicles at guard in the rear; the others went in jeeps to tell old men where to dump firearms and old women where to find water, to lead Squadron ambulances to bloody civilians and guide Group Engineers to the Headquarters they had to make safe against booby traps in the dungeons of what had once been a medieval jail.

In his overcoat Riglioni chauffeured Lindemayer who, wild-eyed and laughing at all the noise and misery, had found some euphoric corner of dementia in which to hide from any thought of his frenzied descent yesterday into mass murder. "Hold it here, boy, that's the house, that's the son of a bitch I want."

Lindemayer hopped out and made for a small brick house with his rifle pointed. *German descent,* Riglioni thought, waiting at the wheel, and pictured himself in Italy, berserk over the death of friends, massacring civilians and raping women who spoke his mother's language. Sense of guilt, something like that, a feeling of personal responsibility for a people who killed one's friends. To dissociate yourself from your own blood . . . like Hitler punks turning their parents in . . . like Italo-American newspapers yelling for the blood of Mafia suspects. *Not me, not me,* he thought in the midst of bumping traffic that represented suddenly the whole *institution* of Stollman and TNT Powell and reduced him in humility and guilt to reflections on the woman he had taken in her terror. *Let me alone,* he said to himself, *get off my back . . .*

The faces of women appeared in the doorway; abruptly hungering, he felt unwashed and predatory, as vile as all that he saw right up the chain of command, and as mad as Pete Lindemayer who pushed through the women now and came along in his loping gait. Circling around the jeep, he stopped a weapons carrier in midstreet.

From the house a short woman emerged, wearing boots. She was round; her body was round in a floppy green coat, her nose was round, her cheeks were round and her head was round in its matronly shawl. With a scared glance at Riglioni she began to climb into the jeep, and he said, "*Raus!*"

Laughing, Lindemayer pulled her over to the weapons carrier where the hands of other civilians poked out of the van to help her in. He spoke to the Squadron driver, then came back swaggering like Finch and got in behind the .30 saying, "Cut around a few streets and then head for that church cellar. She'll be waiting for us by that old potbellied stove, boy."

"Her? Who the hell wants *her?*"

"Hey, she's top stuff—you ought to see what Munzer put it to last night. I picked the *doll* of the family for us, boy. If there wasn't so many people in that house now I'd let her show you—"

"That's what you stayed out all night for? What's she see in you, C and K rations?"

"Half that and half she loves it. Put up a big squawk last night, but just for show, and then she gave me a trip around the world. That whole house of people know what she just went out to do and she's a big hero for it, because I gave them a couple of E bars and promised them real rations later. Hey, that's the wrong way, where you going?"

"That truck'll take an hour before they drop her off." He had swung around sharp in a U turn at sight of a Group two-ton truck transporting prisoners—compulsively, in a crazy vision of time expanding and contracting like a human lung, time burgeoning forth and returning again with the Polish woman it had stolen away. He went racing back through time to the canal, and the sound of shots nearby convinced him he was mad, racing right back into skirmishes of this morning and beyond; sure enough there went a man diving for cover—but his tumbling helmet said MP in yellow and it was Craig of the First firing a rifle at him on the run as Lindemayer laughed and babbled in witness.

He circled the big bomb crater at the canal where an eternity ago Enshaw screamed for a bazooka and Proctor said *pretty please*. He crossed a new bridge to pass Billy Field's hedges on the north end while Lindemayer laughed. Little traffic had passed here and the snow was deep going to the barnyard of rainy slaughter and Gingold's naked ass and Saint Ursula's numberless victims in wax. Among parked vehicles within the walls of that shattered community he dismounted to seek a miracle in green wools and threadbare skirt.

Oakes came out of the farmhouse to greet them. "Where's my wire? I expected you'd be bringing some wire. You see Morgdahl around? Man, I found a secret cellar, enough smoked hams and sides of bacon to feed half this town of Krauts, and these bastards here hollering it belongs to *them. Belongs* to them, can you tie that?"

The cellar was down a secluded stair from the regular cellar. Mountains of canned goods were piled under smoked fowl and hams; pork butts in cheesecloth sacks were heaped among slabs of bacon. "How come you don't keep a guard on this place?" Lindemayer said, taking down a ham.

"Oh, they won't be screwing around down here no more. Bastards wouldn't show me the door and I had to shoot holes all over to find it. Old bitch screamed like I wanted her wrinkled ass—it *belongs* to them. Well, they been told they'd be shot on sight down here."

"Who's they?" Riglioni said.

"The farmers of this joint and their two grandmas, besides all the new boarders they drew. Didn't you guys take this joint, Sal?"

"Yeah, we killed a lot of Krauts here. One of them is still out there, but the snow'll keep him from stinking. You ought to give the Polish slaves special treatment, they speak German pretty good and—"

"What Polish slaves? We got no Polish slaves here."

"How come? Didn't Group bring back all the prisoners we sent them? Didn't they send the farmers back here where they live?"

"Yeah, they kept civilians till we could lock up the town, but they sent military prisoners back to Corps, the Polacks with them, I guess. Why? What's it to—"

"Bullshit! Don't hand me that crap, Oakes! I just saw prisoners in their goddamn uniforms riding a Group two-ton!"

"Man, don't be biting at me. That's just yesterday's prisoners. Orders from Army came down that no more—"

"Who gives a damn? I don't want to hear about orders from Army or any of that snow any more. Buddy," he laughed, turning to help Lindemayer gather foodstuffs, "this being a private is a way of life!"

They departed with hams and pork butts and bacon and canned goods all hidden under a blanket. "Forget about that pig in the church cellar," Lindemayer panted in the frost. "With this stuff we can get some young nookie, some clean nookie. She didn't smell too good, that old pig."

He drove and let Lindemayer direct him, for responsibility was no longer his. Pete planned with the wanton, heartless precision of a general and Riglioni drove where he was told, pausing only to listen and laugh among the rear-echelon men who were aghast now in the knowledge that Group's lines to Corps had been cut. From trucks and jeeps they called to each other with quivering cheeks, but Squadron had quit deriding Group about overtaking it up front, and Troop HQ was no longer mocking Squadron. The raillery had lasted only as long as none took the town seriously as a combat front any longer; each joker turned sickly gray once the presence of men from the rear dawned on him as proof of enemy power in the region.

Laughing, Riglioni helped unload their hoard where heaped wreckage shielded them from the traffic. Charred debris was still smoking well enough to camouflage the smoke of the fire they must build against the cold. In the ruin they found a mattress and a rusty tin can of a stove, and in a cellar corner free of rubble Riglioni got diligently to work building their fire while Lindemayer drove off to hunt, armed with foodstuff bait. It was a way of life; drunk with it, he built up the heat until the rusty stove glowed white. "A whole damn way of life," he giggled.

Unwashed and light-headed and hidden from the *institution*, he giggled at Lindemayer's explanation for the bandaged head of the woman he brought back. With his First Aid hip pack he had bound her head to give any suspicious eye some hint of an excuse for her ride in a platoon jeep. He brought her back half paid for, having left her aunts and uncles with two pork butts and the promise, on her return, of a ham and milk for the tot she had to bring along to prevent his hysterics in her absence. Lindemayer drove the jeep off to keep it from attracting snoopers; at his withdrawal the girl's panic multiplied into shudders of pure horror. But it seemed to diminish with the removal of that bandage, and with the removal of her clothes an excited fervor came over her. *Young nookie, clean nookie . . .*

She was not too young and not too clean, but she was clean enough and young enough and in the overhead noise of motors she kept her child quiet by letting him play with her toes while Riglioni loved her on the dusty mattress and felt corrupt.

She was younger than he and freckled right down to her great white breasts; she was all heft and velvet, with body hair the same pale strawberry as the hair on her head. All her panic and grief turned into whimpers of a delight either spontaneous or affected as he loved her. He took her gluttonously amid visions of his dead friends; he took her with a vengeance in the fleeting images of Stollman and Powell and all the old men who strutted their brass in depraved safety all over the world of war. He loved her gratefully, he loved her attentively, and he relished the sense of corruption most of all.

In soot and charred odors they loved until Lindemayer returned with two jerricans of water, cursing Mess Sergeant Goodspane and snapping something in German to bring the woman up sitting. "You hear him bitch, you'd think I wanted the goddamn oranges he holds out on us, or his shiteating pancake flour, instead of some lousy water. You better get that jeep going, Sal. I'm gonna bathe this broad and myself. I'm gonna shave, and go dig around up there for a bedsheet."

Riglioni gave the baby his toes to play with; they were no dirtier than the little son of a Kraut in a flour sack. "Why didn't you find another broad? I thought you would."

"I tried but they weren't selling the good pieces. Boy, I saw one about seventeen, she could be in the movies." He set a jerrican on the stove. "Her goddamn mother wouldn't let her go. The old lady wanted to come herself. I swear she grabbed up a Cross and prayed big tears over that doll of a girl—and right after giving her own fat ass a wiggle to sell it for some bacon."

As Riglioni dressed, the woman touched his arm and chattered off a mouthful of German. "What's she want, money or something?"

"Boy, you got no heart, that's why you screw in a shit-heap. The lady's thanking you for being gentle. Give her a little kiss."

"You kiss her." He rose pulling on clothes, in a hurry to be out of this. He envied Lindemayer the clean hour he was about to enjoy, envied him his ability to make such deliberate preparations. For him the vice of filth had been as attractive as the iniquity of breaking the law against fraternizing and the sin of exploiting the woman's hunger and fear. But full of shame, he was full of justification as well: in love for himself alone he had shoved it up Germany and the Army and even the holy principle that, training him to serve, had tricked him into this living death—all his enemies at once right up the hole, and it was a way of life, by God.

"I said give her a kiss."

Staring at him with pale eyes like Proctor's, Lindemayer looked more insane than ever. "You can give my ass a kiss, Pete."

"Go on, you son of a bitch, get out of here. Take the jeep back—I'll walk. And don't be coming down here for any of this haul, you black son of a bitch, or I'll shoot you in your Dago face."

Hooking his ammo belt, he wriggled his shoulders to fit the pack straps better, then moved in to club Lindemayer down. But instead he turned with his rifle and left the ruin, hardly caring if either one of them lived or died.

At the rear edge of town the platoon house had walls three-feet thick, two sturdy brick stories and a whole roof of tile. Riglioni entered the kitchen in time to see Atman come tumbling down the stairs head over heels with a mattress, Gingold nodding soberly as he watched the boy's descent. Atman lay still on his back like Finch the day his bike struck a dead horse, and Riglioni knew that presently he would sit up grinning and unhurt. He did. Riglioni looked at Moran, who was toweling himself down by the stove, and went outside again scratching his beard.

He roamed to see if Muldoon had positioned the cars well, until he remembered with relish that it was no affair of his. Lighting a cigarette, he leaned on an armored car, its guns pointing west. Sunset bullied through the overcast, pink on snow that hid the railroad track and all the land this outfit had traveled bringing its best men here to die. He had once felt like the best man of all; now he felt only foul, his skin grimy with the itch of corruption.

On the far western heights, where a week ago he had stood

among young trees looking down into the unknown, the sun broke through and made a frail halo, purpling the snow by contrast. He could not remember how he had felt standing amid those trees; disengaged from responsibility now, he was lost to all he had once cared about, all he had ever been. Every new glimpse of hypocrisy in the outfit seemed to have changed him a little, and he wondered if it could be that, reacting too profoundly to the corruption he saw, a man as weak as he only became corrupt himself.

In faint echoes of thunder, the halo of twilight sun on the heights grew brighter, bubbling out of the snow like molten glass.

19

to ken Atman,
with unfailing admiration,
J. Christ

The inscription was on a new 8x10 chromo of the scene at Calvary which had been neatly folded twice for mailing. It was spiked to a wall of the stone-cold cellar above Atman, who lay back smoking a German cigar on seven mattresses he had piled up for his comfort. Like the rest he was ready to move out in full combat gear, for war had returned; cannon were shelling the town. Rifle by his side, his hands were gently folded amid the grenades hung to his chest, and as if lying in state he was flanked by those imposing candles which, thick as dock piles and nine feet high, blazed in majestic tall flame.

"Why only one capital?" Gingold said. "Either two capitals or none, make up your mind."

"I didn't write it, I got it in the mail."

"It's a forgery," Rayhew said.

"Well, everybody forges that name." Moran was at it again.

Crouching in a corner, Riglioni expected some twisted comment from Gingold, but only the whack of an 88 came, striking forward where B Troop had the war now, sharing it with the other squadron in the woods. In Atman's flames he saw city lights. Staring at one flame or the other for minutes at a time, he flowed into the tall shadow that stood sheathed in fire, until he was lost in the heart of a black world pierced by lights. There were static lights and lights in smooth parade; he saw all the mobile highways of his life, and a human grandeur he had failed to recognize in the highways of his swift nights back home.

Seventy-fives cracked off, and a duel began up front. "Bunch of goddamn kids," Muldoon said, entering now with his bald helmet and spindly little carbine. Half blind from the flame, Riglioni saw him in a haze of dancing lights. "Babies, they can't keep the war quiet, they have to throw shells."

"The 75s started it," somebody said.

His eyes cleared up enough to see Muldoon looking for him among the faces of squatting men, then stopping short at the sight of Atman's shrine to himself. Muldoon looked one candle up and down and then the other, removed his helmet, scratched his head, and said, "Jesus Christ!"

"Well," Atman murmured around his cigar, "it sure ain't Saint Barbara."

Men giggled lightheadedly. Muldoon took time to light a cigarette, then said, "What are you supposed to be, Atman, a maharajah or something?"

"I ain't supposed to be anything, sir."

The hint of mockery was in his voice and Muldoon reacted testily. "You think that's pretty smart, that picture on the wall?"

"I can't help it if people admire me, sir. We all have our followers."

From a few sides came laughter that, along with a sudden pattern of explosions around the canal, discouraged any further argument in Muldoon. The enemy guns east in the hills were locating the 75s now, and as if contemplating that fact he stood there gazing over his shoulder at space. An hour ago, before the smaller candles had burned out in separate corners of the house, he had come to stand over Riglioni with the obvious purpose of urging him back into the chain of command, but had lost either his nerve or his interest and departed. Now he was back over him, saying, "Lindemayer still AWOL?"

"Yeah. You gonna report him?"

"He might be in trouble somewhere, Sal."

About to contradict that notion, he decided against involving himself and only shrugged, staring at the flames.

Muldoon squatted, facing him. "I been over to Squadron and saw Churney, the Colonel's dog-robber. He brought only five replacements down for this whole squadron; around twenty of them went to the other one in the woods. How do you like that?"

"Who gives a damn?"

"Churney says the woods is our front and the other squadron has to be at full strength. And B Troop gets the whole five—"

"Hey, hey. You think about it, don't make me think about it."

"Churney's gonna come sucking around like Saturday Inspection, so you better set up more—"

"Tell Rayhew, Rayhew."

"Sal, they broke through our line in that mountain! Can you get that through your thick skull?"

"Yeah, and they'd've gone right around us if the 75s didn't open fire! Colonel's orders, I know—you son of a bitch, go tell him to quit fouling up our sheets and let me alone!"

Everybody was watching now, all the survivors crouching over their upright weapons, some clean-shaven, some still as foul as Riglioni. Rising, Muldoon said, "We can't let them go around us. We're the goddamn pocket of resistance now. This push, this is the counterattack at the whole European by God Theater of shiteating Operations! Don't you realize that?"

"One thing I realize. We're in the rear now. We're *behind* Stollman and, man, that is the rear! Now let me alone, Johnny!"

Cannonfire sounded far up front and Muldoon turned slowly east as if he could see through walls and the long night all the way to B Troop. "No," he murmured, "it can't be 37s. That's the 75s, some of them moved forward." Then he turned back to Riglioni. "We're in the rear? The rear, the safe rear? That keeps shrinking, buddy. It never stays safe—Christ, even *Group* is up front now."

"Yeah. Yeah. All right. I'll take my guard mount like the next man. I'll *die* like the next man. You can't ask more. I'm a private. I swear I don't know what you want from—"

"Jesus, I didn't tell Stollman anything about that. I thought sure you'd cool off and . . ."

He turned to the sound of feet on the stairs. Through the door came hatchet-faced Tobias and two others of the Third Platoon. "Lindemayer," the corporal said with a nod.

Riglioni leaped up to grab Muldoon's arm. "You sent them out looking for Pete?"

"Take it easy. If I sent you guys you'd take it wrong. Where is he, Tobias?"

"Come on out here, Johnny. The MPs found him."

He started to follow Muldoon out, but stopped and returned to sit in his inverted helmet and watch the flames. That would be a joke, all right, Pete Lindemayer arrested for making clean love after butchering civilian families without penalty. The idea tickled him. The men would be angry enough to run a patrol up to Group, a combat patrol to wipe out a few MPs and bring Pete home. That tickled him too, and he laughed, scratching his beard, gazing at the flame until his vision turned black and he watched the lights swim down far highways.

Muldoon came back. Squatting, he yanked at his pants as if he were home in Spokane wearing pressed slacks. Dancing shadows aged his face as he looked at Riglioni and said, "Lindemayer's dead."

Forward beyond the canal the 75s were mobile now to evade return fire growing too accurate from the hills where German observers could pick out each flash, count off seconds until the boom reached them, and convey the appraisal of distance to tank-mounted 88s which were also in frantic tactical maneuvers. In the thunder B Troop waited for invasion, in the pines the other squadron was poised at full strength to strike north at the flank of any assault force, and Riglioni, poisoned with wretchedness, luxuriated nevertheless in security. For once the Group stood unified as a power and here at the safe rear men free of combat anxiety could visit the wake of Lindemayer.

Muldoon had hurried right off to Troop, but Tobias stayed to convey what he knew of the disaster. Patrolling, MPs had seen a crack of light and traced it to the cellar of a ruin. There a fancy candle burned atop a pile of canned goods and other foodstuffs. Propped back against smoked hams and pork butts and slabs of bacon sat a man with a rifle between his legs, his mouth burned to a crisp and the back of his head a bloody cavern. He wore only combat boots and the dogtags that identified him as Lindemayer. On a mattress lay a nude woman and a nude baby boy, both shot through the head and bleeding all over a clean white sheet.

Cannonfire must have obscured the shots, Tobias conjectured. More flurries of comment came with each new visitor who squatted before Atman's shrine and stared at flames burning bright. Men drifted in from the First Platoon on the south flank, men came from the Third on the north, and all brought civilized condolences. The death of Lindemayer was more of a shock to the outfit than any death in all this gruesome year; without a combat situation to extenuate it, this death was naked tragedy.

Even Moran was appalled, and made no sardonic jokes. But he laughed when Reilly said, "Last wake I was at, my uncles disowned me because I wouldn't dance with Aunt Kathy. It was her wake."

Moran laughed and Riglioni came out of the flame of highway lights in a horror of seeing him go berserk with morbid jest once again. Laughing, Moran cast him a troubled glance and turned to Reilly saying, "I got drunken uncles too. I used to throw punches with them at wakes, they'd kick me out if I didn't. Uncle Jack, he kicked me out of his house once, me and my brothers and sisters. *He-he-he.* Used to give us coffee around a big table. He loved to see us all and give us coffee. His was three quarters brandy. So this one afternoon, we're drinking coffee and he's grinning himself off, watching us. Then he takes a sip of coffee and starts hollering we poisoned him. Choking and gagging and kicking over chairs, he hollers we poisoned him and kicks us out. We all thought he was crazy except my brother Bob who fell down the stairs, drunk. He got Uncle Jack's cup by mistake. Uncle Jack got his and without brandy it tasted like poison. All his life he drank coffee with brandy and—"

"Yeah, yeah," Riglioni said. "Yeah, yeah, that's enough."

Moran blinked with injury, then stood up and walked away in the crowd. Riglioni stared at the flames for a while until somebody whispered, "Sal." It was Moran again, squatting before him, eyes white in the silhouette of face and helmet with his back to the enormous candles. "Sal, did you know I was once a musician? I played tenor sax."

"Well well well well well."

"Jazz quintet, Sal. Big time, we were moving up to big time, Sal, the real big time. Wild bunch of guys. Crazy drunk all the time. One night we took this singer, she had a night-club spot the first time in her life, she was trying to act big time so we took her to a motel and lined her up, the five of us. Not just once. All night, hours and hours, just taking our turns all night, Sal."

"Yeah? Listen, do I look like a chaplain to you?"

"Let me talk. Don't be ignorant, Sal. You know what we did to that kid? Five guys around and around? Feeding her booze and bennies to keep her jumping in that sack? She went under, Sal. We couldn't wake her up. Hardly any pulse beat. So, Sal, you know what we did? Somebody got a bright idea. It was morning already so he ran to the drug store and bought mustard. We gave her a mustard bath, Sal. And you know what happened? She died in it, Sal. Died. She died there. We left her there dead, Sal, a kid nineteen."

"Well well well well well. Did you feel brave, and grown up?"

"No, Sal, listen . . ." But he said no more. Those white eyes blinked; he backed off and turned to hide in the flames, and Riglioni wanted to call him back and forgive him, or accept his apology, or confess his own plunder in a thumping butcher's cellar. But most of all he wanted to sit right there in his helmet and stare at a flame.

Before long Oakes was pulling at his arm. "Hey. Snap out of it, boy. Hey. Were you in on that with Pete, Sal?"

"What?" The sling was loose on Oakes' rifle. All around the cellar men leaned on rifles with dangling slings and the fact terrified him. It galled him unreasonably. Slings had to be tightened in battle conditions, but there was time enough for that and his reaction now was psychotic; he was at the brink of a madness like Scarbro's—appalled by the familiar, deranged by the obvious. "What . . . what are you, all of a sudden, an MP? Who sent you?"

"Man, you're funny today. I just asked. You hauled all that pussy-bait out of my cellar with Pete."

"Why don't you let him alone?" Moran turned on his haunches to say. "Can't you see he doesn't feel like making conversation?"

Oakes giggled foolishly and drew back to talk with others. Moran turned again to the candles which, despite the low-grade wax, had not burned down to any noticeable degree; Riglioni stared at a flame telling himself that all their arguments seemed to have canceled each other out in pointlessness. He and Moran were alike once again in a pesthole, hiding in flames of fancy and unconsciousness for respite from all the sheet-fouling, death-dealing enemies of the race and also from the knowledge of their complicity in the whole foul game. Now Gingold, skeptically perusing a letter from yesterday's mail, no longer seemed quite so absurd in his reeking vision of the world. But to view Gingold as rational, he had to conclude, only proved his own insanity—and justified him all the more in unburdening himself of responsibility. It was a way of life, all right.

More visitors arrived. Riglioni could not believe his eyes, for they were a pair of rifle-bearing men with *MP* lettered in yellow on their helmets. MPs right in the maw of a line outfit—they were taking their lives in their hands. Behind them came Captain Churney, the Colonel's aide, barreling in like Santa Claus with a *ho-ho-ho* and pearl-handled pistols under his ponderous girth. In a voice snappy with authority, he ventured that this was the fightingest combat platoon he had ever enjoyed seeing poised for action, and enlarged on that theme with condescending laughter until his eyes focused on Atman's shrine beyond the confusion of all those faces. "Great Scott!" he piped. "What on earth are those?"

"Candles," someone enlightened him.

"Candles! Who's that man?"

"Atman."

"Atman? Hello, there, Atman. Getting to know your buddies? Good lad. Where's Sergeant Riglioni?"

"We got no Sergeant Riglioni. And if we did, those two PX commandos couldn't get near him."

"Munzer? Corporal. Is that you, Corporal Munzer? And Rayhew, yes sir. Sergeant Rayhew, yes sir. Where's Riglioni? I just want a word with him, men. Don't mind these lads, I'll vouch for them."

Oakes said, "You better have them wait outside before they get their asses shot off in here."

The MPs looked around with eyes that flashed tension in the candlelight. Churney spoke softly, inaudible in the rumble of shellfire and other voices, then guided his bodyguards out the door and turned, protected by nothing but his pistols. He adjusted his glasses, hitched up his web belt, and came forth with a clerkish grin. He looked at faces without comment and, spotting Riglioni, picked his way over and dropped his rump right down on the concrete floor. *Even more a regular guy than Stollman.*

"Now what's all this, Rig, what's all this?"

"It's a wake. Pete Lindemayer died today."

"Yes. Yes, I just heard about that. Awful news. God-awful. One of the best, I know. Those things . . . in war, you know . . . but Rig. What I meant . . . you know, we have to take some things in our stride or we'll go all to pieces. What I meant, Rig, is this business about taking a voluntary bust. I've been visiting the whole—"

"Who sent you, Captain? Muldoon?"

Modulating his voice to a sudden low drone of grave sincerity, Churney panted more than ever. "Nobody sent me, Rig. Nobody sent me. I'm just making my customary rounds." Extending his legs, he crossed one over the other, and leaned back on both hands like a bathing beauty. "We like you up at Group, Rig, we like you. You don't want to go and turn down your rank, pal."

"Yes, I do. I don't feel so good. Little touch of combat fatigue, maybe, but Jesus I think I might blow my top and shoot up this whole town if people don't start leaving me the fuck alone!"

"By *God*, I wish we had a dozen like you, Rig. *Ho-ho-ho*."

"Well, go make your customary rounds up where those shells are hitting and you'll find some like me." He swung the rifle around and, opening his mouth wide, stuck the muzzle into it. Aghast, Churney lurched forward, gaping until Riglioni lowered the rifle.

The panting of Captain Churney was a voluptuous flutter, too intimate, like a carnal secret betrayed; he got up on his knees and in his solemn low tone said, "Don't think I'm not aware of how it all goes through a man's mind. Don't think it for a moment, Rig. It's always your squadron that's committed, your troop, your platoon—that's how it always feels. All right, A Troop took this town. Without assistance, and at great losses. But Rig, if we committed other troops, yes, we might have taken the town a day earlier, but Rig, at what cost? Twice, maybe three times the losses we sustained with A Troop going it alone and—"

"Hey, Fat."

Slowly the Colonel's aide turned to face Moran, a squatting shadow in his helmet of rags, his hands busy with a K-ration can. "I . . . I don't seem to know you—you must be an *old* man." Churney extended a humble laugh at himself for that remark. "Moran? Is that you?"

"That's me, Fat." He freed a cake of cheese from the tin and bit into it, chewed for a moment, and said, "Get out of here now, before we disappear you like they do in the Air Corps."

Forward, the guns dueled. Churney rose, his hands stealing down to his pistols until Moran, still munching, pointed the Thompson at him with one hand. "Rayhew, Sergeant Rayhew. This man—"

"Go on," Rayhew said, "get out of here."

"Oakes! You tell—"

"Get the hell out, you bastard!"

"What," Churney said, backing off, "what are you men doing here anyway? This is supposed to be the Second Platoon, not—"

A rifle shot exploded with a cannon's hollow voice and Churney yowled. Another shot crashed and he fell, yelling, "Guards!"

When the MPs charged in Riglioni tensed for the shots that would kill them. The pair came with rifles at port like Buffalo Bill and it was the drizzly first day in this town all over again, with Moran taking Proctor's place to defile the *institution* and inflame others in a momentum of defiance. "Drop those rifles!" Oakes roared. "Drop them on the floor!" In the pungent gunpowder fumes the two rifles clattered on concrete and nearly thirty men, half of them standing now and half still crouching, lowered their pointed weapons. "Now drag them out of here, muzzles first. Captain, you want to stir us up, by God you better do it through proper channels!"

Outside, an approaching motor growled and careening wheels screeched. Churney cried, "This is incredible! The Colonel—"

A 75 blast just outside cut him silent; again the motor sounded, then the receding grind of wheels. Churney said not a word. He only hunched his shoulders protectively as the night crackled to the flight of an 88 seeking the 75 that had come here to launch a shell and run. In the sudden hush Churney ducked into the brick arch of the doorway, the MPs went flat against the wall, and the 88 walloped with a wrenching moan nearby as another 75 cut loose not far off. Panting, Churney said, "The Colonel, you realize I'll have to—"

"Hey, Fat," Moran said, pointing his Thompson with its loose sling. "Tell the Colonel if he shows his face back here, I'll shoot him on sight."

Cannon dueled and Churney stammered, fighting for time to hide here in the deep earth from shells perversely falling now on this safe rear, but in explosions of rabid mirth the men drove him and his guards out into the night of thunder, into the very teeth of their dread while Riglioni fled to the flames of tall candles.

He vanished in a flame dreaming himself off to remembered lawns and porches, to afternoons of sunny dialogue with strangers, to the random visits of cousins from San Fernando vineyards, to ancient faded calms with Lorraine—a walk with her once down Olvera Street where burly Mexicans played guitars and sang sweetly of half-forgotten loves. Aloof to the enormity just committed, responsible in his privacy to neither law nor reason, he ran home through flame, deaf to shellfire and the jabbering men, until officers began arriving and brought him back as if from sleep.

Muldoon was the first to show up. "It looks like a goddamn

motor pool outside," he said, complaining about all the jeeps tucked in crannies of the wrecked district. He was on a mission launched by Stollman at Churney's behest, that was obvious, but he could find no comfortable way to begin in the dark pierced only by the matches of men while Atman stood on his mattresses and pared the giant candles with his bayonet. Deep puddles had drowned the flames: the wax, melting fast but only close to the wicks, remained cool on the outside. Thus Atman explained it, handing what he called the foreskins to Gingold, who molded them around cord to create a spare candle. Muldoon paced the shadows, muttering gingerly warnings about trouble soon to come from Squadron and Group, and Riglioni tried to fade away in a blossoming flame.

"Bullshit," Dixon rasped, "Churney ain't about to bitch to the Colonel about getting his fat ass chased out of here."

"That's why he ran to Stollman," Muzakis said. "That's why you got sent here, Lieutenant, so don't snow us now."

"Oakes, what the hell is this?" Bringing the din of shellfire with him, Morgdahl arrived, freshly shaven, a razor-nick patched with a strip of toilet paper on his cheek. "Get the men out of here at once!"

"Blow it out your ass, Lieutenant!"

"Did you say—"

"Blow it out your ass, that's what I said." Giggling, Oakes cast glances to all sides like a little kid suddenly the center of attention. "I got three positions set up out from that barnyard and I'm keeping my reliefs going. Mission accomplished, so wipe that chickenshit off, Lieutenant."

Morgdahl laughed with the laughing men, playing the only cards he held, totaling the only figures he could find, like the shrewd Certified Public Accountant he had probably been in real life. "Real life," Riglioni muttered, "oh boy," and followed his dimmed and drowsy eyes into the flame. He dreamed of Hollywood night clubs to dance in with Lorraine like a couple about to be married on Christmas Day and keeping their chins up, bravely drunk on toasts to the boys in the foxholes.

"Hey, you."

Someone hung there above him; but blind from the flame of his dreaming he could not make out the face. Presently it began to emerge, first the lantern jaw, next the drooped eyelids, and finally the black hair slicked down and parted in the middle like that of some Roaring Twenties dasher. Lieutenant Spiro had arrived to stand over him with his helmet at his chest, a small-town alderman posing with his derby. "There's Dixon on the other side, Lieutenant."

"Who needs him? You're the wise guy. What, you're starting a revolution? What do you want, hot chow? Tomorrow you get hot chow."

Riglioni waited, but nobody laughed. The man was fantastic, but solemn eyes were focused on the moment from every side. The night was deformed and spooky, with laughter in mourning and silence in hilarity. "Lieutenant, I don't want anything. I'm not bothering anybody. Why do people come climbing up my back?"

"Because you're a crack in this whole crock of shit now," Gingold called over heads, and snorted.

Spiro turned to Gingold and over his helmet said, "No siree, he's just a dogface like anybody else." And nobody laughed; they only stared, as inexpressive as Spiro himself. Having foiled digression with dispatch that way, he turned back to Riglioni. "What's this you're lousing up the morale here? Stollman complained the morale's bad. What do you want, movies? Red Cross girls with doughnuts? What."

"I loused up morale? Me?" He shifted in the bowl of his helmet, leaned forward on his rifle. "Tell Stollman to come and say that to me. Tell him to come around in person with that crap."

"He can't come, don't talk foolish. He stays in the middle, he can't come to an outpost. He gets too sickly."

Nobody laughed. Riglioni stood up but collapsed on stinging numb legs. With his rifle and Spiro's hand to help him, he rose again, saying, "Sickly, yeah. You know it and I know it. Everybody here knows it. He's too scared to go in himself but he sends us in like cattle and you fucking officers hand his orders down to kill us off—"

"Is that nice? Is that nice? Fucking officers? No fucking officers around here, Riglioni, what's the matter with you? And to say—it's not nice to say he orders men to get killed. No such thing. He figures out they shouldn't get killed, not they should. They shouldn't. That's why he's so stingy with platoons—if one could do it why should two? He's plenty smart. He knows his onions."

"Hey, Lieutenant. Hey, Lieutenant." The man looked like a moron and spoke like one, yet succeeded in making him feel childish. Riglioni could not seem to shut himself up; while everybody watched without cracking a smile, he said, "Why doesn't the son of a bitch run an attack in person once in a while?"

"Sickly, scared—what's the difference? I told you. Don't say son of a bitch no more. What do you care if he gets scared and stays in the middle? It's skin off your nose if he stays in the middle?"

"What do I care? Hey, *I'm* scared, I'm scared *shitless!* Let *me* stay in the middle! Man, I'm *scared!*"

"No, not like him. He gets so scared he could go crazy. It's a sickly thing. What good would he do somebody? This way he don't interfere. You're scared, I'm scared, but we don't go crazy, let him—"

"Rayhew. Rayhew, it's eleven o'clock. My guard, right?"

"What do you want, movies? Doughnuts? It's the front line

—that's who we are, that's who he is. Don't take it so serious. It's only life."

"It's only life?" He bent for his helmet and put it on as he rose, reeling slightly. "It's only . . . Hey. Hey, Lieutenant, tell that to Stollman, tell him it's only life. Then maybe he'll be—"

"Never mind. You know you talk too much? I heard you're such a big-shot soldier. You got no brains. Rations he gets. Ammunition he gets. Hot meals? Why should he commit cooks, they'll make in their pants and get killed from it. If it's quiet here tomorrow, you get hot chow. What more you want, movies? Doughnuts? Toss a coin, that's life—this way, that way, what can you do?"

"What do you want from me, Lieutenant?"

"I want it without revolutions around here."

"You're putting in a complaint that I busted myself down?"

"I should worry."

"So goodbye, Lieutenant."

"Goodbye, Riglioni. But Stollman says no busting yourself down. Do what you're told, and give me back my men around here."

Nobody laughed. Riglioni walked out with his rifle.

The moon, as bright as a flare, lit up the entire turret—the breech of the cannon, the fixed pair of .30s, the elevation and traversing wheels, Atman's shined paratroop boots and Gingold's private pile of notepads, cartridges in their long belts and the racked shells and, above, the .50 like a black prehistoric bird contemplating flight to the roof of the sky.

Through the slits Riglioni saw the world in soul-wrenching peace beneath snow, an apparition of purity rolling off into the mute black pit of night. The town was silent now, and the enemy hills. It was all a weird dream: the silence and the white world, the frozen moon, the warcraft forged in metal around him, his veiny hands miraculously inviolate amid all the ghosts from Sandorian to Lindemayer.

In the hours just past, one man had caught another's giddiness like a disease in some lunatic's dream, until Spiro awed them all with a black magic of nothing but stolidity. "It's only life," Riglioni muttered, laughing in spite of nausea. "Jesus!" He began spinning wheels, elevating the cannon, traversing the turret. Lightheaded, he grabbed an armor-piercing shell and laid it in the breech gutter ready to be locked home and triggered, though it could never pierce the armor front of a Tiger; it would only bounce off like a pebble and none of it was real life and here he was waiting again for the spook . . . waiting, waiting, though it was only life and not even real at that.

He had been in the turret only a few minutes when the jeeps began to pull out, one after another until he knew that all the visitors were gone, not only Spiro's men but Morgdahl's too. For nearly an hour he had not laughed, but now his cheeks were wet from laughter and he cranked the wheels, aiming one way and another without slamming the breech and firing, because he was here only to wait. It was a way of life, and it was only life.

He turned for a look at Jesus, the print inscribed *to ken atman with admiration* back when Christ was still Savior and before He graduated Atman to a capital initial. To judge that or anything else as making no sense was ridiculous; was Atman's secret mocking game mad and Spiro's dull logic sane? He grabbed up one of Gingold's notepads and thumbed through it.

For Jessie, Gingold had scribbled, *culture was a duty, not a joy. Yet better that than to take pleasure in clever lies.* The moon was bright and Gingold's hand was legible; he read another entry: *I don't get on well with anyone whose conscious-*

ness revolves on an axis of self-defense. That made him laugh again; obviously it had been written before Gingold came among men whose lives were war. He flipped pages crammed with penciled notes. Some short entries made no more sense than Atman's private game: *The Nebish Syndrome,* and *Man with "sharp" taste.* Then near the end of the pad he found *Death makes you want to die,* and knew that he had reached Gingold's current entries.

Under a separating line he read: *Those haunting fringes of sleep—just before sleep falls and the first instant after sleep. There's true lucidity in the small note of me in that split instant, and it's my conscious mind that by comparison is lost in hallucinatory murk. It's as if, locked up so long in my skull, the pure tiny sum of me goes free and calls, "Paul! Paul!" desperate to tell my huge worldly self a truth he's too complex to isolate. And in that split instant the cumbersome self of me, desperate to learn, goes plunging around to grasp the fading little prisoner and save him, but stumbles, gapes, clumsy hands floundering, unreliable eyes too slow, and the little bell of truth is silent, even its echo dimming fast.*

"Rig. Relief, Rig."

Swiftly he dropped the pad on the others and, like a sneak, rose scratching his beard. Hoisting himself out of the turret, he saw Gingold in the barren night of the moon and said, "I was just reading your notes."

He dropped to the ground before Gingold, who whispered, "Is that nice? Somebody's notes you shouldn't read."

"I'm sorry, Paul. There they were, and I didn't have anything to do."

"Nothing to do? Oh, that's bad for the morale. Here, you want to read my Dear John letter? It's a scream."

"What?" Gingold's smile was the broad kind one wore in joking, but in the context of his remark it conveyed a bottomless misery; he was not joking about the letter, yet stood there grinning in the cold and implausible moonlight. "You're off your rocker a little, aren't you, Paul?"

"I'm off your rocker, not my rocker. You shouldn't be so sickly."

He laughed, embarrassed at not having recognized Gingold's burlesque of Spiro immediately. "Why didn't they laugh, Paul? He was funny. How come nobody laughed?"

"Shit as plain and simple as that, people take seriously. It's only life, don't take it so serious." Climbing up, Gingold said, "Rig, the Old Man phoned in. He's coming here to see you."

"No shit."

"Don't mention it."

"Goodnight, Gingold."

"Goodnight, Riglioni."

They laughed together and he hurried down the street, running for the cellar to reach those tall flames, to escape Gingold's demented grin of despair and the silent white night that was like a dream of death.

20

The cellar was desolate. The pitiful few that remained seemed the survivors not merely of the Second Platoon but of the entire troop. They kept losing identity for Riglioni so that at intervals he could not even name them with confidence, his brain clouding over and the night losing substance before him until he woke with a start in Atman's flame. Wrapped in his blanket, he sat staring at the flame without seeing city lights. Atman snored and told jokes in his sleep and snored again as men sat in gaping stupor. Smith and Brubak went out, Gingold and Kallenson returned, and still there was no Captain Stollman.

"Did he show up?" Gingold said, settling down with a blanket.

"No, the game-playing creep. That's a politician's trick, to tense me up so he can out-talk me."

"Yeah. Sleep, sleep."

The candles, pared by Atman fifteen minutes or so in the far past, were still about six feet tall. Smaller candles, lumped together from shavings of the parent lights, stood on the floor waiting to be lit when necessary. Tired of waiting and waiting they lit themselves and revealed midget Mexicans by the dozens all naked in bed with naked Lorraine who fondled them with the compassion of a Madonna. Casting them one by one out a window, Riglioni said, "I got nothing against Mexicans," knowing with pain that none of them believed him. Lindemayer came into it saying, "I got a built-in howler, boy," and Riglioni laughed saying, "Boy, it's been a long time since." Lindemayer stared, standing tall in all his gear, and tactfully Riglioni laughed on to keep from exposing his knowledge that Pete was dead. In full gear he stood tall with his rifle at port, but Riglioni knew that the poor guy was no longer waiting, that it was only a pose, that he was done with waiting, that Cesare would be done with waiting all too soon, that he himself would never be done with waiting until his sister came to the window and he stepped through it to see her face. A shell exploded in silence and the blaze diminished rapidly and turned into Atman's flame.

The shelling was loud. It was everywhere in the town. Atman's candles were pared down almost a whole foot; time had raced by. The shrine of mattresses was empty. Atman was gone, but amid the dozing men Captain Stollman puffed on his pipe. Riglioni rubbed his eyes; he was awake. Stollman was there, all right, squatting right before him with a wrinkled brow.

"I didn't want to wake you, Sal, but I would have had to in another minute. They'll be coming at this town soon. I meant to get here earlier, but Group called the Troop Commanders in for a briefing."

Riglioni lay there, glancing around. Only a couple of the men slept; others watched the flames and smoked. He saw Rayhew, but could not find Joe Moran. Lying there, he saw the back of Gingold's head and knew beyond doubt that the man was dead. *Died in his sleep, heart attack dreaming his wife leaped up to gun him down.*

"The enemy is in considerable strength."

"Yes sir."

Stollman put one knee on the ground, and leaned on his carbine. Removing the pipe from his mouth he said, "It's your duty to retain your rank, Sal."

"No sir."

The 75s were not far forward, but the shellfire they drew was sparse, the 88s concentrating all the way up front, and if Stollman was taking his time here then it was as safe as Burbank. He had left Burbank to win a town for Stollman, for Powell, for old men playing private games—small games, big games, all of which they called America. "Sal, Rayhew can run this platoon well enough. I have faith in Rayhew. But it's more than just this platoon. Oakes and Dixon will be watching you if we have to move forward. You must keep your stripes."

That was nonsense. "Lieutenant Spiro can control his men, sir."

"Dixon threatened to attack Spiro. Tobias struck Morgdahl in the mouth. A Troop—there's no question about it—is about ready for a long rest back in Belgium . . . or France . . . or whatever's left to us if we ever stop this drive. But let's face it, Sal. Insubordination started at a particular point in this mission. It has grown like cancer since then. If you—"

"What are we doing here, sir? Why did the 75s open fire on them? Why didn't we just let them swing past us?"

"Because it became the Group's mission to stall them. We succeeded in conveying that we'd hit their flank if they tried to swing past. Now they have to strike this town. We have to engage them when they do. Sal? Are you listening?"

"Yes sir. I just have to keep my eyes closed to stay calm. I'm cracking up, sir. Take my rifle away till you leave, sir."

Nothing happened for a moment. Then he felt the rifle slide out from under his hand. "Sal. Bastogne is besieged. On the way there the enemy took no prisoners, Sal. Reports say that even unarmed Medics were machine-gunned. We can believe it, because this is go-for-broke for Mr. Hitler and they can't afford food or so much as a drop of gasoline on prisoners. Do you hear, Sal?"

"I hear, sir. I'm just keeping my eyes closed so I won't see your face. This is the rear. Why are you so worried, sir?"

"This won't be the rear very long, once they strike. It's going to be a heavy one, Sal. They have tanks. You must keep those stripes!"

"I can't handle them, sir. I can't run men in for you, sir. Shovel your own shit, sir."

He tried to sleep. He wanted very much to look at the flames and imagine city lights, human grandeur, but he could not bear to look at Stollman. "Sal. We all have our capacities and we all have our jobs. I've done mine just as you've done yours. I took this town in one week, and without finding much time to sleep. It required bold and calculated tactics and I worked them out. Committing more power in single skirmishes would have meant that much more in casualties without any quicker success. If you want to challenge my way of leading a troop, do it at the right time, not now. I took this town in good—"

"You got decorated for it, sir. Congratulations. Only we never needed this town. We died for it and got trapped in it for senile old men. And you were their pratt boy to make us do it, sir."

"Damn it, Sal, now you *see* why we needed it!"

"Sure, you knew beforehand that this big push was coming! You must think I'm simple! We belonged in that mountain, plugging up a hole. The Krauts in this town wouldn't have budged toward that mountain with the half-ass strength they had."

"Sal, sit up. There's no use—Sal, sit up and listen to me. *Sit up!*" At that a few men turned to look. Without moving, Riglioni took long glances around; at his tilted angle he saw them slack-jawed and dim in the eyes, like drunks. He could not find Moran among the mesmerized faces. "Sal, there's no point in arguing. I need you . . . and you need me. You're intelligent enough to realize that."

Sitting up fast, he felt his brain dip glutinously and fell back against the wall in hollow, hopeless nausea. "Captain, why didn't you become a conscientious objector instead of a phony hero? You have the guts to hide out and collect medals, but not to stand up and *say* you can't stomach a fight."

The Captain stiffened. "Riglioni. I'm trying my damnedest to be patient. Do you realize what you're doing now?"

"Sure he does." Moran had been right beside him all along, sitting there in a blanket with his Thompson. "He's saying exactly what you said, Captain. That he's intelligent enough. Only you don't really mean it when you say it. Trouble with stuffed shirts like you, Captain, is you think everybody else is simple."

The shelling was heavy on B Troop and probably on the forest too, a solid barrage. In the noise of it Stollman had been talking openly with Moran in plain witness, undoubtedly aware that it was Moran who had threatened the Colonel's life but afraid to provoke him with a command that he move off. Now Stollman rose and looked around. He moved a hand for Riglioni to follow him, with a direct gaze that made his gesture unmistakably a command, and shambled away

"Go on," Moran said, "you got to go. Just don't let him run our ass up front."

The Captain was sitting on Atman's mattresses, facing the raggedy men between the two candles. Riglioni could see the pools of molten wax that would soon drown the flames. With rifle and blanket he climbed up on the mattresses and leaned back against Atman's inscribed print. Sitting there like a sidesaddle horse rider, Stollman said, "That's not true. I don't think you're simple at all. I don't have to tell you that Moran's not all there, do I? You know what anarchy is. You know what nihilism is. I don't think you're simple at all."

Riglioni heaved the weariest sigh of his life. To belittle him as shallow, this slimy college boy was sarcastically putting questions to him in the form of statements. Gunfire laced through the cannonade up front. "No," he said, "I don't know what those things are. I never got past the fourth grade, Captain, and that's where you're screwed."

Stollman puffed on his pipe, but it was cold. His back to the men, he stared. Then he whispered, "Run this platoon. If we move up, talk to Oakes and Dixon—tell them the prospect before us. When this action is over—just this action and you have my solemn word on it—you move up to First Sergeant, Riglioni."

There it came, and it was strong. The Captain was talking turkey, abandoning logistics and morality and all affectations of ethics to invite him over the fence to the other side of the *institution,* where all the super-realists staked their claims. "What about Stearnes?" he said.

"Stearnes is a moron. He can't fill out a simple report. He'd be happier back as First Platoon Sergeant."

Super-realist wrinkling his brow. Puppeteer. But Riglioni saw himself in a deep brick fortress drinking coffee from a tea cup in the light of battery lamps. *Momma I'm safe, Poppa don't die, wait for me.* Scratching his stubbled chin, he stared at one flame, then at the other, then at the men between them. Moran was cleaning his Thompson; Gingold, dead of a heart attack a few feet down the wall, suddenly kicked and snorted and lived again. "If I can stay together long enough, Captain, I'll move this platoon. I'll get Oakes and Dixon to move theirs. Right behind you, Captain."

"What do you mean by that?"

"I mean I go where you lead me, not where you send me."

Small arms fire was building a steady pattern in the shelling. The Captain smiled, getting to his feet, and wagged his head with all the kindly restraint of a superior. "If we move up I can't be everywhere at once, Sal. It's a question of deployment."

"Yeah? And Lucky Strike green has gone to war. Talk yourself off, Captain. I'll take your orders, but I won't pass them on unless I see you right where I am."

"Look, Sal. I don't have the time to . . . look, we both feel justified, we both argue for what we have at stake, and each feels he's right. But for Christ's sake, up here it can't be a matter of who's right and who's wrong. Use your head, it's—"

"That's right, Captain. It's not a matter of who's right and who's wrong any more. It's a matter of what happens if all us expendable slobs just fold up under you guys pulling the strings. Anarchy can't kill *us* any faster than we're dying. Nihilism can't drown *us* in more shit than you throw."

The Captain puffed on his cold pipe again, meditatively,

staring coldly at Riglioni as if preoccupied with those bold and calculated tactics of his. Then he nodded curtly, and said, "Do you want those First Sergeant stripes or not, Riglioni?"

"You take those stripes, Stollman, and shove them up your precious pink ass."

"That about does it. I'll see you again, Riglioni. I'll see you when this is over."

"But you ain't gonna get us up front, Stollman. You're gonna have to pray the other outfits hold without us. Then you're gonna have to tell the court martial something. That I refused to shovel your shit no matter how much you bribed me." He spoke from the heart of madness. Here in this crypt of brown light and shadows he was not even awake but acted as if he had just showered and shaved in a silence miles and years away from that din of enemy attack. It was a dream, but real; it was madness, but so was the whole reality of blind gaping men. He swung the rifle around to point with it and said, "Go on. It's a long walk to that door."

Stollman turned to look at the crouched men. He faced Riglioni again and rubbed his puffed weary eyes in the crazy dance of shadows. "Cool off. I know you won't shoot me in the back. Let's both cool off, Sal. There's no time for us to be—"

"Go on. Nobody's gonna shoot you. We need you to lead us. Come and get us when it's time to move up."

The Captain turned away, but did not depart until he had some private talk with Rayhew, who came over moments later and said, "Sal, he wants me to be the Actor in this psycho platoon. I can't push these guys over your head, Sal."

"Yes, you can," he said, moving back toward Moran and Gingold. "What you can't do is get me to take you by the hand. Get lost."

Moran laughed. "You told him to shove them. *He-he-he*, I heard you tell him to shove them. Just because he's so sickly?"

He sat propped back against the wall in his blanket and promptly started to sink layer by layer into sleep. "No. Not just that he's yellow. No, that's nothing. But he's a phony, that's it. If he came right out and said we're here to save his ass and die, it might be different. But no, he has to give us a snow job that he's in this just like us, the lousy string-puller. The top man is a jaw-flapping hypocrite, and he knows I know it now."

Several times Riglioni woke to thunder and new voices as the men returned hypnotically to the candles with talk of platoon movements that he heard before vanishing again in Atman's flame. Now it was 5 AM; long past his guard hour, Atman was back in his shrine wearing paratroop boots that gleamed between the candles. From the north Oakes had rolled into the area with his entire Third, which a platoon of B Troop had relieved taking over the walled community. A platoon of C Troop had displaced the First, sending it in tighter from the south, and all but the men mounted on guard came to gape at the shrinking candles. Oscitant and stubble-chinned and foul with muddy gear, they smoked, they nibbled on rations, and they met with silence or impatient grunts the remarks that Rayhew made half-heartedly from the field phone, which rang occasionally to give him news. "Tanks cut off the woods," Riglioni heard him say, dozing off into the flame. "Get over to your own houses."

Oakes said, "Shut up." He had a voice like coarse salt and a beard which, as old as this mission, hung scraggly and rusted like the burlap on his helmet. "In one minute flat we can hit our cars and run them any which way we have to. Now let us be."

Dreams and flames later, he heard Rayhew say, "Listen to that noise! Weldon says there's tanks in the town now. The

75s are dodging down alleys to catch them sideways. We better get ready."

"So what do you want," Dixon rasped, "movies? The Johns are sleeping at the CP with Stollman. They'll be running their asses back here after us soon as it gets hot. Let us sleep," he said, and leaned on his rifle to watch the flames. They all leaned on weapons and slept in Atman's flames—Tobias, Reilly, Austen, Muzakis, Goldring, Craig, and more whose faces he recognized and then lost to vagueness until they were just numbers on gray tin dogtags, a pack of madmen surrounded by enemies, and enemies to each other too in this trap. There was nothing left but to sleep in the church of Atman's flames, to hide from the knowing of the coming of the spook.

"What do you mean by that?" Lindemayer said, coming out of the haze, and Gingold answered him, risen from the hedges in burp-gun chatter: "He told me we been waiting and waiting all our lives, a way of life." Atman stood there grinning in the drizzle with someone else waving hands to lead them in song, Atman saying, "He told me people all over the world are waiting for the same thing. We're lucky. At least *we* know what we're waiting for." With a carbine slung to his back, its stock sawed off, and a greasegun slung on his shoulder, the bandleader pumped both hands to build up the music in a clucking crescendo, and then he cut it all dead with a flourish. Riglioni saw only the man's back, yet recognized him as Grury because of the greasegun and short carbine he always carried. Grury, or Proctor, or one of those—it was hard to be exact. The man turned slowly, turned to reveal a mask of bloody orange rivers in which the blue face was Sal Riglioni's.

He leaped to grab Gingold before he could get back into the hedges and said, "Write this down—it's Grury! No, you know those smoke-pots? Hey Moran, you remember the snow, the sweetness and light in that place? It blinds you like smoke-pots!"

He was awake again in the cellar and men sat before candles in a thunder full of automatic fire. "Hah, what's the matter?" Gingold said, rubbing his nose, sitting there against the wall in blanket and helmet. "You want us up in those cars?"

"Me? I don't want anything. Let me alone." There were no officers around; some of the men had pitched over and slept now where they had sat, but most of them kept studying the flames. His watch said 5:25; he had not slept long and tried to sleep again, but Rayhew came over and said, "Sal, all we got now is Jevere in the forward jeep and Spoldren in the car on the back edge. The Krauts are in the town, B Troop pulled back twice already, and the other squadron sent a troop in from the forest. What are we sitting here for?"

"For the candles, kid. To watch them. See Atman up on those mattresses? Not a worry in the world. Now get the hell away from me until Stollman comes to run us somewhere."

The barrage faltered up front, and in the relative quiet the screech of racing wheels could be heard. Rayhew just sat there gaping at him. Men crouched over their upright weapons or lay sleeping. For several minutes the shelling diminished until it came in separate barks. Gunfire flared at different points in the town. Over by the seven mattresses and Atman's truncated candles the phone tinkled.

"Gingerbread," Rayhew said. "What? I can't get a move out of them, Johnny. What? Yeah, wait a minute, Johnny." He looked up with entreating eyes. "Sal, he wants you."

Oakes was watching him. Tobias and others in the lunatic crowd turned. He got up aching in all his joints, and limped over to take the phone. "Riglioni," he said.

"Sal, you hear what's going on? They're moving around. They're looking for a soft spot, Sal, and then they're *really* gonna come on."

"Ah, that's what the Krauts probably said about us, and we took a whole week. What's Stollman doing in the CP if he's so worried?"

"Following orders, and goddamn it, you do the same for a change!"

"Me? I'm a private, what do you want from me?"

"Never mind that shit! I'll be there in a few minutes; you get the men deployed in the vehicles!"

"I ain't deploying nobody, you son of a bitch! You can tell . . ." But Muldoon had hung up. Rayhew gaped at him. Atman kicked in his sleep. Everybody else seemed to be watching Riglioni through the sputtering flames. Brubak was chewing something with deliberate calm; Heggenrich was smoking a short cigarette without using his hands—they made the perfect picture of heroes game against all odds, and it was the little bit of them in every man that added up with all the Buffalo Bills and Stollmans and Colonels like Powell to keep a war rolling.

"What are you gonna do?" Gingold asked as Riglioni sat back against the wall. "Don't cut off our nose to spite Stollman's face, Rig."

Moran sat watching the flames with his mouth open and the Thompson in his lap all cleaned and ready. Cannon barked. The men were all watching Riglioni. He said, "Go ask Rayhew, he's in charge here. Stollman never expected Squadron to move us forward, the little phony. He wants us in the cars to protect his CP, that's all. Oakes! When you gonna man all your cars?"

"Soon as the whistle blows." Oakes giggled like Proctor.

Gingold said, "Rig, let's go outside."

"Let me alone, let me alone." A shell slammed outside and he fled through his eyes to hide in the dancing flame. "I ain't stopping anybody. But I'm sitting here until I see Stollman." Another shell shattered something to crumbling debris nearby, and he trembled and grew abruptly hollow with the old sense of respite ending, luck and all traces of hope vanishing to leave him naked in the storm. "I ain't letting Stollman sweat me out till I bust and save his ass just to save mine."

Turning to him, Moran stared a while and then said, "Just one thing. If a guy believes in the afterlife, how come he's still afraid to die?"

Riglioni giggled in the ascending rumble of shells striking the near north end. "Like when you're a kid. You can go to the movies, but you don't want to break up the ball game. I ain't afraid, I'd just rather stick around with my friends and neighbors."

"Your friends and neighbors? *He-he-he.* What do you want, movies? Doughnuts? *He-he-he.*"

Their laughter ascended in spasms and Riglioni was lost in the dark heart of a flame before he realized that he as well as Moran had fallen silent again in the bombardment. Out of it came Lieutenant Morgdahl in a rush, shouting, "Up and at it, men! Let's go! Let's go!"

Nobody moved. Oakes merely grinned up at him and then turned again to the candles. Gingold whispered, "Rig, this is crazy."

"Don't worry your head. Just look at the candles like everybody else. It's a way of life, boy."

"No, that's shit, I had enough of that. I been *hypnotized*, for Christ's sake, I thought I was home sleeping in my mother's house. I don't want to drown in it any more. Come on, Rig."

"What's the *matter* with you men?" Morgdahl cried, and ran out when Oakes laughed, watching the flames.

Shells struck close by. Somewhere the thin crack of a 37 sounded. Wheels shrieked, the deeper boom of a 75 broke, and motors groaned. Men turned to stare at each other and Riglioni found a flame to focus on until somebody blocked his view of it and Lieutenant Spiro said, "Get up. Move out, Riglioni, that's an order."

He said nothing. He closed his eyes and huddled in his blanket, slipping his hand down the pistol-grip of his rifle to keep it away from the trigger. He quaked in every muscle with fear and some demented exultation. Moran said, "Spiro. Go talk to your own noncoms. Don't be picking on a private like that."

"You shut your face, Moran. Get up, Riglioni. I warn you."

Riglioni opened his eyes to see Moran point the Thompson and Rayhew leap to haul Spiro around in a quick circle saying, "Lieutenant, Jesus, you'll get yourself . . . don't you see they're all . . . talk to me, not them. Jesus, you crazy?"

The shelling ceased. Echoes rang and whined off to silence. Spiro stood there blinking. Over his shoulder he looked at Moran, then at Riglioni, and said, "I don't understand. I don't understand. You're crazy? The whole bunch of you? Crazy? *Get in those cars!*"

The flames sputtered. Atman sat up and shouted, "Look me up!" Gingold leaped up with a snarl, a hysterical growl, and Atman fell back again to sleep under Calvary.

"Listen," Gingold panted. "Stop looking at those lights. You guys stop looking at those lights and get up. Stop looking at Riglioni and get up. He's crazy. It's no good down here!"

"What's good?" Moran laughed. "Why good, why good all the time? Why not bad once in a while? Why good? What's good?—Stollman? This apple-head Spiro? Good for who—Powell? Why good, Gingold?"

"Rig, please!" Gingold began to cough, choking. "Get up!"

"Huh, let Stollman get up there. I like it here, it's a way of life. Let me alone, let me alone."

"A way of—it's a puddle of shit!" Gingold whirled and ran and threw himself into a candle, tumbling with it. Then over the mattresses and Atman he scrambled to knock the other candle dead. Again shellfire broke in the forward areas, a heavy barrage. Matches flared. Munzer and Atman lit some of the small candles. Gingold said, "Riglioni, you idiot, I figured something out but I got no time for you. I'm going."

"Wait a minute." Gingold frightened him. Feeling grimy in all his joints and sick to the depths of his soul, he had a dizzy vision of a desk in some Troop CP, the most heartening way of life possible, and felt even sicker. "Come on, we'll take a look. Doesn't sound like the Krauts are advancing at all. Just poking for holes." With eyes upon him men rose in the flickering brown light; some fell again on dead legs. Riglioni went upstairs with Gingold toward the noise, muttering, "It can't hurt to look."

In the bleak blue dawn he felt a hundred years old. Echoes of shellfire formed an umbrella under which the street lay still in rustic tranquillity, even the ruins sublime in the mists, the wheel-gutted snow a criss-cross of purple shadows. Vehicles of the entire Troop sat toylike in their brick shells of cover. It was like going home guilty after an all-night card game with everybody bag-eyed and blue-lipped and full of enlarged pores like an old man. Faintly in the thunder he heard a crackling patter as he walked west with Gingold, who cast him a wary glance and suddenly broke into a run just as Muldoon came trotting from the back edge of town.

And Riglioni knew he was going home all right, home to the end of his waiting, for the crackle was gunfire and Gingold was in mid-air leaping for a jeep in the far booming and near *crack-adakalak* like cap pistols unbelievable in the dawn where some element of the enemy had circled around to this safe rear. And now with perfect timing like the arrival of Scarbro's brother the sky cracked open for the corkscrew ride that ended in a blast behind running Muldoon, panicked Muldoon, who got nearer and nearer and then lifted his chin to spew out a red geyser and fell headlong and flat with a shudder, arms straight before him as in obeisance and bald helmet rolling away.

Corkscrews tore the sky to shreds. Shells crashed in patterns now to gobble up houses of the district. Running, he saw the armored car of Spoldren, fat-assed with silent guns, leap in a flaming red cough and come down again quivering on its wheels with Spoldren up in the turret raising hands in surrender to nothing but hills of snow on the plain. But the snow crackled to echo tiny flashes of fire that cut Spoldren down, twisted dead in an instant across the .50 he never fired. And running and running Riglioni leaped at last like Gingold into a jeep and swung the long .30 to rake at tiny flashes of fire where there were no men against the blue snow of dawn. Now in the uproar the spook itself came without men in numberless tongues of flame across dawn snow, and he raked at the blank plain and Gingold braked up across the street and hammered his .30 at the snow shrieking, "Aim lower! Aim lower!" hammering shots to kill the snow a thousand times over until a gigantic billowing anger of red and black engorged him and spat the jeep of Gingold against a house. Motors came from behind where men communicated in shrieks, motors too from the side and "YAAAAAAA!" a scream in his throat because it came cannon first around the boulders of wreckage, an enormous Tiger armored with concrete, and all at once he saw the spook's countless faces and all at once shrieked to the bite of a sudden insect on his own private Sal and fired in lower trajectory, for bodiless faces of the spook were close upon him and his gunfire knocked faces down and then at last he saw whole men to kill in their uniform whites that Reeves never got for Proctor's time or his. Something tore a hole in his cheek and he bled his blood to the stings of a hundred rifles *but I will know I will continue beyond and exist and think.* In the roar of a shell that rocked the Tiger, a blessed 75 that blasted and burned it from behind, he squeezed to kill spooks of the white world lost while the end of his death came grinding out of demolished stone, a second

Tiger listing blind and monstrous with a sweep of its great inexorable cannon which stuck out a flaming tongue and vomited to end the thundering music.

The last sound was of rain to which he raced his brain for old days to hide in, days of rain which like tall altar flames were salvation from the final hammer of reality. He was Sal in those days with Lorraine in a locked room while rain beat tropically at the windows. But now, stunned in the mouth of the spook, he fled the amber locked hours of their hotel room for moments of the next afternoon when the storm broke again and drove them into a hallway for shelter. Her wet cheeks brought his love up naked to the moment. Her eyes, pinched by the storm into the purest look of innocence, told him that those moments were the height of his life . . . but though he sensed it then the whole truth of it reached him only now, and now in the dead bowels of the spook he yearned, and sobbed, and she faded away on a tinkle of glass and laughter. The continuing sound of rain was a promise, an abundance, but he sank away and left it behind.

21

After its break-through in the rear the main enemy power was obliged to cross open ground at the canal, and there the tide of battle turned at noon. An ambush waited in the sheltering near streets, from which the 75s and armored cars rolled forth to outmaneuver the cumbersome Mark VI Tigers with point-blank cannon and machine-gun fire that demolished foot troops and armor alike. In the forward quarter fighting continued all afternoon, until a last Tiger operating evasively there was knocked out and the surrenders began.

It was Monday, December 18, 1944, a day of appalling devastation in Major Jimmerson's squadron. C Troop lost thirteen men and four vehicles fleeing to the canal from the rear penetration. B Troop suffered casualties of half its strength holding the forward line. A Troop was completely destroyed, save for one man wrecked so badly that he was not expected to live out the day.

At sunset, advancing westward from the canal—where three great Tigers sat burning amid scores of white-clad corpses—men of the other squadron found the lone survivor falling and rising again to search the snow as if he had lost something among the burning cars and all the twisted bodies. The front of his helmet was staved in, but with his one workable hand he kept them from baring his head. The helmet was removed finally by Group surgeons in the woods to which HQ had withdrawn early in the day; the helmet and everything else was cut away from this bloody man as part of the surgery that saved him.

It was discovered that he had no dogtags. Days later, after Infantry had broken through from the west and lines were open to the rest areas in Belgium, HQ began its investigation to learn why A Troop had collapsed. Its failure to stall the rear penetration was indirectly responsible—since C Troop had to be committed in that quarter—for casualties as far up the chain of command as Group, where Captain Churney died in action. With his new aide beside him ready to take notes, Colonel Powell attempted to interrogate the survivor. But when asked his name the man only snorted and through clenched teeth said, "Up yours, Hebe."

Gingold had awakened to a silence which he took as the sound of death, and the terrible cold convinced him that he was in the tomb. But then he felt pain and took that to mean life.

The pain was mostly in his face; it seemed his jaw was broken. He thought he had no hands until he found them on a wall and called them to him like puppies. Only one came; he had to drag the other and remembered that the first bullet had struck his arm. He was sticky all over with blood and surmised that he was broken in half like Proctor. Without any idea of how he knew, he was certain of one thing—that if he removed his helmet the whole top of his skull would go with it. But he was mentally sound because at once he knew the body on a turret to be Spoldren's. *Clear as a bell ding-dong,* he thought he said and darkness fell and then he found himself walking in a din of shellfire, though all was motionless in the sunny murk before him.

What's this? I was just walking and now . . . Get up again. Instead he dragged himself through snow and rolled over laughing. *Hey Joe, what time's it getting? Hey Moran. Boy do you look stupid, sitting up dead like that* against a jeep with his Thompson on his lap. Armored cars burned somewhere before him and looked full of dead. The shelling was ceaseless. *Oh listen to that.* He was a spectator at Chateau Thierry, a hero to be so close to it without blanching, and that one there without a face, that black burnt crust, was Morgdahl: *I'd know you anywhere. Look at Oakes—the bastard's smiling, a real nut. I was always scared of him. I think I'll drop dead.* Darkness fell again, day came back; he kept dying and waking and greeting dead friends like Jevere and Heggenrich—*what an outfit they sent these kids to*—until he fell over tangled steel to find Riglioni at last.

Hey Rig, you son of a bitch, there's your friend Joe across the way. Boy there's nothing left of you. You are a mess, boy. But what teeth. You got good teeth. Something I wanted to tell you but I can't remember. Not that Kraut broad you trimmed in the cellar. Ha, muscles on her legs, she gave that crazy kick . . .

He moved off to escape the falling night and look for Atman, but stopped at the sound of motors and struggled to rip off his dogtags. *They're coming now. Don't want to give away my blood type, you know.* He found himself crying in the bright winter sun where all his friends were dead. *I never used to do that until this town. Funny how a clown like Buffalo Bill can ruin good men. Think I'll go surround a machine-gun nest for Stollman. Come on, Brubak, call your friend.*

There went the shelling again, and gunfire. There sprawled the remains of more men who had come out to fight. Reilly, Tobias, Craig, more losers who decided too late, all lined up and shot without killing a single Kraut. *No, Krauts must have come back for their dead; Moran would have hit them. Here I go, goodbye, goodbye, I'm going now going now . . .*

He came up from a dizzy haze facing again the parts that remained of Riglioni. *What's this? I was just looking for Atman in that crater. No, that's right, I have to tell you about Atman, Rig. I mean about a way of life you said and it's all bubbles now in my mouth, but just for the hell of it . . . Wait. Listen, Rig, that's just it, a way of life you said. You can live and live until you get suckered into some proud goddamn way of life. I know it's hard to face, it's a hell of a thing to face, but every way of life is the end of the road, the puddle of shit to drown in. Ha. If I tried to tell you before, you'd never hold still and listen. But you're holding still now, Hebe, you're holding still now. Ha, look at you. Look at us, Rig, and goodbye. We made a fatal error.*

After another death and waking he decided to go home and look up Atman.

Dear Dr. Pennybaker,

In answer to your request, I am going to jot down some of my innermost thoughts, in my own words as you so generously privileged me to write them. My purpose, of course, is to reveal the reasons for certain mysteries that trouble you about me, thus to warm the cockles of your analytical little heart.

To convince you at the outset of my complete and painstaking honesty (a quality attracting greater veneration than truth does these days, from what I read in *The Stars and Stripes*), I must come right out and say that yours is a preposterous name, even for a psychiatrist. Penny alone would do; Baker would be better. With astuteness you have already uncovered a strange preoccupation with names that seems to be a side result of my wounds. Since this is one of the mysteries you're determined to solve, let's begin right there.

The reason I'm suddenly willing to discuss the question of names is that I've run out of all the good ones without any success at having you accept one. Buckalew Kooby made you laugh. So did Merwin Fingerhut. Zalig Rakusin made you angry, for a reason that you ought to search your soul for some afternoon when there's nobody else around to pump. Jesus Josephson induced you, presumably through professional insight, to start bringing the chaplain around, and after that the rest became anticlimactic.

The reason you can't get my real name out of me is threefold. First, I don't feel like talking, even though my jaw is not broken as I once imagined. Second, I threw away my dogtags. Third, a principle tenet of my religion is to always confuse the enemy—which is why I threw away my dogtags in the second place. When it appeared that I would soon be captured, my first thought was to keep the enemy from learning more than my name, rank, and serial number. As an Army officer you're aware, I trust, that military law forbids captured soldiers to divulge more. Yet my Government Issued dogtags plainly indicated my ancestral religion, the hoodoo of my fathers for which the enemy might have boiled me down for soap.

The reason I don't feel like talking is that while all my friends were getting ready to die my wife took it into her head to desert me in favor of a portrait painter who waxes his eyebrows to make them look devilish (she thoughtfully sent me a snapshot). That sort of hurts, you know, in spite of the humor attached to the so-called Dear John letter, a specimen of which she sent me with uncanny timing while circumstances were twisting me into shape for this very psycho ward that you have found it expeditious to make my cheerful home.

The reason I ventured home instead of just dropping dead as did all those friends and enemies of mine was to look up Atman on the preposterous notion that he might not be dead. I keep dreaming (that should titillate you) of a song that goes: *Who is Atman, what is he?* I also dream (and this should doubly titillate you) of you, my compatriot, with your hearty mien and your bounce and those searching eyes of yours which I've seen on dead men.

Last week, for instance, I dreamed that you were a Mark VI tank chasing me through all the years of my life. You caught up to me at last with a tremendous explosion that turned into words, words and words—oh, how you talked! It was you all right; the tank was gone and there you stood in hospital pajamas calling me "Tourist" and telling me about men who submitted to fantasy and died of it. "En route to death they passed right here," you said, "tourists like you in a vast enigma, and like them you journey nowhere but to death."

Suddenly I found myself garish in sportswear and gleaming

with camera, sun glasses, binoculars, gold rings, gold watch—an anonymous stereotype, the vacuous provincial himself, marveling at the countryside in some lolling paradise of sun far from home. I was mortified, but you didn't mind and went on prattling about doves and eternity and wild roses and trumpet creepers. I tried to offer you money. You refused it with a ceremonious wave of your hand and began to analyze the reasons for "the headlong intercourse with fantasy that killed them all." You knew it all; you had it right at your fingertips. I sweated, sensing abasement somehow in your very facility of expression, so I tried to laugh you down. I ridiculed your bucolic conceits, your transparent hints at allegorical if not downright anagogic implications. I laughed in the dream to show my insight and individuality, to establish beyond a doubt that I'm nobody's bonehead, and by intruding so crudely only proved myself a narcissistic boor without taste. You continued with a sublime confidence possible only to the wraith of a dream, subduing me. Talking and talking, you finally insulted me with some crack about my 7X binoculars—something like, "For solace they ran to the light that blinds, compelled by a fatal persuasion that your 7X myopia only *seems* to spare you."

Well, I tried to get out of there, but I was suddenly paralyzed by a horror at realizing that all you spoke of belonged to me, that I and not you had known those men, that I and not you had seen them hide in pathetic diversions of light. I shouted in protest, but you interrupted with bland words that insinuated a kinship between us, and insisted I stay to help you ponder ghosts that are and always have been mine.

In my bitterness I began contradicting everything you said: the sky that day had been white, not blue; it was winter, not summer. Affably conceding all that, you called me "Captain," and that was when I let out a shriek. "I wasn't the Captain! No! No!" You laughed, oh, how you laughed, grabbing me by the slings of my paraphernalia, shaking me, saying that in war

—I must approximate here, of course—saying, "In the final storm all personality and faith is reduced to the absurdity almost of your silly glints and gleams and leather ways of life. HAHAHA! HAHAHA!"

Drowned in that maddening laughter I woke at last, but only to the eerie aftermath of nightmare, that moonlit gulf that feels like truth, in which I saw the enormity of your arrogance. To make flat pronouncements on an incident so elusive in significance seemed the foulest arrogance, seemed a solution to life as degrading as war itself. Did you represent war itself in the dream? I speculated. Or Death? But waking more, I soon realized that you were of course a reflection of my deeper self (it was my dream, after all, not yours) and that I was the actual stranger in the dream.

I hate to butt into your trade, Pennybaker, but it seems obvious even to this lay mind that my yearning for just such an unabashed perspicacity as that of the wraith you played is what I transmuted from conscience into dream. It would also seem that I reversed our positions to make a point of the dream all the clearer: I became you, you became me, and here you may have the chiefest reason why I never answer when you come sucking around with questions about the collapse of A Troop and of my identity.

You see, for months I've longed to ponder aloud that mass suicide in hypnotizing light. But I've been afraid that my sense of the incident could never reach the smug, methodized clod I played, taking your role in the dream. I really hate to insult you so, but for me you resemble everyone to whom you hunger to adjust me. No doubt you'll take it as a figment of my maladjustment—obviously I'm a hurt man—but I find you the perfect image of all the happy affirmers that I see grinning from the pages of magazines. To me they all look like neon signs obtruding with arrogant glare and slavishly advertising lies. There were bullets in my body. Something drove half my helmet into my forehead and impaired my sense of taste. Now I lack the taste to be reserved and pamper the hybrid breed that you represent for me.

Half Yahoo and half Houynhnm, each of you lusts to dominate and longs to follow. You cry morality from every public lectern and secretly practice the most obscene egoism any age has seen. You claim the dignity of uniqueness, yet together you all huddle to perpetuate every misanthropic convention. You are a lard-assed fathead who sees an Adonis in his mirror, and the braver your narcissistic cult grows at being what it lets tawdry standards of fashion make it, the more a community of hypocrites you're destined to become.

That much of truth my agony abstracts. I hate the world you make—and yet, just as your basic characteristic is an inability ever to detect in your own bloodstream the cold neon tube of falseness, so I resented bearing your mantle in my dream: that plea of kinship I made from self to self must indicate that somewhere in my soul I know I'm brother to this blundering fool I fear, too often neon-lit myself and prone to seek the safe womb of unanimity rather than dwell aloud on the outlandish ways in which we let fakes and clowns bleed us to death.

So, my sanctimonious kin, as much as I tremble at your blind power, come again with your questions and I'll try to tell of men turned into wax by hypocrites; I'll talk if only to keep from blinking red and green to spell out AFFIRMATION like some suicidal Cain always busy compensating. I'll try to provide the most antiseptic kind of performance, which you with half a brain and half a doubtful education have learned to expect from those whose taste your way of life destroys.

Come, but before you do, dream yourself as I did in the role of that hollow boor so confident of complexity and depth. I can picture you seated before my bed with folded hands on your belly, neither in love with justice nor concerned for the human race, your 7X binoculars turned backwards and focused to a blur, your snapshots of reality taken long ago and framed, your gold rings glinting proof enough to you of personal value, your gold watch tick-tick-ticking away as you ignore it, saying with a yawn, "All right, entertain me."

If it'll comfort you I'm willing to bear the identity of the Captain whom, so anxiously, I denied being in the dream. Or even that of the Colonel—what difference, really? It may very well be that the sins and faults and failings which repel us so in others are those that exist to the most revolting degrees in ourselves. I'm you and you're me; we're one at least in what we journey to. Come brother, come enemy, and when I try to tell of the flames my friends were driven to hide in, remember that the ghosts they left behind are yours as well as mine.

Just one thing: please come without the chaplain this time—one priest is enough for a man whose condition attests to the failure of both your crafts in this world. During my bad time with those bottles and pipes and comas, that gentleman looked as if he were hanging around just to say the last rites, so now he's a depressing memory. When I was younger than my pain and as obsequious as the next neon sign, I used to humor his kind of superstitious dogma. But I can no longer suffer that infantile hoodoo and, God willing, I'll get rid of your depredations too, go home, remarry, get us a child, and have someone of my own around to call me Gov'nor.

Just in case you've been playing it straight and the Army is actually so fouled up that a simple process of elimination has not yet produced my real name, I am

Sincerely yours,
Sydney Australia

ABOUT THE AUTHOR

GEORGE MANDEL born in 1920, is a native of New York City, where he studied at the Pratt Institute and The Art Students League. After serving in World War II, he attended the New School. He is the author of two novels, *Flee the Angry Strangers* and *The Breakwater*, and a short novel, *Into the Woods of the World* (in the collection *3 Short Novels*). Mr. Mandel presently lives in Sarasota, Florida, with his wife and their two daughters.